Tara Without Lies

Naughty Book Five

Christine Young

Chapter One

London 1840

Tara MacLaren swayed in time to the music, tapping her toes, satisfied to watch the ball progress. Her spot behind the potted palm gave her the opportunity to observe without being seen. While she enjoyed the music, she didn't wish to be here. Because of her bum leg she couldn't dance very much. Longed for the security of her home. Wished she could flee to the highlands.

She was in London with a ferocious protest. Staying at the castle on the other side of the island was her preference. Her older half-brother, Liam, called her a loner. She was. Her other male sibling, Kenzie, simply told her she was feeling sorry for herself and should snap out of the snit then get on with her life. She told him she wasn't in a snit nor was she pouting. The drama of a London season was more than she was up to enduring. She was old enough. Should have a few choices.

In London everyone expected her to be looking for a husband. As a debutante at twenty years of age she was already on the shelf, though she admitted easily she wasn't horse-faced. Aunt Ella was her chaperone. Though The Duchess, as she was beginning to be called by family as well as friends, played more the role of matchmaker than chaperone. When she thought one of her charges had an eye for a certain man, she found a means to put them in a direct line that could never be avoided. So far, her success was unmatched.

Aunt Ella took on the role of chaperone to the family females after the original duchess, Charlotte, passed on a few years back. Neither duchess seemed to be able to control their charges once the female in question decided on the man she wanted. Tara didn't think for one moment that either Charlotte or Ella cared about that little *faux pas* they made. Ella put Lyssa in a compromising situation with her now husband though she didn't realize Nickie ran off with the McInnis. Drake and Ella along with others chased after them to demand a wedding after she was compromised.

Tara didn't want a man. A wave of pain at the memory of her loss shook her to the core. In the past the horrid recollections would have sent her to her knees. Now, she somehow learned to look inside herself when the past overtook her. Looking around the room, she caught the eye of Liam, her half-brother. He nodded then set off in her direction with Jeremy, one of his best friends, in tow. Her brother would be determined to make her laugh. Laughter was a hard commodity for her to come by, particularly so close to the anniversary that changed the course of her life forever.

After the two rogues reached her, Liam kissed her on the cheek while Jeremy picked her up then whirled her around in gigantic circles several times before he set her on her feet. Once her feet touched the ground, she swayed slightly, closing her eyes and shaking her head to get rid of the dizziness. Jeremy supported her for the minute it took her to recover. She leaned her head on his broad chest catching the spicey scent he favored. Tara wished she could feel more for Jeremy. She couldn't. Never would. Jeremy was a good friend she could always count on. That was all.

"You're beautiful. More beautiful than I recall." He kissed her cheek. "Dance with me, Sprite. I know you want to whirl around the room. Make a few of the dandies want to hold you in their arms. They will be jealous of me. Maybe you will meet someone."

"Of course, for you anything," she told him smiling shyly as he twirled her into the crush of people on the dance floor. It was then she saw a man, tall and darkly handsome. He was the most beautiful man she'd ever seen. Her heart lurched to her throat. His eyes narrowed as if he scorned her as he watched them dance away into the crowd. Why would he look at her in that manner? He seemed to accuse her of something. She didn't understand the dark look.

"Who is that man?" Tara asked while she looked over her shoulder to get another glimpse of the man who had just caught her attention.

"Who? Has someone taken my place in your affections?" Jeremy searched the room for the object of Tara's question.

Tara tried to see the man. He disappeared into the crush. "I don't know. He's not there any longer." She was thoroughly disappointed. Knowing the man's name seemed important.

"Is your dance card full?" Jeremy asked, looking down at her while she tilted her head up to see into his eyes.

"It is if you dance with me for the rest of the ball. Otherwise, it's empty. Don't care to have men I don't know or want to know maul me. I'm not a debutante with a wealthy dowry. I'm not looking for a title. None are going to want me save for one purpose. I'm not willing to give any of the men what they are after." It would take a very special man for her to want to spend time with. She didn't believe one existed for her.

Jeremy's crack of laughter surprised her. "Maul you?" he asked still laughing. "With Lady Ella hovering over you, doubt if any man here would dare do such a thing as man-handle The Duchesses' niece. Besides isn't that what big brothers are for, protecting little sisters? Liam is here, not to find a debutante but to help Ella protect your good name."

"I wouldn't know. Liam is out having fun and playing at being the lord while Kenzie is chasing sunrises just as father used to do...still does. Now he does it with mother on his arm. I'm not at all certain why Liam showed up here." Maybe he was looking out for her best interest. Liam was closer to her than her other brother. He understood her whims, her depressions. Always tried to lighten her day. Kenzie was Kenzie, flamboyant and devil-may-care rogue.

"You've been alone for far too long. Are you feeling sorry for yourself? You need to get over the grief. When that happens, you can start to live again. Lord knows you deserve that. You're a beautiful young woman who should be out having fun. Finding a man you can love."

Tara gasped, a bit startled by his callousness. "No...yes well...maybe a little. It's almost been two years. In a couple of days..." her voice trailed off while she felt sadness collide within the part of her that needed healing. Her heart ached for what she would never have.

"Sorry, I didn't mean to remind you," Jeremy said, his soft-spoken voice holding a wealth of regret. "Would you like some fresh air? We could go for a walk in the gardens or stand on the balcony. Whatever you would like."

"Appreciate your concern. What I would like would be to go home, back to the highlands. Nonetheless, Aunt Ella won't let me. Mother and father aren't there. One would think a twenty-year-old woman would be allotted some independence. I'm most certainly capable of taking care of myself," she said in a strangled huff that almost turned to tears. Tara fought them back, pushed them away with all the strength she could muster from deep inside. She turned all her thoughts inward, searching for an inner peace before she unraveled in front of this large crowd of people.

"Is that a nod to the fresh air or a nod to staying here with no one on your dance card?" he asked with the persistence she was coming to associate with her beloved Jeremy. If she could have another brother, she would pick him. At one time he wanted more. She didn't have more to give.

"Liam will dance with me as soon as he can pry himself away from all the young ladies who are hoping to become a countess. You know with my leg...I can't dance the night away." Her laughter caused Jeremy to grin. She touched his lips with the tip of her finger. "What about you?" She needed to direct the conversation away from her and to something more suitable. "You should find a suitable young debutante to dance with. You're not getting younger."

"We both understand, Liam is not looking for a wife as yet. Neither am I. Unless of course, I could somehow convince you I'm a good catch." His voice was wistful. His smile charming. It was too bad she felt nothing except friendship.

Her soft sigh didn't go unnoticed by the man dancing with her. She understood a relationship with this wonderful man would never be. "Would hate to ruin our friendship. You understand you will never be any more than a very good friend." Tara knew Jeremy wanted more than friendship. It just wasn't the same as before. "In every way except by birth, you are a brother to me. Just as Liam is, a brother by another father."

"Mother too, much to my chagrin. I understand." Once again, he picked up the pace as the music moved from a slow waltz to one with a bit more stamina to it.

She laughed, clinging to him as her cheeks heated with the exuberance of the dance. Perhaps she needed that fresh air to cool her flaming face. Walking out onto the terrace with Jeremy would set tongues wagging. Tomorrow, the *on dit* would be they were a couple. She wouldn't allow that to happen. Wouldn't hurt him in that way. She owed him part of her sanity. He and Liam helped her through the darkest times of her life. Though Jeremy would just laugh and tell her that people could believe whatever they wanted to think. He didn't care what people thought of him. However, she did need to guard her reputation. It was all she had left.

Jeremy leaned close to her. The scent of his breath was mint when he whispered, "Would you like some punch. I'm certain it's spiked." His voice was a bit husky.

"Because you and Liam spiked it?" she was quick to ask; another tiny bubble of laughter was generated. They would do exactly as they pleased. They both had a bit of wicked inside them.

"I would never confess even to you, sweet sister."

The laughter sparkling up from deep inside couldn't be helped. The amusement healed the ever-present ache that seemed to be part of her soul. "I would like some. Just don't fill the glass to the brim. Don't want Uncle Drake to have to carry me out of here. Nor do I wish to make a complete fool of myself."

"Whatever you would like, my little sprite. Come with me." He led the way moving between people. With deft precision, he guided her, keeping her hand in his so she'd stay close.

They ended up at the table with the punch along with the food. He poured them both glasses then he filled a plate they could share. She should eat something, anything if she was going to imbibe the spiked punch. She was hungry. When had she eaten last? She didn't remember. Food was never important to her, held no appeal until she was too weak to remain standing.

Together they wandered to the balcony then found a table. She leaned back staring at this man who helped her with so much of her grief. Helped her through the worst part of her life. He held her hand when all she could do was weep for something that would never be. Sometimes he walked with her through the gardens at the MacLaren keep just to ease her wounded spirit.

"You are a wonder. You know that don't you? Some lucky lady will find you then you will be glad I turned you down."

Jeremy coughed, clearing his throat. "Not a wonder...not enough to be more than a friend to you." He waved his hand in the air to silence the retort that was on her lips. "No, don't say anything else. If all I can ever be is a friend, that is what I want for us. Drink your punch. Eat the food. You'll feel better after you do. I know you must be starving. After that, I'll see if I can fill your dance card with a few suitable names. Have you seen that man you asked me about earlier? If you would like a dance with him, I can see what he will say."

"No, no! No, don't ask him if you find him. Don't search for the man. I was only curious. There was something dark as well as brooding about him. Gave me shivers." Tara was more than curious. On first glance she thought him the most handsome man she'd ever seen. His face chiseled, his lips firm. His eyes though, his eyes blazed and simmered when he looked at her. With his broad shoulders and lean hips, he cut a dashing figure. She wanted to understand what he was thinking at that moment, when their gazes met then held for seconds. She felt somehow connected to him.

"Anyone else catch your fancy?" Jeremy asked.

"No, though Liam will dance with me. Since he's my half-brother he can have more than one or two twirls around the dance floor. I don't care to dance with anyone else." She lied. There was the man who caught her attention. He stared at her through veiled dark eyes, menacing eyes. The man was someone who was used to keeping to himself, shuttering his thoughts from everyone. For that brief moment that he looked at her, she felt as if he saw into her soul. She touched a finger to her lips, wondering how his mouth would feel against hers. After that she shook the insanity from her head.

"As will your cousin, Ashcroft. Do you have any other relatives among the guests here?" Jeremy asked.

Tara didn't understand why that solitary man caught her attention. Somehow, he intrigued her like no one had ever done before...except... except the man she once called her fiancé. That time was long ago. She could never call the moments back though she wished she could.

"Tara? Where are you? You haven't said a word in the last five minutes. Is the punch getting too you?"

Tara snapped back to attention. "Oh, yes, there is Colby. I suppose Steven and Kane might also attend. I could dance with Colby. He'll be around for a little while longer. Aunt Ella wanted everyone to be here for a short time to lend me a bit of moral support. Aunty understands this is the last place I'd like to be. Colby is not interested in debutantes as yet." Not that he ever will. She didn't know why she had that thought. Colby walked to a different tune. He needed adventure. Always had. Didn't care about sunsets or sunrises. All he cared about was the thirst of new adventures, seeing what was over the next mountain. He wanted to go to the United States. Wanted to see Montana as well as Wyoming.

"Your dance card will now be filled with relatives. The Duchess will never understand what you are about. You shouldn't sulk or give that impression. If it can't be me, there has got to be a man out there for you somewhere."

"She understands. Aunt Ella just doesn't agree. There he is. Don't look at him that way. He'll know what you are about." The man stared at her, his eyes still dark, still brooding. She felt as if there was a subtle threat issued. He nodded seeming to think she was attracted. It wouldn't do for her to show too much interest.

What did a nod of his head mean? He acted as if he understood what she was thinking. He didn't. Couldn't. Tara looked away, her heart in her throat feeling uncomfortable with the situation. The breath she stole from the air singed her lungs burned when she exhaled.

"Care to dance?" The deep voice startled her out of her reverie. She jumped.

7

Her breath caught then hitched. When she looked into his eyes, relief washed over her. She felt as if she could breathe again. "Ash! Yes. Of course, yes. You surprised me. Caught me unaware. I..." She held her bottom lip with her teeth. "It seems I was lost in thought."

"You were staring at a dangerous man. You would be well advised not to make his acquaintance. He has a reputation you wouldn't wish to be associated with," Ash told her, his voice solemn.

"Rumor has it he frequents the shadier parts of the city. Has been seen with some of my father's associates. He's shifty. Suspicious. Arrogant. The man is a bounty hunter. He is a danger to anyone he associates with. Stay away!"

The order put her back up. "Your father's associates are either in the parliament or they are spies. Besides, the *on dit* about you puts you in many of the same places. Are you also a spy? Following in your father's footsteps?" she retorted. "You've no idea what you've just started by your words. You've issued me a challenge I mean to accept. What is his name?" Tara didn't understand why she decided then and there she would discover as much about this man as was possible.

"Case Ferguson." Ash spoke his words soft and low while he turned to look at the other man. "Dance? I'd rather not get into an argument here."

With as much haste as decorum would allow, she stood, smiling at one of her favorite cousins, tilting her head as she meant to flirt. "Thought you would never ask. Need Liam to come around for a dance too." Tara set her hand on his shoulder. "Case Ferguson, you say. Nice name."

"Tara, best you listen to me." He tried to argue again. "You could be getting in over your head. He steals women's hearts then leaves them with the shattered pieces. The last thing you need is your heart traumatized again."

"Heard you do the same."

Ash bent down to kiss her on the cheek. A few seconds later they waltzed around the room to a romantic ballad Tara loved. She hummed as they moved across the floor. Ash smiled down at her. "You need to..." he cleared his throat. "Suppose a man can wait longer than a woman to wed. We are of the same age. No one is insisting I attend galas to find a wife. Everyone understands a man of twenty isn't ready to settle down."

She bristled at his careless words. "I'm not going to marry. Not ever. No one. Had that chance. It's gone." No, would never settle for second best though she would like to find someone she could share her hopes along with her dreams.

"Enough of that." His boyish grin made her smile in return. "I'm only here at the ball for you. Got a lot of life to live before I set my sights on a debutante. Hope to get as lucky as father did when he found my mother." Ash whirled her in a tight circle dancing her through the throng of people.

Tara inhaled, a deep breath of air filling her lungs. She allowed him to lead. Ash was good. He'd been trained well. He was the heir apparent to the dukedom. Some day he would become the Duke of Richmond. His schooling was impressive. By the time they finished and he brought her back to her favorite potted palm, her breath was heaving. Aunt Ella wasn't there. When Ash left, she would be alone. Tara slid a deep breath of air into her lungs.

"Mother is dancing with father," Ashcroft nodded into the crowd of colorful swirling gowns. "Will you be alright if I leave you?"

"I won't swoon or do something else that might be construed as foolish. This palm and I are the best of friends," she spouted but she just might seek Mr. Ferguson. A challenge was a challenge. Tara would see what would happen if Mr. Ferguson did approach.

"No, I didn't think you would. I'm off to find some interesting entertainment for the evening."

"In other words, you're going to gamble and drink with your friends then...if the right woman comes along, you'll spend the rest of the night in her bed."

"You know me so well." He tapped her on the nose. "See that you don't get into trouble while I'm not around to bail you out."

"You know I won't," She was watching her aunt and uncle. "He seems to love her as much today as he did last time I was here." Thoughts of her lost love pummeled her. She sucked in a long draught of air that always seemed to have a calming effect on her.

"Would you like me to wait here until mother returns?" Ash was looking toward the door as if he needed to escape as soon as possible. Brent, one of Ash's friends waved to him before motioning with his arm. "Think I'm being summoned. As I told you, we've a night planned out on the town. You take care. Heed what I said about Case Ferguson. Don't want you to get so far in over your head you drown. He has moves that will leave you breathless as well as at his whim. Despite your advanced age, you're an innocent still. He's an experienced man. He could eat you for breakfast then spit you out just as fast."

"You go on. Have fun." She rose on her toes to give him a quick hug then kiss. "I'll manage just fine. Maybe I can take the carriage home sooner than later. I'm through with this affair. The only ones I haven't danced with are Liam and Colby. They both seem to have disappeared. They most likely have plans."

"You would have to gain permission from The Duchess to leave so soon." Ash laughed when he used the name others were giving to his mother. "We both understand she won't give that approval until the wee hours of the morn." He looked at his watch. "It's only one o'clock now. You've got hours to go before permission will be granted."

Aunt Ella along with Uncle Drake were acquiring quite the reputation. They knew so much about every member of the ton, the thought boggled the mind. They knew who cheated on their spouse. Knew who owed money and those who committed fraud. The list went on. Drake was involved with the government. Once, he was a notorious spy in the Secret Intelligence Service. Uncle Drake always called it SIS if he mentioned it, foregoing the long words. Though most of what he knew was top secret. Now, he was in charge of recruiting new spies. Even though the men weren't called spies. They were more often called agents. What was a bounty hunter? Was this man Ash referred to like her uncle? Dangerous?

While Tara watched Ash leave with Brent, she fingered the amber necklace. The man who gave it to her told her it was the exact color of her eyes. The day still vivid in her mind, she clung to the images as if her life depended on doing so. She held on to the past. Jeremy was right in his assessment. Sometime she would need to put that past behind her. Tonight, she could not.

The hour was growing late. Way past the witching hour. Tara felt as if she'd done her duty. She meant to find Aunt Ella then tell her she would retire for the evening, take the carriage home. Waiting for consent went against the grain. She would send the ducal vehicle back for her and Uncle Drake.

Tomorrow's sunrise beckoned to her. She needed to get home so she could change her clothes into something suitable to ride. Rushing out to watch a sunrise was too much like her father for her to feel comfort. When she watched the sun begin a new day, it was one of her ways to remain calm to soothe her fragmented nerves. She didn't seek adventure. Tiny, her Irish wolfhound, would go with her for protection though the huge dog was too friendly by far. He loved everyone to the point where they would have to push him away.

He slobbered.

"What? No one to dance with?" The hard-edged voice surprised her. Her heart jumped to attention as the man she had watched earlier stood in front of her. He was here... "Thought your dance card would be full."

"It's not," she said, surprised the man would approach her though earlier he did stare at her. She thought about Ash's words. He did look dangerous. Was he the challenge she needed to help her through each day? Tara supposed she should discover the truth. She needed to learn more about this man who beckoned her with his ominous dark eyes. He held secrets no one except him knew about.

"Wasn't the last one a bit young for you?" he asked sending her a look that covered her from the top of her head to the tips of her toes then back. "You're too old for him."

"He's my age." Tara's back was up, felt the fine hair on the nape of her neck bristling. The interrogation was not to her liking. He had no right to judge her or her cousin. She'd dance with Ash anytime she liked. What did his age have to do with anything. Why was this man she didn't know concerned about who she danced with?

"Young," he said succinctly, his threatening stare boring into her. "Can't you handle a man? Boys are easy to take advantage of. Suppose some women need to be in control. That won't happen with us. You won't control me. Dictate how I act around you."

What the devil was that supposed to mean? She let the air she'd been holding since her first gasp of surprise go out in a slow stream as she tried to process this new information he shoveled at her. Everyone knew that Ash was her cousin just as Colby was, "What do you want?"

"A dance, that's all," he said, his voice filled with sarcasm. "Nothing more than what you've been giving others."

The dark edge intrigued her enough to encourage her to take the bait he offered. "Just the same as your suitors. Want to understand why you..." Seeming to think better of what he was about to say, he swept his hand across his chin. It didn't seem he wanted to say anything more.

Tara held the distinct impression that wasn't all. She wanted to know what he didn't finish saying. Didn't Ash just tell her the man was treacherous. Knowing him might be hazardous to her wellbeing. A spark of something went through her as if it was a lightning strike. Heat roared to life. "I don't know. Suppose I could make room on my card for one more dance. Though I was looking for The Duchess to tell her I was going home." Until Case approached her the air had become stagnant. The room boring. Monotonous. Now the air was exhilarating.

The slow smile creeping across his lips sent another wave of fire surging. He spoke, his voice low, as if he knew exactly what she would do. Understood she would fall into his plans. The challenge was on.

"I'll take you home after the dance. No need to concern The Duchess." He held out his hand in silent invitation. The deep blue of his eyes sparkled with fire and heat. She hesitated, knowing this step might very well be irrevocable. There might be no going back.

Another challenge. Was he testing her? For what possible reason? No single young woman would accept that blatant invitation. He overstepped. She wasn't a debutant. Once there was a fiancé in her life. "Can't. That wouldn't be appropriate," she murmured wondered what the *on dit* would be if she accepted the brazen request. The ton would have her wed to this man before she could breathe. Uncle Drake would make certain he wed her just as he did Nickie and Colin.

"From what I've seen, you don't seem to care about your

reputation. You flirt with anyone wearing pants. So, what would a ride home with me matter? Nothing would change."

The words unsaid did more to catch her attention than the ones he enunciated with a clear even voice. He didn't know anything. Nothing she did tonight would create a scandal.

"You...you have no idea what you are speaking about. You don't know me." She found herself shaking her head in disbelief.

"Am I right?" His question challenged again. He crossed his arms over the width of his chest waiting with what seemed to be never-ending patience for her to answer. "Would like to know you much better. Interested in all of you." His languid gaze raked over her body.

She caught the underlying thought. Snatched her breath a long with a nasty reply into her lungs. "I don't even know your name and you are insulting me as if we've known each other for years." The lie caught in the back of her throat. She held out her hand thinking she would like an introduction of sorts. The introduction would have been better coming from Ash as he seemed to know this man. Despite his attitude or perhaps because of it, she did want to get to know him better. "I'm Tara MacLaren and you?"

He brought her hand to his lips, kissed the back before turning it over to place a damp kiss on the heart of her palm. One more time she jumped. Startled from the unexpected contact, her body vibrated with a need she never felt before. The one kiss packed a wallop. She swallowed down a lump in her throat. Wished she dared fan her face which she knew heated to a raging point. Last minute thinking caused her to tug on her hand. He let it go with a deep masculine chuckle.

"Case Ferguson. About that dance you owe me? Shall we?" he queried as he pulled her toward him, tugged until her body was flush against his. She set her hand on the hard plane of his chest to steady herself. Far too close to be appropriate. He wasn't allowing distance between them. When he looked down at her, she felt his breath wash over her, caught the scent of spearmint as well as man...dangerous man...spicey as well as arrogant.

Hazardous!

The devil, she needed to know what the man was thinking. *He's a risk to me. Ash told me to beware of this man. What do I owe him? A dance? I don't think so.*

"A dance, you owe me a dance," he repeated, his voice deepening, huskier than before.

Why? Tara found herself held within his hot embrace. With singlehanded purpose, he wove a spell around her. This was not like the other dances she shared with her friend as well as her cousins. He held her far too close. He was too imposing, too male. Intimidating. Handsome. His hand that was now settled on the small of her back heated her through the thin layer of fabric that lay between them.

He moved with ease around the floor. Her feet flew. At times she felt as if they didn't touch the dance floor. "Tell me about..." Her heart caught in her throat.

Tara stumbled as he moved too fast. She was awkward. Her other dance partners took that into consideration. Case wouldn't understand. He caught her in his strong arms. Brought her up against his hard muscled chest. She closed her eyes then lied again. "I'm sorry. Don't usually have two left feet." Two left feet was her middle name.

"Nothing to be sorry about," he replied with smooth calm continuing as if nothing happened. He stopped in front of Aunt Ella. "Duchess," he nodded politely at her aunt as if he knew her. "Tara says she would like to leave. With your permission, I'm taking her home."

"That would be nice," Drake cut in looking amused at this new development. "See that the two of you behave."

To say she was startled again would be an understatement. Her breath caught in the back of her throat. "But..." She reached out as if asking for a different answer only to find herself whisked away again. His hand rested on the small of her back, guiding her with ease across the dance floor to the entrance. She felt as if he couldn't get out of there soon enough.

"You changed your mind?" Case asked as he led her to the coatroom. "You do have a wrap? Right?" One of his dark eyebrows lifted skyward.

"No...yes... I wish to leave here. It's just that..." She swiped her tongue across her parched lips. "It's just that..." Tara still couldn't get the words out that she was thinking. Her brain and her mouth didn't want to cooperate.

"Did you have too much of the spiked punch? Or...you didn't expect The duke and duchess to give me the opportunity to be alone with you?" He paused for a few seconds as if he expected her to talk. "I work for the duke. If anything happened to you on my watch, he'd skin me alive. You're safe with me."

"Oh."

She found her shawl.

He draped the fabric around her shoulders, touching her. His fingers brushed against the tops of her breasts. She sipped in air, the caress mercuric.

~ * ~

Case wasn't at all certain what to make of Tara MacLaren. By all standards he recognized she was an enigma. In time he would get to the bottom or the top of what made Tara so reclusive yet at the same time appealing. When he looked into her eyes, they seemed haunted by something intangible.

She was acting.

Had to be.

There was no other explanation. No woman could lie with that much conviction. By watching her this evening, he understood he would be last in line for her affections. Not for long though. He intended to have her then let her go. Sassy little flirts like Tara were good for a fun romp in bed. She would be good in that capacity. That's all he wanted, a good lay. A way to spend the evening. Most any woman would do. Though he liked the ones that would pose the greatest challenge. Tara would be a challenge to him. She held herself aloof. That was a contest to him.

In the coach she sat on the opposite seat. Played with the fabric of her satin ballgown. Stared at him as if she was trying to delve beneath his skin. He needed conversation if he was going to begin to understand her. "Tell me something about yourself."

Lifting her shoulders in a feminine shrug she understood he

would notice. "Not much to tell," she murmured as she seemed to focus on a point outside the carriage. The definite feminine lift of her shoulders, the slight sway of her breasts appealed to all his masculine senses.

"I'm certain that's not true. The way you look at men tells me you've experience." Crossing his legs, he stretched out. Case let his leg rest against hers. She moved away, giving him more room. He thought about pursuing this avenue. Changed his mind. Physically, it might be prudent to move slower. At times, she seemed to be a flighty little thing. Hesitant. One moment she was certain of her environment, the next she acted a shy virgin. A virgin she was not.

"What's Jeremy to you?" Cutting to the most important information, he wanted to ask if she slept with him. If the man was her lover. In time he would know. The question was abrupt. He wasn't surprised when she flashed him a deep dark scowl. Her brows drew together.

Her eyes darkened as she seemed to search for a polite or maybe not so polite reply to his impertinent question. "You overstep."

Yes, where she was concerned, he meant to exceed all polite boundaries. Until he found a way to take her to his bed, he would continue to test her, to challenge to confront. She would be his delight for a few months or for however long they were mutually suited for each other. He believed it would be a while before she bored him. "Perhaps," he hedged not wishing to give away his plans.

"Why did you wish to bring me home?" she asked for the first time, her voice sparked of curiosity. "We mean nothing to each other. Why put out the effort? To impress my uncle?"

He drummed his fingers on his leg, wondering how much truth he dared tell her. "The Duchess suggested we get to know each other better. Told me you planned on riding out to see the sunrise this morning. Seems she thought you should have a protector along for the morning ride. Since I'm good at that type of thing, she approved." He smiled at the glower she returned. Wondered if the way her anger was building, her passion, when he finally made love to her, would be as intense.

"I've Tiny to protect me. Don't need a protector...or a man. I stand alone."

"Another of your lovers? Tiny?" he asked wishing she wasn't quite so promiscuous. Curbing wayward proclivities to be with one man at a time would be his mission. He knew Ashcroft warned her away from him. The young pup told him he would do that. Told him to stay away from her and that Tara wasn't for him to play with. The boy shielded her. Ah, she said they were the same age. He wondered how old she was.

Sitting back, he watched her with more intensity. While she didn't deny she had lovers, she didn't confirm his thoughts either.

"Why of course. I have so many," she murmured, her face turning dreamy while she did corroborate his thoughts. "Would you like me to list them? I've only about ten at this time...give or take. I will need to think. Maybe would help if I...used my fingers."

Case heard the sarcasm in her voice. He didn't read too much into the tone. During the following silence, Tara played with her gown. The ball gown was lovely, the ice blue complimenting as well as enhancing her features. When he touched her, the tops of her full breasts, the flesh was silken. Her waist was narrow. He was positive her hips would flare with enough provocation to arouse him. Hell, he was stimulated looking at her dressed. How would he feel when he saw her naked? Her golden hair was swept into a knot while strategically placed tendrils framed her small oval face. Her nose was pert, tipping a *wee bit* at the end. It was her lips that drew him. He needed to taste and savor, leave a dewy trail of moisture on their fullness. He wanted to nibble on her top lip while he listened to the soft sighs of pleasure he created. Needed to see what lay beneath the fabric. In time he would see as well as do.

"We are here. I don't want a companion this morning. Don't need a chaperone. Need to be alone with my thoughts," she told him as he helped her from the carriage. "You cannot go with me."

"Promised The Duchess. I wouldn't want to hear her scalding words when she discovered I didn't accompany you. That I was derelict in my duty." Case set the steps by the carriage door. Held out his hand to guide her downward.

"Why? Why is she acting this way?"

Because The Duchess formed plans of her own. If he didn't miss his first guess, and he rarely did, the woman was playing matchmaker. In this case, she waisted her time. If she hoped to marry off this beautiful woman to him, her plans would fail. Nonetheless, he would enjoy the adventure along with this wooing as well as the bedding.

"You will have to ask The Duchess. I'm certain she has a reason for everything. Since you are one of her charges, she will do what she thinks best. What are you to her?"

"You don't know?" she asked as he held her elbow escorting her to the front steps of the large townhouse the duke and duchess owned in London though they didn't spend a great deal of time in the city.

The question surprised him. "Should I? Why would she sponsor you?" It didn't appear she meant to tell him or give him a clue. Something else he would discover by himself.

"If you did your homework, you would know the answer. I'm going to change my clothes. If you still want to ride with me, meet me in the stable. Don't be late. Punctuality is important." She flounced away from him, her skirts swaying as she strode through the hall then up the stairs. The devil, he'd like to know her thoughts.

What she didn't know was that he occupied one of the guest rooms on the second floor. Once she disappeared, he raced up the steps to his room. Just as she was a guest of the Montgomeries, so was he. With a hurried pace, he changed to buckskins and a white shirt. Instead of boots, he pulled on a pair of knee-high moccasins he purchased at a trading post on his way to Colorado. It wasn't his intent to be late. He figured he would beat her to the horses. His clothing was so much easier to take on and off than hers. Just so he wouldn't seem too eager, he poured a small snifter of brandy. Once he finished, he strode to the stable.

Inside, the large room filled with numerous horses was lit by a lantern. With muffled steps, he strode down the length. Listening. Watching with intent. It smelled of leather and liniment. The scent of horses wafted through his nostrils. The murmuring two stalls down caught his attention.

"Why, you big oaf, I'm rubbing behind your ears just the way you like. Isn't it enough that I give you the bulk of my attention. You still want more. Always more. What else can I do to please you?"

Another lover she's brought to ride out to see the sunrise. He recognized her voice. Anger simmered deep in his gut. The lady would have to learn that while he was seeing her, there would never be anyone else. Second thoughts hit him in the gut. He knew exactly what she could do to please him. He would make certain she understood sharing pleasure was important to a relationship.

"You're drooling, big guy. Can't you ever control that slobber? No, I suppose you cannot," she giggled, her laughter sending a wave of heat to his belly. The sound was so pure and delightful.

Drooling? That didn't bode well for a lover.

"You're supposed to protect me not drown me." Once more, her laughter was light and airy, filling the confines of the stable.

Case liked the way her voice trilled, liked most everything about the woman except her penchant for men. Ah, but that would also work in his favor. She was an experienced little jade. Passionate. Hungry for a man. Wooing her into his arms wouldn't be hard. Experienced in his own right, he would seduce until she panted, until she wanted no other man in her bed. They would both give and receive pleasure. Then and only then would he walk away.

Whoever this lover was, he meant to rid himself of the man before they left to watch the sunrise. He wouldn't be going with them on this first jaunt as he was never a fan of threesomes. His anger simmered only skin deep. He swung open the gate to the stall where the two lovers were trysting, murmuring sweet nonsense.

His jaw dropped. He rubbed his chin speculating why he thought she was speaking with a man, a lover. What he witnessed explained the drooling.

In the corner of the stall, he gazed at the largest dog he'd ever seen. His paws were on her shoulders. He was licking her face. She was laughing so hard her face was a rosy glow. Tara pushed at Tiny. The dog was immovable.

"Tiny, stop that. Get down, you big oaf!" She was still laughing, to no avail trying to push the animal from her. It seemed the dog was an immovable force. Amused, Case leaned against the fencing. He watched. Delighted with the ensuing event.

Tiny's head was above hers. The dog could kill her with one blow or one bite. Case moved forward, deciding it was time for the dog to behave. "Down, Tiny!"

The dog dropped. On all fours, he stood eye-level to her breasts. Tiny looked at him with clear brown eyes, his tail wagging as if he hadn't just been disciplined. Tiny barked a greeting then sat as if waiting for another order.

She was breathless when she spoke as if she had been rolling around in the hay with her lover. "When did you come in?" Tara asked brushing wayward locks of golden hair from her eyes. "I didn't hear you."

Case grunted. She was too occupied entertaining her huge dog to hear anything. "You were too busy talking nonsense to that big hound of yours." He wasn't about to tell her he thought she was entertaining another lover. Though a tryst with her in the hay would be fun. As long as he thought of her as his, he would never allow her to be with another man.

"Well, are you ready?" She sauntered past him to another stall where a horse was saddled and waiting for her. The mare was a russet color. Pretty as her owner but in a different way. "Come along, Sunrise. We're going to see your namesake. In the meantime, we have to let this man keep us company. The Duchess' orders."

Not giving her a chance to mount by herself, he grabbed her by her slender waist before tossing her on the horse. "Glad to see you're not riding sidesaddle." A woman could kill herself riding that way. He didn't understand why more females didn't opt for a safer and more comfortable means of riding.

She nodded in the direction of another stall. "I had your horse saddled. The big black stallion you ride is waiting."

Bloody eyes, he'd been so busy listening to her banter with her dog, he forgot about having Black readied. He was pleased though that she accepted his company. Time spent with her could be enjoyable. He would see into her soul.

After he mounted, "Lead the way."

For the first few minutes, he elected to follow. Tiny ran along beside them, barking then chasing after whatever seemed to appeal to him. Case enjoyed watching her back, the way she rode with ease. If anything, she was an accomplished horse woman, at home on her mount, her movements fluid yet feminine too. The britches she wore, fit nicely to the curves of her hips and her delectable fanny. There was so much more of her he was going to see. He could wait. Patience was the name of this game he played. He needed her to want him as much as he wanted her.

By the time they left the city, he was abreast of her. "Where to? Where is this beautiful sunrise you're taking me to view?" Curious, he was interested in the destination. Tiny seemed to have lost interest in chasing butterflies as well as bees. Now he trotted beside them, his tongue lolling from his massive jaw. The dog was too friendly. Would never do his job of protecting his mistress unless he drowned someone in his drool or jumped on the person to get his ears rubbed.

Tara flashed him a beautiful smile. He could get used to seeing that smile. She didn't do it often.

"Into the country. Are you familiar with the Montgomerie's country estate?" she asked, sugar coating her words, her eyes looking through him as if concentrating on something only she understood.

After he shook his head, "No. Can't say that I am." Bloody eyes, he wished he could see into her pretty head. One moment she was smiling, the next she was sad. He needed to understand why she looked haunted as if she was in constant pain, as if a ghost disturbed her. Needed to see inside her soul. Needed to discover her falsehoods as well as her truths.

"Just this side of the drive we'll veer off and go overland. A few miles into the countryside there is a lake that spreads out across the rolling land. That's where I mean to watch the sun's rebirth. There is a boulder that has my name on it."

The sun's rebirth.

"This isn't the first time you've watched the sun rise over the lake, is it?" he asked becoming more curious about this fetching woman. She had many facets to her. It would take time to learn what she hid from view.

"Nope."

Case mulled all her words over in his mind, liking the sound of them. In many ways Tara was different from the other women of his acquaintance. Not that very different though. She was a better actress. Could hide her true feelings. All women were after what they could get from a man, wealth, privilege as well as a title. Women needed to feel secure as they aged. This woman could no longer claim to be a debutante yet she did. While he didn't have a title, he had more money than he knew what to do with. He could never spend it all unless he started gambling. Something he would never do. Tara wouldn't know about his wealth unless The Duchess told her. Case held the distinct impression The Duchess told her charge next to nothing about him. She didn't even know his name when he walked up to her at the ball. After thinking about it, he would have expected Ashcroft to fill her in on his name as well as profession. Ashcroft would warn her to stay away. Since he rode with her this morning, the man didn't mention anything about him or his exploits. Either that or she didn't appreciate being told what to do.

As far as he knew, the MacLaren clan were not titled though they did own a castle on the east coast bordering the highlands. She had a half-brother by the name of Liam as well as a brother named Kenzie. That was about all he was able to learn at the ball. The Duchess didn't tell him anything more about her. Discovering all the intriguing facets of this lady would be amusing.

This lady's agenda with a man could be anything. Maybe all she wanted from a male was good sex. Perhaps she wasn't looking for marriage or commitment. He sure as hell wasn't going to go down that path. He could give her good sex as soon as she asked. Once he learned about all the men in her life, he decided she would have to beg. Given time she would. The problem for him was keeping his hands to himself until she did plead.

They crested a hill. At the glorious sight, he sucked in his breath. The sky was just beginning to glow with golds and oranges as well as various shades of pink on the horizon. When the sun rose even higher, the site to greet them would be spectacular. Tara chose the place well. She did say she'd been here before.

She stopped. For a few seconds, she stared at the beauty in front of her. A smile grew on oh so kissable lips. Tiny ran for the lake. In one great leap coupled with a bark of pleasure, he landed about four feet away from the beach making a splash as big as if a cannon ball landed in the water. Her laughter rippled around her. The sound so pleasant, he felt something in his mind change. During those moments watching, listening to her, he thought she was different than what he expected. Tara certainly took pleasure from the simpler things in life.

Still laughing at her big dog, she spoke through giggles. "He's such a big oaf. I love him so much." Her words held sadness within them. When she pulled in a ragged breath of air her small frame shuddered. The haunting of her breath terrified him. It was as if she lost her soul in that moment.

Case saw that same sorrow at the ball when she spoke with Jeremy. The man knew something about her that seemed to be a secret between them. Her eyes haunted with pain, she remained very still as if she savored this moment. It seemed she thought of some other time or place. Perhaps a moment with another man.

To find a place inside her head would be nice. Case didn't think she would enlighten him as to her private thoughts. A time would come when she would confide in him. Wondered what it would feel like to be loved by her.

The thought that she was burrowing into his head disturbed him, would waylay his plans until he could control his baser drives. He reminded himself she was just like every other female, out to get what she could from a man. His mind traveled back ten years ago to the woman he thought to love for the rest of his life.

To the betrayal.

To the heartbreak.

He dismounted then helped her down. When she slipped into his arms, he brought her close enough so he could feel the softness of her breasts pushed against his chest. The sensation wasn't the same as when they danced. She wore nothing beneath her shirt, not even a chemise. An invitation he meant to ignore for the time being. If she was truly that needy, she would have to wait to find her pleasure. Tara was a brazen little thing, displaying herself this way. If The Duchess didn't know about her charge's proclivities, he wasn't going to be the man to explain things to Ella.

Tara didn't seem to notice the bulge pressing against her belly while he still held her, his hands cupped around the lushly feminine curves of her bottom to steady her. Either that or she didn't mean to give his need for her credence. When she turned her face so she looked at him, she was flushed with a rosy glow. Mayhap, she did notice.

Case set her away from him. She moved with a few awkward steps toward the boulder as if she was in pain. After that, she seemed to get her feet beneath her. She relaxed.

"Any special place you watch this spectacle from?" His hands rested behind his back while he rocked on his heels, studying every subtle nuance that was Tara MacLaren. She was the perfect study of innocence coupled with sensuality. Her passion would rock him until he couldn't breathe or think. He wasn't positive how he knew this.

He just did.

Tara pointed, "Over there, by the boulder. See, the big rock has my name written on the side. I usually sit on top until the show is over. After that I appreciate the solitude as long as I dare before I go back to the estate. Never want The Duchess to send out a search party."

"How often do you come here?" Case followed Tara to the boulder. She moved with fluid liquid grace. Her hips the perfect size for her frame. Sometime during the ride, she had unbuttoned the top two buttons of her shirt. He wanted to look at her more closely, so he could see what he could see. The slight swell of her breasts would be evident. If he had his wishes, she would go for one more button.

"Whenever I visit the duke and duchess." Her long fingers pushed her hair away from the small perfect oval of her face. "That's not often though. I like home too much."

"You're here for the season?" he asked expecting a round of lies. She was too old to have a season. The lords searching for a wife were looking at younger women, malleable women. Tara wouldn't be easily swayed by any man. Case didn't want to change her in any way, just wanted to experience her company. Needed her to grace his bed for as long as they both wanted each other.

He helped her navigate the boulder then jumped up beside her.

"No, not here to find a husband or to parade for the men who are searching. Don't want a husband. Told The Duchess I didn't want a season. Unfortunate for me, she insisted." She leaned back, her hands supporting her, the view provocative, challenging him to keep his hands to himself.

Case believed her even though the sigh following her words held a bit wistfulness in them. There might have been a time she felt different. "Why ever not?" Seemed she never failed to surprise him. "All women want a husband." A bit of his jaded self-came out in the tone of his voice.

"Don't believe there is a man out there I can fall in love with. Have to be in love to marry." She let out another breathy expulsion of air that brought more questions to Case's mind. "Won't marry for any reason except love." She turned to him searching out his features. Her gaze locked with his.

"What about you?"

A dark shadow swept through him as he thought about the woman he once thought he loved. She killed love for him. Taught him love wasn't real. Love was an imagined emotion. He learned women betrayed men to get what they wanted or needed. He pointed to the sunrise as he spoke. "Love doesn't exist. Don't want a wife. Guess we're a matched pair in that respect." He was surprised he told her as much.

When she turned to look at him, the concern in her eyes shocked him. He didn't recall knowing a woman who was ever concerned about anyone except themselves. A slight tilt to her head coupled with vertical crease between her brows, she asked, "What happened? Who hurt you so terribly you lost all hope for love? Love does exist. All you need to do is watch Ella and Drake when they are together."

The question coupled with her comment hit him as hard as if she swung a sledge hammer into his gut. This conversation was at an end. He wasn't about to talk about his past when the future would prove to be more gratifying. Nor did he intend to debate love. "Suppose we should enjoy the rebirth of the sun as you put it." Revealing a past to any woman was a mistake he wasn't going to make. He wasn't stupid. Doing so would give the female an advantage. Case wasn't a man to allow himself to become vulnerable.

"That bad?" Tara leaned back again, her hands behind her. Once more in that provocative pose he enjoyed. She'd crossed her legs so she sat Indian style. Her breast pushed forward against the fabric of her shirt. Nipples hard and tight showed against the tiny barrier she called a shirt.

Case appreciated the view. While her breasts were not large, they would fit in his hands. She was more beautiful than the sunrise that now splashed color across the horizon. More intriguing. If he could paint, he would paint the sunrise with Tara's face part of the parade of colors. In his mind, he imagined the portrait.

When she turned abruptly, she caught him staring at her. He wasn't about to answer her question. What he experienced with his first love was more than bad. The encounter changed his life forever. No one needed to know. Everyone who did either left him or had passed on. Ella Montgomerie knew part of the story as did Drake. No one except Case Ferguson knew it in its entirety.

When he joined the SIS, he'd had to enumerate a few of his reasons. Drake Montgomerie had been privy to those reasons. Ella, well Ella was a different story. She had this way about her. Somehow and for reasons he didn't understand, he confided in her. Mentioned parts of his life that surprised him. The Duchess promised not to tell anyone, not even the duke. Husbands, especially Drake at his finest interrogation, had a way of drawing unwilling truths from people. If the devious pair put the information they knew about him together, they would know everything.

"What happened is in the past. Doesn't need a recounting of details." Case supposed that much of what he read in Tara's haunted and sad eyes revolved around the past. She wasn't recounting details either.

"Is that your way of telling me it's none of my business?"

"Yes."

They both held secrets close to their hearts.

To his surprise, she leaned into him. The gesture was almost as if she wished for comfort. He wrapped his arm around her, pulling her close. Her head on his chest, he heard a throaty little sigh of contentment that surprised him.

Lost in thought, he barely noticed she'd fallen asleep. Minutes passed. His arm was growing numb. He didn't want to wake her. From some of the gossip he heard last night, she arrived at the Montgomerie's with just enough time to prepare for the ball. She hadn't slept last night. He decided it wasn't the company that put her to sleep.

As carefully as possible, he lifted her into his arms. At the base of the huge rock, they'd been sitting on, he sat down. His back against the boulder, he relaxed. She smelled of lilies coupled with sunshine. To his surprise, she snuggled in his arms, her hand set on his belly. His gut tightened. Heat spiraled straight to his loins. He held tight to control while her small body was cradled against his.

Case wanted to chuckle when he heard the little snore. If he confronted her with that fact, she would deny she snored. He closed his eyes, content to hold her for as long as she slept. Maybe not as long as she slept. The Duchess knew where they were. Would expect them at the country house at a respectable time. If they didn't show up, there wasn't a single doubt in his head that Ella would send someone after them.

The brilliant colors in the sky faded, turning to a vivid summer blue. A few clouds dotted the horizon as the sun inched its way upward. The breeze was slight. Leaves in the trees above them rustled to the stimulant. She burrowed into him, running her cheek across his chest. He flamed from the insignificant contact. If this was any indication of how they would do together, she would heat his bed to an inferno. He should wake her soon. Didn't know her well enough to know how to go about doing so.

"Grant..." she whispered, her hand roaming, exploring across his belly.

Grant?

Case tightened, jealousy surging ahead. Who the devil was Grant? The man had to be another one of her lovers. He would have to discover who this man was as well as what he meant to her so he could let him know that Tara was hands off until they no longer wanted each other. That time would come.

When he looked down at her sleepy-lidded eyes, slightly dazed, she whispered again. "Kiss me. It's been so long. I've missed you so much. Life isn't the same when you're gone."

Case fought the urge consuming him until he could no longer control the impulse. The man must be in her past. "If that's what you want, baby, then who am I to deny you your carnal pleasures. Your sensuality is why we are together. This might be the first kiss but it won't be the last."

His lips feathered across Tara's mouth, light butterfly caresses, teasing nips, flirting sultry touches. His tongue to her mouth urging her to give more of herself. Her fingers wound into his shirt pulling him closer. Her warm breath entered into him. He placed undemanding kisses on the corners of the sweet curve of her mouth. With his teeth he nibbled on her top lip until she opened more fully for his attention. Even in her sleep she knew what she wanted. She gave all that he asked then a *wee* bit more.

A broken sound then a soft mewl was his reward for his tender attention. His body hardened with need as well as restraint while he steeled himself to seduce not respond. With this little vixen he found that feat impossible.

As the day progressed, she'd unfastened buttons on her shirt. Now the sight of the rounded swell of her breasts were visible between the two sides of her shirt. Touching and tasting were in the forefront of his mind. That could wait. One thing at a time.

"Oh, Grant..." she sighed again, running her hand across the expanse of his chest. "I've missed you."

There it was again. Tara needed to learn the man wasn't Grant who was kissing her, who was giving her pleasure. He deepened the kiss, smoothing his tongue over hers as she opened for him, giving him easy accesses. Inside her mouth she was hot, a sultry inferno that begged for discovery. He touched all of her, tugged on her bottom lip, caressed her teeth then delved deeper into the inferno that grew with each passing second.

When she was arching toward him, her hands winding into his hair while she accepted the intimacy he offered, he pulled away, the movement slow. Case was watching her eyes. Needed to see the moment she realized he wasn't Grant. He was so close to her. His wishes confirmed. Knew the exact moment she opened her eyes. Her hand touched feather light on his cheek. She stared, confused for the moment. Eyes widening, she sat up, her head hitting his chin.

"You're not Grant!"

No...he wasn't.

"Who is Grant?"

~ * ~

Ella paced the sundeck where they were eating a late breakfast. She continued to stare in the direction of the lake, worried about Tara. Case was notorious for his womanizing. She'd put them together for a solid reason. Drake agreed with her. That thought didn't make her feel better. Acting as matchmakers could be disastrous. Ella understood why Tara shied away from men. Knew also why Case didn't want a solid relationship with a woman. The two of them both needed healing. They were perfect for each other. Perfect unless Case seduced her before she was ready.

"She is in good hands," Drake told her as if he meant to encourage better feelings. "Case is a good man. He won't do anything Tara doesn't reciprocate."

Ella understood her instincts in this affair were right. Still, doubts whirled in her head. While Case might never allow himself to be hurt by a woman, Tara was vulnerable. "That's what I'm afraid of...his hands...his mouth," Ella retorted as she continued the frenzied walking from one end of the patio to the other.

Drake tossed his head back, barking with the laughter that she knew all too well. "He won't hurt her. Won't take her virginity, at least not yet. When the time is right for both of them, if the pair continue to see each other, they will come together. Tara needs to wake up to the fact Grant is no longer alive. If that means the loss of her innocence, so be it. We both understand she needs to move on with her life. Who better to do that for her than a notorious rake?" He lifted his broad shoulders in a

29

very male shrug accepting the inevitable without feeling a moment's guilt.

"I know. I agreed with you because Tara believes her life ended with Grant's life. It very nearly did. We are all thankful she is still alive. Something or someone has to shock her into living again," Ella said, though she knew Tara had come a long way in doing so on her own. The girl did agree to come for a season even though Ella knew full well that Tara would have been happier wandering the trails around her ancestral home and hunting. Since her fiancé's death she'd become such a loner. Seemed she hid from life.

"When the right woman comes along, every man falls," Drake mused seeming to think of how he fell for his wife.

"I just hope that she doesn't have to give up her innocence before the wedding." Drake was so positive there would be a marriage. Ella wasn't so certain. There were things she knew about Case that she didn't think her husband had learned or if he did, being male he wouldn't understand.

"You gave up yours," he said blandly as he patted his thighs, an invitation to her to come to him.

"You didn't give me much of a choice," she retorted ignoring the invitation.

"No, with good reason. In Paris they will have company of sorts. Ashcroft has left for the city. He will have things prepared for them when they arrive in a day or two. How long do you think it will take Tara to ready herself."

"Bah! Our son will be no chaperone to that pair as well you know. He will be out to whatever party he can find, testing his manhood in every feasible way. What makes you think Tara will agree to go?"

"I don't know. What does she have here except a broken heart? Case offers a warm heart. Companionship. Hopefully love. She needs everything."

"More likely a warm bed is what he is extending to her."

"I saw the way he looked at her. Yes, the man wants her in the most basic way. Our Tara won't give herself so easily into his hands. He will have to work to get her into his bed. By then he will have fallen in love."

"I know." Ella gave in and sat down on Drake's lap. "I hope they will heal each other."

"Kiss me."

Chapter Two

"What!" Tara pushed away from him but he held tight. She didn't understand what happened. She'd been kissing her fiancé. This man wasn't Grant. She woke sleepy and oh, so dreamy in his arms, the man she loved. His lips explored. He tasted of mint. His scent she remembered from when they danced together. Waves of guilt poured over her. She should never be kissing another man.

"Who is Grant?" he persisted, giving her a tiny shake that sent her hair cascading around her shoulders. "When I'm kissing a woman, I want her to know it's me doing the kissing not some other man."

Telling him anything about Grant was never going to happen. Tara couldn't share what was private. Wasn't ready to explain to anyone who didn't know the truth. Without conscious thought, she rubbed her leg. That horrible day it seemed she broke every bone in her body. Grant though, he didn't live. Jeremy told her he died instantly. She didn't know if that was true or if Jeremy was trying to ease some of her pain. Tara couldn't bear it if Grant suffered. Jeremy would understand that. For such a long time she thought Grant was the lucky one. Now, she was beginning to heal. She didn't believe her heart would ever forget or move on. "None of your business." When Tara pushed away, he held her tight.

"You are not going to see that man again." His voice was gruff, demanding. He held her close. Touched her cheek with his knuckles, continued that caress down her neck to the spot where the frantic beat of her heart leapt. "He's in your past. The man will stay there. Do you understand?"

Case was right about Grant being in her past and staying there. He still didn't have the right to issue orders. She gulped in a huge draft of air just so she could talk. "You've no right to make demands. I don't owe you anything. You don't mean anything to me." Tara recalled that he told her she did owe him. She'd owed him a dance. She delivered. "Why were you kissing me?"

Case grinned at her, his smile shooting sparks of heat into her. His fingertip trailed to a spot between her breasts. She jerked. "You asked me to kiss you."

"Did not!" Tara was furious. He lied. He had to lie. She would never... She held his hand trying to tug it upward. He lied. He needed to stop his exploration of her body. She would never ask another man to kiss her. "Stop touching me!" Her heartbeat raced with frantic speed. Even when she spoke the words, she understood her body heated, places she forgot about since Grant's death ached with unfulfilled need.

Did I ask him?

"Well, believe whatever you want to believe. Think what you will. You asked. I delivered. Will do so again if you're nicer to me. What do you want to do now? Another kiss?" he winked at her as his slow charming smile grew on his handsome face.

The man had the audacity to wink. She wanted to hit him. When she moved away from him, cool air caressed her flesh. Her shirt was open close to her navel. Bloody hell?

He shrugged those broad shoulders of his, his eyes glinting in the sunlight. "Couldn't help myself. The offering was too sweet, succulent. You opened the buttons."

"Did not!"

"Hmm..."

This was far too much for her to take in at one time. She'd been asleep, dreaming of another time, a different man. Tara knew she might have done what he said. The kiss, yes, if she thought the man holding her was Grant. Unfastening buttons was not...she did unfasten the first two. She was hot, needed air. Not as hot as she was now.

"We need to go back." Tara pushed to her feet. The stab of pain in her thigh stopped her before she could take a step. She fell to the ground in a heap of agony she couldn't hide from Case. Her eyes filled with moisture. She didn't want him to see her this way. His shadow loomed over her. This was something very few people knew about.

"What the devil?" Case asked, his question filled with concern.

"What's going on here?"

Tara heard the apprehension in his voice. Didn't want him to know why sometimes she couldn't walk. The last twenty-four hours taxed her strength. The ball, the ride all caused her muscles to tighten as well as cramp at the most inopportune moment. How long had she been asleep? Her mind jerked from one thought to another with blinding speed. She had too many questions.

"I'm fine. Nothing for you to worry over." Tara tried to push away from him as she attempted to stand. Once again, her leg buckled, gave way.

Crouched beside her, he massaged her leg. With a long finger under her chin, he lifted her head so he could see her eyes. "Tell me what's got you stumbling. Bloody hell, you can't walk let alone ride. Can you?"

"Why don't you go on ahead. I'll be just dandy in a few minutes after I stretch out the kinks. Tiny will be here with me. I'll follow as soon as I can. Don't wish for you to watch me sitting here embarrassed. The shame..." Tara felt humiliated to the tips of her toes. It wasn't enough that she asked him to kiss her, had unfastened her shirt, now she couldn't walk. She closed her eyes trying to will the pain away. First hand, she understood the ache would recede. Understood that as long as she hurt, she knew she was alive. The alternative was not to her liking.

"No, I'm not going to leave you to fend for yourself," he spoke with sincerity, his voice stopping when she flinched. "Hurts here?"

"Don't want you touching me!" Tara's voice was tight while she tried to hold onto the single thread he was unraveling.

"Didn't mind the kiss or the other." Case was looking at the still open shirt seeming to memorize what she looked like beneath the fabric. "I'm not leaving you here. If I have to, I'll carry you in front of me on Black. Sunrise will follow. Now," he paused, his eyes boring into her even while sitting back on his haunches giving her room to breathe. "What will help? Do you need to walk a bit? In that case, I can hold onto you. Doubt if you can manage on your own."

"Yes, the massage helps. Though I usually do the manipulation myself. If you like, you can help me walk. A few circles around the boulder will be enough. I'll be good as new." Tara hoped a few circles would be enough. She didn't know. Couldn't say for certain. She'd never be as good as new.

Case began the massage again, kneading her muscle in just the right places. His big hands worked wonders. For the first few seconds she gritted her teeth against the pain. As the rose color in the sky lessened, the knot began to ease. The muscle relaxed. She couldn't stop the soft sigh of pleasure as she began to feel normal.

"Do you want to try out that bum leg now?" Case stood, extending his hand to her.

While she didn't want to take his hand, in the process accept his help, she didn't have a choice. There was no way she would be able to stand without help. "No, but I don't see where I've got a choice. Have to get back to the estate before The Duchess sends out search parties. Don't need for her to worry about me."

"That's true. She won't worry. She *kens* you're with me. I've been approved. Take my hand, my help," Case told her. "I won't bite unless you ask. Won't speak of this again. Nonetheless, I would prefer if you explained the problem to me that you wish to keep private."

Tara didn't want pity or sympathy from anyone, least of all Case Ferguson. Until now, she managed to hide her pain from everyone except Jeremy. He knew too much. Had been with them when the accident happened. She'd never be able to hide the agony of that day from the man who knew the truth.

With a fierce tug, he brought her to her feet. Unable to help herself, she swayed into him. His hands on her waist, he steadied her. She needed air, drinking it in as if she couldn't get enough of it. His scent rioted with her senses.

"Whenever you're ready, we can start." Case seemed patient with her. He didn't urge her to do something beyond her abilities.

The nod of her head seemed to give rise to the arch of his dark brow. "If only I believed you." He wrapped his arm around her waist, waiting for her to test her strength. "Take a few steps. You will be able to tell in a bit if you can ride by yourself or if you need me to take you on my horse. Be honest."

Her heart raced with the effort she made. Panting breaths accompanied each step. Tara wobbled around the boulder where they'd been sitting. If she didn't have Case to lean on, this would all be for naught. All the while, she listened to the soft curses bombarding the air. She wished she could do better. The fact remained she would not be able to ride by herself. With every step she grew weaker, her muscle tightening with each motion of her leg. She would need at least a day of recovery.

Leaning into him, absorbing his strength, she placed her hand on his chest. "I won't be able to ride Sunrise. This will get worse before it gets better. From experience I know that." Willing this to a quick end, she closed her eyes listening to the sounds around her the rippling of the water, the bees, the birds. Her head against him, she heard the strong beat of his heart, the strength of the breaths he inhaled. This man was power personified. She represented weakness.

His stoic expression didn't surprise her. He said nothing more about wanting to know what caused her problem. Tara wasn't at all certain why she didn't want to say anything. Except that talking about that day hurt. Still hurt her with such intensity she felt as if a knife stabbed her in the gut. He must have accepted the fact she didn't like to talk about what caused her injury. He never asked again.

The time was measured, second by second, minute by minute. She was learning to live again. Each day was fractionally better than the last. Debilitating memories surfacing only when something or someone reminded her of that day or of Grant.

With easy strength that she marveled at, Case swooped her into his arms. He carried her as if she weighed nothing at all. Before she could catch her breath, she was sitting on Black and he was behind her.

"Can you sit astride, *Lass*? Would it be better if I held you on my thighs?" The sound of his voice was so concerned. "I'm at a loss. Want only to do what is right for you. Don't wish to add to the injury."

Two years had passed since she heard that type of concern in a man's voice. In a few days, she would feel the brunt of her loss more severely than the days before and after. It was the anniversary of that horrific day. Her nerves stretched to the breaking point at his unease.

"I'm sorry." Tara understood he wouldn't accept this apology. She wanted to shrivel into a tiny shell until all the pain vanished. "I don't like to be weak or humbled. Don't want to ask for help from anyone. Not just you. Need to live on my own. My independence is important to me."

"Your courage is admirable but your way of thinking is faulty. Sometimes a woman needs help." Case positioned her so she sat on his lap. "You've nothing to be embarrassed about. While I'm not a mind reader, it's obvious that you had some type of accident that injured your leg. You don't have to speak the words. Nonetheless, I swear to you I will find out what happened. There are people who know. I will talk to them. Everyone who is close to you. Between us there should be no secrets."

More than her leg was brutalized in the accident. She didn't wish to share this secret with him. The pain deep in her soul still agonized over that day. Her heart broken. The organ would never heal. "I don't want to talk about what happened to me...to you or anyone. That fact won't change." Tara closed herself off to thoughts that centered around the horrific day that changed her life forever.

"That would be obvious to a two-year-old. I'm not two. Be it known if you ever want to talk, I'll listen. No judgement."

She would never talk about this to him as long as he was nothing to her. When they reached the stable, one of the hired help came out to give assistance. Case swung his legs over the horse before dropping lightly to the ground with Tara still in his arms. "Feed and water Black as well as Sunrise. Groom them." He didn't set her on the ground.

"What are you going to do?" Tara asked, her voice wobbling on the last words. So unsure of herself or Case, she didn't want for anything more to be made of her injury. Aunt Ella would come see her. She understood what would happen. Questions would be asked. Queries she didn't wish to answer. All she wanted was a hot bath.

"Find The Duchess. Second, take you to your room then make certain someone is there to look at your leg more thoroughly than I'm positive you would have allowed me to do." His voice was gruff when he spoke.

His anger as well annoyance didn't go unnoticed. As far as she was concerned, Case had no reason for fury or irritation. Whatever it was he was feeling was because she didn't explain to his satisfaction. Her past was none of his business. In this life, Case was nothing to her. Most likely would never be important.

"If you put me down, I can try to walk on my own." She didn't wish to be carried into the house. Didn't wish to appear vulnerable even though she was.

The soft spoken explicative she heard made her flinch. "You said this would get worse before better. So, you think you can walk now? Only rehashing your words." His sarcasm blindsided her.

At this point she didn't know what to think or say. Everything he said was correct. She didn't like to admit her shortcomings. She would have to do so now. "No."

"Foolish woman!"

As it turned out he didn't need to look for Aunt Ella. She appeared almost the second Case walked through the door into the foyer. Her lips were pursed. She looked as if she expected this.

"Her leg is hurt. Bad. She refuses to explain. Tara can't walk. If you show me to her room, I'll put her on the bed. Believe a hot bath might help ease the muscle strain along with another massage." There was a short pause before he spoke again, "What happened to her?" Case asked.

Ella wouldn't answer him. She was shaking her head. "Ask Tara. That is the only way you will find out what you wish to learn. When she wants you to know, she'll tell you the truths that you are looking for. Until then..." Ella lifted her shoulder in a half-shrug. "You will have to proceed in the dark. Follow me." Ella led the way upstairs to her room in the east wing. "Set her on the bed. When the hot water comes, I'll help her undress."

When she was on the bed, stretched out, embarrassed, humiliated, Ella pulled the bell cord. The maid arrived within seconds.

"A hot bath," Ella said then turned to Case. "Thank you for your help. Was the sunrise nice? I hope the scene was worth this."

"Spectacular," Case said as his gaze swept from her to Ella. "I had nothing to do with the pain. This is all Tara's doing."

With a nod of agreement, she spoke, her voice soft. "I believe the duke needs to speak with you," Ella dismissed him without a blink just as a duchess should.

Case nodded. "Where can I find him?"

"He is in his office this time of day. If not there, try the library."

Tara watched him disappear from her room. He was so handsome, strong. She liked his gentle side. Did she ask him to kiss her? She'd been dreaming of Grant. The kiss was nice. No, the kiss was more than nice.

"What happened out there?" Ella would want more than an answer to the obvious question. She would expect to learn everything.

"Nothing, maybe not nothing. Seems I did too much." Tara spoke so soft. She wasn't certain her Aunt Ella heard. "Forgot the strain dancing and riding put on my leg. I'd been in the coach for several days with no exercise. The muscle gave out."

"You told Case nothing about the events that caused this. Sit up. I'm going to help you out of your clothes. The bath should be here within a few minutes." Ella worked matter-of-factly, helping her to sit then remove her clothes.

By the time the steaming water was brought into the room, Tara wore nothing except a pale blue satin wrapper. The hot liquid would feel as if heaven descended on the sore muscle that ached and throbbed. The bone broke through the skin, tearing muscles, ripping them apart. The doctor who set the bones was excellent. He told her she might always have trouble walking. She was awkward, favoring her other leg. When she could, she hid the fact. If she was alone, she babied the injured leg.

"Thank you for helping, Aunt Ella. I know you think I should speak of that day more often. I cannot. Those who know, know only because there was a need. No other reason. If I had my way, no one would understand the events of that day except Jeremy. I don't relish sympathy. Don't like to see the expression on a person's face when they learn what happened. Realize what I lost. Don't want pity. Just wish to be left alone."

"Jeremy..." Ella assisted her in removing the robe then helped her into the water. She sat on a sofa near the tub. "Case will have to know sooner than later. He asked me what happened on that day. You heard him. Events will evolve so you will need to tell him."

"Why?" Tara was shocked by her aunt's words. She didn't see how anything could happen that would cause her to reveal her darkest secrets. "Case doesn't need to know anything about my past or my future. The man is nothing to me. Never will be."

Ella's soft breath of air told Tara there was more going on here than she'd been told. "Drake asked me to wait to tell you his plans. However, I disagreed with him. Men, they are all about strategy. When it comes to a woman's mind the male approach doesn't work. Though in my case what he did to get me to the altar was well planned. His machinations accomplished what he desired. I was well and truly compromised before the wedding day. He gave me an ultimatum. When I agreed to his wishes, I understood I might be risking a great deal."

A sinking feeling swept through her hearing her aunt's words. "What's going on? I've a right to know. Is this something I have a choice to accept or deny? Has my uncle plotted to such a degree that all involved will fall into his schemes? What are they?" Tara found herself sitting up in the bath, waiting with a great deal of impatience for the truth. Tiny was snoring by the fire, soaking up the warmth given off by the smoldering embers.

"Tomorrow, if you can walk, the next day or the day after, you and Case are going to Paris. It's what Drake wants. If it is what he wants..."

Aunt Ella's words sunk into her musty brain. "No!" Tara nearly bolted from the tub before recalling that she was naked. "No, no way, no. What are the two of you trying to accomplish by putting us together? We aren't suited. He is always brooding. Staring into space or at me. I don't want another man in my life. One loss was enough." What she was terrified of was falling in love again then losing that man. His kiss haunted her. Heated her just thinking about the sensations.

"You are fluent in French. Am I right?" Ella was nudging her into agreement. "You know the city. Am I right or wrong?"

With each moment, she was growing more concerned this was a plot she would never get out of, she nodded. "Yes, to both."

"You've been to Paris a number of times. You can be a tour guide for Case. He will have to begin to learn the city. To know as well as understand the people along with the culture. You are that one unique person who can accomplish all that."

"Yes." Tara was careful, unwilling to give anything away. Nonetheless, it seemed Ella knew far more about her than she could have guessed. "Where are you going with all this. Tell me." Her heart was in her throat. She both wanted this as well as feared what she suspected.

"Well, Case works for Drake at the SIS. Three days ago, he and Ash were assigned to Paris. Drake doesn't see immediate danger. For Case, the time spent there will be a working vacation. While there are no pressing matters at this time between the French government and the English, he will be expected to keep Drake informed of all the goings on in that town, everything he discovers behind closed doors. The English are still vigilant, wary of the French. No one wants another Napoleon to rise up out of the ashes of that failed government. Louis Philippe I is the reigning monarch. However, as you well know, there is little to no trust between our governments. Even though both countries are playing at being friends. What we do know is that the financial situation of the country is in chaos."

"Where do I come in? Don't see a reason why I should be involved." Tara paused thinking about the ball last night along with the dance she had with her cousin. Thought of his words to her about Case. "His work, is that why Ash told me he was a dangerous man?" Her curiosity was growing by leaps and bounds. She wasn't looking for a relationship. Everything about Case intrigued her.

"To answer all your questions; first, you will appear with Case as a showpiece on his arm. He will escort you to all the invitations he receives, which should be many. Drake has put out the word that Case will be there. Second, I believe Ash understands the danger that goes with this type of job. In Paris there should be no threat. Yes, in other respects Case might be a danger to your heart. If you don't guard it with care, he might well steal it from you. In case you didn't notice, he is a very handsome man. Charismatic. Compelling in many ways."

Tara snorted. "Arrogant."

"That too. Just like Drake. As your father is also."

After she set her head on the lip of the tub, Tara did some more thinking. "I've no choice in this matter, do I? What my uncle wants he always finds a way to get. After all, he wanted you, didn't he? I would enjoy going to Paris. It's been several years. I was there with Grant along with his family the year before he..." She couldn't bring herself to say the word. That was three years ago. Grant was still a major part of her heart.

"No, not much of one. If you adamantly refused to move your feet in the direction of Paris, Drake would be displeased, maybe furious. More than irritated. Annoyed. We both believe you are the perfect woman to grace Case's arm at the affairs the two of you will be invited to. Your fluency in the French language will give you an advantage over another woman who cannot speak French. Oh! Did I forget to tell you? You will be compensated for your efforts. Not as much as your male counterpart but enough to put a smile on your face." Ella held up her hands. "Don't ask how much. I can't tell you the exact stipend."

"I don't know. It would be fun to go to Paris one more time," she mused again reliving the strolls down the city streets, the visits to the museums. Has Case been there?" She would like to be able to show him around. To see Paris with this man would be a delight to her senses. "Does he speak the language."

"Enough to get by in a pinch. You would also be expected to translate and write correspondence he dictates to you. You have a dreamy smile on your face. Does that mean you are agreeing? Have I convinced you that late spring and early summer in Paris would be a delight to your senses? The flowers will be starting to bloom, the trees budding. Sunshine for long walks. Fresh air to fill you. Make you come alive."

"You read me well, Aunt Ella. Believe I am coming around to your way of thinking...Drake's that is. You and Uncle Drake are right. I need a change of scenery. Need to have something else in my mind." Case was...is a nice man. She would enjoy spending time with him, showing him her favorite haunts in the city. They could go to Bordeaux for fine French wines or Epernay where they make champagne. She hauled in a lump of air. After today, getting sick in front of Case would humble her even more. She understood somewhere along the line they would have to board a ship. She was a terrible sailor. Her feet loved land as did her stomach. "How will we get there? You know I don't do ships well."

"As you say. We would have liked to put you on one of Drake's ships then sale you right up the Seine to Paris. That would be the safest for all involved. Since time on a ship would be disastrous for you, Drake has arranged for a carriage to Dover. He has booked passage on a ship that will cross the English Channel. You need only be sick for the few hours it takes to cross the channel. After that, you will go from Calais to Paris by carriage. He has a special agent waiting for you in that city. Ash left last night as he was eager to get on with his first assignment with the SIS. With the help of a few servants who have been gainfully employed for the last week, he will have the apartment where you will be staying ready for the two of you by the time you get there."

"You trust Case with my virtue? I don't understand." Tara cut straight to the major question she had for her aunt.

Ella coughed then turned her head as if she wished to compose her features. After she looked back, "No, I don't. Neither does your uncle." She held up a hand to shush her while she continued to talk. "What I do know, is that the only way you will lose your innocence to Case is if you love the man. I also understand and trust in the fact that while Case is jaded in many ways, as long as you say no, he would never force you. So, in my opinion, your innocence is in your hands not Case's. If you decide to have sex with him, it is your choice."

"I suppose I should trust in your judgment."

"No, trust in yours and nothing will go wrong. You'll see."

"My judgement," she said her words whisper thin. "Yes, trust myself. Who else is there to trust?" Tara understood what her aunt was telling her. If she didn't want him to make love to her, he wouldn't. Though the man was more charming than any male had a right to be, though he might sweettalk, in the end what they did or did not do together was up to her.

"How do you feel about the man? Do you like him? You looked

content in his arms, trusting him while he carried you."

"He is easy to look at," Tara said in response to her aunt. "Nice to me, though he thinks I'm a flirt."

"All women flirt when they see a man they'd like to learn more about. It's in our nature. I flirted outrageously with Drake."

Tara wondered how much she should tell her aunt concerning her feelings. If her mother was sitting with her, she would feel comfortable confiding. As if making the decision, she began, "I'm curious about him. He intrigues me as well as compels me to be different from the way I've been the last two years. I've closed myself off, distanced myself from men, until Case. He's handsome but not always charming. At times he can be blunt as well as rude." Unconsciously, she set her finger on her lips, recalling the kiss, his taste, the scent of him. When she looked to Ella her aunt was smiling.

"He's kissed you."

"Yes, is it that obvious?" Tara didn't know what she'd done to prompt that conclusion. Case told her that she asked him to kiss her. At first, she didn't believe him. After she thought for a while, she realized she'd been dreaming she was in Grant's arms. He didn't like the fact she called him Grant.

Ella rose then fetched a warmed bath towel, setting it on a chair near the tub. "I'll leave so you can get out of the water which must be growing tepid. You can see if walking is a possibility. If it's not, pull the chord. If it is, meet us in the drawing room as soon as you are ready. There are crutches by the door if you need assistance."

Tara nodded, thinking sleep would be nice. Her aunt didn't seem to notice she could barely keep her eyes open. She supposed she could take a nap once her future was decided. In the next hour or so that was what would happen. In a few days, she would be alone with a very dangerous man in the heart of Paris.

~ * ~

Case walked into Lord Montgomerie's office wondering about the summons. He'd been told he would get his next assignment in a day or two. His gut told him this was the moment he would know where he was going next. He thrived on danger. It gave him the means to forget his past, a past that he needed to put behind him. Tara's giving nature haunted him just as her eyes held so much pain. If he could get her to open up to him, he would. She needed someone to care about her life. Just as he did. Case shook that sentiment from his head.

Part of what he liked about the job was the ever-present threat of danger. Living on the edge was a thrill he loved. Even in this time of relative piece, there was intrigue involved, one government pitted against another. Strategies instigated that would give one country an advantage over another. The political games fascinated him. The men involved played a game of chess with the lives of the citizens of their countries. He was part of that game.

He hoped his assignment would keep him in London. Moving on before learning more about the intriguing Miss MacLaren wasn't to his liking. If he was leaving her behind, he might have to change his strategy. As things stood between them now, they understood next to nothing about each other. They both harbored secrets they were loath to reveal. Unraveling took trust. He would never trust a woman again. While they shared an amazing kiss this afternoon, she'd been thinking of another man. That fact bothered him more than the haunted look in her eyes. Next time he kissed her the only name on her sweet, kissable lips would be his.

Ah, well, if he was sent somewhere, he would return. There was always another day, another month or year. It would not be too difficult to find her. He knew where she lived. By the time he finished this assignment, he would have time to explore opportunities such as Tara. For a month or two he could do as he pleased.

The door was open to Drake's office. Montgomerie rose when he saw him, beckoning him to enter. Case's gut clenched as he stepped inside. Tension filled the air in the room. Something was not to the duke's liking.

"Drink?" Drake offered with a bland smile greeting him. He motioned for him to take a seat while he waited for Case to answer. "We've much to discuss. Your new assignment for starters as well as the companion I hope will be traveling with you. Believe you will appreciate my choice."

A partner? I don't do partners.

That wasn't his style. He worked better alone with no one to slow him down or complicate his decisions.

"Brandy would be nice." Once again, his thoughts returned to Drake's edict. Case didn't like to work with anyone. Until now Drake understood. Didn't suppose he had a choice in the matter. "Who is this traveling companion you've picked out for me?" He ran his finger around the collar of his shirt feeling closed in, claustrophobic. Suffocating.

After accepting the drink, he sat down on the chair offered to him by Drake. The duke came around to sit partially on his desk, his pose relaxed as well as confident. The steel of his eyes bore into him telling him he would have nothing to say about the decision. Case waited while Drake sipped his drink. Tension built around the escalating silence.

"I would think..." Drake began, "that you might appreciate my choice of associates. The person I'm thinking of will compliment you quite nicely. Perhaps..."

"I am interested," Case broke into the sentence having heard enough. "Usually work alone. Not looking forward to taking care of another man's mistakes or having to work twice as hard because of a failure. Complications from an inexperienced agent can get a man killed." Case held a cynical view of the situation that was now being forced on him.

Drake frowned watching him through slitted eyes. Tapping his fingers on his thigh, he spoke again, tossing out a unique view, "What if I told you your partner was a woman. One I believe intrigues you."

A woman?

His heart skipped a beat while he digested the information. It would be foolhardy to speak without thought. "I would tell you that you were crazy. Women don't belong in the field. Life is too dangerous for the fairer sex. They are fragile as well as weak. Delicate. Given to impulse rather than logic." He didn't need to protect or coddle a woman. Nor did he want to.

"For the most part, yes, I would have to say I agree with you. Though many women have strength and abilities that would complement any man." Drake stood. He walked to the door then back to his desk. After he leaned back, he picked up a pen, moving the stem around in his fingers for a few seconds.

"If that is the truth, why are you paring me with a female?" His voice grew harsh as he asked the question. In this situation, he saw nothing except failure. The devil, he never failed. This would be a first time.

"How well do you speak French?" Drake's voice was bland as well as casual while he put out the one question that might change his mind. Drake's posture was more relaxed as he set the pen back in its holder.

The question was not only pertinent but important. "Can get buy in a pinch," grudgingly he admitted his failure. "Is this woman French?" That thought intrigued him almost as much as spending more time with Tara did.

"Fluent. She will be your interpreter. Will write all your correspondence. You will be her escort to any social gatherings you are invited to attend while she lets you know with exact precision what is being said. She will show you around the city. The woman knows Paris. Believed she lived there for a year."

All that. A paragon. Sounds too good to be true.

Resigned, he would have to make do with this model of French language as well as culture. This paragon would have to be horse faced to have all these sterling qualities. "Very well, if you insist when am I to meet the woman." He found himself holding his breath while he waited for an answer.

Breathe, you idiot.

"That's the thing. You've met the woman I hand-picked to be your guide in Paris. Spent the morning with her watching the sunrise over my lake. What else did you do besides watch the scenery?" The expression on Drake's face didn't reveal much. "What do you have to say about that?"

"Tara? Tara is going with me?" Astonished would not describe his feelings to the degree his body heated with the news. Not only was he dumbfounded but he was pleased, pleased immensely. Now he found himself looking forward to the new assignment. The duke was putting the woman he wanted to seduce in his arms. The major question was why on earth would he do such a thing? "Does The Duchess know what you've planned for her charge? She might have something to say about this arrangement." He was positive Ella had to approve of this or it wouldn't be happening. An answer would not be forthcoming.

"As we are speaking together in this moment, my wife is telling Tara of the plans we are discussing in my office. Tara loves Paris. Will be quite delighted to travel with you. I'm certain of the fact. The only hiccup is the trip on the ocean. I'm going to have to send the two of you via Dover to Calais. It's the only way she will go."

Did he dare ask why? Thought it better to wait and discover for himself. If she's afraid of water, he would be there for her. She might not be able to swim. Drowning might be a real fear. "When do we leave? I would need time to pack." Case found himself more than eager to begin this new assignment. Spending more time with Tara MacLaren suited him just fine.

"Tomorrow morning, if at all possible. You will have to pack your things tonight. If anything is left behind, I can arrange for you to get them later."

Did Lord Montgomerie know about her leg? When he left her in her room an hour or so ago, she could barely walk. "At this moment, Tara is having trouble standing let alone walking. Doubt if she will be ready tomorrow morning to partake the journey you have in mind. Carriage rides can be unsettling, straining to overtaxed muscles."

One ducal eyebrow arched skyward. His smile widened. "To sit in a carriage? Unsettling?" he asked his tone bland, "There will be no walking until you reach Paris. Even there, you can forestall the tour of the city until she is quite recovered from her ordeal. We all know about her leg. She doesn't wish to dwell on the topic or be coddled because of it."

Case wasn't about to say carriages for him were unsettling. They made him nauseous. Gave him claustrophobia. He would elect to ride his horse whenever possible. "So, the trip will take three to four days? Maybe longer if Tara needs more rest. Do you have a list of suitable inns where we can stop? I would hope your driver would..."

Drake waved his hand in the air in order to stop the comments. "All that is taken care of. I'm not expecting you to push Tara beyond her limitations. Let her decide how far she can go each day. Stop when she needs rest."

"Good," Case said thinking about the trip, the closeness they might share at night. He would let her set the pace of their relationship. That didn't mean he wasn't above a *wee bit* of subtle seducing, a touch here, one there. One meant to coax a coveted response. One meant to protect. Where women were concerned, he knew what he was about.

For the next hour, Montgomerie went over a list of his concerns along with what he expected Case to write to him about. He included men who would be a benefit to cozy up to as well as men who would just as soon stab him in the back as befriend him. It would be up to Tara to decipher with complete accuracy the words spoken to them at the various events they attended. She could accompany him everywhere.

"You should take the opportunity during the journey to learn more French. I'm certain you understand commonly used phrases as well as euphemisms. To carry on a valuable conversation is above your talents."

"You've summoned up my talents," Case said his voice dry. "Mean to make the most use of Tara as possible." Yes, the best use didn't just mean learning the language. It meant learning about her then capitalizing on what he knew.

"My son will also be there though his role is basic. He will provide support if needed. Eyes as well as ears where you cannot be in two places at the same time. Otherwise, his presence is a glorified holiday for him. I know he has plans to visit friends in Bordeaux. A bit of wine tasting as well as exploring would be in order. Don't expect too much of him yet. He needs to test his wings before he can fly. He is still young."

Case bristled when he learned Ash would be there also. He wanted to be alone with Tara. Needed privacy. Didn't need the young pup in the vicinity with his tongue hanging out panting for her. In this instance, he could argue with the duke. An argument would never do any good. The only thing worse would be if Jeremy was coming with them. That thought gave him good reason to groan. Jeremy was a threat Case couldn't ignore.

Female chatter from outside the office stopped the discussion of his assignment. Both men stood for Ella and Tara as they walked into the room. Tara was helped along with a crutch beneath her arm. The tightly drawn lines around her mouth as well as her eyes told him she was still in some pain. Though she looked better able to cope now than she did a few hours ago.

"Ladies?" Drake began while he stood. As if he couldn't wait for them to speak, he asked, "What did you decide, Tara? Would an adventure be in order for the summer?"

Before she could answer, Ella walked into his arms for a brief hug. Case always understood the couple were in love. He didn't believe he could ever love. Once he thought he loved a woman. That ended up in complete disaster.

When Tara looked at him, her smile started Case's blood pumping hard. All of it sent lightning straight to his groin. He didn't like the fact that a simple smile could arouse him at such an intense level. Control was an attribute he prided himself as having. With Tara, he lost all semblance of restraint upon seeing her.

When she clapped her hands together in obvious delight, Case understood without hearing the words she agreed. Was pleased to accompany him. So, she was fluent in the French language. She lived in Paris or had been there enough to act as tour guide to the city. Where would she take him? He had some ideas on that question. She might not agree.

Sheepishly, Tara looked from The Duchess to him then back. "I believe going on this trip would be fun. Paris in the spring and summer is an absolute delight."

"How is your leg?" Case asked as he watched her hobble with the help of her crutch to a chair. He should have helped her. Tara didn't want help. Nor sympathy. Or pity. No, Tara wanted to be ignored. When he looked at her, she dropped her long sooty lashes to cover her eyes. She also didn't want anyone seeing into her soul. Her thoughts were private. She fell into the chair. Her eyes held dark circles beneath dark smudges. The duke and duchess expected too much of her. She should be upstairs napping before dinner.

"Better. I'm doing much better than when you carried me up the steps," she murmured, as she lifted her lashes to look at him. "The hot bath worked wonders."

Case was far from convinced this plan was sound. He had questions. To his misfortune, the duke made all the decisions where his assignments were concerned. If he wasn't careful how he handled this, he could end up wishing for salvation. "You do want to be my escort in Paris?" Bloody eyes, this whole deal fell into his lap. Convinced him that her chaperones understood her proclivities for entertaining men. They would both be beneficiaries in this adventure.

"I thought you were escorting me," she told him then presented a question of her own. "Do you not want me along?"

The Duchess handed her a glass of sherry. "*Merci,*" she murmured with her gaze still fully resting on him, seeming to wait for an answer he wasn't sure he wanted to give her. "Case? Would you rather I didn't go? If my presence will make you uncomfortable, I can always remain here."

A penny for her thoughts would be nice and neat. Of course, he wanted her with him. For him, her presence would be a dream come true. "A *wee* smattering of French. You can give me a few lessons after dinner. As you've most likely been told, I need help. Can utter a few basics along with some cuss words." He lifted his shoulders. "Other than that, I'm at a loss. What do you think? By the time we leave Paris to return home, will I be fluent?"

"If I could keep my eyes open, I would begin your lessons after dinner. Fluent?" she questioned. "If you are good with languages and you apply yourself you might be. As soon as we finish eating, I'm going up to my room for another hot bath then bed. Promise though on the way to Dover we can start instruction."

Instructions, yes, coaching in amo*ur.*

"I'll be pleased if you begin the lessons. Though I dare say, I will spend little time in the carriage. Much prefer to ride." Case wanted to tell her that there were several types of instruction he had in mind that didn't involve language lessons. With the duke and duchess sitting in the same room, he didn't dare.

Tara stifled a yawn, her hand over the lips he'd like to be kissing. He watched as she tugged in a deep breath of air. While he appreciated her riding attire, she was beautiful in the gown she wore. The small sleeves accentuated her white shoulders and creamy skin. The roundness of her breasts were invitingly revealed. When she noticed him looking at her, she flushed a fetching rose color, matching her lips. He wondered at the shade of pink of her nipples. Were they the same color as her lips? Wondered how they would tighten for him when he touched her or breathed a kiss across them.

"I cannot keep my eyes open. Should have had a strong cup of tea instead of the sherry. The potent wine is putting me more to sleep," she murmured even as she finished the drink then turned to speak to The Duchess. "Don't know if I can manage to stay awake through dinner. Could you have something sent to my room, something light that I could eat if I wake up in the middle of the night starving?"

Case wanted to keep her awake a bit longer. Time with her was something he was coming to adore. He searched his brain for questions that would keep her in the room. "What will you show me in Paris? The sites that are most fetching."

She smiled a secret little smile that told him she was thinking of something scintillating. He hoped she had a few places in mind for private trysts. He didn't wish to spend all his time in museums.

"The walk along the Champs Elysée is always pleasant. We could stop and have lunch or a glass of wine out in the open while we watched the people stroll by on their daily business. There are boat rides on the Seine. We could rent a carriage for a ride to Sacre Coeur. Montmartre is interesting too. So many places I would love to take you, it's hard to list them all."

"I would like to taste French champagne," he told her. He could toast to their budding relationship the newness of it as well as all the budding possibilities. Case loved the way her eyes flashed with enthusiasm when he mentioned something she liked. "You like French champagne?" The look was different from last night when she flirted showing no shame with every male body in her vicinity. Ah, but he would almost have her to himself. The thought of Ashcroft being in the same home as the two of them created definite problems. Was wrong. Disturbing. The green bud of jealousy blossomed then spread.

"There is no other champagne except French champagne. We could travel to Epernay. The city is famous for its champagne. Rent a carriage to take us there. Stay for a day or two..." her voice trailed off as if she realized how inappropriate her comments were. A young woman should never travel alone with a man. "Ash could go with us. A chaperone. We would need a chaperone." Tara covered her *faux pas* with ease.

Tara would tell The Duchess she didn't need a chaperone, someone to guard her innocence. If The Duchess new her charge, she would understand Tara was not the virginal maid she tried to imitate. Didn't need someone to look after her. Probably did when they first discussed the situation she was getting tossed into. Well, The Duchess would understand what Tara was about. Who she was beneath the beautiful façade. If she didn't get her out of London, scandal would have no choice but to follow. That might be the reason the pair were not concerned with keeping her chaste. They understood who she was.

If they traveled to either or both Epernay or Bordeaux, Ashcroft would not be going with them. A third party was not something he would tolerate. If they traveled, the journey would be private. He didn't see Ashcroft adjusting well to the role of a chaperone.

"Dinner is ready."

Drake extended a hand to his wife. Case walked to where Tara was seated, helping her to stand. He took the crutch from her. "Lean on me." He would escort her wherever she needed to go including to dinner then later to her bedroom.

"I thought..."

"Would like to have you eat with me tonight. The day has been long. I get that. I know for a fact you ate no breakfast. Unless you had food while you bathed, you've eaten nothing today. If you go to your bed then fall asleep, there will be nothing for your stomach. Come, it won't be too long. When we finish the meal, I'll see you to your room so you can sleep."

While he listened to the sounds of her heart, he thought she would protest. He wasn't going to give her an opportunity to deny the meal or his company. Just as he did by the lake he wrapped his arm around her, supporting her. She was right. Her leg was doing much better. Stronger. He felt the ragged breath of air she inhaled; the fine trembling of her body so close to his. Her breasts pushed against his chest. They were soft. Firm. He remembered the way they looked all creamy and touchable. He squeezed her waist, setting his hand on her hip.

"I'm glad you decided to take up this challenge. I wanted to see more of you today."

She snorted as if she recalled the fact he saw the sweet curves of her breasts where she unbuttoned her shirt.

"Now, while we are in Paris, we can be together quite as often as we like. I would learn more about you." Case spoke, his voice tender, hoping she would pick up on the concern, the breath from his voice caressing her cheek. He felt her body react to the understated caress. The duke and duchess were ahead of them, leading the way to the dining room.

She flinched before she looked at him. Her tongue ran across her bottom lip then her top. The gesture was delicately beckoning to his desires. "I don't know what you are talking about."

Nibbling that beautiful top lip of hers was a priority. Devouring her as his evening meal ranked right at the top of his wish list. "I think you do understand what I'm talking about. I'm also going to discover truths about you. Facts I wish you would tell me but seem to want to hide. Lovers should have nothing between them." In his arms Case felt her stiffen when he mentioned they would be lovers. That would change. Discovering who Grant was to her was another marker at the top of his list. After that he meant to learn the details concerning her bum leg. Soon he would look at her thigh. He needed to know the depth of the scar tissue.

While he was speaking, she stiffened, withdrew to a safer distance. The happy turn to her mouth now pointed down. Her eyes were haunted, filled with pain. He didn't understand. If she was acting, she was a damn fine actress. He needed to find a way to break down her reserves, get under her skin so he could learn exactly who she was.

Tara was more than he thought. Less than he needed to believe. There were parts of her no one touched. He would touch them all. For as long as they wanted each other, she was his. If or when she cried off, he would heed her wishes. He would make damn sure she didn't see a reason to end the relationship they were going to have any time soon.

After searching Tara's expression for clues, he couldn't help but think of his first love. The only woman he would ever love was a philandering whore. Since then, every woman he'd ever been with wanted him for what they could get from him; money, power, sex the list could stretch forever. He always gave his lovers good sex, in return accepted pleasures from them. After that he moved on to new a woman.

Tara was no different. She acknowledged the offer to go to Paris with him because the journey would benefit her personally. There would be parties, social gathering for her to attend to her hearts content. Women loved parties and balls. Plenty of new men to flirt with to test her feminine wiles.

She wouldn't go anywhere without him. If she tossed her sassy little looks in a direction other than his way, he would make damn sure she never did it again. While he was with a woman, he was possessive. He never shared. She was his.

While Tara was his lover, there would be no one else for her to sink her pretty manicured claws into. He would make damn sure Ashcroft understood the parameters he would build around Tara. The young pup would have to search somewhere else to ease his sexual appetite. He would have more trouble keeping her away from Jeremy than the young man who appeared to care about her more than he should. She wasn't meant for him. Tara seemed to have a deeper connection with Jeremy. A closeness he couldn't touch with his thoughts. He would discover that truth too. Given enough time, he would uncover Tara MacLaren.

The conversation at dinner revolved around interesting things to see in and around Paris. The Palace of Versailles was brought up. Drake thought they would enjoy visiting The Louvre. Until the thought of spending private time with Tara, he'd never been a museum visiting type of man. Could one find a private and well-hidden corner in one of those museums to have a quick dalliance? It might make museum hopping more stimulating, even thought-provoking if he could find private hideaways to toss her skirts.

"You look as if you're going fall asleep where you're sitting," Case said watching Tara with an eye of a hawk. "I'll walk you to your room." He was glad he insisted she come to diner. Tara ate well, her plate cleaned. He'd been right. She was hungry.

Tara told everyone how tired she was. He convinced her to eat. Tomorrow would arrive sooner than expected. He hoped to get a quick start in the morning. Now, she needed her sleep. He meant to see to that too.

When Drake started to object to his invitation, The Duchess put her hand on her husband's arm stopping him. That one gesture gave Case a moment's pause. Was there more going on than he understood?

"You don't need to walk with me? I'm a grown woman, capable of reaching my room by myself." Tara seemed to be protesting, her back bristling.

"Don't be foolish. You're not only exhausted but your leg could give out on you again just as it did this morning. Don't want you falling down the steps."

"Go with her," Ella said softly with a fond expression that he didn't miss. "Make certain she reaches her room without mishap. You're right. We don't want anything happening to our young lady."

Eased by Ella's encouragement, Case took her arm, guiding her to the steps. "How do you feel. If you wish, I could carry you up the stairs." Case enjoyed holding her.

"Feel as if I'd like to try out my legs. Need to have a working knowledge of what I can and cannot accomplish."

"I'm going to hold on to you. Not let you fall."

~ * ~

"She's what!" Jeremy shouted at Ash when he discovered the duke's plans. Jeremy couldn't tell Ash the exact nature of what he saw in Case's eyes when he looked at Tara. The man didn't want a platonic relationship with her. His fists tightened. If he hurt her, he would kill the man. Tara was more than special to him. If Grant had not found her first, fell in love with her, he would have courted her.

"They should be here any day now. According to father, Tara wanted to go with Case. Wanted to see Paris. She said she needed time away from London since she didn't want a season in the first place."

"That's not a good enough reason to put her at the mercy of a virtual stranger...a dangerous stranger. The man has a reputation with the ladies. He doesn't ever keep one for long. Seems he uses the women of his acquaintance," Jeremy gritted out as he paced the drawing room of the apartment where the two along with Ash would live for the next few months. Jeremy had a flat about a mile away.

"Case is not a stranger to my father. He's worked for him for the last eight years with numerous assignments in different foreign countries. Bloody eyes, I don't know why I'm defending the man. I've had the same impressions as you. Though Case Ferguson might be the one person who can get her over Grant. That needs to happen for her to go on with her life. Tara needs to live again. We both understand you can't accomplish that feat."

"I wanted to be that person," Jeremy muttered. "Don't know why I'm here. The Duchess suggested I might keep you company." The way Tara looks at him...damn if she'd ever looked at me that way, he would have made certain she was his.

"I'm not in need of a chaperone," Ash said blandly while he slow-eyed the maid who was cleaning the rooms.

"You understand servants are off limits." Jeremy said with a chuckle. "Your father wouldn't be pleased."

Ash nodded, his head still grinning, still watching and wishing the rule wasn't ingrained. "I understand. It's been a Montgomerie policy for years. Since I can recall looking at one and having carnal thoughts, I was told quite early in my formative years the nature of maids the dos along with the do nots. Father informed me when I was thirteen. What happens in Paris stays in Paris. Sounds like a good saying to me."

"Don't get in too deep. You might drown. If the duke gets wind of any philandering, you'll be hauled home quicker than you can blink. Your father has spies everywhere. If you dally, with the wrong pigeon he will know."

"You?" Ash pointed a finger at the older man. "Are you free to do just as you wish?"

"I can do whatever I please. Drake isn't my father. Nor is he my employer." No, Jeremy planned on overseeing the fledgling relationship between Case and Tara. She meant more to him than any woman he'd ever known. Tara needed protection. He was the man to shelter her from harm.

However, Tara had always been in love with Grant. He thought when Grant passed on, she might see him other than as a brother. At first, she was in too much pain from sustained injuries. After that, her grief consumed her. Grant had been her entire life. Her love. She wasn't ready to move on.

"So, you plan on seducing the maids?" Ash questioned with a chuckle in his voice. "Suppose if I found one of yours attractive, father couldn't lecture me on the topic."

"Not your maids, especially not mine. I'm not letting you into my home if that's your intention." Jeremy said unemotionally wishing he wasn't having this conversation with the young pup. Ash had too much energy as well as curiosity. The boy wanted to sample the world all in one bite. He hoped Ash would always land on his feet. If he had the Montgomerie swager as well as luck, he would. "You need to stay close to Tara when they get here. I'm worried about Case taking too much for granted where she is concerned. She is still vulnerable." His mind went back to the woman he'd loved for what seemed like forever. The woman who would never love him.

"I'm not watching over anyone, especially not my cousin. If Tara wants to sleep with the man, it's not my duty to keep her from doing so. Good God, she's twenty years old. Most women are wed with a baby or two by that age. She deserves to live her life the way she wishes with no recriminations. I'm not cut out to be a chaperone of a woman who is my age."

"If Grant had lived..." Jeremy let the words in his mind fade. Yes, she would have at least one child, most likely another on the way.

~ * ~

"My heart fears for Tara. She is just now beginning to learn how to live. After the accident that tore her life apart..." Ella told Drake while she lay in his arms. The big bed in the master's chamber had always been wonderful. Tonight, after they were both sated, she felt as if she sent her charge into a situation she might not be able to handle. To fall in love would be difficult for Tara but not impossible.

Drake stroked her hair, wound the strands around his fingers while he tugged her head back for another kiss. "Tara is solid. She was so in love with Grant it was hard for her in the ensuing months. She managed to close off all her emotions so she could survive each day. I don't see her suddenly falling for Case's charming ways. Any possible budding romance will take time."

"He's a rogue, a handsome devil," Ella muttered while she tried to wrap her mind about what her husband was telling her. "I saw the starry-eyed look she gave the man when they left the dining room. Even though Tara might not know the truth, she is smitten. Case is just the man to pull her out of the horrific depression she wrapped around herself. He is the man to bring her back to life."

"We both understand she was protecting herself, her heart. Do you think she could fall in love again this soon?" Drake asked running his thumb across her bottom lip. "Guess it's been almost two years since the accident."

"I hope they both fall in love. Case has also closed himself off from any world not of his creation. Maybe the two can heal each other."

"If that's the case neither one knows it yet. Though I look at Case and see the desire in his eyes. Desire isn't always lust. Nevertheless, given time lust and passion can turn to love." Drake was running his hand along her shoulder, caressing her until she wanted him again. He cupped her breast in his hand, stroking the hardening crest. Teasing.

"Her mother would be fit to be tied if she knew that we are tossing Tara to a wolf," Ella muttered then sighed softly as Drake's exploring hands found more sensitive flesh.

Drake barked a laugh. "He's not even parading in sheep's clothing. That man doesn't pretend to be anything that he isn't. What he's thinking is straight forward, to the point as well. With what he thinks and wants where it concerns Tara, he will be up front and honest. There will be no deception."

"He could hurt her. I hate to see what will happen to our niece if she falls in love with the man and he's incapable of loving her." Ella played with the crisp dark hairs on Drake's chest, running her finger through them. His chest was broad. She teased one of his small nipples until he groaned and pulled her closer.

"Vixen..."

"Beast..."

Without warning he flipped her over. She was beneath him. He was deep within her. "I can't get enough of you, sweetheart. Never could."

Chapter Three

Chase stood at her door. He was so close to her she drank in the scent of him, pure male, dangerous. She recalled Ash's warning. A soft sound escaped her when his knuckles skimmed her neck, touched upon all the silent yearning that had been a part of her since seeing him at the ball. Why, she didn't know. He enthralled her. Somehow, he touched her heart when no man except Grant had ever gotten close to her. At his suggestive touch, she sipped air. Needed him. His presence filled a gaping hole in her heart. It was all she could do to ignore her desire for the tall, dangerous man.

His tender evocative touch sent thoughts spiraling through her with lightning speed. The kiss they shared this morning enchanted mercurially. She wanted him in ways she never thought about wanting Grant. A wave of guilt pulsed through her pounding heart. Grant was the man who deserved her love. When she was with Case, she never thought of Grant. Except to compare. That shouldn't happen. In her mind, Grant's memory deserved better from her. He'd been her fiancé. Her friend. The love of her life ever since she could remember. They made plans for their future together. Talked about children. She came within five of marriage to him. The pain knifed through her. Thoughts. Memories. Hopes coupled with dreams. Lost dreams.

"What are you thinking?" Case asked as he ran his fingertip across her upper lip. Touched the sensitive inside. She gasped. "I hope it's about our trip...or me. I would wish you're as excited as I am to be able to spend more time with you."

Tara wanted to tell him all she could think about was Paris, the days with him. The sweetness she could almost taste that hovered between them. She set her hand on his chest. What she did know was that she needed to put a little distance between them. Space, so she could think. "I'm exhausted. You need to go now. Morning will come all too soon. I want to leave as soon as possible."

"As do I," he gazed at her. Let his hand move down her arm then back to her shoulder. "Did you order another bath?" His eyes gleamed, dark. Secretive. His body tightened then heated at the stark desire she read in the deep blue glimmer of his eyes.

"You keep your thoughts as well as your feelings to yourself. You expect me to reveal my most inner private feelings," she berated him, her voice a whisper. "I would have a few secrets from you."

"Secrets are for people who don't care about each other. We aren't those people."

Tara swallowed the lump of air that seemed to be lodged in her throat. Her secrets were necessary. It was too soon for him to care about her. Too soon for her to care about him. He would never love her. Love was what she needed.

Case reached behind her to open the door. His breath rushed out as if disgusted with her lack of comment. "Go get your bath along with your rest. The hot water will sooth that injured leg of yours. I will see you first thing in the morning then we will be on our way. We can discuss this notion of secrets later."

Disappointment at his words coupled with his abrupt withdrawal made her want to call him back. Prudence kept her mouth shut. The man was striding down the hallway before she could respond. Tara felt bereft as she missed out on something tender as well as special. When he stood in front of her his finger on her lips, she hoped he would kiss her again. He didn't. The huge chasm between them deepened. Though, she sensed that he didn't feel the canyon separating them.

The emptiness surrounding her left her cold. Frozen to the bone. She rubbed her arms in an attempt to erase the evening's chill. The intense heat exuding from his big body was something she needed. If he would only enfold her in his arms, wrap himself around her, protect her from her past, she might be warm again. The sensations brought her back to the night Grant died. Closing her eyes, she did what she always did when she was overwhelmed with emotions. In her imagination, she watched a rose bud slowly opening to the sun's warmth. The vibrant colors ignited by the steady and ever-changing sunlight. One petal at a time would reveal itself. The process never failed, soothed her frayed nerves

Brought back to the present, she jumped aside as the servants carrying her bath water stepped up to the door then strode inside to fill the tub. *Case...* Once the tub was filled, she poured in her favorite scent from her favorite flowers, lilies. Tried to push the bold and very dangerous man from her thoughts.

Tiny pushed his nose into her hand, begging to have his ears rubbed. She bent down to skim her cheek against his. Laughed. "You up for a boat ride, big fella? We're going to Paris. I would never leave you behind. Do you want to ride in the carriage or run along behind. Too far for you to run. Suppose we'll have to share the mode of transportation with you. You'll try to take a seat for yourself. Naughty boy, you must stay on the floor." She shook her finger at the big dog. To emphasize her point, "You are not to take over any of the seats. Your place is on the floor." Tara didn't think he believed her. Tiny always believed he was her equal.

Tiny whimpered his agreement before sauntering to his favorite place in front of the fireplace. He stretched out, made a few more grunting sounds. He closed his eyes and was soon sound asleep. Tara wished she could fall asleep with that ease. Tiny had nothing to worry about.

At times it almost seems as if Case wants me. Just now he turned away. At other times it seems as if he dislikes me or resents me for some unknown reason. I don't ken what to think. Who is the man? What fills his head?

Humming, Tara slipped from her clothes then into the steaming water. The need to purge Case from her head at least for the rest of the evening was strong. She massaged her thigh muscle working out the stress from her walk down then up the stairs. Picking up the scented soap she washed herself then her hair. Keeping her eyes open was a chore. Her thoughts rambled. There would be no time in the morning. Once, she jerked awake having drifted to sleep, thinking about Case. The way he touched her. Held her so close.

The bath sheet was nearby. After she stepped from the water, she wrapped the big towel around her. While she sat on the hearth, she combed out her hair. Once her hair dried, she dressed in her nightgown. The sheets on her bed were turned down, ready for her. She snuggled into the warmth chasing asway the chill left from thoughts of Case.

When she fell asleep, she once more remembered the heated searing kiss she shared with Case this morning. Disoriented, she woke to the pounding on her door. For a few seconds, she didn't know where she was. After that it all came back to her. She wasn't in her bed at castle MacLaren. The trip to London for the season changed that. Meeting Case and wondering why he so disarmed her.

"Time to get up!" The voice was Ella's, worry evident in the small break in her words. "Breakfast is on the table. If you like, I'll help you dress. As you know your trunk was taken down last night. Case is eating and impatient to get on the road. Impatient, he'll be pacing the floor in a few more minutes waiting for you. Imagine no man likes to be kept waiting."

"Come in. Yes, you can help me dress." A new adventure awaited her. She pushed at covers, swinging her legs over the side of the bed. "The traveling dress I picked out has buttons up the back." Now that she thought on it, the gown was a foolish choice. She wouldn't be able to get out of it without help. Only a contortionist could reach all the tiny buttons. She picked it out because the soft apricot color accentuated the creamy whiteness of her skin as well as the amber color of her eyes. Blushing, she realized she chose this one with the purpose of impressing Case. Bah, the man was to confusing. She'd never impress him. Didn't know why she wanted to make him think favorably of her.

"Beautiful choice. Yes, you will need help to get out of this one." Ella mirrored her thoughts. "Did you save out another gown? Something a bit more practical." Ella asked her as she held up the dress for her inspection. The slippers and bonnet went nicely with the choice. "You will have no one except..."

"Case?"

"Yes. I'm not fond of that notion."

Feeling foolish, Tara shook her head. It surprised her that Ella said she wasn't fond of her needing Case to unfasten her dress. To Tara, she felt as if her aunt and uncle tossed her into this situation with eyes wide open. What was she thinking of now?

"All is packed. I should have put a few things in a small valise so I wouldn't have to unpack the trunk at our few stops before Paris. I'll have to figure something out at the first place we rest." Having Case's hands helping her from her gown was an unnerving thought. She didn't understand the underlying attraction she had for this hard, dangerous man.

Ella's soft laughter surprised Tara. "Yes, seems it's been a while since you've been on a voyage. How are you going to do for the crossing? Drake is worried about you. Have you ever been on a ship where you haven't lost the contents of your stomach?"

Tara couldn't stop the small groan while she shook her head. "Keep my eyes focused on the horizon. After that, pray I don't embarrass myself. Suppose I have my seasickness to look forward to tomorrow morning or this afternoon. As to the second part of your question, no, it's one of the things that have kept me landed over the last two years."

"Believe Drake has a ship waiting for you in Dover. It's supposed to set sail as soon as you arrive. If all goes as planned, later today. If not, first thing in the morning," Ella told her with a slight grimace.

Minutes later, Tara walked into the breakfast nook. She hesitated at the door. Case had finished eating. He looked relaxed yet impatient to get on the road. His long muscular legs were stretched out in front of him, his hands behind his head while he listened to Drake expound on the finer points of his mission. It appeared his mind was engrossed with her uncle's words. It didn't look to Tara he knew she was standing in the room.

When Case saw her, he stood a, welcoming smile on his face. He motioned to the table. "You're ready. The tea is hot. If you want, help yourself. I'll have another cup while you eat. Seems in honor of our trip the cook here has made croissants...chocolate croissants."

Unable to stop herself she grinned back. "Almost. You're right There is the question of food...and...croissants are my favorite pastry."

"Ella had their cook pack us a luncheon along with some snacks for the ride to the boat. We certainly won't starve," Case said as his gaze rested on her. "You look nice. The color becomes you."

Tara was certain his contemplation lingered on the swell of her breasts. Decided to ignore the impact of his gaze, she spoke, "*Merci.*" Tara curtsied. She sat in the chair he pulled out for her. He understood polite manners. Even then while he stared at her, his focus was hard, his eyes dark with something other than pleasure.

I wish I never sensed the vulnerability beneath this man's hard surface. I wish Case was as unfeeling as he seems to be at times. If that were the truth, I could ignore him, letting his hungry glances and touches slide off the coolness I've worked so hard to achieve. I ken he's hiding secrets too.

At her comment, Case hooted, his laughter confusing her again, setting her on edge, changing the direction of her thoughts. "I'll have one word memorized before you know it. *De rien,*" he told her. "Those are the easy words. I'm looking forward to something more complicated. Maybe a complete sentence or two would be in line. What does *embrasser* mean?" His grin widened as he baited her. The question heated her, challenged her. Without thinking, knowing it would give him more reasons to grin, she touched her hands to her heated cheeks.

To ignore the man was her first instinct. From how he said the word, the infliction in his voice coupled with the half-smile, he understood the meaning. "You will eventually get complicated sentences. First, I'm going to need to discover what you do know. From your last question united with your smirk you understand it means to kiss." She placed her napkin on her lap. Appreciative of his impatience to get on the way as well as putting distance from the Montgomerie estate, she ate.

By the time she finished her meal, the carriage with the ducal seal on the doors waited for them in front of the mansion. The driver put the steps down for her. Case held her hand while he helped her inside. Tiny took up most of the floor. When he saw her, his tail thumped with loud smacks on the carriage bottom. With baited breath she watched Case tie their horses to the back of the carriage. She would welcome the chance to ride rather than sitting in the vehicle for the entirety of the day. The mistake she made was in choosing her clothing to make an impression on Case rather than the practical side. She had not thought at all.

After he stepped inside then seated himself across from her, she let out a soft sigh of relief. Tara had not been looking forward to riding in the carriage by herself with only Tiny as her company. If she thought farther ahead, she would have worn riding clothes; not her britches, but an elegant riding habit that might serve to impress the man in a different manner than the gown she chose.

"I'm heartened you don't intend to leave me quite yet. I wasn't looking forward to no one to talk to except a huge dog who just listens as if he believes I'm touched in the head."

In response to her words, Tiny thumped his tale and looked her then slobber slipped from his mouth.

"Don't be surprised if I only last an hour or so. Inside these vehicles, I get nauseous as well as claustrophobic. My head begins to pound within the first hour. It won't be long before I need some fresh air to breathe. Need to stretch my legs. Feel the wind against my face. Afraid I won't be a much better companion than Tiny."

She thought about the same things he spoke of. All of that would be welcomed. "Next time," she began, "I'll put on something I can ride in. This dress," she fluffed the material around her legs, "this dress was not practical. I did not think."

Case leaned forward, picking up one of her hands. "Your britches are fetching. I enjoyed the view. The dress you chose is even more enjoyable. When you sat down at the table, I noticed the long row of buttons down your back. Did you pluck that out of your armoire with multiple reasons in mind?"

Heat flooded her face while he rubbed gentle circles on her wrists and she thought about what he said. He noticed. Words caught in her throat as more heat flooded her. A change of subject would be more than appreciated. Distance from thoughts of tonight and getting out of her gown without help would make her life more comfortable. "Tell me about yourself." It would be nice to idle away the long hours to Dover gaining information about the man as well as what made him so hard, so very dangerous. Ash was right in his assessment.

He kissed the back of her hand before giving it back to her. His shoulders lifted a slight movement as it seemed to Tara he meant to avoid her question. "Not much to tell. I grew up in the highlands. The life is not something I wish to recount to myself or anyone else. The time is not worth the memory." That seemed to be all he meant to say on the subject of his life.

"Your family?" she prodded with a question that she somehow knew he wasn't about to confide when his smile and laughing eyes changed to a cold hard stare. "Why don't you wish to speak about them? They are the people closest to you."

Within a second Case withdrew into himself. Heavy silence lingered for what seemed an eternity to Tara. After that he spoke, "I have a mother of sorts. No family to speak of." He didn't say more. "There is no one close to me. I keep to myself. That way a person doesn't get hurt." For a few seconds, he turned away from her.

Tara realized that was more than he wanted to tell her. He'd said too much. What he told her, it seemed he said only because he hoped that would end the questions. By the shuttered expression on his face when he spoke, she knew the sentence that gave little information was more than he would want her to know. The memories were dark. Still, she proceeded, hoping he would give her something she could grasp. "Everyone has a mother. What does the 'of sorts' mean?" Good manners told her she shouldn't pry. After all, she didn't want to let him into the privacy of her life. The secrets she kept from him were her secrets.

"Is that meant to be some kind of enlightenment? There are real mothers then there are the ones in name only. Everyone has a mother as well as a father?" he asked his tone bland, revealing nothing to her he didn't wish to divulge which was nothing. Again, it seemed he was telling her more than he planned. "Yes, biologically she was my mother. In no other way could the woman be called a mother."

"My mother and father are off chasing sunrises, the ones they've never seen," she offered intending to change the subject matter to something more comfortable for Case. The information was not something he'd asked of her. Tara didn't know if he would care. "Last time I heard they were in Hong Kong. They both love adventure. Now that their last child is grown, they can pursue their interests."

"Is that what you do, chase sunrises? Like your father? We did see a beautiful sunrise yesterday morning." Now that the conversation was about her parents, he visibly relaxed. The stiff tilt to his jaw, the hardness in his eyes, vanished. "You named your mare, Sunrise. What else do you want to tell me?"

"I love a good sunrise as much as the next person. Not going to chase around the world to see a new one. They are all beautiful in my backyard or my front yard. On the rugged coast where I grew up the sunrises shimmer across the North Sea. In the mornings, I like to walk to the cliffs so I can watch the spectacle. One can also watch them from the battlement." To Tara that was the truth. Grant used to think her penchant for getting up early to see the sun crest the hills was foolish. A few times, he rode with her. Didn't seem to understand the startling beauty of the vivid colors stretching endlessly across the horizon. "I like sunrises better than sunsets."

Case understood. Appreciated. This wasn't something she expected.

"Where in Paris would be a good location to see a sunrise or a sunset?" Case was obviously interested. "In your opinion are sunsets as beautiful as the rising of the sun? You said you like a sunrise the best." He was studying her through narrowed eyes.

"That's two questions," she murmured drinking in air, relieved the tension was evaporating. "To a connoisseur of colors both are worth going out of the way to see. Yes, in their own way they are just as remarkable." Tara paused tapping her finger to her chin in careful thought. "As to places to see, either one needs a hill or an expanse of space where there are few buildings. Sacre Coeur overlooks a broad stretch of land." Even to her ears her words sounded breathless. Trocadero Square is beautiful. It's also an enjoyable place to walk. There are fountains.

"Sunrise or sunset?"

"Let's do both. Sunset is *coucher du soleil*. Sunrise is *soleil se levera*. We have all summer to go places, to walk in the endless parks, to visit places in order to see either the beginning or the end to the day."

She was looking forward to everything. "They are beautiful over the *Notre Dame* Cathedral." Tara couldn't help herself. She clapped her hands together. "There are so many places I hope to take you."

His smile was broad, endearing to her. After the first conversation, she thought he would leave to ride his horse. Now, he seemed more interested. Pleased to move on to a new and different topic. "I would like that, to see both from Sacre Coeur. This is a monument in Paris?"

"*Oui,*" she said her voice soft as she watched the harsh lines of his face slowly disappear then change to amusement. She hoped if she was transparent about her family, he might share. "There is darkness in the MacLaren family too. My oldest brother Liam was born a bastard. Father adopted him. The story is long. My mother was not at fault. She was forced. Raped. Liam's biological father was a horrible man."

"Just like me...a bastard," he blurted as another wave of shadows covered his face. "I never knew my birth father. The man who raised me disliked me, more than he disliked the woman who cuckhold him," he said his voice so obvious, so bitter.

With those words, Tara understood that his life as illegitimate offspring wasn't as easy as Liam's. Her brother was loved. From all Case told her, she didn't believe anyone loved Case. The harshness returned to his features. She wished she dared to probe further. Could only hope that in time he would reveal more of his past. As it was now, he was mute. "Liam is now the heir to the Rathen fortune along with the estates. He's quite wealthy, an earl. He is the only one of the MacLarens who holds a title. The debutantes are quite taken with my half-brother. If he wanted to, he could crook his little finger at any one of the many willing females and they would fall into his arms."

"There is more to the tale I assume. I can read the truth in your eyes. Your eyes never lie. Do they?" His voice was husky by the time he asked the question. "You are incapable of hiding your feelings. It's an interesting trait in a woman. One a man doesn't see often. My mother lied easily as did my father's youngest sister. Oh, I forgot, he's not truly my father."

My eyes never lie?

For Tara it was easier to speak of the past, another's past though it concerned her, than it was to talk about herself or her lost love. She didn't like the notion that she couldn't hide her feelings. As to her feelings about Case, she didn't know what they were. She would be safe. "Yes, my mother was forced by Liam's father. She ran away to a convent ashamed as well as disillusioned. Hoped to become a nun. My father was in love with her. At the time, he couldn't help because he was in America with a good friend. Father even arranged for a guard because he was afraid something would happen to her. The guard didn't make it to the ball in time to protect mother."

"Where did she go?" He sat forward more interested in this conversation than it seemed revealing anything about his past. Most of the time, he appeared to close himself off from her...from everyone.

Perhaps the man was right. The present coupled with the future was the direction she should go. Dwelling on the past gave her nothing but pain. Jeremy wanted her to learn to live again. Though he wished that learning would include him. "Mother thought...well no, by the time she understood she was increasing, it was too late to become a nun."

"A nun! Christ's sake." He jerked upright, his eyes focused on her. "Why would she want to do something so foolish? Your father must have had something to say about that."

The venom that he elicited made her smile. "Ryder is my father's name. The good sisters, where mother took refuge, sold her baby to the grandfather. That's right, Liam's grandfather."

"Dear God, what else. There is more isn't there?"

"Always. The nuns told mother the baby was born a girl and was still born. You see, Liam's father was a wastrel, in debt to the extent his father cut him off. Liam's father hoped mother would have a dowry that he could use to wipe away his debt. She didn't." Tears filled Tara's eyes. Whenever she thought about the things her mother endured, she couldn't help but cry. Even though her life turned out wonderful the tears would still be there.

Case pulled her into his arms, stroking her, soothing the hurt. Tara sat on his lap, cradled in his strong arms. With his hand he set her head against his chest. "You don't need to tell me anymore. It's obvious the memories are painful."

While he stroked her back, she pressed against him, craving the comfort he offered along with the warmth he provided. Tara had been loved and cherished her entire life. She didn't need to cry about things that held no meaning now. From what little he told her, she didn't think there had been love of any type in his childhood. Perhaps not even in his adult years. Yet, here he was the strong one. Tara wondered if he ever shed a tear.

She looked up. Found herself reflected in the hard clarity of Case's eyes. Reflected...measured...examined. His eyes were not as soothing as the slow rhythm of his hands rubbing warmth into her chilled body.

"There is more. Mother was shot in the arm trying to find her son. So much more." Tara didn't think she possessed the energy to say anything else. She felt weak. Felt as if she bared her soul yet told him nothing about herself.

"Things turned out for the best. Where is your other big brother? Kenzie? I believe I heard Ella mention him once during the ball. Shouldn't he be looking out for you? Shouldn't someone be concerned you are going to be guiding a known rake around the streets of Paris, living in the same apartments? Why is everyone so quick to ruin your reputation?"

Held within the circle of his arms, she stiffened. Her thoughts plummeted and shattered around her as if someone opened a lid on all her feelings and they tumbled out. In his arms, she stiffened trying to shake the uncanny feeling this man wanted something more from her. Not just sleep with her, he was looking to prove something. "No one except myself needs to look out for me. I make decisions for my life. Because we are living in the same apartment doesn't mean we are sleeping together. Don't care what anyone believes. Don't care about a reputation that will only affect me if I return to London. I won't. It's what I believe about myself that counts."

"I disagree. You are alone with a man who is known as a womanizer, a man who can be dangerous. Although I've never taken anything from a woman she hasn't bargained with me to give. You are sitting on his lap while he would like nothing more than to kiss you, touch you in places that would have you begging for me to be deep inside you. *Veux-tu coucher avec moi ce soir?* Tara, if any one needs a chaperone, you do. Though, I'm heartily glad you don't have one because I do want to sleep with you. Maybe not tonight but in the future. Before the summer ends."

She sighed, her breath floating from her lungs in a whisper, soaking up his words. Tara knew then, eventually, not tonight, she would want to sleep with Case. For these few learning moments between them, she wasn't going to dwell on that fact. Thinking about making love with the man would serve only to make her nervous. "Kenzie is like father. My brother thinks the sunrise he's never seen is better than the one he is looking at. He wants to experience the entire world before he turns twenty-five. He doesn't have much time left though he is close."

"How much?" Case kissed her forehead, tilted her head so she looked into his eyes. Didn't wait for her to answer. He kissed the smile on her lips, touched the corners with his tongue. The caress was both gentle as well as seductive. He backed away as if to give her the opportunity to answer his question or to tell him no.

"Two years." She looked into the depth of the dark blue eyes that stared down at her. Her breath caught in the back of her throat. She needed him to kiss her again, touch his lips to her mouth as he did yesterday and just now. This kiss was too tender. She wanted him to make her feel more than a small quiver of desire.

Instead of another kiss, he tapped her nose with the tip of his finger. "How are you feeling? The carriage getting to you yet?"

The change of subject told her this interlude was finished. He was going to leave her now. Enough had been said for the time being. He learned about her family. She gathered very little about his. He was a closed book. She would have to wait for a more opportune time.

"Kenzie will not settle down soon I gather. Where is he now?" His hands rested on her hips, his fingers squeezing, generating a deep, dark pulsing inside.

Tara breathed a bottomless sigh of relief when he brought his hands back to her shoulders. They weren't quite so intimidating there. "I don't know. Last I heard he was in Australia. Before that, South America. He not only chases after the sunrise, he loves looking for valuable gems; diamonds in Africa, black opals in Australia. Who knows what else or where. I can't keep up with him. Nobody can. Not even father."

"You? What do you like looking for?" his question probed. She needed some secrets. To answer she wasn't looking for anything tangible. The answer wouldn't suit Case. Though it was the truth. She wasn't searching for another sunrise or gems or even a husband. To a man like Case, he would expect for her to tell him she wanted a husband with a title or vast wealth. None of that would be the truth. She wasn't greedy for anything except happiness along with love. Once not too long ago, she held everything she ever wished for in the palms of her hands. Now she held onto nothing.

She found herself shaking her head, denying the question.

What was it she was looking for? Tara knew the answer was love. All her life she'd been loved as well as cherished. She expected to have a life with Grant. That same love would have been the cornerstone of their marriage. Their children would be loved as well as treasured.

Grant was gone. He died before her dreams could be fulfilled.

"Love," she told him honestly without blinking. Surprised she shared with him. To Tara the answer was obvious. Wasn't everyone looking for love. "I think I'm looking for love." Tara didn't believe a man such as Case could love anyone.

"Love?" he queried with one dark eyebrow lifting upward. "Love isn't something one can hold on to. Love won't pay the bills. Love won't purchase a new gown for the next ball. What is it you want from a man?"

As if he read his mistress' discomfort, whimpering, Tiny adjusted himself on the floor of the carriage. Seeming to realize there was an empty seat, he took over the place where Tara had been sitting. The dog looked at her with his big brown eyes then had the nerve to smile at her, his tongue lolling from his huge mouth.

"Beast!" she exclaimed laughing, pleased the dark tenor of the conversation vanished. "You took my seat."

Case knocked on the top of the carriage to bring the vehicle to a stop. "I will see you when we stop for lunch. Feel as if the walls are closing in on me. You can have my seat." Then he was gone.

~ * ~

They reached Dover along with a tempest that lit up the sky. Thunder rolled along the white cliffs while rain pummeled the roof of the carriage. Blue-white light slashed across the darkness over then over again until thunder tumbled around the village. Case had to give up and go inside or he'd be drenched to the skin.

When he stepped inside the coach, he saw her, leaning against the side of the vehicle, her eyes closed, sleeping. She looked at peace. He'd never seen that look on her face before. His heart lurched to a sudden halt. Seconds passed before it seemed to beat again. Tara's loosened hair spilled across her shoulders. Her breaths were slow, even. Steady. He wondered how it would feel when she wrapped her long legs around him, holding him tight within her heat.

He shook water off his shoulders and arms. Tiny looked up at him as if to say stop getting me wet. To get a seat, he had to push the big oaf of an Irish Wolfhound to the floor. Tiny groaned but went along good natured as if he knew his time of leisure on the seat was over. The master returned.

Tara opened her eyes. They were sleepy. Dazed. Not quite focused on him. Her tongue roamed across her upper lip right where he'd like to nibble. "You've decided to come back inside? Why?" she queried.

"In case you haven't noticed there's a storm outside." A bolt lit up the inside of the carriage as he spoke. Years ago, Case stopped believing that he would ever find a woman who told no lies. He didn't even know he was looking for one until he met Tara. All he knew was the hunt then the capture.

"Didn't think you cared how wet you got. Thought all you wanted was to be away from me," Tara said her voice a gentle sound next to the booming thunder. She looked down seeming more interested in her gown than him.

Once inside, he settled back on the seat, arms spread across the back, closing his eyes. He felt the heat of her gaze pierce through his hide. She was angry with him. He understood. If he had to ride for the entire afternoon alone with only a mangy dog to talk to, he'd be furious too. She didn't hide her emotions well. Either that or she perfected the art of acting. He didn't want to open his eyes to talk to her or answer more questions. Putting all he knew about Tara MacLaren into perspective was too important.

Tomorrow they would board the ship. With the storm thundering around them, they would not cross the channel this evening. He would have the night with her, separate or sharing a room. He would leave the logistics up to her. As the carriage pulled to a stop in front of the inn, he decided he should say something to his silent traveling companion. He didn't know what to tell her. She wouldn't forgive him if he apologized for his absence. Tara would understand he didn't mean the words. Earlier, he did tell her he couldn't ride for long. After he stepped from the vehicle, he praised himself for lasting as many hours as he did. At lunch she didn't talk to him either. He could only hope she would relent for the rest of the evening.

"Are you hungry?" he asked as he riffled his mind for something intelligent to say. His muddled brain was a blank slate. He looked outside as if the storm would give him an idea or two. "I'm famished. All that riding..." The sound of his voice talking nonsense faded away with the same intensity as the frown lines increasing on her forehead. The mention of his riding put a damper on the need to ease the tension.

Case's dark gaze lingered over Tara's lips, the grace of her neck rising out of the apricot muslin gown, and the soft tendrils of hair curling around her shoulders. He swallowed the lump growing in his throat. The soft curve of her brows beckoned to him. He wanted to smooth them. After that ease the scowling lines that brought her brows closer together. His focus drifted to the swell of her breasts barely revealed by a modest gown. Modest by modern standards.

"You going to talk or just sit there and pout? Don't like to be around a woman who sulks," he blundered once more into treacherous territory. She didn't intend to give him any leeway. The downward curve of her mouth grew. Her golden-brown eyes smoldered, shot sparks of fire.

Thank God, the carriage stopped. He could take no more. Small talk was not his forte. To say he was horrible at making light conversation put the fact mildly. Needing to leave the small intense confines, he leapt from the door. Beat the coachman with the stairs. When he extended his hand to help her, she hesitated, tilting her head to the side as if assessing the situation. With grave reluctance, she extended her hand when his remained within easy reaching distance. Her fingers were long and slender with neatly buffed and trimmed nails.

They were cold. Frigid.

Talk to me, Tara.

Tell me what has you glowering.

Once she was safe on the ground, he pulled those long slender fingers into the crook of his arm before setting his hand on top of hers. If she was going to sulk, he meant to ignore her pique. "The Dover Inn, a very unique name for this part of the country, don't you think? We will stay here tonight. Drake has made all of the arrangements. We've nothing to do except enjoy ourselves."

Case wasn't all that certain but he thought he heard a snort of amusement. Maybe things between them weren't all bad. Tonight, could be looking up. A good meal. A bit of small talk. He thought of the long row of buttons she would need help with tonight unless she wished to sleep in her clothes. Her corset too. Foolish woman, she should have forgone the torture device for the day. There was no one she would be seeing that would be impressed by a wasp thin waist. The corset wouldn't be at all comfortable. He would make certain to see to her ease. Tomorrow, she would dress more practical.

Together they strolled up the steps. Tiny followed. The lobby was large. Off to one side tables were set up for dining. His stomach rumbled. He wondered if she'd eaten any of the food that was packed for the long journey. After lunch, Case couldn't bring himself to sit in the carriage again.

"Let's get our rooms first. The coachman will bring our trunks. You can freshen up." If she wanted a bath, she would need to ask for help with her gown.

"That would be nice." There was definite edge to her voice when she spoke. Instead of this pout, he'd rather she yelled at him. He wondered if the long hours in the coach cramped her leg. He would have to keep her injury in mind.

Her mope wasn't going to be over any time soon. He would have to make do. "While you are..." hell, he didn't know what to say. "I've got to speak with the captain of our ship. I'll be back for dinner."

"You're running out again?" Tara tossed after him, a bit of anger in her voice. That pleased him just fine. "Seems you could come up with a better excuse to leave me with nothing to do or no one to talk with except Tiny."

Fury he could deal with. The silence unnerved every pore. He was the kind of man that would have it out then peace would reign. "Tending to business would be a better description. The captain needs to know we're here. That we'll be aboard the vessel first thing in the morning. I'll be back here to escort you to dinner. Don't doubt it." Case didn't want to find himself angry with her. Instead, he'd rather kiss her senseless.

"Fine. If that's what you have to do." Tara waited behind him while he registered then received keys to their adjoining rooms.

Case thought it was interesting that Drake gave them adjoining rooms. Though in a rough seaport, adjoining rooms was prudent. She would be safer with an unlocked door between them. He didn't like to think of problems that could befall a young lady in a hotel such as this one. Knowing the duke as he did, this would be the best as well as the most expensive hotel in the vicinity, also the safest.

Up the long stairs and to the right he found the room. Opening the door, he beckoned her inside. The adjoining door was open. Case leaned against the door frame, his arms crossed on his chest as he watched her explore. She would pick a room. Whatever she wanted was hers for the night. Perhaps they should eat in this room. The small table in front of the fire looked cozy. He liked warm and comfortable. The privacy would be nice, a bottle of wine nicer. A tryst with her even better.

When she stepped back into the first room then stopped in front of him, he smiled. "Will this do?"

"It's nice. From Drake I wouldn't expect anything else. He's thought of everything. Likes to keep his wife comfortable." She held out her hand. No doubt expecting the second key to the room. "You have something for me?"

Tara didn't need a key. She wasn't going anywhere. Case handed her the key. She slipped it into her reticule. The trunks arrived. A maid entered to start the fire in both rooms. She left water to wash.

Unable to stop himself, he lifted her chin. His gaze met hers. "I won't stay away any longer than necessary. Shouldn't take me more than thirty minutes to talk to the captain and come back. Be ready for dinner when I return. We'll eat here. I'll order the food on my way out the door." He wished he had time to kiss her the way he longed to do. Kiss her so hard and deep the pique would vanish, he touched his lips to her cheek. Was pleased with the startled sound coupled with the widening of her eyes. Her breathing changed. He saw the pulse at the base of her neck speed. The sight pleased. "There could be more of that later if you've a mind to it."

Before she could toss him cheeky words, or curse him, he turned. Whistling. he strode down the hallway to the stairs. Skipped as he made his way to the bottom. He felt the heat of her gaze on the back of his neck. That pleased him too. Tonight might prove to be interesting, he thought, while he recalled the first kiss they shared after watching the sun move away from the horizon. Remembered the sleepy-eyed look, the moisture on her lips. The scent of her rippling through his senses, lilies coupled with spring rain. Intoxicating. Next time he kissed her the only name he would hear from her would be his.

He ordered dinner along with a bottle of Bordeaux. He knew she was used to good wines. Learned while he was at the Montgomerie residence that one of Ella's relatives owned two wineries, one in France the other in Italy. Gifts of wine were often sent.

Once outside, Case pulled his slicker around him and the hood over his head. The street was muddy so he kept to the boardwalk. Rain continued even though the worst of the storm was now far out to sea.

Damn the weather. The night wasn't fit for man or beast. Tiny didn't even spend more time than necessary moving from the coach to the inn. Walking up the gangplank he boarded the ship.

"Case Ferguson, here to see Captain Sanders," Case told the man who must be the first mate. Drake told him the captain was one of his best. Been in his service for years. He helped find the McInnis when the duke and duchess searched for Nickie. Case found it interesting that Montgomerie threatened to hang Ian from the yardarm of his ship when he spirited his niece away. With Tara, he seemed to be tossing them together, putting Tara in a position that she would be easily seduced. Nothing made sense. Though he liked the way this was being orchestrated. He couldn't complain. Of course, Tara wasn't a niece. That might well be the difference.

The man nodded, "Was told to be expecting you. Follow me." He turned then strode to a cabin. The man knocked before calling through the door, "Mr. Ferguson is here to see you."

After Case stepped inside, he was greeted by a great bear of a man. He was tall, broad of shoulder. His face was tanned from the elements. The beard he wore was trimmed short. Dark brown eyes shimmered with intensity. His deep brown eyes seemed to see everything. The captain studied him, looked him over.

"You made it. Too bad we can't sail tonight. Would have liked to make port before dark. Storm's too bad." He held out his hand. "Was told to take no chances with his charge."

The men shook. Case cleared his throat before he spoke. "The little lady with me doesn't like ships much. At least that's what the duke told me. Thinking we need calm waters when we sail. This trip isn't an emergency. So, there's no rush." Case thought about the man he was supposed to locate for the duke. A man who escaped to France to avoid a conviction of murder. Several convictions. His capture wouldn't be an issue. Had to find the man first.

"The missive I received said she was my first priority. Not to do anything that wouldn't be good for someone who doesn't like traveling by ship. The little lady is to be kept comfortable. I've a cabin for the two of you to stay in during the crossing." The captain scratched his head as if he tried to figure out some perplexing thing. "Don't understand that myself. Seems it's a fine way to travel. The only way if one has to cross open water. Since a person can't fly...what else is there?"

On his way back to the inn, Case let his thoughts wander back to the woman waiting for him in the adjoining room. She confused him. Baffled him at every turn. It seemed she had her actions all down pat. *Except for her pouts and sulks all her worried glances, the caring little gestures, the apprehensive looks, the determined smile, the words...*

Case might have begun to believe her sincerity if Tara hadn't softened and flowed over him like warm honey at his first touch in a sheltered glade with the spectacle of vivid colors and soft breezes entertaining them.

When they spoke in the carriage and she probed to bloody deep, he held the distinct impression she cared. That couldn't be. Her soft sighs and tiny sounds of empathy twisted his gut. He needed to think of her as the woman she was, not one he hoped she might be. When he spoke of his mother, she seemed sad. When he spoke of his mother, he made himself vulnerable. Cursing himself, he gave himself a harsh reminder that he never spoke of his family to lying jaded women. Women who were out to get whatever pleasure or monetary gains they could from the man they were with. There was nothing different about Tara. Maybe if he told himself that enough times he would begin to believe.

Is Tara pretending to feel sadness and determination to carry on because of something she won't speak about? Has she found my Achilles heel where other women have failed? He drank in air. Needed more as he sifted through his memories and encounters with the female mind.

Has she somehow sensed that there is nothing on earth I respect except the guts it takes to climb out of the deep dark pits life drops you into? He was beginning to think that was exactly what she'd done. Tara wouldn't speak of it though.

Case stopped at the bar to tell the manager to serve the food. Two-stepping his way to the rooms they would share tonight; he shook off the plaguing thoughts that had him second guessing this woman. When he stepped inside, she was sitting on a large wing chair staring at the blazing fire in the hearth. Lights danced across her face, that except for the flickering fire was cast in shadows. After she turned to look at him, he saw the wariness in her eyes coupled with the exhaustion.

The suspicion he recognized in her gaze she came by naturally.

During the ride he'd been surly and at times rude. He baited her when she didn't deserve to be challenged. All he wanted was for her to show her true colors. After she stopped acting, they could carry on in any way that pleased her as well as him. Her performance never varied.

"You're back," she said with no emotion in her voice. "I wondered...no, you wouldn't leave me. You'd have to explain your actions to the duke. If you left me to fend for myself, you'd be a dead man."

"Are you all right?" Case asked as he became concerned for her health. When shadows didn't hide her face, he noticed dark circles rimming her beautiful whiskey-colored eyes. "You need to eat then sleep. How is your leg?"

"Tired," was all she said, lifting her arms before letting them fall back to her lap. "Tired of being alone. Not used to spending so much time confined. Enclosed." She stopped herself, the pause significant. "No...that's wrong. I like privacy as well as being by myself. It's just at home I've places to go. I can walk in the woods surrounding the castle for hours without seeing anyone. Swim in the nearby creek. Tiny always keeps me company. I'm not by myself inside a vehicle with no way to get out. Being there is claustrophobic. The feeling doesn't suit."

For Case the thought of Tara walking alone in the woods caused his gut to clench. Tiny would never protect her from anything. He didn't like the notion she was left to fend for herself by wandering parents. Alone, she was vulnerable. Her mother was forced. Had an illegitimate child. Didn't Tara learn anything from her mother's mistakes? This was a moment when he wished he could shake her as if that would give her the good sense to stop her wanderings.

"Dinner is here," the voice from the hall stopped his meandering thoughts. He'd left the door open.

"Set the tray on the table."

Neither said anything while the maid saw to the food. "Set the tray with the dirty dishes outside the door when you are finished." The woman curtsied then left.

Case opened the bottle of wine. Poured them both generous amounts setting the glasses by the plates. "Come?" He held out his hand for her to join him at the table. "Let's enjoy the meal."

The winsome smile she slanted his way didn't bode well for his hasty plans for the evening. Taking the ensuing minutes one step at a time might serve him well. He pulled out a chair for her. Waited.

After he sat down, he lifted his glass. "To the crossing tomorrow. May the water be peaceful." He was surprised when she paled, her face very nearly a death mask.

She lifted her glass, touched his glass with hers after that she smiled. "How about we toast the landing, to dry ground. If you must know, I'm not looking forward to tomorrow. Keep telling myself the sooner I get it over with the better. Won't have to worry again until fall when we return to London."

"The duke told me you don't like ships. What are you afraid of? Did something bad happen?" He sipped his wine then set the glass on the table, keeping his focus on her eyes. "Is it worse than he said?"

"For me, yes, much worse." She was toying with the roast beef along with the peas on her plate, pushing them from one side to the other. The boiled potatoes she cut into tiny pieces. Nothing seemed to reach her mouth.

He wanted to reach out to her. Take her hand in his in order to calm her jerky movements. "You have to learn to relax. There is nothing for you to be afraid of. The captain is one of the duke's finest. The weather should be calm in the morning." He hoped the sun would shine, the winds enough to speed them on their way. Nothing to rock the boat.

Her snort of laughter gave him pause. She stared at him before she spoke. "Easy for you to say. I take it ships don't bother you."

Well, perhaps this was easier for him than for her. She rose, walked around the room holding her glass of wine stopping to take a small sip every two or three steps. She turned a curious light in her eyes. "Where are you planning on sleeping?"

Replaying his dream would be to have her sleep in his bed. Without flinching, "The opposite room from you. A different bed. Different covers as well as pillows." The relief he saw in her face startled him from thinking he could seduce her into his bed. That was counterproductive. He needed for her to come to him, to charm him beneath her covers. "Are you planning on finishing your dinner?"

Tara sat down again, doing justice to almost have the food he dished out for her. He topped off her wine. "What time do we need to get up in the morning? I should go to bed." She played with her skirts again. Looked at him as if she wanted something before turning away.

"Dawn was the time the captain told me we should head to the ship."

"Dawn," she murmured seeming distracted. "It will come too soon."

"Do you need help with your gown before I leave?" Case tried to keep his voice bland. She couldn't undo the tiny little buttons fastened in the middle of her back. Could she? Was she a contortionist? He didn't think so. "I could help out."

"No, no, I can manage. You go on to bed. I'll be just fine." She drank long and deep of the wine in her glass before adding some more. "If you don't want anymore, believe I'll take the bottle with me."

Case didn't believe her statement about unfastening the gown. She would need help with her corset too. If she wanted to sleep in her dress, that was her business. Doing so would be damn uncomfortable. If she still wore her dress in the morning, she would want to change. Help would be forthcoming. All she needed to do was ask. He left the bottle of wine on the table so she could take it with her.

Shrugging, Case walked into his room. Her comfort wasn't his business. He undressed, folding his clothes. Just in case she needed him in the middle of the night, he set his robe at the end of his bed. The woman was too pig-headed stubborn to come to him for help. The thought shook him to the core. He decided he understood her less the more he got to know her. He should walk in there, unfasten the gown then leave. If she didn't sleep, she'd be irritated in the morning. Lousy company. Case knew he wasn't good company when he didn't sleep.

She was a sassy little flirt.

A beguiling woman who intrigued him more than he wished to admit.

Why the devil did she hold him at arm's length? That was a question he didn't have an answer for. Nor did he think he would anytime in the near future. Normally, women threw themselves at him. He was a good catch even though he was *sans* a title. So far, she wasn't like any other woman he'd ever been close to.

She melted in his arms when he kissed her. Made bewitching little sounds that told him he pleased her. The tiny hitch he heard in the back of her throat told him he gave her pleasure. Certainly, a woman of deep passion along with vast experience would do the same. Tara was exactly who he thought she was.

It was late. The bed waited for him. Tomorrow could be another trying day. If she kept asking questions he didn't want to be reminded of, he might toss her overboard. With a long deep breath wishing to sleep, he eyed his bed then the door separating the rooms. When he stepped beside the door, he heard her pacing.

Shrugging his shoulders, he went to bed, pulling the covers high.

Dreams swirled in his head. Past missions. His childhood. The dislike he felt from his father. He tugged at the blankets. Pounded the pillows. Turned over then over again. Thought of the little witch in the next room. She didn't know any of the facts. Drake Montgomerie head of the SIS, sent him to hunt man not to sidle up to French aristocrats. Rolling over he saw that it was well past midnight. He closed his eyes again, hoping for sleep that seemed illusive.

"Case..."

His name said in a whisper sent fire to his loins. His lashes flew open, his body tensing. Where the devil was she? He thought she might be standing next to him. Lilies along with spring rain filled his nostrils. Case groaned.

"Case...please..." Her soft beguiling voiced filled him. The bewitching sound gave rise to desire.

One more time he pounded his pillow trying to ignore what had to be his imagination working too hard.

"Case...I need help. Wake up..." A small hand rested on his shoulder. Shook him a few times. "Case..."

He heard his groan. Her scent washed over him. He bolted to a sitting position nearly hitting her chin. "Good God, Tara? What the bloody hell are you doing here!"

When he pried his eyes to open, he saw her fiddling with her skirt, biting her top lip. "I," she seemed to be swallowing. "Can't get the buttons...um...undone. Need help if you don't mind. I...I want to go to sleep. Um..."

Of course, he wouldn't mind. She should have asked sooner.

The least she could have done was come to the conclusion at a decent hour. A glance to the clock told him the time was past two. As it stood now, she wouldn't get more than a few hours' sleep before he woke her.

He tossed off the covers before he realized he was stark naked. Bloody hell! He grabbed for his robe.

Tara gasped, her hands covering her heart when she saw him. Yeah, he was hard, at attention, anticipating something that wasn't going to happen. Let her stare. She wasn't a dewy-eyed virgin who'd never seen a fully aroused man before. There was nothing innocent about her. He tossed her a half-smile. "Old territory?"

Even with limited light, he saw flaming color settle on her cheeks. They were very red, a brilliant red. His grin grew wolfish. He tamped it back a notch. Taking his time while she stared opened mouth, he slipped on his robe. He should have stayed the way she first saw him. Naked.

"Come here." He motioned with his hand. "Turn around so I can get you more comfortable. So, you can sleep."

To his immediate surprise, she did as he asked.

Tara stood in front of him, her back to him. Her small body trembled as he looked at her wishing for more than he intended. "Hold up your hair."

She did.

The devil he wanted to take his time with this endeavor. He meant to tease her senses until she was as aroused as he was. After he unfastened each button, he touched her back with his knuckles or his fingertip. Minutes passed before he reached the last button. He smoothed the material from her shoulder so he could see the creamy expanse blinking at him.

"Corset?" Case asked in an attempt to keep the bland in his tone.

Giving anything away about his hunger would be disastrous.

"Um..." She nodded up then down then again. Her hands held the gown to her breasts.

"Is that a yes? A no? Be specific." Before he did anything more, she would have to give her approval to his endeavor. Always she would have to tell him, yes. If not, he would do nothing.

Tara nodded. That had to be good enough for him. With infinite patience, Case pulled the strings from the eyelets. One at a time he watched more satin flesh revealed to his gaze. When the corset hung loose, opened for him and he gazed at her back, he began at the base of her neck touching each vertebra as he made his way to the flare of her hips.

Her shivers told him she was affected by his tenderness. He watched her suck in a deep breath of air. If he wanted, he could have her in his bed. He would wait until she asked.

He bent close to her ear where his breath would whisper against soft warm flesh. "You should leave now."

~ * ~

The next day the weather was just as Case had ordered. Bright blue sky, soft billowing clouds high above coupled with a soft breeze would make the day's sail more enjoyable for Tara. There would be no cresting waves to frighten her. The night's storm washed the air clean of chimney soot and smoke. On board, waves lapped easily against the frame of the ship. To a man like Case the rhythmic sound soothed.

Tara leaned on the railing staring across the channel. They would land in Calais before the day ended. The crossing didn't take very long under good weather conditions. The steamer they were on was more reliable than old sailing ships. In Calais they would either stay the night or begin another journey by land via coach. Drake would have arranged more transportation along with a driver. The head of the SIS never left anything to chance.

"Relax and enjoy," Case whispered to her as he set his arms around her, his hands on the railing.

She jerked startled he assumed by his close proximity. "I...I can't relax. As soon as we start moving... Maybe I should go below." Tara didn't want to leave. She liked the feel of him so near. Knew she should still mourn Grant. Case had this way of making her forget. Her back was pressed against his chest. She caught his scent on the wind. Let the spicey smell flow over her. Tara could feel the flex and play of his muscles where they touched her.

"The fresh air will make you feel better." Case skimmed his finger down her back, following her spine as he did earlier this morning. Without thinking too hard, he recalled the way her body shivered at the gentle yet evocative touch. He knew she wore nothing save her chemise beneath the gown. "You're not wearing a corset."

"No," she sighed then leaned back against him. "Wanted to be more comfortable. Not restricted. Yesterday, I learned my lesson. Don't plan to try to impress..."

As Tara moved her head in a reflexive gesture, a subtle fragrance drifted up from her hair to Case's nostrils. They flared drinking in her scent. Memorizing. Desire ripped threw him. Case refused to show the hungry raw passion swamping him. A man who showed need to a woman was a fool. He was glad her back was too him and she couldn't see into his eyes.

At this instant while soft waves rocked the ship, he was the one who needed to calm himself. The time to seduce her was not ripe yet. She was like a rose opening to him. When she was fully exposed that would be the time to take her to his bed.

"Good, that's the best way to try to calm your fears. Breathe in deeply. The salty scent of sea air can pacify any shivering of the soul." He ran his hands along her arms, up then down. After that he massaged her shoulders trying to work out the kinks he felt, the tension he didn't understand. Her fear wasn't tangible. The sailing would be smooth. The waves buffeting the ship were small. If he didn't know better, he would believe she wasn't afraid.

Another act?

He didn't want to believe she would make up her fear about the sailing. Though the evidence was startlingly clear to anyone willing to look past the most obvious.

They stood together watching the white cliffs below the town of Dover move farther away. As they edged farther into the ocean, he felt her stiffen. Saw her gulp air. He turned her. Tara's eyes were wild. She clutched his wrist, her nails biting into his arms.

Tara held her hand over her belly, her face turning a sick shade of green. Other than the morning of the sunrise, this was the only time he'd been with her this early. His imaginings turned to places he'd rather they didn't travel.

"Are you alright?" he asked concerned that she might lose what little breakfast she ate before they left for the ship.

"No! Let me go!" She pulled in a long deep breath of air. "Have to go to the cabin. Now! Let me..." She tried to duck under his arms. He was too strong. They closed around her. "Case! Please, if you don't..."

He wasn't about to let her run. He needed to understand. "What's wrong?" Case started to shake her but was brought up short by the pallor of her face. "Talk to me. I can't help you if I don't know what bothers you."

"Where is it?" Tara escaped the jail of his strong arms then started for the interior. She twirled her head searching blindly. "Tell me," she whispered as the wind stole the words. "Where is our cabin?" she gulped again.

While he didn't understand what was going on here, something was wrong. Any idiot or fool could tell she was distressed. He wasn't stupid or an idiot. He scooped her up then strode with fast strides to the cabin the captain showed to him last night when he visited. Once in the stuffy confines, he set her on her feet. Held her shoulders. Frantic, her eyes wild, she was shaking her head, seeking something.

Tara turned in a circle seeming to search for something. When she found the desired object, she rushed to the basin. Just as she reached the basin, held it in front of her, she lost the contents of her stomach.

Shocked, Case didn't have words to say to her. Bloody hell, all he had were questions. Questions that needed to be answered, sooner better than later. He didn't like the direction of his thoughts. While she retched, he held her hair in his hands.

Once everything in her stomach was emptied, all that was left were dry heaves. Case brought her a glass of water. Tara held up her hands shaking her head. "I'll just lose that too. I can't put anything..." She broke off as if she didn't wish to say more.

"This happen often?" he asked hoping for a negative answer.

She nodded her head, sipping a tiny bit of the water he offered before handing him back the glass. Less than a minute later she lost that too. Tears pooled in her eyes. Her arms on the counter overlooking the churning ocean, she set her head down. Her entire body shook with the sickness.

He stroked her back, hoping to give comfort to her. His voice was soft when he spoke, "Are you pregnant?"

The jerk her body made told him most likely she was increasing. What could a man expect from a sassy little flirt who needed men as much as she needed to breathe. If she was with child, he would have to wait longer to make her his woman. This was no game he wished to play. Being labeled the father was not to his liking.

"It's all right." Case tried to soothe her, attempted to calm himself. For some reason he didn't understand that while he wasn't in line for a virgin, he didn't like the fact that someone else had her before him. Until now, that information never mattered. Until now, he understood she was just another cheating, lying woman who he would give pleasure to then move on to the next woman. His heart ached. Case didn't understand what he was feeling.

She was part of the chase he enjoyed. The challenge that kept him on his toes. The contest that kept life from becoming boring. He enjoyed a beautiful woman in his bed. Soon he would enjoy Tara. He would have to wait. In the long scope of his life, she didn't mean anything permanent to him.

Chase until the capture. After that depart. Don't get involved. Leave your emotions in tack. Don't give away your heart.

Pushing hair from her face that was a tiny bit less green, she spoke. She was looking at him now. Staring into his eyes as if she could read his thoughts. "You don't understand. I'm not pregnant. Just..." Tara raced for the basin again.

"You certain?" Casually, Case leaned against the bedpost. A bed they would not be sleeping in. "Don't see how you can be positive. Sense you're are throwing up your breakfast, that would be a solid sign."

"Positive," she said without a moment's hesitation.

"Positive?" he quirked an eyebrow as he speculated.

"Yes. There is no way I could be..."

Chapter Four

The big oaf. He thought I was pregnant. Thinks I'm pregnant. My telling him that no, I'm not didn't have an impact. Once the man has a notion put into his male sized brain, right or wrong he rolls with it.

You could have told him then and there that you hadn't been with a man in that way. Tell him you're a virgin. If you tell him all your truths, he'll treat you differently. Now, he's holding you at arm's length.

Could have. Didn't want to tell the arrogant beast what he wanted to hear. Not going to play into his hands that way. Besides, doubt if he would have believed me. Appears he has his mind made up about my character. About all women. What do you think? Would he accept my word?

No, nonetheless, it will be you who pays the consequences for keeping secrets. You're right though. That man would never believe you. He will have to discover that fact on his own. There is only one way for that to happen. Are you ready for that?

Only if I'm willing. Right now, I'm not willing.

You like his kisses. The way he touches you.

Going to stop liking them...it...him.

You should have told him about that day. The significance. He would understand that part. Tell him what happened.

I can't. I couldn't.

You're going to have to tell him sometime.

Her fingers clenched as she recalled two years ago...pain and helplessness. The rage. Wanting to die.

No. it's too soon.

Once they deboarded the steamer, Tara's stomach settled. Just as she knew it would. Solid land under her feet did wonders for her disposition. True enough, telling him she always got horribly sea sick would have been prudent. Would have explained everything without explaining to him the one truth she couldn't face. Tara thought Uncle Drake told him. How was she to know he'd think she had morning sickness and was carrying some unknown man's child. He must think I'm a whore.

Impossible man.

True to form he spent most of the trip from Calais to Paris riding Black. Because she learned her lesson the first day of the journey, she wore a riding habit each day so she could join him outside the carriage. During those times their conversation was limited. Stilted. While she wished he would tell her more about his childhood, about the part of his life that held dark secrets for him, Case remained mute. So, in retaliation, she refused to say anything more about herself.

The air outside was more pleasant than that inside the carriage. Every day a nice breeze cleared the air. While inside the vehicle the atmosphere smelled stuffy. Confining. Riddled with untold truths. Tara would ride Sunrise until she was exhausted enough to fall asleep. Until she knew if she stayed on the mare any longer, she would be unable to walk. That would lead to more questions she was unwilling to answer. She found the journey tried her in more ways than one.

He woke her each morning at the crack of dawn. That was good. Every morning they enjoyed a sunrise along with a brisk ride. Few people were up that early. That time of day was special to her and she hoped to him as well. Some moments she felt as if she grew closer to him. Other times they were separated by chasms.

Now that she was no longer dreading the channel crossing, she was coming to enjoy Case's company. Along with his sense of humor. His wit. The moments when he forgot himself and smiled. When he smiled it transformed his face. To Tara he was always handsome. Oh, but when he flashed his smile, he could melt her heart.

She looked forward to the morning jaunts. At times they would race far ahead of the carriage. Though conversation was limited, Tara was getting to know a few of his idiosyncrasies. His daily habits. What she said that would inevitably make his anger flare. The way his hard gaze seemed to study her when she was feeling alone. The anniversary of the accident grew closer. He grew darker the more he asked and the less she told him.

I wish I never sensed the vulnerability beneath this man's hard exterior. I wish that Case was as unfeeling as he seems to want me to believe he is. If that were true, I could simply ignore him, letting his hungry glances and touches slide off the serenity I've worked so hard to achieve. If that were a fact, I wouldn't long for something more with this man.

Case rode up beside her. "We're almost to Paris. Are you happy or excited? Where do you want to go first?"

The questions surprised her. Over the last few days, since he asked her if she was pregnant then disbelieved her answer, he kept distance between them that she couldn't break down. Never asking for more than he was willing to give.

"Do you care?" The question felt like a slap to his face. Tara didn't want to sound so bitter. She was though. She missed the carefree banter they sometimes had before they left. Though those occasions had been rare. Since the pregnancy incident they were nonexistent. In part that was her fault. She couldn't find a way to forgive him for leaping to that hurtful conclusion.

"I'm sorry I offended you. Don't know what I said to cause your wrath to surface so instantly. You might give a bloke a chance to defend himself. Tell me what I said." He tipped his hat to a man who was riding in the opposite direction.

Her back stiffened when it seemed he blamed all on her. "You know bloody well when you insulted me. You're doing the same now. Pretending you don't know what you said." Tara thought if it wasn't so stifling riding in the vehicle, it would be a good place to escape. She didn't lack courage. She wasn't going to hide from him. Confronting the man and telling him the truth would never mean he would accept her word.

"Morning sickness is usually a sign to be noticed. You were quite sick that morning. The conclusion I came to was logical as well as realistic. Tell me where I'm wrong."

"I haven't been sick since," she shot back too fast. "Haven't you noticed?"

"I pay attention to more than you think."

"Really? You could have fooled me."

"That's why you've given me the silent treatment. Tara, it ends now."

"At your command, Captain, Sir."

When she turned on him to confront him with the fact she was never sick in the morning, he held up his hands to stop her. "Hold for a moment. I understand now that you didn't have your sea legs. I had to ask the captain if he knew what was wrong. He told me the duke informed him of the fact when we were going to ride across the channel with him. Told me you get horrible bouts of seasickness."

"An understatement. ...and, I don't believe your apology for one minute. You don't mean the words. You thought you were right. Thought...think I have indiscriminate sex with any man who suits my fancy. Why should I dissuade you from that bizarre notion? Under the same circumstances you would do and think the same thing. Nothing has changed. You still believe I might be with child. I tell you now that there is no way in hell that could be true!" Even to her ears she sounded bitter...too angry to think straight. The last few days had not been pleasant. Some of the anticipation of showing Case Paris vanished during those hours.

"Can we start over?" His voice was soft, tender.

Tara knew he could be sweet as well as gentle. She should never allow him to suck her into his world. He could also be a royal pain in the ass. He'd shown both sides to her. This time he sounded sincere though something in the tone and tenor of his voice told her there was something he wanted from her. She heaved a big breath of air then prayed she would never regret the words. She understood what it was he hoped to receive from her.

She drank in her fear of the unknown. "I'd like that. Starting over. Make this a new beginning." Once the words were spoken, Tara realized what she acknowledged was the truth. She missed his teasing smiles along with the dark hungry looks he sent her way when he knew she was looking. The last few days she'd seen little of his lighter side.

Case seemed to like her answer. He closed the distance between them before pulling Sunrise to a stop. His hand slicked behind her head. After that all she managed was to feel his mouth pushed hard against hers. He touched her lips with his tongue, pressed until she opened for him. A broken sound fled her throat. She moaned, the noise a soft whisper while a sensual languid heat flushed through her. When he let her go, she touched her finger to her lips awed by the sensations coursing within. Her eyes were wide, filled with the wonder along with the magic he created when he kissed her.

"That's a promise I mean to fulfill. A promise I mean to keep."

"Um..." Tara didn't understand what he said. Though she thought if another kiss was promised, she'd like that. Even Grant's kisses didn't move her with such deep intensity and as quickly as those Case orchestrated.

For the remaining hour they didn't speak much. Her mind along with her body were still reeling from his attention to her mouth as well as his potent words of promise. The time was just a little later when they stopped in front of the building where they would live for the summer months, maybe even into the fall. Drake told her they would be here for however long it took for Case to complete the mission. Knowing her uncle, she understood there was far more to his assignment than what she'd been told. They weren't here to test the climate of the French government or to send missives about the goings on of the aristocrats. That might in part be true. Tara knew her uncle. He would never send one of his best agents on such a trifling mission if something else wasn't involved.

After dismounting, Case set his hands on her waist then lifted her from Sunrise. He didn't let her go. Instead, he held her close to him, her breasts pushed against his chest, her hips next to his. His arm was wrapped around her waist. His fingers squeezed. There was little to no space between them. She felt his arousal against her. Knew he wanted her. Remembered from the times Grant held her this close.

This time when he kissed her, the caresses were like butterfly wings touching on her lips. Light. Airy. Tara knew she wanted something else. She was hungry for a real kiss, a proper caressing of lips.

Needed to feel his tongue inside, playing with her, teasing her to hot hungry desire he evoked the few times he kissed her.

After he pulled away, he tapped her on the nose. His smile revealed straight white teeth. "Don't want to make a spectacle of ourselves or start the *on dit* in Paris that we are a couple when we are not. What do you say? Should we take a look at our residence?" he asked while he handed off the reins of both horses to a boy who was standing in front of them as if that was his job.

Not a couple? Why did his words hurt? She wasn't certain. He was right, they weren't a couple nor were they lovers. "I would. Do you think Ash will be here?" Tara would like to see her cousin. She needed a little grounding after the two shared kisses today. After hardly speaking to the man for the last days on the road, the intimacies made her legs weak and her hands shake.

The distance should make her more comfortable. She did but she didn't want the separation. Tara wasn't a woman to jump into his bed. To her it was clear he wasn't a man to expect something like that. He looked out for her reputation.

When she asked the question, Tara saw the tightening of his mouth coupled with the narrowing of his eyes. "I hope not. The less I see of the young pup the better. Ash can go to the devil as far as I care." His words were issued in a low growl.

Possessively, he placed his hand on her waist, drawing her close to him. Another sign of affection that had been missing. That instant she thought he was going to kiss her again. His eyes darkened, turning deep blue as they always did in her short experience when he shared his lips with hers.

Tara's voice trembled with emotions along with curiosity, "Why don't you like Ash? Has he done something to earn your displeasure? He's always nice to me. Though when I visited as a child, he could be a rascal. He liked to hide my things. He teased me. Sometimes I hated him." She stopped walking so she could study his features again.

"Like the boy just fine," he gritted out through what appeared to be clenched teeth. "It's the way you act around him I don't like. Don't enjoy watching you flirt your wiles with everyone in britches. You can be sassy with me. No one else."

Her brows furrowed. She blinked a few times before tilting her head a bit as if that would give her better perspective on his thoughts. The gesture failed. "You don't want me to act myself around Ash. How do you expect me to be?" After that with an indignant huff, "I do not flirt with everyone wearing pants. I'm not sassy. Don't know what that means. Don't know what you are talking about. I'm not like you think."

"If the truth is what you want, I'll give it to you straight out. Don't like the way you trip over your feet to give him what he wants. You kiss him when you come into a room. Your eyes sparkle with pleasure when you see him."

"His cheek. Yes, I'm happy to see him. We've known each other for a long time, a very long time. Don't recall when I didn't know him. It's been that long." She didn't understand where he was going with this.

"Jeremy is worse though. You share a bond with that man. An attachment I don't understand and you refuse to explain. I don't like what you feel for him or how you act when he's around. You climb all over him when he's in your path. Push yourself against him."

"Do not!" Tara was floored. Indignant she didn't know what to say to his denouncements of her behavior. Tara thought for a moment then, "Jeremy is a friend, not a lover if that is what you are getting at. The man has never been a lover or in close running. You're not a lover either and have no right to think to put restraints on the friendships I had previous to meeting you." She heaved in a deep breath of air. "Where do you get off making accusations of that sort?"

"This is where I get off!" he shouted then pulled her into his arms.

His mouth crashed hard against hers, possessing hers. He pulled her hard against his body. Tara felt the length of him pressed against her body. A sound hitched in the back of her throat. When he deepened the kiss she splintered into thousands of pieces, moaned. Sounds fragmented. His big hands cupped her bottom, holding her against him.

Tara felt the solid evidence of his desire pushed on her belly. Told her he wanted her in elemental ways she never experienced. Grant wanted to wait until they married. The ways she understood would cause a woman to increase if she gave into the hungry passion a man could illicit from a woman.

Case's fingers wound into her hair, tugging her head back, making her more vulnerable to his possession. Unable to stop herself, not wanting to end the kiss, Tara wrapped her hands around his neck before sliding her finger into the dark hair at his nape. She wanted him, another kiss, more...so much more that she didn't even understand.

"Give me what I want, sweetheart. Melt all over me. We'll both be happier when you do. Touch me. Push that sweet tongue deep inside me. Moan with the pleasure I give you." His voice was a low growl. "I want all of you, Tara. All you're willing to give me. Just let me know when you can give more than a kiss."

His muscular legs pushed hers apart. She felt his thigh move along the inside of her leg to the apex. The caress titillated. Gave her unfamiliar feelings. Mercuric sensations flooded her. Tara moaned again. Let her tongue meet then dance with his. The devil, he tasted good. Disjointed sounds shattered from the back of her throat. Case absorbed them into his.

Tara found herself clinging to him, fighting to keep her knees from buckling. "Case..." she sighed his name into his mouth.

"Give it to me, Tara. Give me everything you've got. Don't hold back."

Her mind was blank. She thought she was giving him all she could. He sucked her tongue inside his mouth. The moment was dark and secret, sultry. Seconds passed while they dueled. She touched his teeth with the tip of hers, felt the soft interior while he rubbed his tongue across hers. Mindless, until more heat than she could ever imagine inflamed every part of her shattering her, she jerked when she realized his muscular hard thigh rubbed across her intimately. Inside she clenched, squeezed as if expecting something.

The loud, rude clearing of a masculine throat behind her startled her more than the private, secret caress between her thighs. She clung to him. Her face pressed against his chest. All the while her heart clamored beneath her ribs. Tara didn't want to look up. Didn't want to acknowledge the man who had been watching them kiss.

"It's alright, sweetheart." With his big hands he soothed her, caressed her back in a calming gesture. "Hold on to me as long as you want. I've got you."

Tara nodded telling him she understood what he was saying. She'd never done anything like this. Still pressing her cheek on his chest, she felt the hard ripple of his muscles. His arms stayed around her, keeping her close for as long as she wanted. The strong steady beat of his heart comforted. When Case was sweet and gentle, he was very sweet and gentle. She liked him that way. At other times...

Second after second whipped by, with her hands flattened on his chest, she moved a breath away. "Who is it? Who...?" His breath whispered, teasing a response. Tara was stunned she could speak. She didn't want anyone watching her kiss Chase. The sensations were too private, too new.

"Jeremy..." The harsh tension in Case's voice was obvious. He was angry. Angry they were interrupted. She felt his body stiffen. It was obvious he held no tender feelings for her friend.

Jeremy? What is he doing here? He is supposed to be in London.

Distressed at the other man's presence, she pushed away. "Yes, didn't know the man was coming to Paris. Did you?" The accusation was clear. He expected that she invited him. She did not. It was just like Case to think the worst of her.

"No. I didn't know." After she turned around, she was shocked by the tightness in Jeremy's expression, by the fists clenched tense by his sides. His lips thinned. A pulse beat at his temple. The flashing darkness of his eyes focused on Case sent another message. Jeremy was also angry with her, with Case. The man didn't have that right to judge anything she did or did not do. Tara didn't understand what was happening right in front of her. All she comprehended was that she didn't like seeing distrust between these two men who she cared about. Jeremy had been her friend for forever. Case was becoming more than a friend. If he could ever get over the bitterness he felt toward women out of his system, they might have a better chance of understanding each other.

Proprietary hands held her at her waist. He squeezed. One arm circled her stating his point with emphasis. She was his. In his own way, Case claimed her. Telling Jeremy in no uncertain terms to keep his hands off, to keep his distance. The man didn't have that right. Nonetheless, he was taking it. She wasn't complaining.

"What do you want here? What is your business?" There was no forgiveness in Case's voice. "You need to go home to London where you belong. There is nothing here for you. If you believe you're here for Tara, think again."

"Tara might need me," Jeremy said as his hard stare softened when he focused on her. "She might need a friendly shoulder to cry on when you're through with her. You will cast her aside. You don't understand all she's going through."

"She's got me."

Jeremy's shoulders were squared, the taut angry lines around his eyes and mouth remained. It seemed he realized he would have to back off. In a taut voice, he spoke to Case, his gaze focused on the man who held her. "If you hurt her, you'll answer to me."

"I won't hurt Tara. We understand each other. Go on, go to wherever you're staying." He nodded in a direction away from the house. "You're not wanted or welcome here."

Jeremy seemed to be waiting for her to say something. She turned to look at Case. After that she stared at Jeremy. Wondering what she should do. It was clear Case didn't want anything to do with Jeremy. While he tolerated Ash, he seemed to detest Jeremy. To end this conversation amiably would not happen.

Tara went with her gut. She had to agree with Case. "You should go, Jeremy. I'm fine. Tomorrow will come and go no matter what you do. I'll remember things I don't want to remember. Feel things that I'm trying to forget. You can't help me. Nobody can. I just need to live through that day." The truth of her words to herself were harsh.

Once more Case's fingers tightened where they held her. "I will be here for Tara if she needs anyone's help."

"You don't know what she needs," Jeremy spoke through gritted teeth displeased that he was finding himself tossed out.

"Please, Jeremy, just go. Leave. I don't want you here." Dealing with two hostile men who were acting like children was not something she could relish at any time.

Case bent close to her ear. His breath tickling the fine hairs at her nape, "If you would explain what happened on that day two years ago, I would..."

His speech stopped when she turned. Put her hand on his cheek. Felt the vibrance of his energy surge into her. If she could, "I want to. I can't. Maybe someday. Telling you about that day would take trust. I can't trust you. not yet." Tara drew in a deep breath of air as she searched for courage to go on. "I just can't talk about what happened. Maybe someday. For now, you have to try to understand. You're still a virtual stranger to me. A stranger with moods I don't comprehend how to deal with. One moment, you're smiling. The next you are angry with me for no reason. Sometimes you appear hurt, vulnerable. At those times I want to hold you close, tell you all will be fine. Other times your arrogance exceeds all limitation."

Once more, the distance between them felt as if a chasm opened. A black hole that could suck her down. She needed to stay away from the danger. His back was straight, his jaw taunt. "Very well." The words were stark, unfeeling telling her the agreement wasn't heartfelt.

Her courage evaporated like the puddles left from a summer rain storm after the sun popped out. The cringe of despair filling her sent moisture to her eyes. Remembering that day left her speechless, weak with debilitating hopelessness. He wanted her to share something so tragic she couldn't breathe each time she thought about the moment changing her life forever. She couldn't. Tara leaned into him, shaking until Case seemed to understand her unspoken words. Any minute now her knees were going to give out. She might crumble to the ground if he didn't hang onto her.

He tightened his hold around her waist, speaking without words to her that he was indeed there for her. When he spoke again, he talked to Jeremy in her behalf. He moved his hand along her back, soothing. "Tara needs to rest. The trip was difficult. She doesn't like ocean travel." Case turned with his arm still wrapped around her. When he bent close to say. "If you need for me to carry you, tell me. Is your leg bothering you?"

"I can walk," Tara said the words but her voice shook as much as her body.

"You could lie to me."

"I wouldn't do that. Not about this. Not about anything," she said looking up into his eyes. "I don't lie, Case." She didn't tell falsehoods but she understood he was well aware she left out a lot of information.

So did he.

"When you don't want me to know something you just don't speak. Understand perfectly. No words are better than lies. At least I know when you tell me something it's the truth." His words spilled out with a harsh frankness. They were all true.

Tara wanted to blurt again that there was no way she could be pregnant. Instead, she kept quiet. Though the steps were measured and slow, they were walking. Tara felt the heat of Jeremy's gaze following them to the porch then up the stairs. The short walk seemed to take an eternity. All the while, she leaned into Case, absorbing his strength. His heat. He held so much power in his body. Power along with strength she wished she could have.

Once inside, he left her sitting on a large chair. Tara let her head fall against the back. With great effort she sipped in air. She heard a voice from the hallway. Case was speaking with another man. It wasn't Ash. He never told her he expected visitors. She reminded herself while she was here for rest along with relaxation, Case was working. The man left. The door shut. Heard his footsteps as he strode to the room.

Case hunkered down in front of her, taking her hands in his. When she looked into his eyes, she saw deep concern. "We'll have tea in a minute, a few refreshments to eat before dinner. The butler tells me the cook knows how much you enjoy berry tarts. Seems strawberries are coming into season. Is there anything else you would like? By the way, I was speaking with the butler. His name is Timms. Ah..." he tapped her on the nose. "You thought someone came to call. I'm sure Drake put out the word long before we arrived that I would be here. However, it's up to me to summon the people I need to speak with. They will not show up unannounced."

Tara ignored his declaration. He was right. She meant to concentrate on the here and now. Secret alliances were not her forte.

"Timms, nice name. I think he was here a few years ago when I was with..." Tara broke off, lowering her lashes, not wanting to mention Grant's name. Not today. Not after the kiss that left her week in the knees. In time she might tell Case about the man she loved.

"With who?" His voice was soft now, gentle. He spoke as if he didn't care. "Who were you with? Your mother and father? Your brothers? A lover?"

She supposed he couldn't help the last question. Case held such a deplorable view of her...of women in general. Today, she wasn't of a mind to correct him on his assumption. "Nothing. No one of any importance." To answer him was too painful. It would bring back more memories of times she was trying to forget.

"With who?" he persisted, stroking her cheek with the back of his hand. "I'd like to understand more about you. I can't if you remain silent."

"Case...not now." She wiped away the tears that were starting to fall. "I don't want to talk about what happened two years ago tomorrow. If that is what you are trying to do, don't. The pain... I couldn't do anything to stop it... It just happened and my life changed. Thinking about that moment hurts."

"What does Jeremy have to do with any of this. Why the bloody hell can you tell him and you won't tell me?" The gentle softness vanished to be replaced with his anger. The fury so evident it sent chills down her spine.

When she looked up at him, tears slid down her cheeks. She gulped for air. "He knows because he was there. Jeremy saved my life that day. For days and days, I cursed him for doing so. Wished he would have let me die." Tara turned her face away. She told him too much. Hiding from this man who somehow gave her reason to live again. Jeremy helped but nothing like Case. When she could look at him again, Tara said, "I owe him. Owe him my life though I was ungrateful at first. Now I understand what he did was for the best."

"You don't owe that man a damn thing. He's milked you for all he is going to get. Was he your lover then? Is that why you cling to him?"

With that question Tara bristled, her back straightening. She wanted to tear into him. Struggling for the calm that was the only way she could get through this time, "No!" she bit out with harsh venom. Jeremy wanted more from her, always wanted more. Wanted to be what Grant had been to her. "A friend. That's all he is. All he has ever been or will be. Not a lover. Never a lover!"

"A friend with benefits?" Case questioned again his eyes hardening. He didn't bend, didn't let up. His mind was set.

Tears were still falling, streaking her cheeks. She couldn't stop crying. Tara found herself shaking her head, persevering when she knew she should walk away. "No. Don't know what you mean. He's just a friend. Don't understand the part about benefits. Has been a friend since we were children. What's a friend with benefits? I don't get what you are asking."

Tara looked up from her questions to find herself reflected in the hard clarity of Case's eyes. Reflected and...measured. Condemned. His eyes were not so soothing as the slow rhythm of his hands rubbing warmth into her. She needed to distance herself from this man before he swallowed her whole.

The tea arrived. Poured. The strawberry treats arrived. Different pastries were arranged on the table. Tara held her cup in shaking hands. Set it down to steady herself. She filled it with milk and lemon, one cube of sugar.

Case sat in an opposite chair, nursing a brandy and staring at her. His gaze bored into her. Tara felt as if he tried to see into her mind, to unravel her secret. She didn't care if he knew. It was just that she couldn't bring herself to talk about that day. True, he deserved to know. In such a short amount of time, Case was becoming an integral part of her life. She didn't know what she meant to him. He kept such a distance between them.

~ * ~

Anger simmered deep in his gut. Tara melted all over him, warm as well as soft. She wanted him. He understood the raw desire packed into such a delectable sweet body could be summoned with ease. The passion simmering between them was fast and deep. She wouldn't tell him a simple secret. Not for a second did he believe all Jeremy was to her was a friend. The other man's possessiveness was not hard to miss. Bottom line, Jeremy thought of Tara as his. Wasn't willing to give her up to him despite the fact Tara sent him away. Today though, today, Jeremy seemed to realize, at least for the present, she was his. The man could have her back after he moved on. Lilies and rain water, he would always think of her when it rained in the spring. When he saw lilies blooming in gardens.

"What would you like to do tomorrow? I suppose you have an agenda." Case thought it prudent to change the subject. She was mute when it came to this second anniversary of hers. Apparent to him, it happened two years ago tomorrow. In due time, she would enlighten him. He could be patient. Tomorrow he would make certain she didn't have time for old memories. They would be making new ones. He would keep her busy, her mind occupied. He wanted to explore Paris with her.

Her first smile since Jeremy arrived sent his heart spinning wild and uncontrolled. She was willing to make plans with him. That was good.

She ran her hands along her dress, smoothing imaginary creases, rearranging fabric over her legs. "You don't want to do something tonight? I thought we could..." She was looking at him as if she forgot what tomorrow would bring.

Surprised, "You would? What do you have in mind?" He was eager to spend more time with Tara, private time, just the two of them. Case was up to doing anything she would plan.

"Well," she tapped a finger against the tea cup. "A glass of good Bordeaux on the Champs Elysée then a walk. Maybe some food if you've a mind to eat. There are all kinds of restaurants on the street. We can buy some pastries for breakfast tomorrow from one of my favorite *boulangeries ou bonbons.*"

"That would be nice," he said with a bit of hesitation watching the smile on her face replace the tears. Kissing her smile came to mind. The corners of her mouth. Case wasn't positive how to approach her now that she'd done a complete about face. "You're not too tired? You're leg?

Don't want it to give out on you."

"No and my leg is just ducky," she said, her voice tart.

"Good then what do we do now?" He tried to think of what she might want. He was hot and dusty. She had to be feeling the same. Too bad she didn't wear tiny buttons and a corset that needed his tender attention. He would be pleased to help her with her gown.

"A bath first. After that...after the bath, we can stroll, watch a sunset on the Seine." She smiled at him.

Case still wanted to know about the anniversary. They needed to find common ground before she would confide. Since the crossing he'd not done very well with communicating. Tara took umbrage with the fact he asked her if she was increasing. The question was legitimate. Case wanted to wrap a curling tendril of her hair around his finger. After that he would take his time releasing it, letting the silk and radiance of Tara's hair caress the sensitive skin between his fingers.

"When we have the glass of wine, we can talk about tomorrow morning or the afternoon. Montgomerie told me there was a ball tomorrow evening given by Lord Montesquieu. If we feel rested, we should attend. I need to get to know all the important players in this city."

"Drake doesn't waste time. I knew that. Just didn't expect the day after we arrived in Paris we'd be called upon to start fraternizing with the locals." Sitting back on the sofa, she sipped her tea. Tara appeared to be pouting.

This woman amused him as well as sent his body thinking of all types of activities they could do together in bed. "I'll be working most of the afternoon," he told her. "Lord Montgomerie has an itinerary of people for me to see. I have to do business first." Case wondered how much of his mission here Tara knew about. Did she think they were here to have fun? If she thought that, she wasn't as close to the duke and duchess as it appeared at first glance. What was her relationship with the almost royal pair?

"Very well, I'll take the time to scope out the new restaurants along with the sights we wish to see. I'll take a carriage to the monument S*acre* Coeur. After I've researched the city, I'll have a better idea as to what to prioritize."

He leaned forward, setting her tea cup on the table then taking her hands in his. With gentle ease, Case rubbed his fingers on the sensitive skin of her wrists. "That's out of the question." He sucked in air before he proceeded on a track she would take exception with. "Tara, you aren't to go anywhere without me. You have to understand that fact or I'll have to find a man to guard you at all times. Will you promise?" There was some danger in this mission. The man he was looking for could know about Tara. Bloody hell, he couldn't tell Tara anything else. She wouldn't know she might be in danger.

She tugged on her hands. "Let me get this straight. If you aren't with me, I'm a prisoner here in this room. What about Ash? I could go places with him. Could I not?"

Telling her Ash could accompany her stuck in his throat. He didn't want Tara to go anywhere unless it was with him. That very reason was part of why Ash was sent to Paris with them. Ash's assignment was an easy one meant for a new recruit which was exactly Ash's description. Ash would entertain Tara when he could not. Ash would protect her when he could not. If Ash's French had been better, Tara wouldn't be here.

"You could. It wouldn't please me." He gave her a tiny shake. "I want you to promise."

Her eyes sent daggers that could pierce through him if he let them. "Let me get this straight. I'm in Paris. Stuck in this apartment while you do your business does not please me," she retorted, her thoughts clear to him. "If you are through, I'm going to take that bath now. You did order baths when we came in. I need to put this conversation behind me. Find a way to calm myself. Hot water might work."

With a sigh at the lost ground, Case nodded his head. Future conversations with her would go much the same. "They should be ready any minute now. We'll have to plan our schedules so I can spend as much time with you as possible. I don't want you to feel as if you've been jailed. Don't wish to see you bored to tears. Your time here should be fun for you."

Light shining in her eyes, Tara brightened. The quick change didn't surprise Case. "I would like that. I find that when you are not being a royal ass, I like your company."

With her words he barked laughter. "Ass? Did I hear you say ass?" Case knew he wanted more of her sass. When Tara let lose, she was such a delight. As he spent more time with her it was clear to him her older brothers played a part in her upbringing. He was certain that what one brother didn't teach her the other did. What other delights were up her sleeve? Waiting to discover more would be more difficult than he thought. He wanted to spend as much time as possible with her. Needed to pursue without her knowledge. Keep her on edge waiting. Unlike most women, Case would have to let her set the pace.

"It's what you are at times. Does the truth hurt your tender sensibilities?" she asked as she started toward her room. Her fingers toyed with the ribbons holding the bodice of her gown together.

"I can be exactly what you called me." He waved his hand in the air, grinning at her antics. "Go take your bath, I'll join you here when you're done then together we will take a tour of the nearby cafes. Scope out the best places to eat. We will find a nice out of the way *resto* to enjoy a glass of wine then discuss what we will do tomorrow. Make a list we can go over for future reference. If you'd rather not go to the ball, I'll decline the offer with graciousness."

On the minute, an hour later, Tara waltzed into the drawing room wearing a soft blue silk confection that showed off all her beautiful curves. The corsage was modest showing a hint of her swelling breasts above the pale ecru lace. The skirt fit to her narrow waist then flared in soft folds around her legs. Case wanted to pull out all the pins in her perfectly arranged hair. After that, he wanted to sift his fingers through the silken mass while the strands slid through the sensitive flesh between. More than anything else, he would have liked to lower the bodice. The small glimpse of her breast he got when they rode out for their first sunrise together just wasn't enough.

Case rose. Set the brandy he'd been sipping on the table. "You look lovely. The color as well as the cut becomes you."

She beamed at him, curtsied, before twirling in a slow circle for his ardent perusal. "Thank you, you look quite dapper yourself. Are you ready for the first stroll on the most famous street in Paris?"

Tiny barked when they left him behind. Case knew Tara seldom left her pet. He was certain the big dog stood guard at the door waiting for their return. "Tiny doesn't like to be left to fend for himself. If he was a better guard dog, I might consider negotiations. As it stands now, the big boy is too friendly."

"You mean it?" Tara clutched his arm as they walked down the steps in front of their summer home. "I like to take him places. He likes to go. If..." She stopped speaking to frown.

The small creases on her forehead didn't go unnoticed. He wished he could smooth the small indentation with his thumb. "Not really, if you listened you would have heard the single word if. Tiny befriends everyone. He is a pussycat. He would never forgo a pat on his head to defend you. Too bad he's not more like a lion." By the time they returned, the big dog would have found one of the beds then made himself at home. Case would have to tug him off. Would need to somehow teach the beast that he didn't belong on beds. Tiny thought he was human.

When they stepped out on the street, Case felt as if a weight of sorts had been lifted from his shoulders. He knew what he was doing here. Understood that whatever happened, he might have to fall back on Ash for help. Jeremy, if he was a smart man, would stay far away from them. It would be best if Jeremy sailed back to London, the sooner the better. The man was a liability, not a help. Case didn't think the man would leave any time soon. Jeremy thought of himself as Tara's protector. He wasn't. Protecting her was his job now.

After Tara wrapped her hand in the crook of his arm, they strode through the streets. She pointed out places along with things she remembered from other visits. Boats sailed down the river Seine. Tara told him the sunsets here would be beautiful. Case planned on at least one kiss before they returned to the apartment.

"Look over there." She pointed to a two-story building, brilliant flowers in planters on all the windows. "I remember. Madam Pipelet lives there. She used to bring me jam every year when I visited. She would go out in the late summer, pick the berries then make jam. Every time I come here, she brings me a jar of each kind. Can we knock on her door and see her?"

"I'd like to taste some of this jam." Case wanted to taste Tara more than the jam. "People like you, don't they?" The statement composed with the question surprised him. If she were the lying woman he thought she was, Tara would not be so well liked. An elderly woman would never look twice at a woman who was out to please herself.

Her laughter was soft and floated around her like a delicate spring breeze.

Rain.

Lilies.

Spring.

Case would always remember the scent of Tara. It would be scalded into his brain for eternity. After he left her...

"I am a nice person. Not sure you've noticed that yet. Of course, people like me." Tara leaned into him while they strolled. She set her head on his arm.

She was amazing, all woman. She didn't lie. Case never met a woman who was without lies. "That you are...nice," he spoke with as much tenderness as a man like him could do wondering how this woman was getting under his skin. That never happened before. He didn't allow a woman to get close enough that he would have gentle thoughts about her. His thoughts hardened.

"There she is!" Tara let go of his arm. Lifting her pale blue skirt, she half skipped half ran to the woman he guessed must be Madam Pipelet. She tossed her arms around the woman before stepping back to look at her. "You look just the same. Don't you ever age?" The question was spoken with humorous accusation.

"As do you, *ma petite. Non, plus belle.* Every time I see you, you are more beautiful than the last."

Case heard the comment. Beautiful Tara, yes it seemed to him every day with her she grew more beautiful. He agreed with Madam Pipelet.

The two women spoke for a few minutes before Tara turned to glance his way. Using her entire hand, she waved for him to come. He held back to give her some private time with this woman though he did want to meet the lady who seemed to captivate Tara.

Madam Pipelet was short, stocky. Her hair was graying but she showed him a warm smile. By the time Case reached them he saw her light gray eyes twinkling with merriment. The woman would make a perfect grandmother. A child would relish her hugs. He never had a grandmother or a grandfather. Never had a father either. His mother never loved him.

Tara grabbed his hand before tugging him forward. "Come. Hurry up. This is the woman I told you about. The jam lady. Oh, but she is more than that. She always let me talk to her. Told her everything."

The delight in Tara's face warmed him. She told this woman everything. Madam Pipelet would know about the anniversary tomorrow that Tara wouldn't talk about. "The woman who makes the most wonderful jam in the entire world?" Case arched a dark eyebrow as if speculating the taste. He knew this was the woman she spoke of earlier.

"*Non...non...*not the most wonderful. *Mais oui, la confiture est bonne.*" Madam Pipelet was all smiles when she spoke directly at Case. "*Tu es tres beau,*" she giggled. When she turned to Tara, "You bring your man by whenever you wish. We'll have tea. You can tell me how the two of you met. He is your man? True? If not," she turned to Case, "you are not *tres* intelligent."

Case hugged Madam Pipelet. He thought she might swoon at his feet. The woman was sweet. Had some spice to her. This woman, even in her prime, would never be after what a man could give her, looking out only for herself. Not like Tara. No, she would want to give of herself first. After a few more hugs along with promises to come see her, Tara put her hand through the crook of his arm again. They strolled down to the river. Walked along the banks for a while. Silence except for the sound off the river along with the cry of a few birds kept his mind alert.

"Isn't she wonderful?" Tara beamed at him, her smile caressing him. "When you are not able to escort me, can I take Tiny and see her. She is only three doors down. You can't have a reason to tell me no. What harm could there be in a short visit?"

With her question coupled with her ill-advised statement, he stiffened. A second later he brought the back of her hand to his lips. Tara didn't understand the issue here. He couldn't explain the scenario to her. "I'll think about it," he told her knowing that he couldn't put his answer off forever. He would have to tell her no. The no would last until he found the man he searched for. The duke called Case a bounty hunter. Case was bloody good at his job. Made a great deal of money when he brought a man to justice. By most standards he was wealthy. Women looked for men with money as well as titles. He had one, not the other.

They found a table at a small café on the street. He ordered a bottle of their finest vintage Bordeaux. She ordered baguettes with cheese and meats. They sat at an outdoor table. Arm in arm, people strolled by. Chatted. Kissed. The evening was pleasant. The warm air brought fragrances from the bakery across the street.

"So..." She began between bites of food and sips of the wine. "What can we plan around your schedule? In my mind, I've made up a list of places I want to show you. When can we start?"

"Tomorrow afternoon?" Case wasn't positive he would be done with his interviews by then. If he wasn't he would reschedule. The time spent with Tara tomorrow was important.

"Yes." Her eyes twinkled.

A drop of wine sat on her lip. He reached up to wipe the moisture off. He would have rather kissed the drop, touched her with his mouth. "What do you want to do first? You're my guide." Relaxed, he sat back to study the nuances of her face. He clasped his hands together. "Tomorrow morning, I'll be meeting with two of Lord Montgomerie's agents. They'll brief me on what is going on here. As far as I can tell we've the afternoon free."

"While you are talking with people what can I do?" Tara watched all the people walking along the street. "I would go out. Where is Ash? You said he could take me."

"Thought you would know." Case didn't like thinking about another man escorting Tara. Didn't want her to go out with Ash even though the young man was harmless. A pup. "If Ash cannot be found, then you'll have to satisfy yourself with something to do in the apartment. You are supposed to write the correspondence for me in French. I'll have some documents ready for your attention. You can start with deciding if you wish to attend the ball. If not, you can send a missive that we won't be there. What do you think? Should we dance the night away? Should we explore Paris?"

She sighed the sound of dissatisfaction coming from her lips. "I could sit on the balcony and twiddle my thumbs while I wait."

"Why don't you show me your list?"

"*Oui*," Tara began, shuffling through her bag to bring out his request. Once the paper graced the table, she smoothed the crinkles where she folded it. "It is quite long. I've the feeling you won't be able to do everything in the short time we have here. If all you do is work, we will have to decide what is not important."

To his ears, she sounded hesitant. That was something different. "What would we do first? Tomorrow afternoon?" Case brought the conversation around to something he was looking forward to doing.

"What we do is up to you."

"You're my guide. You decide." Case enjoyed the conversation. Tara would do well as a conductor. He watched while Tara went over the long list of places to visit. Her confidence came from experience. It didn't surprise him that she knew Paris. Men liked the types of diversions she was skilled at. It was clear to him. Tara was a woman who made a career out of pleasing men.

As Case sipped the dark red burgundy, he wondered in what other ways she learned to please men. The thought caused desire to ripple through him. He needed to change the tenor of his thoughts, knowing that his curiosity wouldn't be assuaged tonight. Several days might pass before he could reach her the way he wished.

If his suspicions were correct, Tara would dodge and twist, keeping him on tenterhooks until she could no longer do so. The game would be interesting to play. She would tantalize him by remaining just beyond his reach. Not that he minded. Her playing the game so adeptly made the inevitable end of the chase sweeter, hotter.

Chase and catch.

Easy prey wasn't worth the trouble it took to reach out and pick it up. If anything, this woman was not easy. Tara confused and challenged him. She sent mixed signals that needed interpretation.

Tara was talking of the tours. Case found himself half-listening. Her smooth voice swept over him. Peace settled around him. He found she was animated, her hands moving as she spoke of the Sacre-Coeur Basilica in Montmartre along with the Pont Alexandre III Bridge then there was The Louvre. The list continued.

"We will go to Montmartre tomorrow. Walk to the top of the hill. Watch the sunset there. After that we can walk through the streets. Eat something at the bottom of the hill. Find a hack to bring us home. I'll write the missive telling Lord Montesquieu we won't attend his ball. We are too tired from the long journey. That should be a good enough excuse." She set her wine glass down. Rested her head in her hands while she continued. "When would you like to go to Epernay? That is where you will taste the fine French champagne."

It had been a long time since Case sat in a small outdoor café sipping wine with a woman. Most of the time, he didn't drink wine. On most missions he was alone. This was different in more ways than he could imagine. The few times he relaxed in a small café with a woman, she would talk as if she had to fill the silence with words...words and more meaningless words pouring out as she tried to fill the emptiness surrounding her. Emptiness could never be filled. Words could never change the morning after the end of the chase. When it was over, that kind of desperate chatter left Case cold. To be with a woman who demanded nothing of him was as unusual as it was peaceful.

As he listened to his thoughts, he pushed away his empty wine glass. He couldn't fall under Tara's spell. It was too dangerous to do so. If she bewitched him, the game would falter. Case needed to make certain he stayed within the parameters he set. That was how the game would playout. Since he was eighteen he understood the game along with the end. That was when he learned that to be an emotionally honest man in a world of lies is to be a fool.

Tara pushed her glass away. She tapped the crystal with a fingertip, "Well?" she asked. "Does this itinerary meet with your approval? Do you have anything you wish to add or subtract?"

Case nodded as if in complete agreement with her plan. "You will have to remind me though as the days progress. Tomorrow, Montmartre.

Is that correct. The day after that we'll ride to Versailles?"

Case didn't wish to spend more time discussing famous sites to see in Paris. Time to change the discussion to something that might lead somewhere. He wanted to see if she would bend a trifle. Kiss him as she did this afternoon. "Let's find a good spot to watch the sunset. Finish your wine then we'll go."

"There is only a drop left. I'm done."

Together, they walked along the bank of the river. Cool summer breezes lifted her skirts and played with tendrils of her hair. Tara was just like every other woman, just a bit more complex.

~ * ~

"I felt as if you weren't listening. I was rambling off places. Your mind was somewhere else. If you don't care..." Tara looked at Case, who returned the look with interest. In the brilliant time before the sunset his eyes were dark blue, very intense against the darkness of his skin.

"You think I wasn't listening?"

"Have you been to Paris? To France? Is this the first time?" Tara asked wishing he would pay more attention.

"Yes and no."

What kind of answer was that? Case was too illusive for her mind. He left too many questions unanswered. Tara clenched her teeth hoping to keep her frustration in control. Breathing deep even breaths, she searched for the calm she needed to deal with this confusing man.

As they strolled, her shoulders touched his arm. Tara flinched away from him, at this moment not wishing to touch the man who showed her so many varying sides. She never knew what nasty comment he would speak to her. Until Case, she never believed a man's words could hurt her. Deep in her heart, she understood getting close to him would be dangerous to her peace of mind. To resist him was impossible. He cast a spell on her with his brooding eyes the set of his stubborn mouth, the vulnerability she didn't believe he meant for her to see.

When he wasn't paying attention, she saw the deep pain he hid from everyone. They stopped at a solid wall along the Seine. The space between the buildings made it possible to watch the sun descend then show the vibrant colors that signaled the end of the day. She wondered so much about this man. Needed answers to her questions. Understood he would not be forthcoming.

"I've been a lot of places." Case turned to lean against the wall. He stared at her, watching her as if he expected her to run in the opposite direction.

"That doesn't answer my questions. If you don't wish to speak of your past, that's fine by me. Don't. Don't pretend either."

"Some questions aren't meant to be answered." His voice was rich with scorn, his words and tone undoing all the good feelings she had earlier.

Tara started to respond. Her lips opened. With a light touch, his finger pushed against them. She shivered when he caressed her bottom lip. "Hush," he told her. "I didn't mean anything. I've been through Paris. A rushed operation orchestrated by the SIS. In then out. Spent more time in Italy, Rome to be exact. Lord Montgomerie likes to place his agents where they understand the language. Know Italian much better than French."

"That is why he sent me here with you?" Tara was looking to Case for more answers he wanted to give. His mind was a closed book to her.

"Look." Case pointed to the sky. He lifted his face to better see what he pointed at. He closed his eyes letting the sunset wash over his features. After he opened them, he began to speak. "The colors are starting to form as the sun is beginning to hide until dawn where the sun will paint the sky again. So beautiful." He turned to her. His expression told her he thought she was also beautiful.

The air Tara sipped in startled her. Her gaze met his. Collided. She saw the fierce pleasure on Case's face. Felt desire rush through her. The sensation startled her in the instant before she accepted the feeling. Obvious to Tara, if not for her, the man would have never taken the time to absorb and enjoy the setting sun.

I shouldn't be surprised by his enjoyment of life. I chose to live after Grant died in the wreck. Passion and enjoyment of earth's sights are part of life's pleasures. What he is seeing now has nothing to do with me. Just because I haven't wanted a man for two years, doesn't mean I will never want a man again.

Do I want Case?

The question surprised as well as confounded her. He wasn't an easy man to get to know. Hard around the edges as well as everywhere in between would describe Case. Tara held the opinion he liked relationships that way hard and fast. He needed to direct the scene as well as express all that would transpire between them. She didn't doubt for a moment that was the way he always acted. She was just another woman to him, easily taken just as easily discarded. Case held himself back, revealing a limited portion about himself while he expected her to be an open slate for him to read at his pleasure. For her, love with Grant had always been give and share. She knew just about everything about her fiancé there was to know. But then...but then she'd known Grant most of her life. Didn't remember a time when he didn't play some role in her everyday existence.

Even though Tara admitted the emotional intensity of her attraction to Case, she warned herself against acting on her feelings or encouraging him. If she thought she meant to remain innocent for some man in her future, she deluded herself. For her there would never be another man as dear to her as Grant. Case could hurt her. In this lifetime she'd had enough pain. She'd never met a man as hard as Case or as formidable. Her uncle could be hard as well as unyielding. Ella tempered those traits with her love. Beneath that hardness possessing Case, Tara sensed a yearning for beauty, for warmth, for...love? Without that deep-seated longing, she would never have been attracted to him. If she didn't see the chink in his armor, she would not be here. She didn't delude herself into thinking she could change the man. Attracted, she was.

Like a moth to the flames of fire.

Even admitting to her burgeoning feelings, Tara understood there were no guarantees she would be the one to touch Case's heart. He could toy with her then move on to some other conquest, another assignment, another woman. There was no guarantee any woman could touch him, could shatter the hard shell surrounding him.

Am I willing to risk my hard-won peace for a man who is incapable of love?

Case was resilient and inflexible. If all he told her was true, he lived a long time alone.

So had she.

Somehow during her thoughts, Case wrapped his arms around her, shielding her from the sharpness of the evening wind sliding across the river. Tara's back was pressed against his chest. His fingers were folded together against her stomach. The hot warmth from his body both shocked as well as surprised her. Needing the closeness, she set her head against his chest, her hands resting on his forearms. For the first time in so long she couldn't count the months or the years, she relaxed. She allowed Case to hold her up. To support her.

A man could do that for her.

The right man.

That was the problem. Tara didn't know if Case was the right man.

She didn't know if she wanted to risk falling for him.

The last of the sun disappeared. Still, they stood on the banks of the Seine staring into the darkening sky watching the colors fade into dark blue. The river flowed, small waves lapping the banks. Stars began to appear in the night sky. The moon hovered high with whisps of clouds ghosting the brilliant orb from time to time.

"Are you ready to go home? You're shaking. Are those your teeth I hear chattering? Fool woman, you didn't wear enough clothes." With no fanfare, Case settled his frock coat around her shoulders.

"You're right. I didn't. Didn't know the wind coming off the river would turn this chilly after the sun disappeared. Didn't realize we would stand on the bank after the sun left us. It's growing dark." Tara stepped beside him as they made their way back to the apartment. They passed Madam Pipelet's residence. The older woman waved to them from her balcony, the smile on her face wide and infectious. Tara grinned back at her.

Tara knew she would visit the older lady, with or without his permission. There were things that needed reminiscing. Advice to be given. The last time she was here, Grant had been with her. Madam would have heard of his death as well as the frightening ordeal she went through. She needed to explain.

"I know what you're thinking." His dark melodious voice washed over her. "Be advised, it won't work."

She blinked, startled by the statement. What did he know? "You do?" Tara realized she would never be able to hide anything from him. If he wasn't around, he wouldn't be there to stop her. In his absence, she would do as she pleased. At least she thought so. There would have to be a few good reasons for her to kow tow to his unreasonable demands on her time. She understood there would be days when he would be too busy for her, days where he would disappear. Tara would be alone to please herself. Her uncle did much the same. Aunt Ella was never quarantined to either of their homes. Drake also had enemies. When Drake was gone, Ella always had a man with her, an agent, someone to protect her back.

"Yes."

"No, you don't."

"I do." His hand on her waist tightened. "Best you rid yourself of those mutinous ideas. I won't have you in danger because of your impetuousness."

"No...you don't."

"Tara, you cannot put yourself in a spot where one of my antagonists might take exception to the fact you are unguarded. While I don't yet know your connection to the duke, he also has enemies. Don't want to see you hurt or killed."

"This is a diplomatic mission. There are no enemies. You're autocratic and taking advantage of a situation you are not in charge of." Uncle Drake did have men who wished to see to his demise. Tara didn't know what that had to do with her.

"Listen to me." Case stopped between Madam's home and theirs's. He turned her. His hands rested on her shoulders. The shake he gave her loosened a few tendrils of hair. Grabbed her attention. The harsh set of his face gave her reason to pause. "Does the idea of danger turn you on? Does danger make you excited? Emboldened?" His voice was harsh, grating in its strength and power.

"No." Tara blinked deciphering his message. Danger never did anything for her except terrify. She hated the thought of risking herself, her life. Thinking brought back memories. Memories caused pain.

"Good. It turns a lot of women on. Glad to hear you have a healthy fear of it. Don't want you vulnerable. Taking chances is not something good for you." The intensity of his voice reached deep inside her.

She didn't want to recognize the truth of his words. Tara's hands were on his chest. To force him away would give her distance. "Does it?" She pushed. He didn't budge. His eyes darkened. "Why? Why would danger...?" Tara was confused by his statement. Her head fuzzy.

The sound Case made was severe. His fingers clenched tighter around her shoulders. "Excitement, sweetheart. The risk tells them they are living. Excitement makes them breathe. The heart beat faster. Makes the world seem brighter. I should know. I thrive on gambling my life."

The shudder whipping through her couldn't be hidden. Case must feel alive when he courts danger, when he takes chances. She didn't. "Or...that someone else is dead," Tara said, feeling the tremors of memories skating through her, seeping into her soul. Tomorrow was the anniversary of the accident that took Grant's life, that crippled her for well over a year. She tried to break from him. Needed to walk away from his piercing all-knowing eyes. Distance. She couldn't look into his eyes any longer. If she did, he might reach into her soul, touch her heart. Find something inside her broken heart. Tara didn't want another person to touch her heart, to become part of her soul. The pain was too intense when that person was lost to her. She didn't know if she could live through that agony again.

Case didn't know anything about her. He didn't want to know. He lived on assumptions he believed were valid. They were not. She caught the distinct impression he detested women, all women. Lumped females into a derogatory category.

He doesn't know me.

I want him to know me.

By the look in his eyes, Case saw the haunted expression she couldn't hide, could never hide when she was reminded of that horrific day. His hands fell from her shoulders. She picked up her skirts and started walking as if nothing had been said that sent moisture clogging her throat or tears sliding down her cheeks. If she could hide from him, now would be the time.

Ghosts haunted her. They haunted him too. She couldn't hide from him or the phantoms in her mind. Didn't want to believe his words when he told her she was just like every other woman he met. The ghosts were an accepted part of her life, he would soon come to acknowledge them just as she recognized the ghosts haunting his.

With a slight shrug to his shoulders, he seemed to dismiss the subject for now. "Go on, we'll talk about this more tomorrow." Case took her hand into his as they walked the remaining distance to the apartment they shared with Ash. He wasn't a man to allow her to hide from him or from herself. He was just as determined to have his way as she was to have hers.

When they stepped inside, Ash greeted them with a glass of wine. "What have the two of you been up to? I could guess," he asked sporting a wicked smile, the devil in his eyes. Ash kissed her on the cheek. "I'll pour you each a glass. You can tell me what you've seen. Where you've been." Ash turned to Case then winked as if he had ideas. "Did she show you all the romantic places in the city?"

Case snorted, taking the glass from Ash. "We watched the sun go down over the Seine. Does that qualify as romantic?"

The moment was romantic until it turned to something different. Cold whipped through her. The ice created by the man she found herself attracted to froze parts of her that needed warming. She was a fool. He didn't even like her. There wasn't one romantic bone in that man's body. Ash thought romance was only about sex. Case was right about her cousin. He would never appeal to her even if he wasn't related by blood. Ash was too young. He called him a pup. She supposed that described Ash.

"Come sit. While you two were wandering the city, I found a permanent cook. The man, Gateau is his name, will be here in the morning. I assigned him the room off the kitchen. We will have omelets in the morning. As for tonight, I found a few places to purchase food.

We've fresh bread along with cheese. There is fruit as well as a few vegetables ripe for consumption. I didn't hold back with the wine. Bought only the best Paris has to offer."

With hooded eyes, thoughts of the few things Case told her this afternoon on her mind, Tara watched the two men. They seemed oblivious of her. That was just the way she wanted this evening to go. If Ash was busy occupying Case's time, she could hide within herself. Exposure of her deepest fears was not acceptable to share with Case.

Ash poured them all a glass of wine. Tara wanted to excuse herself. When she was about to do so, Case wrapped his hand around her wrist. Tugged her to sit. "Stay. Believe Ash is going out on the town tonight. Aren't you, Ash? We can discuss a few things while he's exploring Paris at night."

A momentary look of disbelief rippled across Ash's face before he grinned. "Oh, I see how it bloody is. Yes, believe I'll go find Jeremy. We can see what the city has to offer. Find a wom..." Catching himself Ash slanted a look her way then back to Case. After he rose, he downed what was left of his wine. On his way out, he grabbed his hat along with a coat that would keep off the chilling winds blowing from the Seine.

Heart in her throat, she watched her cousin as he walked from the apartment. At the window, Tara gazed at him as he strolled along the sidewalk before he disappeared into the darkening night. Case stood behind her. All she was aware of was the heat of his body so close to her back. His hands rested on her shoulders. She brought in a breath of air. The scent of him, the cologne he used all rushed through her. Deep in her chest, her heart fluttered.

"What do you want, little Tara?"

Case pushed escaped strands of hair from her neck. His touch was light. Delicate against her nape. The tips of his fingers tantalized. Sent flames she didn't want to acknowledge darting through her. Tara swallowed hard. Grant would touch her like this. She remembered when she wanted to forget. Forming words was impossible. Her fingers tightened on the window sill.

"I know what I want." His voice was smooth, banked to seduce. His fingertip trailed across her back, followed the line of her gown. "Do you also want a kiss? I remember the first one you gifted me with. Do you? The second one as well."

Contrary to what she wished she shook her head. His hands ran the length of her arms then back to her shoulders sending vibrant shivers down her spine. "No." That was the only word she could form. His teeth grazed her neck where his lips had been. At the brief contact, she jerked, startled by the heated sensation. Tara thought she was about to jump from her skin. She whimpered, a low sound in the back of her throat.

"I don't believe you. Your body is speaking a different tune. A language apart from your whispered words." Indifferent now, Case dropped his hands from her shoulders. He walked away. Stood in front of the fireplace his hands clasped behind his back.

Disappointed, Tara turned to watch the distance grow between them. His eyes were dark...damning. He wouldn't take from her what she wasn't willing to give. She was willing. He filled his glass with wine then sat on one of the brocaded chairs gracing the sitting area.

"Would you like more wine?" Case held his glass up to the light as if examining the transparent colors enhanced by the wall sconce. "Ash picked out a good vintage. We should enjoy the bottle."

"Yes." Tara sat in the chair opposite his. He filled her crystal goblet. She needed something that would make her stronger. Something that would fortify her spirit.

"Ah, she can say something besides no. I was wondering." Now Case sounded cryptic.

Her hands shook when she brought the glass to her lips. A bit of the wine dribbled over the top. Her body thrummed from his touch. Tara couldn't help but remember the kiss along with the way his lips played hers when he thought to seduce. It was too soon for her to give in to his tender ploys. Too soon for another man to replace Grant. Was it? Two years passed since the accident. She mourned him all that time. Both Ash along with Jeremy told her the time to move on had passed.

A change of subject would help her forget the feelings he created. The terrible longing... She swallowed the wine she sipped earlier. "The day after tomorrow would you like to ride to Versailles? It is only about nine miles from here. If you clear your schedule, we could fill the entire day. Gâteau could make us a picnic."

"Versailles would be nice. I will clear my schedule just for you. I would enjoy a brisk ride. I'm sure by then our horses will be ready for exercise. Would you be ready for..." he lifted a dark eyebrow. "...exercise?"

"Yes, I love riding, as you well know." Tara puzzled over his expression. The double entendre his look suggested when he mentioned exercise coupled with riding eluded her.

"Umm..." Case tapped his fingers on the glass he held. His smile blinked with wicked avarice at her. "Yes, your passion for riding is well known. What other desires do you have."

"Are you talking about riding a horse?" Tara asked feeling as if he was holding a one-sided conversation.

"What else would I be speaking of?" Case's voice was bland when he answered. "Do you have some other thought?"

Still puzzled, shaking her head, "I don't know." The chasm between them deepened as she caught his smile before he shut himself off from her. His closed expression both irritated her and confounded her. "While you're seeing to your duties, I'll find a hack to take us to Montmartre."

"How?"

Tara blanched as she realized she would have to leave the apartment to rent one for the afternoon. He told her she was his prisoner. Case wasn't making this easy for either of them. "I'll get Ash to do the honors."

"He'll want to come with us. That's not acceptable. Don't want the youngun' trailing after us. Do you?"

Frustrated.

Angry.

Annoyed.

Her emotions escalated. "What do you want me to do?" What Tara wished for at the moment was a fight. Something that would serve to clear the stilted air between them. She needed to throw things, bang a door against the wall, pummel his hard chest. She needed to yell. That was so unlike her. She breathed in deeply...once...twice...three times, controlling her fury. Soared to a place in her mind far away where she could turn inward. Easy in then easy out. Air to her lungs then out. Relax. Her body and mind began to calm. She found peaceful serenity where words along with deeds didn't bother her.

"Wait for me to finish. You'll get used to it. Comes with the territory." At her withdrawal, Case's voice deepened to uncharted ground.

"I'd rather not wait," Tara said, her voice smooth, calm just as she wanted it to be. She didn't like the agitation he so often caused.

Case leaned on his thighs, his forearms resting there, his hands clasped together. When he spoke, he stared at her. "Things happen when impatience sets in. People get hurt when they are exasperated. Accidents...crashes...all mistakes made because of impatience. People in a hurry..."

Tara flinched in the instant before she controlled herself. He hit too close to home with those last statements. Case dictated to her. She would have to obey despite her annoyance.

"Yes, sir," she told him with increasing sarcasm. "Accidents happen. We keep testing our limits just to prove something. Some people like danger. I don't." She didn't know what the hell she was thinking. Grant enjoyed challenging the elements, enjoyed testing his limits. Always believed he controlled what went on around him.

Case's dark brows drew together while he concentrated on her. He meant to get to the bottom of her thoughts. She wasn't going to allow him inside her head. "What accident are you thinking about. I noticed the haunting of your eyes, pain. What I saw looked very real. Tell me. Talking to people always helps."

Tara was surprised he spoke the words. Ash...or Jeremy must have told him something as to what happened two years ago. She needed to banish her emotions, keep them from showing. As long as he thought she was a brazen trollop, sharing with this man was impossible. Grant along with what happened two years ago tomorrow were her memories. No one would change that. She desired something more from this man than he would give.

"What were you talking about?" Tara asked.

He smiled. The change of topic obvious to him. "Nothing."

~ * ~

Jeremy found Ash. Not the other way around.

"Tonight," Ash said, thinking he needed a diversion. Case and Tara were dancing around each other. He saw in their eyes they wanted more. Case he knew well enough to understand the man would make Tara come to him. If he had a beautiful woman on his arm who wanted him, he wouldn't play games. "I want to get foxed. You can see me home. Make certain I get there in one piece. I should be at home for Tara if she needs me. Though she doesn't want me. Won't let anyone inside her head."

"You want to get foxed. What brought that on?" Jeremy hooted his laughter. "Suppose we can start at the tavern I discovered earlier today. The ambiance is nice. The women sweet and well-rounded, showing just enough to tantalize male senses."

"He's going to hurt her." Ash continued walking as well as thinking about what he saw in the drawing room before he was asked to leave. "He's going to push and push until he gets her in his bed. With that accomplished, the game he's playing will be over. Tara will be hurt. If she gives herself to him, she'll want love."

"Case promised me he wouldn't," Jeremy told him, his voice curt. "Come, Tara won't ask for help. She's a big girl. Think she understands the game Case wants to play. She's not an easy mark."

"Doesn't mean he doesn't intend to bring her to his bed. It's obvious to any fool he desires Tara. Who wouldn't? She's beautiful. Intelligent. What I don't understand is why mother allowed this to happen. The Duchess orchestrated this event. With father's help, she set it all in motion." Ash said. He didn't understand his reservations where it came to Case and his cousin. He also knew Tara wanted Case. Since the accident she'd never been the slightest bit interested in a man. Tara was now.

Interested.

Fascinated.

Tara wasn't innocent. She couldn't be. She'd been going to marry Grant. He was her fiancé for several years. They were five days from their wedding day when the accident happened that stripped Grant of his life and left Tara in the hospital for weeks then in bed for longer. During that time, she stayed with his family. Her parents had been out chasing sunrises somewhere in South America. They made it home the day before the wedding. After the tragedy Tara was brought to London for the medical expertise she needed. His mother helped take care of her as if she was her daughter. There were days when Tara didn't want to live. Jeremy was there for her, seldom leaving her bedside. Ash never understood why Tara didn't fall in love with Jeremy. To Tara, he was a friend, more like a big brother though she had two of those. Nothing more.

What Ash understood was that if he had a fiancée, he bloody well wouldn't wait for the wedding night to bed the woman. He was certain Grant didn't wait either. When they were together, they couldn't keep their hands to themselves.

"Tara is still in love with Grant. She won't let Case charm her into his bed. With Case, he's after women for reasons I don't' comprehend. Case wants Tara. There is no doubt in my mind," Ash said as he thought again about what he saw when he was in the drawing room with the two of them. Silent sparks were flying between them, darting between their eyes. He thought the two could set the room on fire with the flaming looks between them. They appeared as if they were about to ignite.

"After Grant died, I would have married Tara. Wanted to help her get over her loss. She wouldn't have anything to do with me. I've accepted that fact. You should too. Tara might be ready to move on to another man. Hope to God it's not Case Ferguson," Jeremy said as he opened the door to the tavern for Ash to precede him into the boisterous room. "If it is, I'll be there to pick up the pieces of her second broken heart just as I was the first time. Maybe then she will see me in a different light. Where Tara is concerned, I'm a patient man."

The pair found a place in a corner with privacy. Ash didn't want a lot of privacy. What he wanted was to find a willing woman to share a bed with this night. The room was loud. Music played from a tinny piano. Scantily clad women circulated, bringing drinks while plying their bodies for coin. He leaned back, content for the moment to watch. It was always a good idea to get the scope of the land, so to speak, before one began to drink or to linger with a whore. Figure out which woman he would like to dally with for the evening.

"Not a great place to find a woman," Ash muttered having second thoughts about his intentions. The place is not what I was told. A pretty little redhead bent over, showing off parts of her delectable body that were quite charming. He didn't want to get the pox in exchange for a little fun. He decided the best place for him to find a willing bedmate for his stay in Paris would be at the ball tomorrow night. Though this girl interested him. Could be the diversion he coveted before he returned to the apartment.

"Bring us two glasses of red," Jeremy said seeming to understand his plight. Amusement was written in Jeremy's eyes as he watched the two dance around each other.

The little redhead sashayed her fanny to the bar. The little walk showed parts of her that should be hidden. What Ash saw of her breasts could be described as perky. Caught beguiling glimpses of the pink tips. Saw her ass as she retrieved the drinks.

He liked that word.

Perky.

With her disappearance through the customers, Ash turned his attention back on Jeremy. "Want to go with me to the ball tomorrow at the Montesquieu's? Don't believe Case and Tara are going. I'll send a response to the invitation if you're interested. Might meet someone to take away the ache."

"You have ulterior motives?" Jeremy hooted with laughter while he continued to scope the room. "You're seeing the clientele here the same way as I am? Tomorrow you might find a widow who could teach you the ways of French *amour*." Could find *coup de foudre*. You know...love at first sight.

"Looking is the only option," Ash snorted thinking that perhaps the redhead with her perky pink tipped breasts might be the exception to this hasty opinion. Love at first sight wasn't an option in this place. He tried to figure out a way to have her tonight along with a few more nights. "Wouldn't mind a feel or two. Discover how much experience she has. Not going upstairs with any of these saucy ladies despite my need."

"You're only twenty. What need could you have?" Jeremy continued to laugh amused by this situation. "I'd be delighted to accompany you to the gala tomorrow. Though even among the rich, a man still has to make certain his partner isn't carrying something unwanted. There are no guarantees except celibacy which is not an option."

The redhead brought their ales. Ash pulled her onto his lap after she set the glasses down. "*Oh la la....!*" she exclaimed pressing herself against Ash. She smiled. At least her teeth were straight and still white. Her breath was sweet, mint scented. "Aren't you the boldest, *monsieur*? How very naughty of you." She ran her hand along his chest down to the top of his britches. Lingered.

"Just want to see what you have to offer," Ash said enjoying the play of her hands over his body. His mind spun with a multitude of possibilities. He had a place in mind to put her for his stay in Paris. If she proved to be clean, he would keep her, take her away from this place. Enjoy her charms for the duration of the summer.

"What's your name, *monsieur*? Lou Lou will give you whatever you want tonight? *Voulez vous coucher avec moi ce soir?*"

"I bet you will, but not tonight, *Cherie*. Going to bed with you will have to wait though I do want you," Ash said, his voice stiff, his member stiffer. "All I want is your company for an hour or two. We will see what will happen later." He gazed down the front of her low-cut gown. Her breasts were ripe, swollen. The aureoles were soft pink, the tips hard. He pulled fabric down. One breast popped free. The globe was round, white and enticing. "Nice." He wanted to suckle the fullness, taste as well as tease.

"You shouldn't..." Lou Lou giggled. She didn't cover herself. To Ash the sound was charming. This little one shouldn't be here. She was fresh faced, new to the game. This would harden her. He could see if she was clean then set her up until he left at the end of the summer. His allowance was enough to keep a dozen mistresses. The only concern he had was for her when he left. He would have to figure something out. He wasn't going to let his little Lou Lou go to just anyone.

"You're right, but I'm not going to cover you back up." He tugged again, bringing both breasts to full view. He cupped them holding as well as weighing, testing the texture, finding her flesh silken. She was turned so he was the only person who could see her. Ash explored her leg with a free hand. She wore nothing under the gown. "Naughty." Ash repeated when he touched soft wet territory. He grinned as the pert expression on her face. Her eyes twinkled.

"Naughty just for you," she sighed, her breasts pushing upward as she arched against him. The nipples hard, pouting for attention.

Jeremy sat back, sipping on his drink perusing the interior as he watched Ash play with what he supposed would be the boy's next mistress. Ash would do as he pleased. He had the coin to lavish attentions on anyone he wished.

"Just for me." Ash agreed before touching the hardened tip with his cheek. "Now, do you have other work to do before we can play?" Ash had a good idea where he was going to put her tonight. He couldn't bring her back to the apartment. He looked to Jeremy who was grinning and also shaking his head, no. Didn't matter. There were plenty of boarding houses that would house her until he found a place she could call her own.

"Have to work until midnight," she sighed when he ran his palm across her buoyant assets again.

He guessed he had a couple of hours before he needed to retrieve her. Ash knew people in the town. With the added time, there wasn't a doubt in his fertile brain that he would find a place for tonight. He could look further tomorrow. He brought her dress back up to cover. "Don't show yourself to anyone. Do you understand? As of this instant, you are mine."

"*Oui.*"

"You going to do this?" Jeremy was still laughing. "You still don't know if she's clean."

"No, a doctor will tell me. I'll have him examine her tomorrow morning."

"Guess that means there is no ball for me. Didn't want to go anyway."

Chapter Five

Tara's flaming red face amused Case. While he felt she didn't know what type of district she brought him to, there was also a bit of doubt in her attitude. Hand in hand, they walked through the streets filled with brothels and taverns. The cabarets would be fun for him to show her. They wouldn't be here once it was dark unless he felt it was safe to stay in the quarter. Case intended to make quick work of the sunset then get her out of the district. Maybe not. He'd like to see her reaction to a real cabaret.

Setting his hand on her back he guided her up the last steps to the top of the hill. "Do you know what went on in Montmartre?" Case tried to keep his voice bland. Couldn't help the amusement at Tara's discomfort. She would find a way to coverup her *faux pas* in bringing him here.

"No." There were tiny crease lines in Tara's forehead. She was scowling. "The duke never let me go here. Grant agreed. I thought it was male arrogance keeping me from the trip." She was fumbling for excuses. "Why did you allow this?"

That too amused him. He had his reasons. Part of which was getting to understand how her mind worked. Also, he needed to test her, challenge the reserve she held in check.

"Who is this Grant person to you? Another brother? A male friend?" Case didn't recall his name being mentioned before. Except when he kissed her that first time. The hell, she called out his name. When he asked, he felt the tightening of Tara's back muscles, the stiffening of her spine. Whoever the man is or was, she didn't want to speak of him or hear someone else say his name. "Does he have something to do with this anniversary of yours?"

"The Basilica," she paused, her voice stretched thin as if thinking of what she wanted to say. "Well, it is...what I discovered in my readings is that Montmartre means the martyr's hill. Denis, Bishop of Paris, was executed by the Romans somewhere on this hill during the early Christian era. Denis was remembered as a martyr and became known as St. Denis."

"So...you do know nothing of the brothels or the cabarets?" Case didn't want to leave that topic behind. "One would think..."

"No."

Case heard the panting of her breaths. The hill was steep. Thought a change of topic might be prudent though not as amusing. "I'm certain the sunset will be beautiful at the top. How is your leg holding up."

"Yes, and fine."

"Do you want to leave now?" They stood at the top of the hill. "We can see for miles around. This was a nice place for you to take me. The sunset should be magnificent. I'm thankful you thought of this place."

"Yes." Tara gulped in air. "We should find someplace to eat where we can watch the sunset."

"I agree. We need food. Before we leave, we should visit a cabaret. What do you say? Are you interested in food along with music, dancers, wine. The entertainment will be something you won't witness again for a long time. You brought me here to sample Parisian culture. *Non? Oui?"* He wanted to appreciate the expression on her face when she realized what she was looking at. "It will be fun. Say, yes."

"We'll have to get up early tomorrow to make it to Versailles before the day gets hot," Tara said backing away from him. "Perhaps we should go home."

She was reading between his words, having misgivings. Seemed nervous. He tugged her closer. His hands on her hips. "We should enjoy each moment at its fullest. Don't you think?" Case maneuvered Tara so she stood in front of him. She was looking up at him. He was tempted to kiss her. She hadn't asked him yet. He would wait until she wanted that kiss more than he did. Wanted it enough to ask for his lips against hers. Seemed he couldn't wait to test her mettle. He would sample later.

Case set his hand beneath her chin. Moved his thumb across her bottom lip. The silken flesh he caressed trembled. He dragged on her lip until he caressed the sultry inside. She didn't pull away. Didn't tell him to stop. Good, Tara was not immune to him. When she tried to back away, he held her at her waist with his other hand. There was no pressure keeping her close.

"Come, relax against me as you did last night. We'll watch until the last arc of the sun fades into the horizon. We'll find a tavern at the bottom of the hill. I want to see the entertainment. Don't you? The dancers will wear...the women's attire will leave little to one's imagination." Case bent close to her. Whispered. Blew with a soft caress. His breath swept across her cheek. Her body reacted. "I promise you've never seen the like."

As the sun set, Tara's back rested against his chest. His hands splayed across the softness of her belly tugging her next to him. So many parts of Tara he wanted to explore, he was lost to the moment. Case wanted her to feel the evidence of his arousal on her fanny. He breathed in her delicate scent.

Lilies.

Spring rain.

He kissed her neck. Light airy shivers gave credence to the touch, to how the caress registered on her small body. His hands ran beneath her shawl and across the soft flesh of her shoulders. He explored along her ribcage then settled back to her waist. Next to him, her body quivered. Trembled with desire, hungry for him. Her breath whispered with a ragged cadence. In then out. A mewl followed. A sweet sigh left her lips. He was pleased with the passion he read.

Tara was where he wanted her. Next to him. Within his control. When she tried to step away, he brought her back. "Don't go. The sunset is almost finished. We will walk down the hill soon. Eat. Drink. Watch the show." He felt her hesitation. Needed her to be with him every step of the way. Didn't understand the feelings...different feelings. She touched the jaded part of his heart. Threatened to shatter all he believed into tiny pieces. He couldn't let her touch him so deeply. If that happened, he would hurt. He would lose himself.

"I've never been in a cabaret or a tavern," she spoke on a murmur of a sigh. "Don't think my parents would approve."

Parents be damned. They weren't here. Tara was twenty. Could make decisions for herself. Perhaps not always the wisest. That would suit him. Case let his fingers brush against the fullness of her breast. Tara sipped air. "You should tell me no...when I touch you. If you don't, I will believe you wish for another caress then one after that."

Her body jerked when his thumb moved higher. She didn't say a word. Nothing. That was his invitation to something more.

He pointed to the horizon. "Look, the last colors are fading. We need to go to a safer place." On the way down the hill, Case held her close. Felt the first shiver from the night air. Close to her ear, "The cabaret will be warm. The food excellent if you've a mind to eat. The drink enough to ease thirst. Perhaps enough to make you a bit giddy. What are you like when you've had a bit too much wine? Do you giggle?"

"Yes." Tara nodded even while she held back. Her steps hesitant. She was thinking. He would give her more to think about before the end of the evening.

A lot more to think about.

"We are here," Case told her smiling, impatient to enjoy the next hour or so. Tara stopped with the door open. "You have to pick up your feet if you are going to reach a table or a chair. They will not come to you."

The trembling might not be from the cold. There was much going on here. Case's need was great. He held open the door as he escorted her inside the tavern. His hand rested on the small of her back, guiding her progress. The touch possessive. At the provocative sight in front of her, she stiffened pushing back against him. Her beautiful amber colored eyes were wide. Tara was seeing the seamier side of Paris. The scene was a little bit dirty and a lot naughty.

Tara pointed to a lady strolling past them. Biting her lip, "She is almost naked. I can see..." Her sentence stopped cold when the dancers on stage turned then lifted their skirts so everyone could see their fannies.

"Pretty," Case told her as leaned close to her ear. He didn't want anyone except Tara to hear. "What would you look like in a gown so revealing? Would your fanny be prettier? I bet your backside would. What about your pretty titties? Are they as sweet to look at as the other ladies here?" His tongue touched the tip of her ear. She drew in a ragged breath. Shuddered. "I'd like to see that. Would you wear one for me? I could purchase one for you to wear in our apartment." Case imagined her in one of the gowns. If Tara put it on, she would not wear it for long.

When he looked at Tara, she was shaking her head. Her bottom lip caught beneath her teeth, quivering. "I don't think so. I've never..."

Her quick denial angered Case. Tara gave her favors away without blinking to other men. Now she would deny him a simple request. "Don't lie now that we are finding common ground, you and I. Who is Grant?" His voice was too harsh. The sound would vanquish the mood he worked so hard to create. He needed to back off. Given time she would open up to him. Patience with Tara was the name of this game. Steps forward then back, he needed caution, needed to temper any anger.

She turned to leave. Case held her close. "No. Not so fast. Come along, Princess." He guided her to a spot where they could see the performances. They were close to the stage. Music blared. Six women danced on stage, kicking their legs, grinding their hips to catcalls from the floor. When their legs went high a man could see everything.

Case pulled out a chair for her. He watched her gulp air as she sat down. He waved to one of the ladies serving drinks. "Two beers." He moved his chair close, meaning to give her a private description of what was going on in the room. Case bent over her, knowing from her indrawn breath that his close presence disturbed her. He was careful not to touch her. He saw her retreat into herself. It was as obvious as seeing her consuming sensuality of her appraisal of the dancers.

Case controlled his craving to stroke the rapid pulse beating in Tara's throat. He couldn't deny the sudden coursing of blood through his veins, the excitement and heat as the chase began in earnest. None of what he felt showed in his voice or his body. In this he was an expert.

Like the prey the predator was capable of measured retreat, knowing always that retreat was temporary. He would go on the offensive when the time was right. She was unaware of his motives or the end game. Tara would not know until the capture was complete, the stakes achieved.

"I don't think we should stay here," Tara whispered, her voice tight with strain. Her shoulders shook as she pulled her shawl around her as if the small gesture would keep her safe. "I would like to go."

Feeling empathy for Tara was not part of his plan. They would stay until he was satisfied she was treated to everything this part of the city offered to men. She brought him here. Romance at the forefront of her mind. "We'll stay just long enough to enjoy this first show as well as have a bite to eat and finish our drinks. I know you are hungry." Hungry for me. He wanted to feel her melting over him like warm honey.

Case was taken by surprise when a woman sat on his lap, pushed her breasts against him. Case laughed, stroked her beneath the low-cut gown. Held her breasts in his hands. Tara stared at him, eyes wide with an emotion he didn't understand. When he pulled the woman to his mouth for a long-drawn-out kiss, Tara gasped. When the lady stood, he tapped her fanny, grinning. "*Merci*," he told her.

"Y-you kissed her. Y-you d-don't know her. Do you?" Her words were spoken with a slight stutter. "Do you?" Tara repeated, her voice now tinged with anger. During his encounter with the woman, her face flushed a delightful shade of rose. Her total embarrassment surprised him. Was surprised she wasn't green with envy. This was something new to think about.

"How would I know the lady? I've never been here." Deep inside, Case was howling with laughter. If he guessed right, she was both jealous as well as embarrassed by the encounter. Tara's eyes were huge saucers of anger or disbelief tinged with green jealousy. He wanted to think some of it was possessiveness. "Do you always kiss your beaus behind closed doors? Never in public, Princess?"

"No!" She started to stand. His hand on her shoulder kept her in her seat. "Don't call me princess!"

Ah, that was the kind of response he wished for. She'd been kissed and not always in the bedroom. "Would you like to sit on my lap? I'll kiss you too. Hold your breasts in my hands just as I did hers. Feel your jewels beneath your gown. Would you like that? Do you enjoy sex in public places?" Case didn't have reservations where Tara was concerned. This was all about the hunt then the seizure. It would not be long before he held his prey beneath him. She was proving herself to be a passionate woman. She wouldn't disappoint.

The moisture he saw on her bottom lip could have only been caused by her tongue running across the tender flesh. Tara was nervous. She wanted that kiss he offered. Case leaned back, his hands tapping his thighs. "Sit? We can see what comes next. I'd enjoy kissing you if that's what you would like. No one will watch. Everyone here is watching the dancers."

Tara pushed on her chair as if to stand. Her lips were stretched in a slender line. Case held the back of the chair in place. With a heavy sigh she sat down. "What do you want from me? This was supposed to be a fun excursion."

"In my opinion this is fun. I'm enjoying myself. You're not?"

"What do you want from me?" Tara persisted with the question.

Case wanted all of her. He wanted what Jeremy once had. What she offered Ash. He meant to be honest. "I want you in my bed to do with as I please for as long as I please. What do you want with me?" Case turned the tables.

Again, she tried to push back on her chair. The beer he ordered came along with a plate of bread and cheese. There were apple slices on the platter along with some strawberries and grapes. Tara picked up a berry. Ate. She sipped her beer. What she didn't do was answer him. She stared at the drink then the plate of food.

Wheels were turning in Tara's head. Case liked what he saw. She ran her hands down her dress, tightening the fabric over her breasts. He could stare at her all night. After she drank again, she looked at him. "Arrogant! Beast!"

"True." He fed her a second berry, ran the tender *morceau* across her lips. "I always get what I want. Whenever you wish for me to kiss you, ask. Sit on my thighs. We'll both appreciate the experience."

"Not this time," Tara gritted out between clenched teeth. Her fists were also clenched tight. She pushed against the table.

"Finish your drink. We'll go as soon as every drop is drained and we've eaten all the food." Case thought tonight would be a good time for the kiss. Tomorrow at Versailles might prove more promising. What he knew was that she weakened every second she spent with him.

"If I toss it in your conceited face, does that count?" Tara asked. Her smile was sweet, syrupy. She didn't mean a word.

His crack of laughter caused her to scowl at him. "Admit it. You want me just as much as I want you. Come sit and ask. I'll give you that kiss you've wanted for longer than you wish to tell me. We'll both feel more relaxed when this is done. After that we can move on to whatever might come next. It's up to you."

This time when she pushed back, her chair moved. Hands planted on the table, she stared at him. "With or without you, I'm leaving." She stood.

"No."

Case pulled her onto his lap. She fell, tumbling into his expectant arms. His hands were tight around her waist. Tara wiggled. Squirmed. Twisted. Pushed at his chest until her breath heaved. He waited, knowing how the tiny fight would end. This was pretense to save her pride. "I think you know what I want. Believe you want it too. Stop denying yourself pleasure."

"There is no pleasure in this."

"There is."

"Obstinate man."

"Foolish woman."

"Are we trading insults?" Tara asked as she leaned into him. "I'm tired of the argument. Take me home."

"Ask for what you want more than a solitary bed. After you do, we'll go home."

"No."

"I promise." He touched the sensitive place behind her ear with his tongue. Nipped the lobe of her ear. Blew on moist skin. At her waist, his fingers tightened. "I promise as soon you ask and I deliver, I'll take you home. Either that or you can tell me what Grant is to you. Your choice, little Tara. Always your choice. Never mine."

Case didn't realize how much he hungered for this kiss. He'd known for a while now that he wanted her with an intensity that frightened him. They shared one kiss that first morning. The one when Jeremy caught them. A few others as well. Nothing made sense. He was a saint.

"Don't know what you mean," Tara told him, her cheek still resting on his shoulder. Her hand on his arm.

Tara was a perfect fit to him. He felt the flutter of her lashes against his neck. She would come to a decision. One they would both like. "Of course you know. Don't prevaricate. Make a choice. One or the other. The kiss or tell me about Grant. That should not be so hard."

"What if I don't decide? Will we be here all night?" Tara asked, testing him. The challenge in the question was explicit.

"If this is a challenge you're delivering, you'll lose. The cabaret is open all night. We can stay here until dawn then into the next evening." Bloody eyes, he didn't want to stay here all night.

She issued the challenge.

He would never be the one to weaken.

Either answer would please him. Learning more about her would strengthen his cause as would the next kiss of their relationship. Whatever her decision, Case couldn't lose. "What will it be? This is about you. Your pleasure."

"A kiss," Tara murmured as she pushed away from him. Her lips were moist. Eyes simmering pools of amber, she stared at him. Touched a fingertip to his chin. Her smile hesitant. Obvious, nonetheless.

Case waited, grinning at her. They tread on common ground. Her experience would shine through. Tara tilted her head to one side then the other as if trying to figure out how to approach the kiss. Her hips moved while she pushed away. The small pink tongue he was waiting to play with slid across her bottom lip, wetting it. She was nervous. He could appreciate that.

"Thought you decided. What are you waiting for? Christmas? Hope not. That's a long way from now," Case said his voice filled with amusement. Tara wouldn't understand what he expected. He wanted her to initiate the connection between them. After all was finished between them there would be no recriminations. No question of coercion or force.

Seduction with this lady would be pleasant but meant for another time. This action was her choice. She would be the one to say *yay* or *nay* to the intimacies they would share tonight at the cabaret.

"I told you that you could kiss me. What are you waiting for?" Tara's indignant voice amused him even more. He bit back the shout of laughter bubbling up from his throat.

"No, Princess, you are supposed to kiss me. Not the other way around," Case said as he stroked the moist bottom lip tempting him. "I'm waiting. Growing more impatient by the second. Do you know how to kiss, Tara? You must have some idea." No woman her age or possessing her potent beauty would have not been kissed multiple times as well as by multiple men.

"I'm...?" She pointed at herself then him. Tara questioned. "I'm supposed to kiss you? Is that how it's done? What you're waiting for?"

"Yes."

The shake of her head was one of denial. Case didn't understand what she was waiting for besides another engraved invitation. Tara appeared baffled by his comment. She blinked, a look of confusion gathering between her brows as they furrowed together.

"I don't know how."

"Liar. Kiss me like you kissed...Grant. Like you kissed me before." Case knew that was a challenge that might backfire. By the darkening of her eyes, he understood he would have to act fast. She pushed on his shoulders. Tried to remove herself from his hold. Wriggled. Tara took umbrage at his words. That was too bloody bad.

"Don't bring up his name again!" Tara yelled, her fury clear. There was nothing soft about her voice that had heads turning to look at them. The chatter in the room stopped as did the music. The dancers stared at them.

They were now the center of attention. Case didn't think that would be something to covet.

"Trouble with your princess?" The little barmaid who served them earlier stood in front of him. "If this one doesn't know how to give you a good kiss, I'll be pleased to show her. Push her off your lap. Give me a chance."

"I know how to kiss a man." Tara set her lips on his, her eyes flashing amber fire. That was all. Case wanted a whole lot more from this encounter than the slight brush of lips on lips.

Case wound his hand through Tara's hair, keeping her head in place when she thought she was finished. He allowed her the tiniest of distance so he could speak. "Princess, that's not a kiss. Put your tongue inside me. Rub the sweet thing across mine. Show me what you can do. Taste me. Give me a taste of you."

Surprised by her gasp, he pulled her close again. Case opened his mouth, hoping to feel the sweep of her tongue plunge between his lips. Moments later, she obliged him. He wasn't disappointed, the taste of her evocative, titillating. He could die kissing her and he'd never know. His body heated. Flamed. Burned to cinders. To his delight, she took the initiative now that he explained what he expected from her.

A whispered mewl.

Soft sighs.

Another gasp when his tongue mated with hers. She pressed against him, all her soft rounded parts arousing him. Provoking a rich dark need a message sent straight to his groin. His free hand roamed down her back, one-by-one counted vertebra. His imagination played havoc with his aroused body. Case wanted her naked. If he wished, he could take her upstairs to one of the rooms. He would pay later. Didn't have a doubt he could find one that was empty.

She would be his tonight.

Taking her in a cabaret was not his plan. Besides, it was too soon. She wasn't begging him. Pleading for him to take her was of utmost importance. Taking her too soon would be a waste of emotions. She would end up regretting the encounter. He didn't want that.

Tara came alive as the kiss continued. Her fingers wound into his hair. Her nails skimmed his scalp. She found the softness of his lip, bit, swept across the fulness with her tongue. Her sigh into his mouth stirred more flames. Ignited. Flared to life. Case pulled away from her. Besotted by the sight of her swollen mouth, he nipped her top lip. He moved back, smiling at her. The loud clapping along with the cheering delighted him but not as much as the flaming of her cheeks. They were no longer rose colored but a deep crimson.

"You're my delight. Now, little princess, that was a proper Scottish kiss. You can do that anytime it pleases you to be with me. Shall we go home?" He set her on wobbling feet. Adjusted her shawl. "Can you walk?"

"I—I think so."

"Good." Case took her hand. He led her from the cabaret, pleased with the first contact in too many days. Tonight, progress was made.

Chase and catch.

By the third step, Tara stumbled, he lifted her into his arms. Hailed a hack then set her inside. Before following her, he gave the address to the driver. Case sat back, relaxed, watching her.

"You liked the kiss?" he asked grinning at her flushed features. Continuing what they started would be fun.

Tara nodded her head, her eyes dazed with the pleasure he just gave her. Bloody hell, it was just a kiss. What would she look like when she had an orgasm?

"Do you want more?" Case asked, curious as to her response. He wondered if she would deny the sweet sensations between them.

The nod of her head made him smile as much as the expression on her face. He waited for an answer. Didn't intend to say anything more until she responded. He wanted that kiss then one after that. Her eyes were closed. Tara looked dreamy as well as sated even though Case knew she was far from being sated.

Her lashes opened. Tara looked confused. A *wee* bit dazed. "What?"

"I asked you if you wanted another kiss. Do you? I would like you to kiss me again."

She nodded again. Then... "Yes. I want you to kiss me this time."

To the negative, Case shook his head. "Tonight, you will do the kissing. The exploring. If there is any seduction, you will do the deed. Do you wish to seduce me? Have your way with my body? Charm me senseless? Sweettalk me until I can't breathe? Until I will give you everything thing you ask? Whatever you want, Princess. It's yours." He wasn't going to fall into a trap of his making. "You can touch me anywhere that pleases you."

"Where would you like me to touch you that I haven't?" Tara sounded confused at the notion of touching him.

"Anywhere. You decide." There were so many places she'd not touched. Tara wasn't anywhere near discovering his body.

~ * ~

Tara liked the idea of touching Case. She also wished he would touch her more. They were in the carriage, riding through the streets to reach their apartment in the city. She didn't know how she felt about the public display in the cabaret. The heat of embarrassment still flushed her face. She set her cool hand on her cheeks. The heat was either from Case or from the lack of privacy. Maybe a *wee* bit of both.

Grant pledged to her that he would wait until they were married to have sex. Her fiancé never kissed her in the way Case did, never dipped his tongue inside her mouth. By comparison his kisses were chaste. Tara never felt her temperature flare so fast. Never felt the intense longing for something more. A ragged breath of air whispered from her lips.

Case leaned forward, taking the initiative as well as assuming she would kiss him again. He brought her onto his lap. His hands tightened around her waist. "We are not done, are we?" One dark eyebrow lifted skyward while he waited for the answer she didn't want to give. "You said you wanted to kiss me again. You should understand. Know that I will decide when and where."

The look in his eyes left her winded, fragmenting in too many different directions, not that she'd been able to suck much needed air into her lungs for the last ten minutes. "I don't know what you mean." Even to her ears she sounded like a prudish spinster. Case would take issue with her lie. Her words of denial rippled through her lips in a husky croak.

"Don't lie to me, Princess. After the last kiss you understand what we are talking about here. Kiss me. Kiss me like you did in the cabaret. Gift me with all you have to give. Everything. I won't accept anything less. You can do whatever you want. No one except the two of us will know." His grin was wicked. His eyes dark. Case would know what she was thinking, feeling.

Tara didn't know if she could give him any more power over her. He already wielded more than she wanted to give him. She understood how easy it would be to succumb to his rakish charms. She saw his eyes dilate at her appraisal of him. Her hands roamed his shoulders then down his arms soaking up the strength he was so cavalier about. She wanted the heat of his arms surrounding her. Needed for him to respect her. The sinking feeling that if she gave into these newfound desires, respect would never be hers. Tara didn't understand what possessed her. She wanted this man. Was half in love with him...a man she'd known for such a short time. All her life had been given to Grant.

She retreated, looking away from the hard sensual line of Case's lips. Tara wanted to say something, anything because she sensed he was looking at her as she looked at him, missing nothing, evaluating everything. This time he saw beneath the façade she cloaked over herself. She hoped he saw more than a casual fling.

With second thoughts assailing her, Tara said in hoarse voice, "I don't think we should kiss again." It wasn't what she wanted. The thought of not kissing him disappointed Tara. If she continued in this vein, she would give him more than a few kisses. She would allow him to take liberties she wasn't ready to hand over to this vulnerable man who had a history with women. A story followed him that was not good.

"Not good enough for you, am I?" Case asked with a sneer on his lips. "Thought you enjoyed the kiss we shared in the cabaret. Was I so wrong?"

The mood changed in a beat. The air became stilted. Vibrated with the woman-hungry passion of his words. He tested her. From experience with the rough side of this man, Tara knew there would be an insult to follow. He wouldn't let her denial go unanswered. The man didn't know her. She should tell him about Grant. If he understood what happened to her two years ago, he might realize she wasn't the woman he thought she was. The pain was too raw today to speak of Grant to anyone. Not today. Maybe tomorrow.

"It's not that. You know it's not," she spoke looking at her hands that were winding in then out of her skirt. Her voice lacked the fierceness that might serve to convince him. "It's not that way at all. I did enjoy the kiss. Thought at the time more would be nice. I've had a change of mind. Can I not change my mind?"

"Should we return to the tavern. After the show you put on, you could sell your kisses to some lucky gentleman. Suppose I should thank you for the favor of your kiss. You give them out so sparingly."

Case's sarcasm made her flinch. "I wouldn't do that. Sell any part of me. To you or anyone else. I'm not for sale. If you believe that about me..." She told him she liked his kiss. Wanted another one. Now she refused him. What was he supposed to believe? He would believe she was fickle. She was a coward.

"Lucky for you I was there," Case said straightening across the seat from her. His hands fisted then relaxed. "Otherwise, you might have had to sell your pretty little...smile...to get out of the tavern unscathed. There would have been a bed upstairs with your name on it waiting for you to occupy. After the exhibition we put on, there would have been a line extending out the door. You would have made top dollar."

Tara gasped at his stinging words. She looked away wondering how he could be so sweet then so damn mean.

Case overlooked some important facts. He was the one who insisted on going into the tavern when she told him no. It was his words that made her give in to the asked for kiss. He wanted to know about Grant. She had to make a choice. She chose the kiss. It was the lesser of two evils. Evils? The kiss was not evil in any way.

"The men I enjoy being around don't pay for my company or my smile. I would never..." Tara tried to finish realizing she gave him more ammunition to hurl her way. He didn't give her a chance for further words.

Case cut her off with a dismissive wave of his hand followed by his baiting mockery. "I'll bet." Case's voice was laced with such contempt Tara withdrew further into herself. To present salient reasons to this man would prove useless. She didn't know how she could ever breach the hard shell he surrounded himself with.

In a way of protecting herself, she couldn't let that stand. She tilted her chin high before she spoke. "You'll lose," Tara said while she watched the expression vary on his face as the long silence between them stretched thin.

He grunted his disagreement.

"I'm not understanding why you bait me. I'm not what you think. I've always tried to do right by the people I know. You make it difficult to be nice to you or even like you. If I don't do what you want, you hurl insults my way."

Other than continuing the rakish tilt to his eyebrow, Case made no reply nor did he remove his avid stare in her direction. His silence prickled her skin. Anger grew.

"As I've told you numerous times, Case, you don't know a bloody thing about me!" Tara understood she could refute his notions until she died. It would never make a difference to Case. He would never change his mind. What he thought about her was what he thought about her. His mind was clear.

"You'd be surprised, Princess. I understand women. Know what they want. How they think. You are not so different," he told her, the tone of his voice never lost the biting edge. "Don't back down now. Keep telling yourself lies. In time you might believe them. If you decide to grace me with one of your kisses, I'll still be here. Women always change their mind when it suits them. When they believe they will gain the most."

His voice was flat but for the slight, sardonic lilt that was as much a part of Case as his thick black hair. Tara wondered what woman had embittered Case so much that he assumed all women were shallow as well as unfeeling. Some day he might let her in on the circumstances of his life that led him to this place. Appeared they both held secrets close to their hearts.

Speculating about the woman or women in Case's life splintered Tara's calm into thousands of sharp pieces. Jealousy became a part of her thoughts. Even though she didn't want to become one of his women, she did want him to come to care for her. In the short time she knew Case, he wormed his way into her heart. If she allowed him privileges, he could take anything as well as everything from her. Tara needed something more from Case, something more than his disdain.

She had no control over Case, his women, or the conclusions he drew from his past then applied to the present about her.

All Tara could direct was herself, her reactions along with what she was willing to give. If she didn't find a way to shutter Case from her thoughts, she would unravel here in the hack. She closed her eyes, concentrating on the images that would always calm her. After Grants death she found solace in keeping the encroaching world from her mind. Now she needed to keep the memories of Case in a place he could not reach. The way he touched a part of her that had been dead for a long time scared her.

Breathe in.

Breathe out.

"Are you going to stay inside yourself the rest of way home?" Case asked as he watched her keeping her lashes lowered. "Thought this ride was going to be a tour of the city. Believe we just drove by Notre Dame. You're not giving me the guided information you promised."

Her mantra fought with the real presence of Case sitting across from her, talking, testing. He challenged her to poove her worth. The way her lips felt beneath his. She didn't want to feel this way. Nonetheless, Case had a way of disintegrating her reserve. Stretching her reserves. Tara thought at any moment she would snap.

Tara was certain he wished to pick up where they left off before the argument. In memory of the heat they shared when they kissed, she touched a finger to her lips.

"You've said it all," she sighed as the words left her mouth. "Suppose I could tell you I'm no longer in the mood for a kiss or two. You've insulted me one too many times tonight. We might be able to start over tomorrow."

"No, it's not that easy to turn those emotions off. Want to talk about this evening. Admit it, Tara. You enjoyed the kisses, even the public display. I could have fondled you and you would have enjoyed everyone watching you, me, us. If I uncovered your breasts, you would not have said no. Would have felt no discomfort...because you wanted me more than you're willing to admit." Case wasn't going to let anything go. He would hound her until she gave in once more.

"You might not believe I was not coerced into the kiss. I was. You might think that I would want you to fondle me in public or otherwise. I don't. I'm not an exhibitionist. I accepted the kiss because I didn't want to tell you about Grant. There was nothing more."

Case stiffened while she watched him. His brows along with his lips narrowed into a thin line. "Shall we put that declaration to the test? As I just said, if I pulled you into my arms and kissed you, you wouldn't resist. If I pulled your corsage down to your waist then touched your breasts, you wouldn't stop me. I could suckle them. You would moan, your body would hum to life then ooze over me as if warm honey. If I touched you in the most secret, darkest part of you, you would be dripping wet with your desire." He paused. Silence hung heavy in the cramped space. "You would not tell me no? What does that tell you?"

Looking away from his hard gaze, she chose not to answer until she could figure out something that made sense to her. While she had not wanted to speak about Grant, he was correct in assuming she wanted the kiss. In ways she didn't understand, she needed him to take the kiss to the next step. If that was touching her breasts...so be it. Those facts did not make her a whore or a woman of lose morals.

"Do you still wish to go to Versailles tomorrow?" Tara asked not understanding how she would spend an entire day with this arrogant man. He would continue to tempt her as well as insult her. Case didn't even like her. While she was losing her heart to the man, he kept a shell around himself, shielding himself from any feelings.

"Do you?" Case asked.

"Maybe." Tara was having second thoughts about the viability of being alone with this man. The notion terrified her.

"I cleared my schedule."

"Why? Why would you want to be with me? You think the worst of me. Insult me at every turn. I don't understand why you choose to spend time with a woman whose character is so questionable."

"A man has needs a woman can attend to. All women have questionable characters. They are all out for what they can get from a man. What makes you think you are any different? What do you want from me?" Case's words were stiff along with unforgiving.

The words stung. Her heart ached.

At least she wasn't alone in his condemnation of her. She would give into him because she needed to spend time with this man. "Very well, we will rise as soon as possible. Get an early start to the day. That way we can return before—"

To her dismay Case shook his head. "No. We'll stay for the sunset. Perhaps spend the night since it would not be prudent or safe to ride in the darkness. Since you insist that I don't know a bloody thing about you, this will give you more time to enlighten me. You could show me who you are, the true Tara MacLaren. It isn't as if I don't want to know who you are. I do." The sincere sound of his voice shook her.

Tara wasn't convinced she could ever tell him anything that would change his mind. "We could start out before dawn, see the sunrise instead of the sunset." Tara watched the muscle of his jaw twitch. Case didn't like that idea. Too bloody bad!

"Either way, I'll have you to myself. Let's rise early. Do you wish for me to wake you? Would you like the honor of waking me? Perhaps we should spend the night in the same bed. If that was the situation, we would wake at the same time." Case continued to provoke, to challenge.

"No." Emotions she didn't wish to deal with vibrated through her. He was distrustful. Still arrogant. Tara couldn't help but wonder what spending the night in his bed would be like.

"Not even a reason? After the last kiss, I would think you would be more inclined to accept the invitation. You want to be in my bed. Beneath me. You want to feel me deep inside you. Don't ever deny true facts. I know better. I can read the truth in your beautiful amber eyes."

Her eyes widened at his descriptive words. Tara realized he relished watching her squirm. The last kiss meant nothing to him and everything to her. She touched her lips. Let her hand fall away before he could notice. She wasn't about to answer. "I'll be up at four. Is that too early?"

Case sat back, his hands folded on his stomach. His legs were stretched in front of him. A beguiling smile on his mouth. "Not too early for me."

She wished she could look forward to the day. If she could ignore him, enjoying the sunrise along with the ride would be easier. As soon as she hardened her heart, he slipped beneath the protective blocks she put around it. Tara wished she understood what drove him to hate women. If she could comprehend, perhaps she could begin to heal him.

Bah! No one could heal the jaded man she was supposed to spend time with, least of all her. She meant nothing to him. For the minutes remaining, she closed her eyes listening to the clip clop of the horse's hooves on the cobbled streets. The scent of the river wafted through the opening of the vehicle. A silver moon hovered on the horizon.

As the horse slowed, she opened her eyes to see Case staring at her. He leaned toward her. "I'd like to know you better. I would." He ran his fingertip along her jaw then down the column of her neck stopping where the frantic thundering of her heart would give her away.

"Would learning more about me change your opinion of me?" she asked knowing the answer before he spoke more words condemning her.

"Probably not." His hand dropped away.

"That's what I thought. Why should I bother? There is nothing in learning more about each other for either of us. You don't like me. So many times I don't like you. We have to be cordial while we are here in Paris. I have to write your correspondence. That is all there is. Nothing more." Tara wanted to believe her last statement was true. It wasn't. The kisses between them told a different story. The way those few encounters made her dream about being in his arms were between them.

"Little liar. There is a great deal I enjoy about you. Never said or meant to imply I didn't like you. Also believe there are things about me you like. You wouldn't kiss me as you just did if you didn't have some good opinions concerning myself. Today you were generous with your feelings. I appreciate that." His voice calmed as well as soothed her battered spirit.

He leaned over. Again, his finger trailed along the length of her neck. One hand bracketed her throat. No pressure was applied. His touch was a simple caress of ownership that frightened. Her toes curled even while she fought against the new sensations shattering her body, her willpower, her control. The heart she didn't want to give to him became a hole of despair. Of loss. Grant became a distant memory. Tara jerked away from him. Case's hand remained, his thumb stroking. Igniting.

Case meant to charm then seduce.

Would never let up on his quest to prove she was a woman of misplaced principles. She didn't know how to convince him he was wrong. Even if she told him about Grant, he would continue his outrageous assumptions. He thought she gave her favors both to Ash as well as Jeremy along with every other man who caught her attention. Any man who danced with her. There were no men who caught her attention since Grant...except Case. Tara swallowed hard trying to push thoughts of Case and the possessive way he was claiming her from her mind.

There was a lot about Case Ferguson that pleased her. Tara was never going to tell him her thoughts on the matter. She did not intend to stroke his enormous ego with flattering words.

If she allowed him his way with her, the act would give credence to his low opinion of her.

"Don't touch me," Tara told him, her voice a sultry moan she didn't recognize. The thinness of the words shocked her. Her breath shivered into her lungs. She moved back but couldn't escape his touch.

"We are here." His voice was gentle. He was still stroking the column of her neck, still running a fingertip along her collarbone. Ignoring her command to stop. "Will you sleep with me tonight? Share my bed? That way we can get to know each other better."

The breath she inhaled wavered. Tara whimpered, wishing she could tell him no with the ease that would convince him. She wasn't going to fall into his bed tonight. Case had too many different sides to him. "No," but the single word was weak. Held no conviction. She should have made her denial sound stronger. He would find a way to twist the knife if she wasn't more forthcoming about her feelings. If she could tell him a resounding no, she wouldn't find herself lost to him. "I'm not going to your bed tonight or any night." Tara didn't want to have this false conversation. Deep in the most secret part of her, Tara understood that if he continued to ask, she would find herself in his bed. When that happened, she would have herself to blame. No one else.

As soon as the hack stopped, she helped herself to the ground. Lifting her skirts, she rushed up the steps to be brought to a halt in front of the locked door. Case stood behind her. Too close. The heat of his breath caressed the naked skin of her neck. His large body touched hers.

A shocked cry.

"It's alright."

"No...no, it isn't."

"The key?" Case handed it to her, a smile on his handsome face. "You'll need that to unlock the door."

Relief. "Thank you. I know." Tara reached for the key he held out. Her hand shook. Case pulled away his hand, keeping the key from her reach. She wasn't going to jump to try to reach the hand he could hold above her head. Wasn't going to play this game. If he wanted something else from her, he would have to speak out. Case told her in the hack what he wanted.

"Not so fast," Case murmured while he touched the key to her nose.

"Now what do you want." Tara watched him, her hands on her hips. If she tried to grab it, he would keep it away. She was losing her mind. "What *wee* game be *ye* playin' with me?"

"What I want?" Case tapped her forehead then her nose. "What do you think I want? For the evening to end different. Don't wish to play games now or ever. Want the promise of your words while we were still in the cabaret."

"What was that?" Tara remembered what he was referring to but admitting to the fact was a different matter. She'd said quite explicitly she wanted another kiss as well as enjoyed the first one.

"Need to *ken* the truth of your words. Lies or truths?"

"You want only your truths. You don't care about mine," Tara bit out, angry with herself, with the escalating emotions this man caused without a care.

"No," Case said.

"The kiss that was promised? Another public display? Is that what you be askin' of me? Should we show the neighbors how we feel about each other or should we make this kiss private? Take the matter inside?"

Case chuckled as he stared at her. "Either is acceptable to me. Public displays can be titillating. I don't mind showing your neighbors how I feel. Wouldn't mind uncovering you if you didn't mind."

"If that is so, you and I will spend the remainder of the evening on the porch. I will no be kisin' you out here where everyone will be seein' me." Some of the neighbors she'd known since her first visits to Paris. She'd been six years old then. Tara wasn't about to regal them with something that should be private. The cabaret was different. She didn't know anyone in the room. Foolish woman. It was different because the man seduced you. Took the choice right out of her muddled brain. If she'd allowed it, he might have... The devil she didn't want to think about that.

Tara bristled heaving in a tight breath of air. While she knew he wasn't threatening, he meant every word. A shiver swept through her. She didn't know if the sensation was caused by the wind or the thought of the kiss. Tara agreed, "One kiss. Nothing more."

"More is up to you. What that will entail is up to me if you become agreeable. We will see what transpires." Case's voice was whiskey smooth. He knew what he was about. Was an experienced man. The sound of his voice charmed. Enticed. Captivated. She was drowning in deep water. No longer knew how to swim. Couldn't surface for a deep breath of air.

If he touched her, she'd be lost to the sensual pull of the generated heat. Tara realized she was lost despite her intention to stay away from him. She couldn't resist him when he was nice. When his smile stretched across his face.

"A kiss," she conceded. "Inside... Not on the front porch." A breathy sigh of relief swept through her when he unlocked the door. Tara wished she dared rush up the steps to her room then close the door. He would call her on that move. That would leave to another round of insults to her character.

"Well, I'll be. The two of you just getting home?" Ash stood, framed in the doorway on his way out, his dress casual. "What have the two of you been up to? Seems like a fine night to be up to something. I know I am...up to something." Ash let his gaze drift across her. Felt the rise of heat. Tara felt certain he knew she kissed Case.

"You are leaving?" Case asked, his voice more demand than question. "Seems a bit late to be starting out on the town. Though the privacy will be looked forward to. Tara and I have a few matters to discuss before we can find our beds."

"Got unfinished business to take care of. My entertainment until we depart Paris awaits me," Ash said as he stepped around Tara. "You two enjoy each other. Will be gone the night. Don't look for me in the morning. If I have my way, the two of you will be alone just as you wish. Hope that's not going to be a problem. Never wished to be a chaperone. Don't know what mother was thinking." Whistling, Ash set off down the steps at a jaunty speed.

Tara watched him until she could no longer see him, her heart pounding hard and fast. "What do you think that was all about? He seems pleased with himself."

"Believe the man has secured a mistress for the duration of our visit. Suppose his nights will be..." Case pushed on the back of his neck. "...better than mine unless I can convince you otherwise."

What Tara knew was that it would not take much to convince her otherwise. "A mistress? Ash? Is he old enough?" Tara couldn't help but shake her head. "We've only been in the city one full day. Does yesterday count?"

Case laughed, his hoot, startling her. "If a man finds the right woman, it doesn't take longer than that to secure a female. One who will benefit from the association. Ash does have a great deal of charm. Ash also has money coupled with a title. Though I don't need to explain that to you." Case bent at the waist gesturing for her to precede him further insides. "We've things to explore. Matters to discuss. Important ones between us."

"Just a kiss," Tara muttered understanding Case would try for more. She needed to stay strong in the face of Ash's abandonment. If Ash stayed, there would be a small buffer between them.

Ash was gone.

He wouldn't be home tonight.

With his hand on the small of her back, Case ushered her inside. He turned her. Undoing her shawl, his knuckles brushed across bare skin. Tara jerked. Her reaction to the gentleness of his touch surprised her. Fragmented sensations shocked her. Heat coiled. Flames of longing kindled.

With little effort, Case could unravel her one tiny thread at a time. She sucked in a deep breath of air. When he touched her nose, he grinned that wicked, devilish grin she was becoming accustomed to seeing. He knew what his slightest touch generated. He knew!

Tara wasn't about to plead that he kiss her so she could get this over with. Case didn't appear to be in a hurry. His back to her, he poured a sherry for her and a brandy for himself. As he sauntered to her, he held out her glass.

"The drink will relax you, Tara. You are just as stiff as the fireplace poker over there. How can a man enjoy a kiss from his woman when she can't soften against him? When she holds herself aloof despite the pleasure he gives her." Case sipped then set the glass down on the table. "Drink."

"Is that a command?" Tara did sip. She did feel the heat of the alcohol slide down her throat. Did believe the drink might relax her. Case was right in all he said. Remembered the heat along with the possessive caress of his thumb. Case would taste of the brandy he was drinking. At the cabaret he tasted of the beer. Heat rose to her face as she recalled the kiss. She'd wanted more. Let him do more without denying him anything.

Stay strong!

Not tonight.

Make him wait.

Control. It was a heady word. After she set her glass beside his, she looked at him. Tried to smile. "I'm ready."

"No. No, you're not. You look as if you have an appointment with Madam Guillotine. A kiss will not be your execution. Promise you will like what we do." He hooked his big hand around her neck then drew her to him.

"No more than a kiss," she repeated, understanding her words would mean next to nothing to him.

"Are you certain about that? I would convince you otherwise." Before he finished speaking, she found herself pressed against him, his hand on the small of her back, holding her close. His other hand around her neck with possession in mind. He guided her to him.

With light precision, his lips brushed across her once then twice. Rendered speechless, the soft mewl couldn't be helped. His kisses had a way of doing that to her. Made her speechless as well as mindless.

"You didn't answer. Are you certain, Princess. If you don't say anything I'll take that as permission to explore."

This was different from the cabaret. There, he wanted to make sure she understood the rules. Comprehended that she was giving permission. He wanted her to say the words that would absolve him from guilt.

What guilt?

Foolish woman. Case would have none. Her arms were wound around his neck. She opened for him. Felt the heated glide of his tongue explore inside her mouth. Grant never kissed her with this much intensity. Knew the gentle bite of his teeth as they tugged on her top lip then soothed. He slanted his head for better access to the sensitive inside of her mouth. Her body caught on fire. He didn't even like her. Said he liked her. She needed to stay strong. She wanted him. She didn't want him.

She couldn't stop the rippled sigh issuing into his mouth. Her fingers wound into his dark hair. Sharp nails raked across his scalp as he deepened the kiss. Touched inside, found the back of her throat. He cupped her bottom with his large hands. She felt the hardness of his arousal pressed against her belly. This was too much too soon. She needed to stop him before she could not.

Case's lips teased her neck then lower. Gentle bites nipped across her just above the fabric of her corsage. When she mewled then whimpered, he moved back to her mouth. He pushed his tongue inside after she gave him permission by parting her lips.

"Are you wet?"

Tara understood what he asked. She felt the heat along with the moisture between her legs. The question jolted her back to the reality of this kiss. Case meant to take more than the kiss. If she didn't do something different, she would be in his big bed tonight.

"I'm not ready. I can't...not yet."

~ * ~

Whistling down the walkway, Ash knew he was leaving his cousin to a wolf. Those two were meant for each other. That was why his mother approved. The thought absolved him of some guilt but not all. In the beginning, he wondered what his mother was doing putting them in such close unchaperoned vicinity of each other. Now that he abandoned Tara to seek pleasures for himself, there would be no buffer between the two of them. They would either kill each other or fall into bed together. How soon made no difference. Case would enjoy the chase. Tara needed to feel alive again. What Ash didn't understand was why on earth Case thought Tara was interested in him as a lover. Bloody eyes, he was her cousin. With a shrug of his shoulders, he dismissed the notion. That problem was between the two of them.

Ash was betting on the bedding.

With little fanfare, Ash procured a room in a boarding house nearby for Lou Lou. As it turned out, he didn't need to wait until midnight for her to be released from her position. Since she was giving up her job at the tavern, she didn't need to finish her shift which would include sleeping with some man. If his little Lou Lou was going to become his Paris mistress, there wasn't going to be a man in her bed tonight unless it was him.

In the morning, he would bring a doctor to examine her to see if she was safe. Ash wasn't positive what he would do if she had the pox. He couldn't take her back to her job. By taking her away before she finished her shift, all ties were cut.

"Lou Lou?" He opened the door to her room. "Where are you?"

She whirled, her skirt swirling around her ankles. She beamed.

Her hand was at her throat as if he surprised her. "You're back? So soon."

"Told you I would be back tonight. Didn't want to leave you alone too long." He set his hat along with his frock coat on the coat stand. Ash loosened his cravat. He didn't want to wait to have his little pigeon. A prudent man would wait a few weeks.

Bloody hell.

"What are we going to do? What are you going to do?" She blinked a few times. "Are you staying here? With me? I think I might like that."

In most women he would have taken the feminine gesture as flirtatious. With his Lou Lou the movement looked different. Almost as if she was shy. Ash dismissed that notion. She was young. She couldn't be innocent. She let him pull down her dress, fondle her in front of the entire establishment.

Could she?

Lou Lou worked at a cabaret.

If she was a virgin, that would negate all his questions. Lou Lou wouldn't have a disease. There were two ways to discover the truth. One of those would be to ask her. She might lie. The other was to...

That was too crass... or was it? If she was an innocent, he could have her tonight. If she possessed the treasured maidenhead, he would not have to proceed with caution. If he seduced her he could discover the truth. Would not have to wait three weeks or more to see if she had the disease.

He could ask.

Lou Lou could lie.

Bloody eyes, Lou Lou worked in a cabaret. What the bloody hell was he thinking? She served drinks. Sat on my lap as if she did that with all her customers. Let me look at her breasts. *Nice titties.* Lou Lou might see him as an easy mark. He supposed he was. Her bright red hair coupled with her brilliant smile caught him in the ballocks.

"A kiss for your protector?" Holding out his arms for her, he dismissed his thoughts. Ash waited while she ran to him, hoping she would be as free with her body here in the privacy of the room as she was in the tavern where she was on display to the public. In some ways he liked that she was free with herself.

"*Oui!*" she giggled, throwing herself into his arms. "*Oh, la la!*"

Lou Lou caught him off guard. With the unforeseen momentum, Ash faltered, stepped back for balance. Her legs wound around his flanks. He hardened. His arousal pulsed against his britches. This was more like what he should expect every day. His mouth covered hers. Like the pro she was, she opened for him giving herself over to his kiss. She met each thrust with one of her own. He cupped her fanny in his hands. The kiss was honied. He deepened the penetration, poking his tongue into the deep cavern that welcomed him. They danced and played. Taking. Sharing. Tasting. Sharing. Taking.

This woman was far from innocent. Untried never. He would have to wait the required time.

With a bit of regret, knowing he didn't want to take this too far, Ash let her body slide down the length of his. The succulent curves of her breasts pushed against him. His Lou Lou was ripe for the mating he wanted. When he looked down, he could see the hardened tips, the blush of rose surrounding her pert nipples.

Ash cleared his throat. His hands still cupping her fanny, he spoke, "We've a few things to discuss before we are intimate."

She flushed a delicious shade of pink matching the skin surrounding the tips of her nipples. "What would that be?" Lou Lou lowered her eyes as if the thought might embarrass her. When she looked at him again, Ash saw the questions. When she looked at him in that manner, all rational thoughts fled.

Thinking hard about all that needed to be said, he cut straight to the most relevant of all his questions. He hoped that however she answered, she would be honest. "Are you a virgin?" Her color deepened to crimson.

Lou Lou let out a deep sigh as if she was annoyed. "I don't know why you are asking me that. It cannot be important. You saw where I worked. What's important is that you want me. That you're willing to make me your mistress. What else is there?"

Air cascaded from his lungs. Just as he suspected, "This isn't going to be easy. Honesty is all I ask from you."

"Why would you want to know such a thing?" She blinked a few times. "You know what I was doing. I would have taken someone upstairs at the end of my shift. Half of what I earned would go to the proprietor. You had to pay him the fee I would have earned last night in order for me to come here with you."

Ash felt very real disappointment at her words. She was just as he suspected. "Yes. Yet you send mixed messages. Are you untried in the ways of love? Are you innocent? The truth will determine how I proceed." Ash understood no matter how she answered he would not be able to trust what she told him. Either he would have to wait or he could find out for himself if she was a virgin.

"I've never had a lover," Lou Lou answered with a caution that wasn't an answer. She looked sheepish then riddled with guilt.

"How many men have you taken to the rooms upstairs?" Ash was blunt with the question he needed an answer to. If it was only one, he would have to fetch the doctor in the morning as well as every day after that for a few weeks if nothing was discovered.

She looked down, playing with the drab gray gown she wore. When she looked up, she smiled, her mouth forming an O. "Dozens? I've been working there..."

"*Merde!*" Ash cut her off with a wave of his hand. That was not the answer he wished to hear.

Lou Lou jerked back at his curse. "You don't want a woman of experience? I can be whatever you want. Don't want to lose you. If you don't wish it that I've slept with another man or hundreds of men, I will tell you I haven't. If you want a woman of experience, I can be that too. The proprietor trained me. Told me I had to please in order to keep my job. Tell me what you want. If I can, I'll give it to you."

The lie was absurd. She was answering in the way she thought he would like the best. "You won't lose me. You haven't had dozens of men. Have you? There is still untried innocence about your reactions. The look on your face when the question surprises you." His hands were on her shoulders. He shook her. "Truth, Lou Lou. I want the truth. There is no right or wrong answer to this."

When she looked away, Ash understood he would get nothing he could bank on from her tonight.

"If I told you no one, would that be better? Would you believe me?" Moisture filled her eyes. A silver tear slipped down her cheek leaving a moist trail.

The second little shake he gave her wasn't enough to hurt her as was the first. He hoped it was enough to rattle a bit of sense into her pretty head. "I would like that answer though I wouldn't believe you. Tonight would have been nice to bed you. Since I can't trust your word, I'll bring a doctor to look at you tomorrow as well as the days after that until enough time has passed to discern the truth."

"No!" Lou Lou was trembling. "No, please don't!"

"I won't sleep with you unless I know you don't have syphilis or any other disease spread by sex."

"No..." Lou Lou stared into his eyes, pleading, "What will the doctor do?"

"Check you...look at...your... Bloody hell! You don't know?" Ash didn't want to be the person to tell her she had to spread her legs so the doctor could look at her. When he saw her as his next mistress, his thoughts didn't go that far.

With her moving from side to side, her bottom lip caught between her teeth, Ash understood her reluctance. "I'm clean," she murmured shaking her head, wringing her hands. "I haven't slept with any man. Tonight you would have been my first. Tonight was my first day of work. I was lucky to meet you."

"I see," Ash still didn't know how to proceed from here. Didn't know what he could believe. "Would you let me look at you?" In time, she would open herself up to him. If she was innocent, that might be too much to ask. He felt caught between two imposing forces. The last thing he wanted was to embarrass or hurt her.

"If we made love, you would see all of me?"

"Yes, however, before we make love, I'll have to find proof of your virginity. Foreplay would help you ease into my..." Ash didn't know how to put the rest of it. Prior to this moment he never spoke to an innocent.

Was she?

Was this girl his first virgin? If so, he would remember her for the remainder of his life. Also...he would take care of this lovely child-woman for the remainder of his life. His father wouldn't be pleased.

Chapter Six

The next morning, Case made sure he rose before Tara. The night before did not end the way he hoped. They didn't share his bed or hers. While she slept, he watched, pulling up a chair beside the bed. The view was enjoyable. Would have been more than pleasant if he was lying beside her. Because he could, he let the cool, satin strands of her hair wind between the sensitive inside of his fingers. He didn't know what he was going to do with this woman who baffled him. Confounded all his preconceived notions of the fairer sex.

He hated to admit to the hesitancy in his mind, Tara was not the woman he assumed her to be. Who the devil was she? Too many times the pain in her eyes pinched at his heart. Yesterday was some sort of anniversary. It was a time she refused to speak about. The minutes they spent in the cabaret she felt pleasure from their kisses. Those minutes she forgot the part of her that kept distance separating them. He would like to reconstruct those moments with new ones.

Tara was an enigma. She perplexed. Puzzled. Somehow, he would get into her thoughts. Discover her secret or secrets if she had more than one. Today would be a good start. While Case understood she wanted him, she kept him at arm's length. He didn't understand why. Intensifying the chase would be exciting. Tara would not be as easy to catch as his other conquests. He had the entire summer to breach her armor.

She rolled over. Her hair slid through his fingers. The cover settled around her waist. She clung to a pillow, held it tight against her chest. Her protection. Armor. A pillow would not shelter her forever. If he could, without waking her, he would pull her tiny bit of protection from her. See what her nightdress would reveal.

After pulling the blanket to her feet, he whispered close to her ear. "Time to wake up, sleepy head. Thought you would be ready to leave at least an hour ago. Here you are, still lying abed as if we didn't have a destination. Do wish for me to join you? We could curtail our plans for something else. Wait until tomorrow."

When she reached for the cover, he stopped her, held her hands. "No, you don't. Wake up, little princess. We've a mission to be off on...an adventure."

A pause in time, after that a small moan followed his words. In that instant she jerked awake. The pillow fell to the floor, her eyes wide pools of amber. "You!"

"Me," Case agreed as he caught site of the gentle curve of one breast beneath the fine lawn of the nightdress. The tip was hard pressing against the fabric. "I could join you in bed if you'd rather."

Tara sat up, pushing thick curling hair from her face. "No! I'll be ready in a few minutes. As soon as you leave my room, I'll get dressed. Meet you for breakfast. Give me a few minutes. Did want to get an early start to the day."

"Now...where would the fun in that be?" He sat back crossing his arms in front of him. His gaze was on her, all the enticing parts of her he could see beneath the nightdress. His body felt the impact of the sight she presented him with.

Her finger that was pointing to the door shook. "Leave!" The command in her voice surprised him. The words did not. He supposed she would be difficult today. He would look for a way to breach her defenses.

Heaving a loud expulsion of breath meant for her benefit, Case stood, "Croissants and coffee are on the table. You will have a minute or two to eat if you dress with haste."

The pillow she let fly hit him on the back before he could step through the door. His crack of laughter followed him into the main living room. Before he closed the door giving her privacy, he leaned in. "Good aim." He grinned at the wanton picture she presented.

While he waited for her, he poured coffee for her then set a croissant on her plate. She was out before he could finish eating. Tara was a pretty picture walking into the breakfast nook. Her skin flushed a tiny bit as she met his gaze.

"I'm starving," she told him, a smile on her face as if she anticipated the day. She sat.

"You look well rested." In silence, he admired the copper-colored riding habit she wore. Matched the color of her eyes. Her hair was tied with a single ribbon behind her neck. She wore tiny jet earrings.

"Amazing isn't it since I felt as if I tossed and turned all night." Tara caught her bottom lip beneath her teeth while she lifted the coffee cup.

"If you slept with me, you would have had a peaceful night." Case understood she would have slept less. He would have made love to her more than once. If she slept with him, they would not be leaving for another few hours. One of his favorite pastimes with the right woman was morning sex.

Silence greeted him. Tara would have no reply. She sipped her coffee. Ate the croissant. After she finished with both, she touched the cloth napkin to her lips.

Case reached to her, shaded the corner of her mouth with his thumb. "You missed a *wee* crumb." Jerking back, she reacted to the touch. He saw the shiver, the heated reaction as if she was thinking about other things.

"My bag is there. I packed a few things for tonight and tomorrow. Do you have a bag?"

"My saddlebag will do fine. Used to traveling light." He extended a hand as he stood.

Tara looked at him as if he'd gone mad. Nonetheless, she accepted the hand. Her fingers were chilled when he held them. Case rubbed the top of her small hand with his thumb, thinking about touching other places. She was soft, soft everywhere. Silk. Soft. So very touchable.

Is there any place on your body where you are not soft?

She would deny his question if he asked. Without speaking more, they strolled to the stable. Both horses, Sunrise along with Black, were saddled, ready for exercise. With his hands circling her small waist, he helped her mount. The feel of her never ceased to affect. He fantasized.

As they left the outskirts of Paris behind them, the sun was beginning to rise in the east. The colors were brilliant. Vivid. Electrifying. Pastels coated the sky with color. Mist skimmed the land in front of him. To Case it was like being in the highlands. He sucked in a deep breath of air registering all the different scents that greeted him.

"I understand why your father chases sunrises. Each new one must be more beautiful than the last," Case said as he drew abreast of her. She was looking straight ahead. Her acknowledgment of his comment came a few seconds later.

"I don't," came her succinct reply. Tara motioned to the skyline in front of them. "None are as beautiful as the ones that rise over the MacLaren castle. When I stand so high above the land and I look out over the ocean from the battlements to watch the display of colors, somedays the sun is covered by clouds or the ground is heaped in misty fog so high it blocks the sunrise. Still, they are lovely. Don't understand why he would think in some other country the scene is more beautiful. It's an excuse to see other places. Father won't admit to that fact. Truth is, he has the wanderlust. My mother goes along because she cannot live without him. She understands him." There was a pause before she could continue. It was what she wanted. "Mother loves father with all her heart."

Case was curious about Tara. Curious to understand why she would agree to come to Paris with him. Case couldn't broker that question. "How did you spend your days when you were home? Were your parents always out seeking adventures?"

"Two questions. You will need to reciprocate. Before I left or during my childhood? The times for me were very different." She looked straight ahead waiting for him to speak. He wanted to know about the last two years along with why she came to London for the season. Her childhood was not something he cared about.

She was still angry about the insults from last night when they rode home. Case thought honesty was the best. He would try not to offend her again. "Both, I guess. Wish to learn about you since you tell me I *dinnae* know anything about you. Help me understand what makes you unique."

"Do *ye* now?"

"*Aye.*"

"Thought you knew all about me. At least that is what you told me." She tossed back his words with a casualness that belied her tone. Tara seemed to have a change of heart, more open than before. "I used to spend time with my mother hunting. We didn't actually hunt, though we practiced with the bow and arrow. I'm very good at close range. Not strong enough to hit a target at a great distance."

"You shoot?" Case didn't like the idea of Tara roaming the woods even near her home. She lived in the highlands. The land was rugged. Untamed. Wild. Men there were often more uncivilized than the wild animals that roamed. Would take advantage of a lone woman they came upon.

"Very well," she laughed the sound trilling in the morning air. "As I said, I can hit most targets if they are not too far away."

Case liked the sound of her laughter. Enjoyed hearing her giggle. Tara didn't laugh enough. He didn't want her to withdraw into herself. Enjoyed the carefree side she was showing him now. A challenge and a forfeit to the looser would be his agenda. "We could have an archery contest." He tossed out the invitation never thinking she would accept. If he won, he knew what he would ask as the forfeit.

"Yes." She beamed, clapping her hands together as if the thought delighted her. She wouldn't know what he meant to ask for when he won. "As long as the distance to the target isn't so great my arrow wouldn't travel that far. I hate to admit to the lack of strength. However, I must be realistic. If we have the contest, I will set the distance for the first round as well as the second. If we are tied at the end of the second round, you will decide on the distance for the remaining round. Would that would be fair?"

"You think you can win against this man?" Case asked, intrigued by this new experiment between them. "You must be very good."

"As long as the contest is won by skill and not brute force, I am a very good archer. Are you? Can you take on this woman then end up the winner?" The pained expression vanished. Tara smiled at him. It was the first time she let down her guard. He felt as if for one thump of his heart he could see into her soul.

When Tara let down her guard, she was a little tease. Almost wanton in nature.

Case enjoyed this side of her.

"You should smile more often." Case said wishing he wasn't part contributor to Tara's pain. He wished he could touch her smile, outline her lips so he would recall what that smile looked like after he was gone from her life. Needed to memorize that smile.

To distance herself from the conversation, Case assumed, Tara nudged her horse to a faster gait. He watched as space between them grew. He would give her some breathing room. There was a lot more he would like to learn about her. In time once more he would approach her past.

An archery contest? That was an interesting thought. He would figure out how to go about setting one up after they returned to Paris. A few inquiries would produce a proper venue for the competition.

Tara wandered the highlands with her mother in the guise of hunting. Case didn't believe the woman would be capable of killing an animal. For a mile, he let her ride ahead of him. Case decided to close the distance so they could pursue the previous conversation.

With ease, he caught her. Tara turned to him. She was still smiling. "Thought you would have caught up with me sooner. Should we share our pasts? I told you something about me. It's your turn now. Share and share alike."

Blindsided, Case's mind stumbled. Sharing a past with someone meant becoming vulnerable. If sharing was the only way for him to make tracks into what made Tara who she was, he could mention a few prominent facts. Before speaking, he paused. "I was also born in the highlands. Farther north than your MacLaren castle. The winters are harsh. We are not close to the ocean. Couldn't see the water if I stood on the highest craig. The land there...well...it's difficult to eke out a living."

"You were poor."

"*Aye*. You were brought up with plenty. It matters not now that we are adults. I have more than enough groats to buy what pleases me."

"True. Now, you have plenty also. Suppose it's my turn to spout a truth as we who live in the MacLaren castle know it. The castle is haunted. Some nights the ghost cries on the battlements. We don't know why. There are rumors. Our ghost followed my mother and father to London when they were trying to get my half-brother, Liam, back."

"A ghost you say? Don't believe in them. It's all foolishness. Though the tale makes a fine story." Case thought what she told him absurd. He didn't believe in anything he could not see, taste, hear or feel. Tara said the ghost cried. "If I heard this nonexistent woman sobbing, I might consider truth in your words."

"Didn't think you would. Nonetheless, if you ever visit my home, you might hear her crying atop the castle. I could take you up to the battlements. That doesn't mean she would cry in your presences. She needs a reason to make her presence known. Something horrible that is happening."

"That hardly counts. Have you heard this ghost?" Case wondered if she meant to tell him frivolous untruths to meet her part in this exchange. Tara needed to tell him something of importance. He needed to learn more about her, not some type of nonsense that told him nothing.

"Believe it does count...but no, I haven't heard her. I put my beliefs on the line for you. Isn't that what this telling of our pasts is all about? I do believe this ghost is real. Mother also does. I trust her." Tara questioned him, her head turned a bit sideways. "I'm supposed to tell you about parts of my life I would rather keep to myself."

"It is. So, it is my turn then." Case pulled in a deep breath of air. Only those closest to him knew this for a fact. Now this woman would also know. What she would do with the information was an unknown. "I'm a bastard," he blurted adding nothing more than the hated words. After all this time he still wasn't used to the thought of his parentage.

Tara's stunned laughter trilled through the air. "Are you expecting me to believe that nonsense? The Duchess said you have a mother as well as a father. Was she lying to me? Are you? Which is it?"

"When were you and Ella speaking of me?" Case didn't like the idea of people gossiping about him when he wasn't there. Anger rose. Escalated. Surged through his blood. He had not thought about this as a possibility.

Tara tilted her head to one side while she thought about his question. Saw his anger...the fury he couldn't keep hidden. "It was the night of the ball when I first met you. Seems like that night was forever ago. For some unexplainable reason, she told me that you were one of the duke's favorites. You worked hard. You were willing to risk your life for your country. On top of that you were honest to a fault. Is that true? Honest to a fault? I haven't seen that side of you." Tara lifted her shoulders, the slight feminine shrug just like Tara. "That's what he said. All those traits he values. The conversation was positive. I would think you would be pleased the duke thinks so highly of you rather than angry that they spoke about you. Everything said was positive."

He let a parcel of air rush from his lungs in an effort to hide his emotions from Tara. Case understood he was too sensitive about his beginnings. "*Aye*, I've a mother. As to my father, she never told me who he is. What she did tell me was who he was not. He was not the man who raised me. Not the man she married. He was the man who detested me until he took his dying breath. The man who worked me to the bone to gain whatever he could pull from me. I was just a small child. The man used me as his slave."

When Tara turned, a concerned look on her face, her eyes were wide, questioning. "The man everyone believes to be your father is not? How?"

"You comprehend. Are you just too refined to mention something that is more common than it is not. I would think most people understand adultery. Why father kept me rather than setting me aside is well known. He wanted free labor. Didn't wish to admit the fact his wife was an adulteress. Although I found out later, he was far from a good husband." Case felt as if he just bared his soul even though there was so much more that shaped his thoughts. The story was baser than what he shared. There were more ugly truths in his history.

"That's why you hate women." Tara caught on to part of his beliefs. "Your mother..."

"Don't hate women or detest them. Love them. Every part of them. Their breasts...their..." He cut her off as well as himself before she could finish her statement. "Those words are two simplistic to describe my feelings toward the fairer sex. What I know is that a woman is out for personal gain at a man's expense. My mother was like that as was my father's sister who came to live with us after my mother passed. It wasn't much longer than that when my father died."

"It was just you and your father's sister."

Case could do no more than nod. He thought he put that time of his life to the back of his mind. "It's your turn to speak of something from your past. Something other than a fanciful ghost. Something important to you personally." Case hoped she would say something about the anniversary which was yesterday.

Instead, avoiding her turn, Tara pointed to the magnificent chateau in front of them. "We are here. There is Versailles. This structure on that land was built to be a country retreat for the king and queen. This chateau was built by Louis XIV. Though in the beginning this land harbored a simple hunting lodge. The first building to grace this sight was constructed in 1623 by Louis XII."

Tara told him more about the chateau than he cared about. What Case wished to know remained in her head. He wanted to learn more about her, not this country retreat which looked like a palace. On the horses they circled the grounds. "Too bad we can't get a closer look."

"You want to go inside? I've heard it is lavish, ostentatious, a sight to behold. Gold inlays everywhere. Expensive paintings gracing the walls. Huge chandeliers hanging from the ceilings." After a slight pause, "I'd like that too. We'll have to wait until the government decides to let peasants see how the wealthy French aristos lived." Tara pulled to a stop on a hill above the castle.

"What now?" Case knew a meal would be nice. He was famished. A croissant along with a cup of coffee wasn't enough to sustain him through the day. The time neared the noon hour. They rode with good speed. Today, it didn't seem her leg bothered her. Tara was a good horsewoman. He couldn't have asked for a better companion. The company and conversation were sufficient to keep boredom at bay. Still, he hoped to learn more. Between them there was so much left unsaid.

"Let's find a small café where we can eat. After that we can stroll through the village. I would suspect most of the people who live here also work at the chateau. Afterwards, you know...get ready for the setting of the sun. After all, the sunset coupled with the sunrise is why we are here." Case had ideas about tonight. He hoped to take the seduction of his beautiful companion one step farther.

After lunch, the time passed too fast. Case lost track of the conversation, his mind set on a different direction than the mundane chatter between them. As they strolled to the apartment he rented, he held her hand, their fingers entwined. Case liked the feel of her hand in his. Tara didn't object.

"There is one bedroom," Tara murmured as she turned to smile at him. "Where are you going to sleep? The sofa doesn't appear too comfortable. A bit short for you."

"The same place as you," he told her, his voice holding his laughter back at her look of chagrin. "What? Not acceptable to you? I will guarantee you that I will not be sleeping with my feet hanging over that couch."

"Oh my, I'll have to get another room." She whirled to head downstairs to see if she could speak to someone about the reservations.

"No. Don't want you out of my sight." He blocked her way to the door. During their stroll through the village, Case noticed a man following them. So far, this person kept his distance. He didn't want to tell her about the man or his mission. This man could be the one who he was after. Then again, he might not be. Case did have enemies. He'd not been able to get a good look at him. Tara would be difficult until she understood the danger.

"I've heard that before. I won't share the bed."

Case nodded toward the sofa. "It's all yours if you prefer it to the soft mattress...and me. My body will warm yours. I'm not the least bit soft though I don't bite. Well, not often but only in strategic places along with tender concern." He figured there would be more discussion as to where they would sleep. The argument could be put off. "Do you have a warm coat? If you recall, the other night you were chilled to the bone by the time the sun went down."

"Yes," she went through her valise. "Here."

"Let's go. Do you have a place you wish to watch the sunset

from." Anywhere was fine with him. He ordered dinner for after the show. "Should we continue our previous conversation? You never told me about the last two years. What brought you to London?"

She produced an unladylike snort. "Believe it's your turn for revelations."

"No."

Tara bristled at his curt word. "I..."

"Told you I was a bastard. You changed the conversation to the chateau. So...by my calculations it's your turn to bare your soul. Tell me why you came to London." Case was hoping to hear something about Grant. Tara was so closed mouth where the man was concerned hell would freeze over before she mentioned him. Where the bloody hell was the man now? Who was he to her? He was about to seduce a woman who must have meant something to him. If he were Grant, he...he would never let her go. That thought startled him. He shook the idea from his head.

Was he a man or a boy?

Did he have something to do with the anniversary where she mourned the loss of someone or something important to her?

That thought didn't come to him before. He could be a boy. Could Tara have a child? If so, she should be with the lad instead of spending time with him in France. No, he didn't think Tara would be so callous. There was no child. Unless the child was the person she seemed to mourn. She wasn't very old. If she had a child and the boy died... The thought stole his breath. His heart staggered. He needed to readjust his thinking. Wished for the truth. No, when he kissed her, she would not have been thinking about a child. Grant had kissed her before as a lover kisses.

"Why did I come to London?" She was shaking her head then shrugged her slight shoulders as if the truth didn't matter. "Didn't want to. Didn't care about the season. I'm too old to be called a debutante. In a manner of speaking, I was forced."

"Yes. Why?" Case persisted searching for more answers. Found himself frowning. Tara was dancing around the subject. He could be patient. Didn't want to. "Don't think anyone could force you if you felt strongly."

"The Duchess asked me. I can't refuse her. It's also why I agreed to accompany you to Paris. Both the duke as well as The Duchess told me joining you here would be good for me. Said I needed to get away for a time. Don't see how this is good for me." She was shaking her head.

Tara was keeping things from him, important aspects of her life. "So, what did you do that caused the invitation?"

"You're not going to let up. Are you?"

"No, you're hiding behind something. What is it? What don't you want to tell me, Tara? It's your turn to open up. Won't tell you anything else about me unless you turn honest about your past."

Case saw her face pale. Her hands twisted in the cape she'd pulled from her valise. He had the sudden feeling he wasn't going to appreciate her answer. Pain distorted her features. Crease lines accentuated her forehead. Tara closed her eyes, blinking back moisture sliding down her cheeks. She inhaled several times before she looked at him.

Damn, Case didn't want her to cry. He wanted to tell her she didn't have to speak of whatever it was that twisted her into knots. Stopped himself. Needed to understand her.

She began. Her words slow and precise. "That horrible day...it was an accident." She walked to the door with slow, even steps. "I didn't want to live. The Duchess told me since mother and father were gone that if I didn't come see them, she would send the duke to fetch me. One way or the other I was coming to London where they could watch over me. That was two years ago."

"You agreed? It was that easy?" Case knew there was more to this story than she was telling him. He didn't like the part where she stated she didn't want to live. "What the devil happened?"

Tara was shaking her head. "Not now. No more. Now it's your turn." She swallowed hard as if she tried to put memories to the back of her head. "Tell me about your father's sister. What was she like?"

Case sipped in a fragment of air. He couldn't go there. Yet, he felt obliged to tell her something. "She doesn't deserve consideration. A monster, if a woman could be described in that manner."

"That bad?" The sarcastic comment brought his attention back to her instead of dwelling on his past.

"Very well," Case said understanding he would have to talk or he would learn nothing more about Tara. "His sister was a bitch...!" A few seconds passed before he could finish. "That woman was my first lover. Fell in love with her. Thought we would be together for the rest of our lives. I was a fool. A stupid idiot. Vowed that would never happen again." His fists tightened.

"You weren't together."

"No, not for very long. Just long enough for her to make certain she was the sole owner of the Ferguson land. She was a lot older. I was eighteen. She was twenty-eight. I was three times a fool. Three times an idiot. Vowed I would never be so again." Case didn't want to say anything more. Tara had leverage to use against him if that was what she might wish to do.

Giving more information as if she owed him. "A carriage. A broken wheel. A cliff. I was thrown away from the carriage." Tara seemed to scrambled for words as pallor ghosted her face. Her lips thinned. Crease lines formed on her delicate forehead between her eyes. Case saw the pain, wished he could reach out to her, help her. Needed to pull her into his arms. Give her the life-giving reassurance that he cared. "The accident was horrible. He died. I didn't."

"Grant?"

"Yes."

~ * ~

Tara was finished with this conversation. To her amazement Case said nothing more. He didn't ask another question. He wrapped her in his arms, holding her close. She closed her eyes absorbing all the strength and heat from his hard body she could. Case stroked her back, the touch soothing. Held within the strong embrace of his arms, she felt cherished. Tara understood the feeling wouldn't last. Nonetheless, she absorbed and treasured the moments as if they would be the last.

Giving in to her tears she let the moisture gather then fall. Tara didn't want to cry. His questions brought the memories along with the images back to life. Vivid. Too real. Held close to Case, her body shook.

"Hush...it's alright. There will be no more questions tonight. We've both said enough. Bared our souls as much as two flawed people can do." Case's voice was light, soft, as if he spoke to a child.

She snuggled into him, embracing the heat of his masculine body. "It won't ever be alright. Will never be fine." With her hands on his chest, she put a bit of distance between them. Looking into his eyes, she spoke. "That day won't ever be alright. The best I can do is live with the memories. Later, I will tell you more. Tonight, I don't want to answer any more questions. Is that okay?"

His hand under her chin, Case smiled at her. With a soft caress, he brushed her lips with his. "Whatever you want, Princess. We've a sunset to watch, after that a meal to eat. We can order food after we watch the sun go down. No more tears. Only smiles coupled with laughter."

Still shaking she nodded her head. His arm around her shoulders Case led the way. They walked up a hill that looked over the valley to the west. Tara leaned into him once more absorbing his strength.

"You'll have to tell me if this is better than the one we saw at the top of Montmartre," Tara said. "We should compare each one."

"What about the one we watched go down over the Seine?" Case asked. "We will have to write a journal with all our impressions. A book for tourists. Tell them where the best sunsets are along with the most incredible sunrises."

Tara felt the rise of laughter as she thought on their words. "You write the journal. I'll read what you wrote then make a few comments."

His chuckle caught her attention. When he let himself feel free, his face lost all the lines of strain she was accustomed to seeing. "That doesn't sound fair to me. I would be doing all the work. You would be coasting on my thoughts."

As the other times they observed the sun vanish, Tara stood in front of Case while they watched the colors slash across the sky. His strong arms pulled her against him. More than any time before, Tara felt comfort along with security emanating from him. Something she hadn't felt since Grant's unfortunate death. She heard as well as felt each breath of air he inhaled coupled with the strong beat of his heart.

Once it was done, he turned her. His mouth descended onto hers. Warmth of the caress filled her. Shivers spiraled. Broke apart in a cavalcade of sensations. Without further encouragement, she separated her lips, opening for Case. Allowed him entry to the dark secret parts of her. She wanted him to explore. Her fingers wound into the depth of his hair.

She pulled.

He deepened the embrace.

When he ended the kiss, it was far too soon. He smiled down at her, a soft smile one that held promise of something more. "Hmm..." Tara didn't want to stop.

In his usual way, Case tapped her on the nose. "We can continue this in our room. Unless...you want an audience as you did last night. I'm feeling as if with little provocation I could toss your skirts right here. Tell me no."

Tara didn't want to tell him no. "You're right, we should go."

He laughed. "As you wish. Perhaps another time you will choose to have spectators. We will see. I'm open to whatever you want."

No one watched. They were alone on the hill. His hand around her waist he guided her toward the village. She stopped to look in the window of a small shop, intrigued by the ticking clocks as well as the music boxes. Thought that perhaps tomorrow she would stop here to buy one. She could give him a gift to remember her by. "I'll get the food," he told her. "I'll be right back. Don't go anywhere."

She gave him a quick nod. Where would she go? "Wouldn't dream of it." Her hands clenched in front of her, Tara watched him stroll toward the café. Case was so handsome he made her heart flutter as if she were a young girl with her first beau. No, she was a woman grown with her second beau. His hips narrow, his long powerful legs striding with purpose. So strong. So certain of himself. So very stubborn and unreachable. Case's shoulders were broad, his butt small. Tara put her hand to her mouth to stifle the giggle wanting to erupt. She never called that part of a man's anatomy a butt. She did call him an ass. He thought that was funny.

What was he doing to her? Changing her in too many ways to

count. She felt a bit giddy as well as lighthearted.

What she saw next terrified. Tara's breath caught in the back of her throat. She tried to call out a warning. Words wouldn't form. She was so afraid she froze. A man draped in black followed him. When he pulled a knife from his boot, she realized he meant Case harm. With a stifled cry of warning, Tara flew at the man, racing toward him.

"Case!"

She bowled into the man. The knife that had been aiming at Case's back slashed across her side. Tara screamed. Oblivious to the pain, she pummeled him with her fists, beating on his chest. "No! Stop! No!"

The man pushed her off then scrambled to his feet. "Bitch!" he cried out as he turned to flee. He ran, disappearing around a corner into an alley. People milled around them. Tara knew Case would want to race after the man.

"What the devil?" Case picked her up, dusting off her cape, his voice filled with concern. His hand came away, blood painting his fingers. "You're bleeding. What happened?"

"I..." Tara fought back the lump of fear in her throat. Tried to speak. "That...that man meant to kill you. I...st...stopped him." Tara slumped in his arms. Her eyes closed. She fought nausea churning in her stomach. Until that moment when Case mentioned blood, she felt no pain.

"Stay with me. Don't faint on me now. You're made of stronger stuff. Got to see the damage. Fix it, you know. Stop the bleeding. See to the damage."

Case picked her up. He carried her. Raced to their apartment.

"Nothing wrong with me. Nothing to fix...he missed you with his knife. Wanted you dead." Relief penetrated her fear. "You're alive." Tara inhaled a deep breath blessing to all the saints she could think of that Case was unharmed.

"The man got you. You little fool. Why?" Case sounded shocked she would try to protect him. "I don't need a woman's protection. What the bloody eyes did you think you were doing?"

Alarmed, dazed, she stared at him for a few seconds before she bristled. After that, Tara nestled herself into his shoulder determined not to argue with him. Pain began to slice through her side. If he didn't say anything bad and she kept her mouth closed, she might succeed in ignoring the throbbing ache. Case would discover she was not hurt that bad. She might have saved his life. This was merely a scratch. Tara moaned as she began to realize it was the excitement that kept the pain at bay.

Once inside the room, he kicked the door closed. "You've been quiet. Would you like to explain your actions. Do you have a death wish?"

Too many questions. "No and no."

He set her on the bed. As she watched he undid her cloak then tossed the garment to a chair. His fingers on her bodice, he slipped the buttons free. He moved on, pushing the sleeves of her gown down her arms.

"What are you doing?" To no avail, Tara slapped at his hands. Case was determined to see to her knife wound. "You...you...can't. Look at me."

"I can. Now, hush. If you want me to check out the damage, you're going to have to sit on your hands. I have to see you uncovered."

"Sit on my hands?" She wasn't at all certain... "Oh."

"That's better. Back on the street you were bleeding. I need to stop the blood then bind the wound. Check for infection. Would you like to finish with your clothing? I'm getting the bandages along with the ointment. Lower your gown to your waist. Undo your chemise."

"You have bandages...ointment?" If anyone would, Case would. He struck her as a man who was always prepared. Tara wasn't certain about the disrobing part of this scenario. Case could not bandage through the fabric. Could not see to the possible infection.

"In my line of work, it's necessary equipment. Bandages, ointment, scissors, needle and thread, tweezers can all come in handy." He returned to see she'd unfastened her blouse. With the rest of her clothing, her fingers were fumbling. "Now lie down on your side. Seems the knife caught you here." He touched where he thought the entry was. Without preamble, Case cut away her chemise along with her corset. She closed her arms over her breasts along with her eyes. Tara didn't believe what was happening. She was open to his perusal. He acted as seeing her unclothed was nothing to him. Of course, this was nothing to the man. He'd had countless lovers. She'd had none.

Her heart thundered. Even when she was engaged to Grant, she was never naked with him. She wasn't naked now. Very nearly. "You..." Tara's voice was thin as it seemed to stretch into nothing. "You're not looking at me. Are you?"

"A flesh wound. It's not very deep. I'll have this taken care of before you can blink." Case cleaned the wound, taking his time.

"I b—blinked. Can you finish? Please?" She was trembling not from the wound but from the languid caressing of his fingers.

Have to get all the tiny bits of cloth I can find out of the wound. Did you know? It's the material that is left behind that causes the injury to grow red and hot. Don't want you to have a fever come morning." He washed the cut.

Seconds ticked by turning to minutes. Tara shivered, her arms covering her. She was turned half way to her stomach as he tended to her. Case worked as if she wasn't naked. He didn't pay attention to anything except her wound. He put a soothing ointment on the slash that seemed to ease the pain. When he finished, he sat down beside her.

"You will live." Case's hand was on her shoulder, massaging. She sighed. "Drink this." He handed her a cup.

"What is it?"

"Laudanum, will take away whatever pain you might be feeling. Just a tiny bit. Later, I'll give you more. The drug will help you sleep."

She sipped. Sighed. Breathed in deeply.

"All of it."

Tara obeyed. Felt the easing of her pain. Felt nothing except the soft stroke of his hands.

He touched her, caressed as if a soft breeze fluttered against her. The feeling so sensual her breath caught in the back of her throat. The play of his fingers traveled along her arm then back to her neck. She remembered the kisses, the touch of his lips where his fingers were now. The teasing dance changed to something more erotic. Tara needed more.

Wanted the new ache to go away.

The sensation caused her to jerk. Her body hummed to life while he sent heat flaming within. His lips touched her shoulder, his teeth then his tongue. He bit across her back, lower. "Case..." a soft mewl followed. She moaned. A whisper of air rippled from her. Her body heated. She should tell him no. Tara couldn't form the word.

"I've been needing to do this for several nights now. What do you say? Should we explore what can go on between the two us if we're not arguing? Don't want to fight with you. Want to taste every part of you until we are both sated. Would you like that too, Tara?" Case turned her on her stomach. He flattened his hands on her back, sweeping them across her in such a light caress Tara didn't know when it began or when it ended.

Tara had no protest on her lips. The no that should be forthcoming wouldn't form. She didn't want to argue either. No, she wanted to explore him, discover who he was. His fingertip traced the length of her spine to the top of the band holding her skirt at her waist then back to her neck.

Shivers.

Tremors rocked her.

Heat filled her.

Case brushed her hair aside. His thumb drew gentle circles at the base of her neck while he held his hand there. She felt the possession. With the pressure of his hand and the motion of his thumb, he claimed her. His lips touched upon her. She tried to push from the bed. His hand on her shoulder kept her in place.

"Don't move."

"I want to see you," Tara whispered.

"You are wearing too much," Case's murmurer preceded kisses down her spine. One then two...three times and more his lips touched upon her. Twenty-two...twenty-three times before he stopped at her waistband. He did the same on his way back to her neck. His fingertip chose the same path as his mouth. "I want you. Tell me no before..." He didn't finish. "Before I won't stop. Do you hurt? I can stop now if you want."

"No, nothing hurts." She felt as if she dreamed.

Tara didn't want to tell him no. Didn't want him to stop the tender assault on her body. She needed to find out what would happen next. Needed to discover how all this would end. Her skirt fell away. Cool air brushed lower. He tugged on the fabric of her petticoats.

"Lift your hips, Princess. I want you naked. Need to see all of you."

The skirt slapped to the floor. He nipped her on her fanny then the other side. The sounds she heard came from her. Her stomach danced with the fire of a million fire breathing dragons. Muscles she didn't know she had clenched then pulsed.

"Oh! Oh...oh...oh, Case..." Whatever he was doing caused her to arch up asking for more. Her body contracted everywhere he touched. Muscles compressed.

"You've only your shoes and stockings. The sight is evocative. You are seducing me. Should I remove them?"

She was nodding but she didn't think he was waiting for the answer. This was all too naughty. With two separate thuds, her shoes hit the floor. Except for her maid, no one since she could remember saw her naked. Well, her mother as well as Ella had seen her naked. Not even her fiancé. Grant never saw her wearing nothing. He could have. He didn't. She'd wanted him. Just as she needed Case.

"Now for your stockings. I'll remove them one at a time." His fingers slid along the inside of her thighs. Higher to the apex. He touched places, deep dark secret spots, sliding his finger between her legs. "You're hot. Wet. I don't want to stop touching you. You are so soft. Soft everywhere. Move them wider. Part them for me. The sight of you like this all damp as well as hot for me makes me hard everywhere."

"Please..." Her nerves twitched. Stretched. Tara wanted to open her legs to give him greater access. She moved. Separated them for him.

"Please what? Make love to you? Unless you tell me no, soon you will find me deep inside you, Princess." He waited. She didn't say anything.

Tara was certain he was waiting for her to tell him no. "Make love to me," she sighed into the pillow beneath her head.

"If that's what you want."

The ribbon holding the sheer stocking in place loosened. His lips touched upon her sensitive skin. Moved up her leg while Case's knees separated her legs. He would be able to see all of her. Higher. Each stroke of his mouth went higher to touch upon her fanny again. After that, he nipped and kissed her thigh, behind her knee then the sole of her foot as he removed the stocking. Case sat back, hands on both rounded globes of her fanny. The touch was nice, soothing, undemanding.

"Shall I get rid of the other one? Wearing only one stocking you are quite the little tease. I like you like that. Tease me all you want as long as you deliver the promise you are offering."

"Yes...get rid of it," Tara breathed.

Case did the same. His mouth touched between her legs. He nipped her most private parts. Licked. His finger slid along her cleft. In then out. The seduction garnered what he wanted. He left no sensitive place on her untouched. Except... His attention went everywhere. He needed to kiss her again.

Tara's body flamed. Moaned. Sighed. Her belly clenched. He finally made his way back up her spine to her neck.

"You please me, Princess. Let's put you on your back. What do you say? I need to kiss those beautiful globes that tease and tempt a poor man's body. I wish to suck, nibble. Bathe you with the heat of my tongue." Taking care with her injury, he flipped her. "Would like to give the sweet rounded jewels on your front the same attention as your backside."

Tara was amazed, shocked when she saw him naked. She'd been so absorbed in the erotic dance he played on her body, she'd not heard his clothing hit the floor. With her elbows supporting her behind her body, she sat.

"Case?" Tara questioned as she stared at him, feeling as if her eyes bulged. Her gaze riveted on his arousal jutting out from a nest of dark black hair at his groin. She never understood how a man would look naked. He was beautiful. Intriguing. His body fascinated her. She wondered if all men were that well-endowed. She wanted to touch him.

"Are you pleased with what you see?" Case set his hand on her thighs. "Put your hands above your head."

"What?" Tara was shaking her head unsure of what it was he wanted. "I...?" She ran her tongue across her lips still questioning.

"On the headboard. Don't want you to touch me before I'm ready. Do as I say. Need you open to every possibility." His voice was husky, smooth. Dark. Vibrating.

"Oh...okay." Tara did as he asked. Her body was stretched out and bared for his perusal. She never felt so vulnerable or safe. Excited too. She clung to the headboard, her fingers gripping the top. "I..."

"Where shall we start? I know." He was between her legs again, parting them. Looking at her. His eyes dark, dark blue. Simmering. He stroked where his gaze rested. "I like looking at you." Her thighs rested on top of his legs. He could see all of her. Oh god, she could see all of him.

"I..." She closed her eyes with a soft moan of pleasure when his fingers brushed her cleft again. Stimulated. Her body spasmed with the thrilling contact.

"Do you like this? You're wet for me. Your moisture glistens here." He stroked her. Case bent over, the stubble of a day's growth brushed her belly.

Tara's body arched giving him the answer he requested. Leaning higher, he supped on one nipple while he continued stroking her. Tara arched. Moaned. Inside her body throbbed. A sweet purr of pleasure vibrated through her. She was beside herself with the ecstasy he created. Body pulsing, heat flowing. He pressed her legs farther apart.

"Soon I want your slender legs wrapped around my flanks." He nipped her inner thighs, laved to sooth the slight pain.

When his nips touched upon her belly, her stomach contracted with the pleasure. Case continued attending to one breast then the other. Sucking on each one. The heel of his hand pushed against her, raising her temperature, increasing her pleasure.

Sensations spiraled.

"Beautiful pussy." He kissed her stomach again then with strange tenderness bit each hardened tip of her breast. "Let it go, Princess. Trust me. Let your body soar until you can't do anything except ride the storm.

Keep your eyes open. I want to see them when you climax. When you have that sweet orgasm you've been waiting for. Did your other lovers give you pleasure? Did you climax?"

She did what he asked and she felt the thrilling sensations climb higher until all feeling broke from her. Her hips bucked and pulsed as he continued to stroke her, nip her, stimulate so thoroughly she could do nothing except ride the tempest. It seemed the sensations went on and on before he withdrew his hand from between her legs.

Now, he kissed her, his mouth framing hers, his tongue pushing into her mouth, dancing the same tune. Heat whirled and flamed inside her once more.

"You..."

"It is our turn now." He brought her hand down to the apex of her thighs. She felt the moisture that lingered there. "You are wet with your desire. Hunger runs through your sweet body. Touch yourself...here... I want to see you pleasure yourself while I add to the joy."

Tara did. She felt the nub where he caressed. Realized the same soaring sensations. He smiled at her before he gave his attention back to her breasts. "When you are ready, tell me."

The moan followed by soft purrs must have told him what he needed to know. He caressed her where her fingers had been a moment before. Tested. Watched her body's response.

"I'm..."

"I know." He thrust into her.

Her cry of pain stopped him. He thrust into her once, twice then a third time. His growl of release penetrated the pain vibrating deep inside her body. When he pulled out, he stared down at her. His face was a mask of fury.

Tara's breath caught in the back of her throat. "Case?" What was wrong? She had no idea why he looked so angry.

"Bloody, bloody, bloody everlasting hell! You're a damn virgin!" He left her. Pulled out of her body. She flinched with the sudden pain as her flesh was pulled. Her legs sprawled apart.

The blood on him was obvious. Tara couldn't move. She was terrified. Hurt by his words. She gave him her innocence. He loathed her.

Despised what she did. She recognized that look in his eyes. There would be no going back from this. He thought she betrayed him. She told him numerous times she never had a lover. It wasn't her fault he never believed what she said. His preconceived idea overshadowed the truth.

While she watched, confused, Case pulled on his pants, his boots. A second later he grabbed his coat. Curses flew from his lips. The door slammed shut behind him. She was left alone.

"I was a virgin," she said to the empty room. "Not anymore." A sob broke from her then another.

I don't know what I've done wrong. I gave myself to him just as he wanted. Just as I wanted. Nothing will ever be the same. I never expected permanence. He made that clear. Still, he will blame me.

The sound of the horse's hooves pummeling the ground raced through the open window. Case was leaving her behind. She would fend for herself. Since the accident that was what she did. Each day passed. Each day she was alone with her memories. With Case she thought she might make new memories. It wasn't to be. He reviled her because she had been innocent.

Case didn't want to see her. That was alright. She didn't want to see him either. The pain of his rejection stabbed her heart. He broke through the shell she kept around it to guard herself from this pain. She would build back the barrier. No one would ever break through again.

Minutes passed while she thought. Planned the next day before she roused herself from the bed. A small basin and a pitcher of water sat on a dresser. Tara bathed her blood along with his seed from her body then tossed the rag into the basin of water. She stared at the blood that was turning the left-over water soft pink.

Proof of her virginity. All that was left of her heart as well as her soul lay in the basin of water. What difference did it make, proof or not? She would toss the liquid away. Case knew the truth. He chose to vent his anger toward her. The man had no right to his fury. He wanted her. She gave herself to him because she thought she might be falling in love. Stupid thought. That was not what he wanted. She should have known better. Told him no. She thought he was different. What a fool she was.

I thought I was falling in love with him. How could I be so stupid?

Let down my guard? Fall for his sweet talking.

Case got what he wanted. No, from the way he acted, Case didn't want a virgin. Now, he hightailed it out of Versailles as if the hounds of hell were at his heels. So be it. I can get home by myself.

I can live with his revulsion.

Dressed in her chemise and stockings, Tara sat down to write Uncle Drake a letter. Given Case's reaction to her, she couldn't stay here longer than was necessary for her uncle to make the arrangements for her trip home. By the time she finished the note, her hands shook. Of all the things she expected in Versailles, this wasn't one of them.

Who would write correspondence for Case? That was no longer her problem. He would have to figure something out. Uncle Drake would send someone else to replace her. Under the circumstances, Aunt Ella wouldn't want her to remain in Paris. With the letter saying as little as possible tucked safely into a pocket of her cape, Tara set to work on the next phase of her return trip to Paris.

A sharp pain in her side reminded her she saved the ungrateful man's life earlier this evening. No, now it was yesterday. She stretched, easing her position on the bed. There were no stitches to secure her wound. Case reminded her she should take care. Excessive movement might mean she would have to have stitches.

He must not consider the lovemaking as excessive. She wasn't certain if she agreed with his assessment. Yes or no, it didn't make a difference now. He was gone. Fled from the room and her. Coward that he was. He couldn't stand for his preconceived notions of all women to be wrong.

Tara gathered her clothing, packing everything including her bloodied riding habit into the small valise she brought with her. Thoughts of running back to Paris came to mind. The road at night would be too dangerous. She didn't mean to compound one bad mistake with another one. She would wait until morning.

A restless sigh broke from her. Sleep would prove elusive at best. Why bother? The thought of lying on that bed horrified her. After she looked outside, she could see the night beginning to lighten. Soon, the roosters in the surrounding area would be crying out that a new day was beginning. Before she could fall asleep, it would be time to leave. Still at the writing desk, Tara set her head on her arms. She closed her eyes, not meaning to sleep.

The door slamming against the wall jolted Tara awake. Her head had been on the small desk in the room. She was still dressed in only her chemise and stockings. Tara blinked a few times when she saw Case, tall and bold as if he commanded all in sight, hands on his narrow hips staring at her. Accusing her.

"Case? What are you doing here? Thought you left." Tara had not expected him to return. She thought he would have gone back to Paris last night.

"Get dressed." He picked up the packed valise then headed outside. "Sunrise is saddled. We're going to Paris."

Her mouth gaped open as she watched Case slam out the door again. She stood at the door yelling at him. "I need my clothes!"

He came back, tossed the valise into the room. "Two minutes." The command reverberated down her spine. He would not wait for her if she was late. What did she care? She could find her way to Paris. Could have found it last night in the dark.

I didn't do anything wrong. He seduced me. He wanted my body just as much if not more than I wanted his. I gave him my innocence. What does he do? The man curses the fact I was a virgin.

Damn man. He was an ass. *Is an ass!*

When she was dressed then stood beside him, he stared at her. His voice harsh. "You should have told me."

"Told you what?" As far as she was concerned, Case was going to have to tell her what he meant...every word. She didn't wish to speak with him. Didn't want to hear any of his thoughts concerning last night.

His hands on her waist, he tossed her on her mount, sent a maelstrom of emotions and thoughts ricocheting in her head.

"You know bloody well what I mean!"

He was still cursing. If he was angry, she deserved to be angrier. "My, my aren't we in a nasty mood today. Didn't get any sleep last night? Neither did I." She nudged her horse forward. The clip she set wasn't too fast. Nonetheless, by the time he mounted, he would have to catch up to her that is if he wanted to ride beside her. Now that it was light outside, she wasn't about to wait for him. Tara didn't care if he stayed here. Didn't care what he did. The bloody man could fall off his horse for all she cared. She wouldn't stop to pick him up off the road. On the dirt was where he was supposed to be. He should grovel at her feet. Apologize for his cursed behavior.

When he rode up beside her, she kept her face straight ahead, unwilling to acknowledge his presence. This day would prove to be nothing like the one before. There would be no sweet laughter or sharing of the past. No inexplicable bonding. Tara thought they bonded in some way.

"How is the knife wound?" Case asked. His voice had gentled. He didn't command an answer. He asked as if he deserved an answer.

As far as Tara was concerned, she was alone. Case swore beneath his breath. Good, he created this atmosphere. Let him live with the anxiety he orchestrated. A mile stretched by in silence then another. Tension mounted.

"Did I hurt you last night?"

Tara glowered at him before she continued the silence. Refused to acknowledge his presence. Refused to answer inane questions that were not his business. Case gave up that right when he stalked from the bedroom cursing her.

"Are you sore?" he persisted.

Since he abandoned her, raced out in a fury of rage, none of the answers to his questions concerned him. How she felt was no longer his business. Even so, heat suffused her face, which she tried to ignore. She'd never done anything like she did last night. Had never been so brazen, so bold. Wanton.

Case reached out to grab her reins bringing her to a stop. The horses sidestepped. Sunrise tried to rear. Case held firm on the reins. "Answer me! Damn you!" All pretense at gentleness vanished with the heated command.

Once more she didn't say anything. Tried to reclaim the reins to her horse. Her angry gaze met his furious one. With a soft sigh, she spoke, more firmly this time, "How I feel is not your bloody concern. By your actions last night, you gave up the right to know. If the wound bothers me, I'll see a doctor when we reach the city. As to the other, when you stormed out without a word of explanation, curses fallowing the air, all tender feelings I might have had for you vanished. You've no place in my life, Case Ferguson. I expect from your behavior you feel the same about me."

"I will take responsibility if there is a child." His words were fierce.

"There won't be." It was plain to see he didn't want a bastard.

Her second attempt to snatch the reins back was also aborted. "You won't rid yourself of the child if there is one."

"If there is one, you will never know."

~ * ~

Tara stormed through the door. Behind her Case was hot on her heels. Stupefied, Ash watched as the pair separated without a word to him. Both slammed the doors to their respective rooms. He heard Tara's valise hit the door hard. After that silence from both rooms.

What the devil?

They would both have to come out sometime to eat. Questions swirled in his head as he tried to curb the impatience to discover what was going on between them. He bet on Case showing himself first. The man would not hide in his room. Tara, on the other hand, would withdraw into herself doing that breathing thing she always did when she was agitated. Once she calmed, Tara might show herself. If not, he would have to knock on her door. He needed to talk to her. Something happened. She would want someone to confide in. He had to make sure she didn't go back to that horrible place she'd been in two years ago when Grant died. No one died today.

Ash was right in his assessment of the situation. Ten minutes later Case stormed from the room to the sideboard where he poured himself a hefty portion of bandy. The man didn't come out to eat. He came out to drink. The situation must be worse than he thought. His mind raced with possible scenarios. He needed to nip this dicey situation in the bud before it could fester.

"Women...!" Case downed the glass. He poured another. "Damn woman!"

Well, Ash thought with the slightest grin, what Case muttered was true. The fact he narrowed his curse to one woman told a major tale. His chuckle brought on a scowl from Case. "Women do have a way of muddling up the works, now, don't they? What happened between the two of you? Both stomping as well as swearing. Is Tara going to come out of her room?" After joining Case with a glass of brandy, he sat down across from him, studying the expression on his face. "Might have to go in after her."

"You'll be a dead man if you do!"

He shouted possession. That was interesting. No doubt about it the man was furious. Confused. Annoyed. He looked as if he could spit fire. What did Tara do this time? All his female cousins had this way of driving a man to drink. The fact Case was on his third brandy in such a short time proved that point. No doubt the fury was directed at Tara.

"What happened?" Ash asked tongue in cheek, beginning to realize there would be no forthcoming answer from this man.

"None of your business," Case growled before tossing back the remaining brandy in his glass.

"You going to get smashed?" Ash asked, dreading the possibility. They had a place to be tonight.

"Whatever it takes to get her out of my head," Case retorted with heat staining his words.

"You shouldn't," Ash said, thinking again about the commitment they all had tonight that it was obvious Case forgot. Tara too.

The interpretation to this interesting situation that flashed through Ash's dusty brain was that the man tried to make love to her and was soundly put down. Either that or he did make love to her and failed to give her pleasure. Neither scenario sounded right. Each one, off kilter the tiniest bit to ring true. In time, he might discover the truth. It was obvious that Case wasn't going to inform him why he was boiling mad, why Tara was in her room in an obvious sulk...furious, too, if he didn't miss his guess.

"Very well. I gather whatever happened can be construed as private. I will keep out of this unless the two of you can't fix the underlying problem. In case you forgot, both of you still have to work together," Ash said unable to keep humor from lacing his tone. This was amusing.

The lady killer meets the innocent maid. All hell breaks loose.

Case's snort told Ash more than Case would have wanted him to understand though he had no salient facts to go with the grunt.

Ash decided he might as well make certain he remembered what was expected. "The ball is tonight. You and Tara are supposed to attend. Do you think the two of you can be civil for an entire night?" Ash was just about to expand on this when his thoughts were interrupted.

"Not going!"

Ash never heard Tara's door open. Never knew she was listening. Though it was clear she'd been in the room for enough time to understand the gist of the conversation. The two answered in unison with the same words. Ash took the moment to grin, the devil inside him needed to understand everything that was going on with the pair. This was all far too amusing.

"No choice unless you wish to bring down the wrath of the Duke of Richmond along with that of the SIS. You and Case are scheduled to meet with a Monsieur Raynard at the ball. He will give pertinent information to you. Information that will have to be acted on in an expedient manner." Ash turned his attention to Tara, "You must read then translate the information for Case so he understands what is said in the missive perfectly. This isn't a question of want. It's your job. There is no choice for either of you."

"Not mine," Tara said as she marched to the sideboard to pour herself a brandy. "Not my job. Didn't sign up for this. No longer wish for any part of this so-called job."

Ash could tell by the tone that his cousin reconsidered. She would feel obligated if not to his father but to Ella. Case held up his glass in salute as if to say, job well done. After the accident Tara would do about anything his father asked of her. Tara swayed on her feet, her face pale, stress lines around her eyes. Ash wasn't at all sure what to do if both of them were two sheets to the wind by the end of the evening. He didn't want to find himself responsible for either, least of all both. If that were the situation, anything could happen. It wasn't his intention to babysit these two adults. He was going to see Lou Lou after he put in an appearance at the ball. After he did his duty.

Heaving a sigh that was clearly one of resignation, Tara spoke. "What time are we leaving?" Then to the maid who hovered in the doorway. "Draw me a bath. You can help me get dressed in about a half hour. I owe the duke. Nothing will ever change that."

"Me too," Case caved into the pressure Ash presented. "Guess there is no choice. Don't want to risk my position with the duke or the SIS."

"Good, we'll leave at seven. The two of you might think about figuring out how you can be civil during the night. This event is far too important for the two of you to be at tenterhooks when you are supposed to be—"

"Shut up!" Again, the two people at odds with each other spoke in unison turning their anger on Ash.

Ash jumped at the venom he heard in both voices. "What devil has possessed the two you? Last time I saw you nothing was this bad. In fact, you seemed to enjoy each other's company. When you left alone, I thought the two of you would return as lovers." When Ash got the chance, he would dance with Tara. She might spill some of the problems between them. "The two of you will be presented together. At least pretend for the duration of the evening that you can stand the site of each other. You have a little over four hours to get yourselves ready, mind as well as body." Ash felt as if he dealt with children. No, angry toddlers who fought over a toy. He would be happiest when he could retire for the night then visit his new mistress.

"Is there any food in the kitchen?" Tara asked as she headed in that direction. "A certain person here didn't allow me to eat this morning. Didn't stop for a noon meal. I'm famished." Tara turned to glower at Case. Emotions sizzled between the pair.

"Didn't stop you from racing here," Case shot back as he stepped in front of her on the way to the kitchen. "If you mentioned hunger pains we could have stopped long enough to eat. Don't blame your hunger on me. If you recall, you wouldn't talk to me. Gave me the cold shoulder."

"Children! Worse, infants!" Ash clapped his hands together to grab their attention. He found himself smirking. "Behave yourselves. I'm certain Gateau has food enough to tide the two of you over until the ball."

"As soon as...she...translates this all-important missive, I'm leaving," Case threatened while he downed more brandy.

Thinking of himself, Ash swore. Case needed to get control of his emotions. Maybe he should lock the two in a room. They could fight it out. Case would never physically hurt Tara. Would he?

"You can't leave. The two of you must dance. Must present a united front. We don't want anyone believing there is trouble with the secret service. There are spies everywhere willing to report discord to their superiors."

Chapter Seven

Ash walked behind the feuding couple. Case attempted to take Tara's arm on their way to the carriage. She stepped aside, keeping her distance. What infuriated him more was when she dropped back to accept Ash's arm. She smiled at the man. Jealousy exploded. He tapped the despised emotion down. The blame for this rested solely on him. Nonetheless, when he attempted to sort out the problem, Tara remained speechless. After he discovered her virgin status, he needed to ride, to think. She wasn't what he thought her to be. He never made mistakes of this magnitude. Neither Ash or Jeremy had been her lover. Even this Grant person she so adored had not made love to her. He was the only man who discovered her passion. Tapped into the sexual hunger that exploded within her with his touch. He was so shocked, he never gave her pleasure...only pain.

Case gritted his teeth. He needed to change this situation. Didn't understand how to do so.

The devil, last night he'd been a fool. Truth was, he didn't know how to handle the knowledge that Tara had never given herself to another man. He never considered himself a defiler of innocents. Made it a habit to never take virgins to his bed. That was what he did while she tromped on his misconceived notions. He didn't like feeling as an ass at the hands of a female. Numerous times she told him that he didn't know her at all. Tara proved him right on that score.

When they spoke about their past, he saw pain in her eyes. Hurt was evident in her speech along with her mannerisms. Now he understood the pain was real. Case still didn't know what caused the raw hurt he read in her eyes when she spoke of Grant along with the anniversary. Someday she would tell him. If the cursed woman would tell him about her past, he'd understand so much more about her. This misunderstanding was her fault. All of what happened was her doing. Now she wasn't talking.

Not tonight. Tonight, Tara MacLaren didn't want anything to do with him. Just as she didn't want anything to do with him on their return journey from Versailles. If he could, he would find a way to ease the pain he caused. *Talk to me, Tara.* Case didn't believe a mere apology would do the trick. He'd never seen a woman so hurt or so angry. Never seen the pain so evident. The look in her beautiful amber eyes spoke of betrayal. Betraying her last night had not been his intention. He should tell her he was incapable of love. Deep in his heart, Case understood Tara searched for love.

That's the conversation, laddie, that needs to be aired before she falls in love with me. After yesterday she would never fall in love with him. Perhaps his mission was accomplished.

True, Tara desired him. He could change her anger to passion with a few seductive kisses if she would allow him close enough for a kiss.

Sweettalk.

Charm.

All would work with the lady. He would be a cad of the worst sort if he took her into his bed again. After a week or two, even a month he would leave her. Tara would never understand why. He didn't want to be the next man who hurt her. Case could not tell her that for him a relationship with a woman was all about the preliminaries. The hunt along with the catch. Once the chase was initiated, the association never lasted more than a few weeks. The sex was also part of it but not the most important. He never failed to give a woman the orgasm she sought. In this case, she felt no pleasure...only pain. He wasn't ever going to give this woman what she wanted from him. Love.

He couldn't.

In the carriage, Tara sat next to Ash. She made a point of staring out the window rather than look at him. Ash tried to make idle conversation. The young pup tried to engage them both in tête-à-tête. Frustration whipped inside, showing itself in a long sigh. Ash spent the ride with a mischievous grin on his face.

Case didn't like the fact Tara sat next to Ash. Didn't want to think about her dancing with Ash or anyone else. She should be in his arms...only his arms...never anyone else's arms. A man shouldn't have to watch his woman in the arms of another man no matter how stupid he'd been.

Tara is not my woman.

Reminding himself of the fact was important. Case listened to the idle chatter between the two friends.

Two friends.

Tara told him she and Ash were friends, nothing more. What about Jeremy? She told him they were friends, nothing more. He never believed her. With proof of her virginity, what she told him must be the truth. She also told them she didn't lie. He never knew a woman who didn't lie.

She gave her innocence away to him. That was a point he couldn't refute. Funny thing was, he'd never taken a virgin. It might be that reason why he stormed out of the room feeling betrayed. Shocked. Disabused. The devil, he left her with his seed and virgin's blood to deal with. He should have been more intuitive. Should have known she might be frightened. Case didn't think she was scared. Mad as a hornet, yes. Frightened, no.

No matter how many times he tossed recrimination at himself, he could not get the picture of her out of his head. When he stormed out, Tara was still sprawled on the bed, her hair in wild disarray around her head. Her inner thighs were stained red with her blood along with his seed.

Case still hadn't made one move to apologize. He could have told her he was sorry. Thought that would have made the situation worse. She'd been too angry and hurt when they arrived at the apartment in Paris. Besides, he didn't have the words. He wasn't a diplomat with flowery words and phrases that would turn a person's mind to his way of thinking. He was a bounty hunter, rough around the edges. Forceful. Uncouth at times. Vulgar. Able to kill when necessary. Tara deserved more. Deserved a man who would cherish her. Dote on her every word.

"We are here," Ash said as he watched the two players in a game that could turn deadly at any time. They were in a foreign country. "You two pretend you like each other. Case, you know a great deal depends on what happens at these soirees." Ash never thought he would end up lecturing Case or Tara. Though Tara was new to the world of intrigue, Case was not. The agent was experienced.

"Don't worry," Case said as he stepped from the carriage, his hand extended to help Tara with the steps that were put at the door by the driver.

It appeared that Tara buried her fury even to granting Case a hesitant, shy smile. She allowed him to help her then graciously held onto his elbow as they walked to the entrance. The introductions were made to the assembled guests. The two in question smiled at each other as if they were not at odds only a few minutes before.

Case bent to whisper close to her ear. A lover's caress was his thought as he saw Tara shiver then jerk away not allowing her the distance she seemed to crave. His touch was soft. His breath whispered close. He touched the lobe of her ear with the tip of his tongue. "Dance or food first?"

"Food," her voice shivered. "I'm starving."

The answer didn't surprise him. A dance would put her into his arms. A place where she didn't wish to find herself. Before the end of the evening, he would hold her close, dance with her. He wasn't going to give her a choice. Nodding to individuals, they smiled as they made their way to the table that was loaded with all types of delicacies, Case directed her. At the table he filled two plates then poured them each a glass of wine.

"*Bonsoir*," Tara nodded to a gentleman who was staring at her breasts.

"*Mademoiselle.*"

Case's gut tightened. He didn't like the possessiveness rushing to his head. Didn't like the man's lecherous stare that ran the length of Tara who seemed oblivious. She sipped the wine before she used her fingers to put shrimp in her mouth. He watched her chew. As if she sensed him staring at her, she looked up. He placed another shrimp in front of her mouth. Smoothed the food along her bottom lip, teasing her.

"Open," Case wanted different parts of her body opening to him. Wanted to give the message to that man. Tara was his.

He saw the shiver spiral through her. She obeyed. He felt her lips press against his fingers as she took what he offered.

"You don't need to feed me," Tara said with a tremulous voice. "I can do that myself."

"I know. Enjoying myself. I find I like the way your lips caress my fingers when you open for me. Wet. Do you recall how wet you were last night?" Case liked everything about the rose stain splashing her cheeks. She wasn't oblivious to him.

"At my expense?"

"Never."

He led her to a table on a balcony that overlooked the gardens. A place where a man could steal a kiss from a willing *lass*. If he hadn't made such a mess of the evening before, the garden paths were romantic for strolling. Far in the distance he noticed a gazebo. On such a balmy night as this one, the place would be far too busy. Privacy would be lacking. Kisses though didn't require privacy. Case proved that pertinent fact the night they visited the cabaret.

Case took her hands in his. Brought them to his mouth, where he kissed her knuckles. He supposed even though he made love to her, because of his *faux pas* the pursuit was still on. He was far from apprehending her. "Will an apology be accepted?"

Tara tugged on her hands, her eyes blazing. When he let her go, she placed them in her lap. "Yes and no. For tonight the apology is accepted. If you've plans to humiliate me again in that fashion, no. An apology will not put me in your bed at another time. I don't make that a habit of allowing any man into my bed. You...you were..." before she could finish, she looked away.

"Your first," he finished for her. An eyebrow rose as he waited for her to answer. To Case the stretching silence told him none of this came easy for her.

"Yes."

"I don't plan on humiliating you or hurting you. While now that I'm accustomed to the fact you haven't had lovers, I do want you in my bed." Though he did want to make love to her more than one more time. Needed to discover if a second time would result in as much raw passion between them. Needed to introduce her to a woman's pleasure. Wished to see her eyes when she climaxed. He could wait until she became comfortable with him. Seemed he was starting from the beginning. He could do this. He was experienced. Case ran his knuckles along her jaw then down her neck. He watched as her pulse raced with the fleeting contact.

She wasn't immune. Together their passion could burn Paris to the ground.

"You have such a glib tongue. Such a sugarcoated way with words. Would you be surprised if I told you that after what happened just yesterday, I've a hard time believing anything you say?" Tara asked, sarcasm coating what she said.

Disturbed by her words, Case ran a finger between the collar of his shirt and his neck. "I am sorry about what happened between us. I take all the blame. You should know that I've never behaved so horribly with a woman." Case thought the confession would ease his way to a more amenable night if not the sharing of his bed.

Her soft laughter surprised him. "Lucky woman, is that what you're trying to tell me? Don't know if I feel that way. Lucky. You left me. I had no idea what I did to cause your wrath. The departing horse's hooves beat in my head for the hours you were gone. I was both terrified and furious."

Ash stood beside the table a smirk on his face. "If you've finished eating, would you dance with me? I'll be leaving soon. As you know, I've no commitment to fulfil here. Thought the two of you might give me some advice."

Without a blink Tara stood accepted his invitation. "Yes, a dance would be nice. I've a need for someone different to talk to. Conversation with Case was growing boring."

"I've ulterior motives, you know. Would love to find out what brought you and Case to fisticuffs. Would you be willing to enlighten me?" Ash helped Tara from her seat at the table.

Case could still here every word. He glowered. His brows were laced together as if one.

"Verbal fisticuffs," Tara corrected. "As to the second part of the question, the answer is no. "What happened is between the two of us. Don't need a third party to intervene. All has been settled." She looked at Case as they walked onto the floor.

He nodded.

"Verbal. I take it there were no blows," Ash agreed with a gallant wave of his hands. Then he drew her into his arms.

Even though Case understood firsthand that Tara never slept with another man, he couldn't help but think about the future. Tara was a beautiful woman. Passionate. Ash was a friend as was Jeremy. What kind of choices would she make now that she lost her maidenhead? Who she bedded would no longer matter. Would it? Would she become promiscuous as most women. Take men to her bed just because? Just because she could.

Now that he introduced her to intimacy, she might decide to test other men. See if they would come to her as willingly as he did. First, he needed to find a means to get Tara over her pique. He thought he understood women. Believed he was a master manipulator. Tara was right. He didn't know anything about her.

Tara bedeviled him. Touched a part of him that had never been moved.

When she was close, he couldn't think. Hell, even when she wasn't close, he couldn't think of anything except her.

While he watched, he finished his plate of food. As the music ended, Ash brought her to the table with another plate of food along with a second glass of wine.

"I'm not going home to the apartment tonight," Ash began while he pulled out a chair to sit down.

"Your new mistress calls?" Case asked feeling delighted he and Tara would be alone. He felt as if he could start to mend the fence he ripped down last night. He didn't have hopes of Tara falling into his bed this evening. Nonetheless, he would have the privacy to talk with her, to reason. Explain. Put out his excuses for the best that they were. They could always plan the archery contest they spoke of on the way to

Versailles before all hell broke loose between them.

Case saw Tara visibly flinch. She stopped eating. Instead, she drank more of the potent wine. He wished to dance with her after Ash left to mingle with the crowd of people they were supposed to meet.

"Dance with me, Princess." He grinned at her expression when he spoke his given name for her. Tonight, she couldn't deny him the pleasure of its use. Her hands were tied. They promised no arguments. When they returned home, he was certain she would unleash all the fire power she could muster. She would use all her cannons to blast him.

"If we must," Tara told him, her smile insincere. "I will dance. It's better than having you stare at me."

"Mayhap I'll stare at your petty bosom." Case looked down to see a shade of rose paint the tops of the rounded jewels he kissed last night. Fondled. Tasted. His mouth watered. He longed to have a second savor of the tight hard buds at the tips of her breasts. Doing so would take a lot of work.

"Do what you must." The resignation in her voice was obvious. "I'm sure there are other women in this room who would enjoy your attention more than me. You should center your interest on a woman who cares."

"I will stare at whatever pleases me," Case told her holding his hoot of laughter back. "As for other women, I don't want anyone except you." He had to possess her again. That one time was not enough. The way it ended must be remedied.

Case whirled her onto the dance floor. Tara was an excellent partner. She moved easily with fluid grace that couldn't be denied. The tempo quickened. They matched each other step for step. Case wound through the couples in intricate patterns. As the dance progressed, he pulled her closer. To his delight, she didn't resist.

He caught the enchanting scent that was only Tara's; sunshine and lilies. His breath stalled. When he reached an opening, he danced her onto a small balcony meaning to take advantage of a moment of privacy. She was pressed against the wall. They were hidden by a potted palm, its fronds shielding them from the view of the ballroom. Her breaths were short pants that sent her body closer to his. Her breasts rose and fell in a delicious cadence.

His hand wrapped around her neck, his thumb exploring all the tender flesh he could find along the slender column. "Would you kiss me as you did last night? I need to taste you again." Case's question was one he'd been wanting to ask for over an hour.

Tara's lashes lowered over her amber eyes. When she opened them, he saw the same desire he admired last night. The same raw passion deepened the amber color to dark brown. With infinite slowness, giving her time to say *nay*, he lowered his head. His lips brushed against hers, once then twice.

"Oh...oh..." she sighed into his mouth as she opened for him. His tongue met hers before he withdrew. Her hands crept to his shoulders then around his neck, holding him close. Tara tasted of the sweet red wine she'd been drinking...as well as something that was uniquely Tara.

Case felt her nails on his scalp. They scraped. All he wanted was to lower her bodice so he could feel as well as see her breasts. He wanted to pull her legs around his flanks then drive into her. This time he wouldn't hurt her, nor would he curse her virginity.

No, I already did that. She's no longer innocent. I saw to that. More guilt than he felt in a lifetime swept through him.

This time he would give her the pleasure she deserved. Tugging on her bottom lip with his teeth, she opened for him again then accepted his tongue inside the sultry heat of her mouth. He ran his hand up her rib cage to hold her breast in his hand. Tara gasped from the contact but didn't draw away. He didn't understand how he got so lucky.

This was not the time or the place. With great reluctance on his part, he put distance between them. One hand rested against her throat. His thumb ran along her lip, feeling the moisture left from their shared intimacy. He wished he could do more.

"You are damp, moisture here. Does that mean what I hope it means?" Case asked, his arrogance easy to read if she was looking.

She would not understand. Maybe she would. Tara was new to this game they played. It would be difficult for her to learn. He made up rules as he went along.

"We should go back to the dance floor." Her voice was

ragged...thin. Filled with raw passion. Passion he discovered rose quickly in this woman. The throes of desire would keep her from thinking about consequences.

"I want to kiss you again," he murmured as his mouth framed hers one more time. He should do what she wanted. She should tell him what that was.

The tap on his shoulder surprised him. He didn't wish to break contact with Tara. Case was certain it was Ash returning to torment them or persuade them to behave themselves. When he turned to meet the man standing behind him, he stiffened. This was it. He would not have tonight to mend fences with Tara.

"Raynard..." Case spoke with a soft Scottish burr. "You are here. That can be meanin' only one thing."

"We were to meet tonight. Monsieur...Mademoiselle." Raynard nodded. "I don't mean to interrupt your...er...discussion. However, I'm on a strict schedule that needs to be adhered to." He handed Case a sealed envelope. "Take care." He vanished into the crowd.

Case placed the envelope in an inside pocket. Tara's hand in his, he led the way to the table where they'd been sitting and drinking wine. Ash was nowhere to be seen. He would have to tell Tara something. Since Ash wasn't nearby, he would also have to escort her home before he left.

"Don't you think that was a bit dramatic?" Tara paused watching him. "This is what we came here for?" Tara asked as they sat. She sipped the wine while she watched him open the sealed envelope.

"Yes..." Case was hesitant to read what was inside. Before the night finished, he knew Tara would have to read the words too. She'd been hurt yesterday by someone who was after him. If this missive gave him new orders, he would be gone. Tara would be by herself. Ash could not be trusted to be with her when she took a notion to go somewhere. Case didn't want to think about Jeremy escorting her anywhere.

He placed the written words into the envelope before tapping it on the table. "You will read this to me when we return home." Case comprehended enough of written French to understand he was going to leave this evening. He would travel to the southern part of France. His bounty was spending his time on entertainment of the seedier sort. Enjoying the ill-gotten gains. After selling a valuable painting from Windsor Castle no less, the man was basking in the sun.

The sooner he finished this mission the sooner he could return to Tara. The sooner the two of them could finish the business they began over a week ago. For her safety, he hoped Lord Montgomerie wasn't amenable to her return to London. Though Case didn't wish to return to an empty apartment. He didn't think Tara would be leaving any time soon.

Some of that was Case's interpretation of what transpired. Some of his thoughts were in a direct line to his briefing from the duke before he set off on this mission with Tara and Ash. Whatever amends Case would be making would happen when he returned. He was certain Tara would still be in Paris.

"Get your cloak." Case stood, his chair grinding against the tiles on the balcony. He was impatient now to do the job he'd been brought to France to complete. Impatient to return to see what would happen between him and Tara.

"We should tell Ash that we're leaving," Tara said sounding a bit concerned about departing alone with him.

"Ash left when we danced. Watched him leave the ballroom. He won't be back tonight. Nothing for us to tell. He's otherwise engaged for the evening."

"His mistress?" she asked, a hesitant smile on her lips. "Hope she is deserving of his attentions. He's a good man."

"Man?" Case questioned with a chuckle. "Ash is a damn pup." Case had more important matters to think about as they said their goodbyes to the hosts. He led her to the waiting carriage. His mind now engaged on the mission he was about to embark on, he gave little attention to Tara sitting across from him until they were almost to the apartment.

"I've been remiss. Should have told you what I expected while I'm gone," Case said just as the coach rolled to a stop. "I have little time now to go over the rules as well as my expectations."

"That won't be necessary. I sent my letter to the duke before we left. Gave it to my maid. She promised to deliver the missive to the post. When you return, you won't be bothered by me. I'm going home."

His smile stretched across his face as he watched her hands flutter. "You understand the duke will never give you permission to return unless you give a detailed reason as to why. Did you do that? Did you explain about last night as well as how I took your innocence?" His gut tightened at the thought of the duke knowing. He might hang him just as he threatened the MacInnes. "What did you tell him?"

"He's not like that."

"What did you tell him?" At the thought she might have written exactly what transpired to procure her abrupt turnabout, his gut clenched. His heart throbbed hard against his ribs while he waited for an answer.

"Not what you're thinking. What happened between us isn't going to happen again nor is it my uncle's business. What we shared is between us. No one else."

"Uncle?" The one word stopped him cold. Sent a chill straight to his heart. Sweat broke out on his forehead. "Let me get this straight. The Duke of Richmond, Lord Montgomerie is your uncle? Why the devil did you never tell me? And Ash? He's your cousin?"

"Yes, of sorts, Ella is my mother's cousin. Don't know what that makes Ash except..."

"Related." Case finished for her, anger for her silence growing. "Ash is a friend who is related to you." Answers to a million questions were now coming clear. "Is Jeremy a cousin of sorts too?"

"Of course not." Tara stepped from the carriage with Case's assistance.

Case placed her hand in the crook of his elbow as they walked up the steps then into the apartment. He felt lighter by far. Questions he had about her were beginning to fall into place. Ash was no longer a problem...but Jeremy? Jeremy was the biggest threat.

~ * ~

While Case packed to leave, Tara sipped several glasses of wine.

Since he didn't have time in the carriage to give her a list of things she could not do, he spent five minutes after he was packed telling her she could go nowhere without her cousin accompanying her. What he expected pretty much boiled down to making her a prisoner in one of the most enchanting cities in the world.

Tara remained silent during his tirade. She wasn't about to tell him he could go to hell. What he didn't know wouldn't hurt the man. If she mentioned to him that his rules along with whatever he decided to demand could go straight to hell, he would turn livid. If she told him he was an ass for telling her what she could as well as could not do, he would laugh. Would figure out some way to keep her confined. Staying couped up in the apartment would not help her mood. He could be gone weeks.

She intended to shop until she couldn't walk any longer. A new wardrobe would be wonderful. It had been two years since she went to a modiste for new things. She would bring back small souvenirs for the cousins who lived near her. There were a few toy shops on the streets nearby. If Ash was amenable, she would let him attend her on those days. Before Case left, Ash had plans to visit Bordeaux. Tara was tempted to ask him to take her with him.

That wouldn't do. The trip was to be with some of his French friends. Male friends Tara added on a second thought. Even Ash wouldn't take up with another female when he kept a mistress. Thinking of Ash's mistress, a wicked thought fluttered through her head. Despite the fact meeting this woman would create an *on dit*, Tara thought she should visit the lady. See if she was good enough for her cousin. Rumors to such a fact would be ripe when Case returned. She relished the very thought.

Oh! Yes! Tara meant to visit Madame Pipelet too. A discussion might be necessary. Not only did she wish for female company, she'd heard other things about the woman. Tara pressed her hands against her flat belly wondering. Case addressed the issue of a possible pregnancy. Until he spoke the words that thought never crossed her mind. She didn't want to have a baby.

While she didn't believe she would abort a child, she needed to be prepared if he made love to her again. If she didn't conceive that first time, Tara meant to make certain conception would never happen. That kind of chance should never be taken if there was a means to prevent a child.

From overheard conversations, Tara knew that Ella got contraceptives from Madame Pipelet whenever the duke and duchess visited Paris. She also knew the woman could concoct a potion that would rid a woman of an unwanted child. Tara was going to visit her. Listen to everything she had to say. Make decisions for herself based on her needs. Case had no rights to comment or demand.

Tara was on her third glass when Case stood in front of her, a small valise in hand. She looked up. "It's time? You're going to be gone in a minute? How nice."

He nodded. Case pulled her to stand. "I want you to behave yourself," he said, his voice solemn. "You can't act like a witless hoyden while I'm gone. I'm warning you. Don't take chances with your life. Until this man is caught, there is danger here for you."

His insult stiffened her spine. *A witless hoyden?* How dare he? "I can act any bloody way I want to act! Can do anything that pleases me. You don't have a say! You're nothing to me!" She tried to wrench from his hold. Case's grip tightened.

"No. No you can't. I'm not nothing to you, Tara. We've been intimate." Case set her glass aside before pulling her to her feet. His lips found hers.

The kiss was hard. Meant to ensure her good behavior. She resisted. Tara wasn't having anything to do with his commands. She pushed on his chest, unwilling to give into the easy rise of passion he generated. Tara didn't want to feel the way she did about this man. She needed to fight the feelings. She had to stand firm against his wicked ploys. Tara pulled her mouth from his.

"I'm not yours to order around!" Tara shot back when he withdrew from her. She couldn't grasp a breath of air.

His hand rested on her throat, running along her jaw then higher to touch the moisture on her lips left behind from his kiss.

"True. Would it matter that I'm just trying to protect you from harm. Would my opinion make a difference if you knew I care about what happens to you?" His voice was beguiling and sweet. Sugarcoated. In a strange infuriating way, tender while he looked down at her with hooded dark blue eyes. Passion filled eyes. Raw desire simmered. "I want you here safe and well when I return. Don't disappoint me."

"I told you I'm leaving. Just have to wait until Uncle Drake arranges my passage. I'll be out of your way. You don't need to worry about me. When you return, you'll be able to do what you please without offending me." Tara said.

"We shall see," he told her, his confidence bubbling over.

"What does that mean?" Tara shot back realizing Case must have some understanding beyond her insights.

"You will be here when I return." His smile widened, his eyes alight with amusement that only he understood.

"You don't know anything." Tara said her voice unsteady. He sounded so bloody self-assured. "What do you know about my leaving?"

"You've said that before. This time I do have insight into this situation. You see. I also wrote Lord Montgomerie. Told him how much I needed you. What an asset you were to the correspondence that I need to write as well as read. Also told him we had a bit of a misunderstanding that would be cleared up as soon as I returned. Just sent the note off with a messenger." Between his fingers he held up a strand of her hair that had fallen loose. He lifted the strands so he could test the scent. "And...I intercepted the letter you asked your maid to deliver. That one will never reach your uncle. True, you can write another one. Mine will be read first. What do you think? He will send for you or ignore your request? Hmm..."

Tara felt a burst of anger then relief. She didn't want to go home. Wished to see what might happen between them if they could cease the endless arguments. The trouble was Case infuriated her to such a degree she did things she would never do under normal circumstances. She acted on her emotions rather than logic. She was impulsive as well as headstrong. Those weren't characteristics she was proud of.

I let him make love to me. Not just one time. I want to...

Heat began to spread on her cheeks then down her chest to caress her bosom. He must have noticed. He chuckled then touched the heated area. Ran his finger across the top of her bodice as if he could see what was beneath her gown. "Your emotions show on your face, in your eyes, on other delectable parts of your body. You want me. You're glad I stole the letter. You didn't wish to go home. Not yet. You want to see more of me."

Infuriated with herself, she stepped back. Control was lacking where it concerned him. Everything he said was true. She did want to see more of him, of his magnificent male body. "You're wrong again. What I am is glad to see you leave tonight. I want to be alone so I can do what I please without your infuriating presence."

"Little liar. No, you're not." Case tapped her on the nose. "Think about me." With that said, he was gone.

For Tara, Case's leaving was bittersweet. She'd been with him night and day for more than a week, almost two. Unable to understand why, Tara missed him. Missed his laughter along with the way his eyes simmered when he looked at her. He just strolled out the door. She should revile the man for taking her innocence then treating her so caustically. She didn't. She wanted him to make love to her again then again after that. The bottom line was that he didn't like her. Didn't like women. She was falling in love with the vulnerable man he didn't want her to see. Case would never show weakness. Yet...he did.

The defenselessness he didn't display often touched her heart. Sometimes he seemed lost and alone. She imagined him as a small child seeking the attention of parents who wanted him for the chores he could do for them. Nothing else. Tara wanted to get inside his mind to heal him. She also wanted to hate the man. She could never do anything but care about him. Tara touched her side where the knife struck her. The knife that was meant for him. She stepped into the line of attack. Because of his attention, the wound was fine, healing.

Conflicting emotions stretched her nerves thin.

He was gone now, strode out the door without looking back.

The first day she spent in the apartment, thinking. She tried to follow his rules. By the second day the walls began to close in on her. For more than thirty hours she followed Case's dictates. Tara looked out the window. The day was sunny. The sky blue. A few tiny white clouds dotted the sky. It wouldn't hurt to go for a walk. She would take Tiny with her. Feeling guilty as she started towards the door, she turned around to look at the room. Self-reproach swept over her. Case would know. He would discover what she did. He would be furious.

Damnation, she couldn't stay couped up another minute. Ash was always too busy for her.

Tiny barked. He too was bored with the walls. Tiny needed exercise. Needed to run. Should chase a few birds he couldn't catch. Tara poured herself a glass of wine, sat down on the sofa and wished she possessed more nerve.

Three days passed since his departure. So far, Tara stuck to his autocratic rules because Ash had been there for her. Ash took her to dinner at a small café. To her surprise Jeremy joined them. It was Jeremy who walked her home when Ash said his goodbye so he could go to his mistress. It seemed Jeremy also had an agenda where she was concerned. Tara could tell by the predatory light in his eyes she was about to be the recipient of a lecture about Case.

"Case is possessive of you. When he returns you need to take care. He could hurt you," Jeremy told her after sitting down in the drawing room of the apartment.

Tara didn't know the answer to Jeremy's statements. Yes, she knew he had a possessive streak where she was concerned. Jeremy's warning came too late. Yes, he'd already hurt her. Tara didn't understand why nor did she comprehend what he wanted from her. Case sent her different messages with every encounter. She poured them both a drink then beckoned for her maid to bring the pastries Gateau always left for her. Even though they ate earlier, she was hungry. Her stomach was always so agitated, she couldn't eat much at any one time. Jeremy was right on one point. Case would probably hurt her again. He did say he was sorry. Tara didn't know how sincere that apology was or if he wanted forgiveness. Didn't have any idea what would happen between them when he returned.

"I don't know what you meant," Tara hedged as she watched the frown lines deepen on Jeremy's face. She didn't intend to give Jeremy a reason to dislike Case more than he already did. The two men were at odds because of her. That fact didn't sit well. Tara adored Jeremy. She'd known him for as long as she'd known Grant. Jeremy and Grant had been best friends. Jeremy rescued her when she didn't want to be rescued. There was history between them that could never be erased.

"Yes, you do. The man wants you, Tara. You need to guard your innocence when he is around." The sound of Jeremy's voice was bitter to Tara. Tara always knew Jeremy wanted her. After Grant died, he courted her until she told him an emphatic no. Told him she didn't feel the same about him. Told him they would always be friends. Nothing more. Jeremy accepted that fact until now. Until another man wanted her. The trouble was that Case wanted her for whatever time he deemed right. It was not forever. Was not for marriage and children. In all he did and said to her, he made that clear. He never lied to her. All she was to the man was a momentary play thing. Tara guessed that as soon as she fell into his plans, he would leave.

She felt a surge of heat race to her face and quickly turned from him. Tara didn't want Jeremy to see the blush caused by his words. Without flinching, Tara gave her body to Case. Until he stormed from the rented room, she didn't regret her choice. Now that she had time to think, she still didn't regret or bemoan the fact she lost her innocence to him. When she discovered she wasn't going to have his baby, she didn't know if she felt sorrow or relief.

"Jeremy..." Tara began as she tried to think of the right words without telling him anything private. "I know you care about me. Nonetheless, I'm not going to allow you to malign Case. He's a good man. Now, as to you and I, I thought you understood we would always be friends...nothing more. In the last months nothing has changed."

Striding to the window, Jeremy looked out on the long boulevard. He turned, "Know that if you need me, I'm here for you. I won't pressure you. You have a sound mind. Trust your judgment not your heart."

Moisture in her eyes, she nodded. "I know and appreciate your concern. You must have faith in me in this matter." Tara saw frown lines appear between his eyes. He questioned. A small sigh of resignation slipped from her. More than anything she wanted to trust her heart. Knew

Jeremy was right in his assessment.

"I trust you. It's that man who has me worried. The way he looks at you as if he owns you makes me want to hit him. He's far too arrogant."

"You don't need to worry about me. Case would never force his attentions on me. He will honor my wishes. If I so choose to be with him, it is because that's what I want." Now that she gave herself to him, Tara understood that he made the decision hers. Case gave her more than one opportunity to end the lovemaking before he took her. She never wanted to say no. That night she wanted everything that happened between them except the abrupt ending.

"Case Ferguson can charm a lady with finesse. You wouldn't stand a chance against the man. If he sets his sights on seducing you, you will give in to his potent charm." Jeremy leaned against the wall, his arms crossed in front of him. Sunlight filtered in from the window highlighting his handsome features.

"I should be insulted by your lack of faith in my judgement. A man cannot seduce a woman unless she wants to be seduced."

"You're not affronted because you understand I speak the truth. You're wrong about the latter. A man experienced in the art of seduction would have no trouble charming you to want what he wants. You are ripe for the plucking," Jeremy said as he pushed away from the wall. When he reached Tara, he brought her to her feet then into his arms. He pressed her face against his chest, his arms around her, holding her.

Jeremy was warm. His heartbeat filled her ears. He ran his hand along her spine. Tara was struck by the memory of Case doing the same, his fingers sliding down her backbone touching each vertebra. The sensations created by Jeremy were different. Different as night and day. With Jeremy, Tara's body didn't stir to life, didn't heat with fire as the potent caresses became more intimate. After his hand settled on her bottom she moved away.

Shaking her head, she looked at him. Tara felt saddened by the weary expression on Jeremy's face. "No," she told him pain in her voice as she saw the hurt look in his eyes. "I don't feel anything."

"I understand." Jeremy pushed a strand of hair behind her ear.

"I'll take my leave now. If you want to spend an afternoon with me, send a message. I will come. Take you anywhere you'd like to visit."

"Thank you, I'd appreciate that. Though I doubt if Case will be gone much longer." For some reason she felt he'd be home in a few days. "If you don't mind, would you walk me to Madam Pipelet's home. I would like to talk to her."

"Whatever for?" Jeremy scowled. "You understand what she is known for in this city. Women come to her for..." Jeremy stopped as if he didn't want her to know the rest.

Tara tilted her head in one direction then another as she tried to read his mind. "Jam...she makes the best jams. She promised me a few jars when I saw her the day we arrived. I haven't been able to get there since. I've been forbidden to walk outside by myself. Ash has been great but..." Tara broke off.

She didn't think Jeremy was satisfied with her answer. Jeremy couldn't know what she gave away to help women. Could he?

After a few seconds he relaxed. "I can walk you and Tiny there. Who is going to see you home? I know Case told you not to go anywhere alone." He lifted his shoulders in a very male shrug. "Ash told me. Volunteered the information. I never asked."

"What else did Ash tell you?" Tara could think of far too many things Ash could relate to Jeremy.

"The night he left, you were fighting with Case, acting like children. He sounded amused."

"I had my reasons and Case thought he had his." Rehashing this was not going to happen. If she could explain, it would be easier. Tara couldn't clarify without telling him about the scene that sent Case racing from her bed.

"Very well, I'll walk you to her home. Once you finish, don't dally on your way home. I'm certain you will be safe. Make sure you leave before the sun sets."

After the door opened, Jeremy said goodbye with a quick kiss to her cheek. Madam watched, smiling while Jeremy sauntered down the steps then to the hack waiting for him.

"*Bienvenu*...come in. I'm pleased to see you," Madam said her voice soft. "Is this just a friendly visit or is there something more?" she asked. "You haven't given up on your other young man. They both love you."

Love? Jeremy might believe he loved her. Case did not. In this Madam Pipelet was wrong.

To Tara it seemed the woman understood what she wanted. A flush spread across her cheeks as she stared at her feet. When she looked up, Tara spoke, "There is more I need to see you about."

She ordered tea.

Tea along with chocolate cookies arrived on a tray. Madam poured each a cup then offered a cookie.

Tara was both hesitant as well as embarrassed to begin the discussion. The need was there yet her tongue was tied. She tried to tell herself she had nothing to be embarrassed about.

Madam reached out to touch her hand. "Take your time. You can ask me anything. It's about your young man, isn't it?"

Relief pooled in her stomach along with the tea. She nodded. "Yes. I..." Tara swept her tongue across her dry lips. "Yes, I need something to prevent conception." Just getting the words out gave her confidence.

"Are you increasing?" Madam asked patting the hand she was still holding. "If you are, you've other considerations. Either way I can help."

Thankfully, "I'm not. Whatever you do, don't tell me to say no to him. I cannot do that. Though, he would stop if I told him no. It's just that..." She swept a large dose of oxygen into her lungs.

"Does your young man know you are here? He should be part of this conversation. Don't you think? Do you plan on keeping what you are doing secret? He might not like that. I've known many men who don't like to think their seed has been blocked short of their destination or worse...killed before it could get there."

Those words stopped Tara cold. She sipped her tea. Set the cup on the saucer while Madam waited. "I don't want him to know what I'm doing. Yes, secret is best. I don't know how he would feel. What I do know is that I don't want to take chances. Don't want to bind him to me in that way. He would never appreciate a baby. The child would grow up a bastard. Don't wish that on any child, especially not his." Tara paused. "I don't think he would care since he doesn't love me."

"Why?" When Tara didn't answer Madam continued. "It is your choice. Why, is none of my business. How I feel has nothing to do with you. You understand I will always help in any way that I can."

Without meaning to, Tara blurted. "It's my body. Not his. He has no right to know. This is my choice."

"Yes," said Madam Pipelet. "You are right about that. Decades in advance of common thinking."

"We're not married. He will never do that...marry me. There should be no pressure. Case can't love. He's incapable of the emotion. He wouldn't want a baby," Tara said, her voice so soft Madam had to lean forward to hear the soft-spoken words. "If I believed he would be part of my future, I would talk to him."

"Yet he could father a child. One that would be born without a last name or a father to nurture him. Your man should know better than that. It's a man's job to protect the woman he cares about along with his child."

"Yes. All you say is true. Don't believe he cares about me. Not in that way. Never that much. What we do is a game to him."

"Very well. Shall we proceed? There are no guarantees with any method of protection. However, this will lessen the odds of conceiving. If you do get with child, what will you do?" asked Madam Pipelet.

"I suppose I'll have to think more about the possibility. I would never expect Case to marry me or claim the child. Suppose I would go home. Raise the baby by myself. Could always claim the father died. My mother and father would support my wishes."

Grant died.

Jeremy would help me if I needed it. He would even pretend to be the father.

"Or," Madam said, "you could abort the child. No one would be the wiser. You would be the only one who knew."

"You...you would know. I'd have to think more about that. In this instance, that is not a problem to be considered."

"Not if you left Paris before you began to show. I would understand that I gave you the tool to end the pregnancy. I would never know if you carried through. It is not an easy thing for a woman to make that decision."

Tara gulped. Tears clogged her throat. "I don't think I could..." Tara knew she couldn't. If anything, she wanted his child to live...if it was conceived. In that case she would always hold a part of him close to her heart.

"You sit here. I'll get you what you will need. After that, it is up to you what happens. Whatever you do, don't be hasty. Any decision you make you could regret. Yes, you could regret a decision that would last forever."

While Madam Pipelet was gone, Tara sipped her tea wondering if she could even use whatever paraphernalia her friend gave her. She ate a cookie. It tasted dry and hard. She coughed. Smoothed the cough with another drink of the tea. A huge glass of wine about now sounded good. As soon as she was home, she would indulge.

"Here we are." Madam dumped items on the table where the tea tray sat. "These can all be used more than once. The sponges are durable."

Tara nodded understanding the sponges would have to be washed after each use. "Yes." Her stomach knotted. Flipped over. Bile rose. Unseeing she stared at the items laying on the table. She didn't know if she could do any of this. Her hands shook. Her stomach churned.

"Soak the sponges in vinegar. If you don't want the young man to know that you are using these, you must put them in your vagina before he makes love to you. If you make love more than once in a night, you must be sure to use a different sponge each time." Madam Pipelet continued, her words matter-of-fact. This was a no-nonsense description of what needed doing.

"That could present difficulties," Tara guessed as she watched frown lines appear on the older woman's face. Madam Pipelet would know what she spoke of.

Do people do it more than once in a night?

"It could. If you don't want him to know..." Madam Pipelet's voice trailed off then she looked at her. "His seed could take root. If that is the case... You understand this would be easier if he agreed."

Tara's hands shook when she put the sponges back into the bag. If that was the case, her life would be turned upside down. Topsy-turvy. "What do I owe you for this?"

"Nothing. It is yours free of charge. I hope you succeed or that your man changes his mind about love."

As do I. Though he won't.

"He won't. *Mercie.* Tiny, come." The big hound leapt to his feet, drool sliding from his mouth and followed. His tail banged against her leg. Once outside, he bounded in front of her. Chased a squirrel to a tree. Stayed at the base and barked until Tara caught up to him.

"You are incorrigible."

Just like someone else I know.

Walking to the apartment, Tara thought about all Madam Pipelet told her. While Tara didn't know if they would ever make love again, what she did know was that they both desired each other. If he suggested making love in any way, all she could tell him was yes. From the words he spoke before they left, she understood they would make love.

Despite the rocky beginning.

There were still secrets that came between them.

~ * ~

Two weeks in the heat of southern France was two weeks too long. Case wiped sweat from his forehead. Perspiration soaked the back of his shirt. He cursed the heat. Exhausted, all he could think about was getting back to Paris and Tara. How would she act? Would she still be silent and hurt. He caused that pain when he abandoned her. Left her... He'd been a bloody fool.

The man he'd been sent after was in chains now. Headed for London. He'd been easy enough to find. Capturing him was one complication after another. He was a wily devil, evading him throughout the south of France.

Case was told to be discrete. He needed to take every precaution.

While the French government would look the other way in most cases, they wouldn't if there was a scandal of any sort. The man was a French citizen. He had rights accorded to him by his citizenship to that country.

The woman draped on his arm was proving difficult to extricate himself from. She'd not taken no for an answer when he told her he didn't want to be her lover even for the short time he would be here. He was set to leave as soon as the tide turned. That was a few minutes away. He needed to board before the vessel left without him. Waiting for the next ship...no, he had to get rid of this clinging woman.

"You could stay one more night," she pleaded, her hand roaming downward to cup his groin. He pushed her hand away. "I've a cozy apartment. Promise you wouldn't regret the time with me. I'll make you happy. Give you whatever you wish for."

Case caught her fingers before they slipped beneath his pants. "No, my ship waits. I'm eager to get back to Paris. I've some unfinished business that needs attending." Very unfinished, he had a woman to woo, a woman who was headstrong. A woman he'd hurt. Had yet to figure out how to go about soothing her wounded feelings.

"*Oui*, a woman? Better than me? I'm the best. You could never do any better. I will give to you whatever monsieur needs, all his desires," she questioned him holding on to his arm as he tried to shake her off. She clung to him.

"*Oui*, a woman," he agreed, unwilling to argue the point. Smiled at her pretty pout. "I don't dally with more than one female at a time. Can be quite painful."

"Very well," she huffed pushing her bosom out as if that would convince him to stay. "You are not so great to look at as you think you are."

Case hooted his laughter, kissed her soundly on the mouth then sauntered toward the ship. He felt great to be on his way back to Tara. His ship to Paris waited for him. At least this time he could sail right up the Seine. There would be no overland adventures to take more time. No woman to share a room at the inns where he stopped. No woman who could befuddle his mind. He was in a hurry. First thing would be to schedule the archery contest. The wager, in his mind was set.

On the flip side, Tara would not have adhered to the rules he set out. There would be consequences. Case didn't know what they would be as yet. All he could do was pray she remained safe. He never wanted to make her feel a prisoner. He was just so bloody afraid for her. She was impulsive as well as headstrong. She believed she had the same strength as a man. The woman was impossible. If she was fine, nothing should be done except a sound lecture.

The captain waved as he strode up the gangplank onto the boat. Wind blew strong whipping the French flag at the top of the mast. Water rippled against the ship. They would make good time.

"*Bienvenue*," the captain roared over the stiff wind as he stepped up to greet him. "I'll have the first mate show you to your cabin then we'll be off. Heard your mission here was a success. Good news."

"*Oui*." Now, he hoped his mission with the woman who bedeviled him at every turn would be a success.

Case contemplated how he was going to win over the fair Tara. She would never put up with anything but the truth. She would have to understand his terms. The thought startled him. Tara was unlike any woman he ever knew. She would have to learn he wouldn't love her. He was incapable of love.

She never lied.

A woman without lies.

A novel idea. He ran that through his head a hundred then a thousand times. A woman with no lies. He never thought a woman like that existed. Case was eager to return. Impatient to see this woman who confused him in every way.

During the short voyage, he took to walking the length of the vessel then back until the captain would stop him to chat. Case sorted through all the things he needed to say to Tara. Needed to figure out what he would do when she told him she disobeyed. Lord Montgomerie charged him with keeping her safe. That was his intention. She was foolish. How could a man keep a foolish woman safe? He tried. That was all he could do.

Failure was not part of his way of approaching life. How could he keep the woman safe if she never listened to him? As to her deflowering, he never suspected she was virgin. He had that to atone for. Case prayed she didn't conceive. An experienced woman would have taken precautions. If he'd known, he would have done the same. As far as he knew he had no illegitimate children. No bastards to account for. He never wished to bring another bastard into this world.

Was that a valid excuse? The fact he didn't know she was innocent?

Case didn't regret that night. He hoped she didn't. He had a lot to make up to her. Meant to spend the rest of his time in Paris doing just that.

Tara could have told him the truth. She claimed he didn't listen, didn't pay attention to her words. He assumed so much about her that was false. Assumptions could get a man into trouble. Had to admit that if she tried to tell him she was a virgin, he would never have believed her.

She was right. He assumed her innocence was a plan to bring him to his knees. Just as other women pretended, he believed Tara did too.

Days later when he saw the city of Paris, his heart leapt. It was midafternoon. She should be home. If not home, she should be with Ash. Her cousin. Case ran that knowledge through his head. He still didn't understand why the duke and duchess allowed her to go to Paris unchaperoned. While Ash was a relative, he wasn't a fit chaperone. The duke along with the duchess must have known that fact. Ash had an agenda of his own which didn't include babysitting Tara when she was with him.

Were the two playing at match maker?

The duke...never. The Duchess...he'd have to think on that.

Chapter Eight

As Case expected, Tara was not at the apartment. When he called out, the only answer was from their cook, Gateau, who bellowed that it was too early for dinner. Even Tara's maid was gone. The quiet rooms felt eerie. His voice seemed to echo bouncing off the walls. Case wandered through the house. As he stepped inside Tara's bedroom, he paused. He had half a mind to look through her things.

Berated himself. Changed his mind again while he strode to her dresser. All kinds of toiletries were strewn on top. Tara was not well-ordered. Case sprayed a bit of her cologne in the air. Sniffed.

Lilies. Summer rain.

Case opened a box of powder, found a tint that must have been meant for her lips. The color was soft pink. There were other cosmetics. He didn't recall her using them except the night of the ball. An envelope, unopened, was beneath a brush and comb with a matching shoe horn.

Unable to fathom the reason, Case felt as if she hid something. He didn't think she'd be keeping secrets. Though the sense was strong. Case shook off the feeling and left. Walking into his room, he set his valise on his bed then stretched out. His hands behind his head, he closed his eyes. Images of Tara flitted across his mind.

He saw her stretched out on the bed in Versailles.

She is so beautiful. I can hardly wrap my mind around it. I've never been with a woman like Tara.

While she was on her stomach, Case recalled touching each bone down her back. Tara...so slim, her waist small flaring to the sweetest hips and fanny. He kissed her delicious rump. Nipped. She moaned. Soft sighs whispered from her lips. She allowed him to do whatever he pleased. She delighted him.

If he could take back his reaction to her virginity, he would. He was an ass. A stupid fool. Tara should have called him out. Should have laid into him before he fled. What she did was look stunned. Embarrassed. Unable to come to terms with her status, he ran. The deed was cowardly. A man didn't act that way.

When the door swung open, he didn't move from the bed. He knew who came into the apartment. It wasn't Ash. Light footfalls, a soft whisper of fabric, the scent of lilies and summer rain... the essence of Tara. He heard Tiny's easy lope to the fireplace where he settled himself in front of it.

Tara was home.

"Case?" Tara called out from the somewhere near the front door. He heard her walk closer. "Is that you? Are you home?" She stood framed in the doorway. Tara didn't move further into the room.

He opened his eyes, saw her watching him. A small smile formed as if she was pleased to see him. After that, her eyes narrowed, her lips thinning. She waved her hand in the air as if she tried to think of a greeting. Tara would understand he wasn't pleased. She was outside on her own with no guard.

"I'm home. Who is with you? Ash? Jeremy? One of the duke's men? You are supposed to be accompanied when you go outside." Case tried for a tone of unconcern. He knew Tara was the only person who walked in through that door. The proper words to say to her fought with the greeting he would like to give her. He would like to drag her into his arms for a long, hard kiss. One he'd dream of over the days he was gone. There was more he dreamed about.

Her chin tilted up. "No one is with me. Why should it matter? I don't need to have someone by my side when I go outside. I'm a grown woman. Don't need protection on a diplomatic mission."

"So, you were you out alone?" Case wasn't surprised when she ignored him. All he saw now was her back her skirt swaying around her ankles as she left. He heard it when Tara hung up her cloak. He heard her walk to the sideboard. She was pouring herself a drink. The devil, he needed one too.

The question for him now was how long did he intend to wait until he began the conversation that would put them at odds. The discussion had to be accomplished. Sooner than later would be better. To put it off would be a waste of good time. Once the conversation was finished, the two of them could discuss more pleasant things.

He reminded himself she was a woman who didn't lie. She might skirt the issue by remaining quiet when he asked a question. Just as she did now. Instead of answering Tara left the room. His anger built.

His feet hit the floor hard when he stood then walked from the bedroom. He leaned against the door watching her rearrange pillows. Plump them. Move on to the next. Tara was nervous. He smiled. Her emotions always showed. Nervousness meant she felt some guilt. That was also good. She should feel guilty as hell for ignoring his warnings that were meant to keep her alive. Alive was better than good.

After Case reached her, he took the pillow from her hands then set it on the *canape*. For a second, he studied her. Watched as she looked to the window. She turned away from him as if she needed to hide.

"Were you alone?" Case held her hands. They were so small. She was delicate as well as fragile. He needed to do all that he could to protect her. She didn't want his protection. He needed to deal with that fact. Was used to fending for herself. She was no longer alone.

Tara tugged on them. He held fast. She looked away again for a brief moment. As if deciding she would give him an answer, she straightened. Their gazes connected. She tucked her bottom lip beneath her teeth. After that she drug in a deep breath of air.

"I was with Madam Pipelet. She is the woman you met the other day. Tiny was with me. You needn't worry. I was only a few houses down the street."

His smile stretched as thin as his nerves felt at the moment. He tempered his words. "Ah...a woman who could protect you from harm. I like that. You chose a valuable companion. One who is more fragile than you. What the bloody hell were you thinking?" Case didn't try to hide the sarcasm tinging his voice. All he attempted to conceal was the anger. "We both understand Tiny is no protection unless he drowns the perpetrator in his drool. Perhaps when he knocks them over as he clamors to their shoulders to lick their face. Perhaps his tail is his best weapon. If he hit a person behind knees with a hard flick of his tail, the impact could send the man to his knees."

"She is quite spry, far from fragile. If you paid attention to who I am, you would see I'm not delicate at all," Tara told him, smiling as if he would believe her ludicrous statement. "I take it your mission was a success. So, there is no danger."

He was looking into her eyes. They sparkled as if she found something amusing. It was obvious to Case Tara thought she held the winning hand.

Perhaps a different tact would be wise as she was just fine. To belabor his point would be ridiculous. The ensuing conversation needed to go in a different direction. "We could discuss the competition."

"What competition?" Tara asked showing no sign of remembering what they talked about days ago.

Case didn't think she would forget. "You know darn well what I'm talking about. Don't pretend with me or hide from the facts. Thought you were an honest woman. A woman who never lied." Case tugged in a deep breath of air. His calm demeanor was about to vanish. He didn't like the game she played. This wasn't acceptable.

To keep from saying anything more he would come to regret, he tugged her close. His mouth brushed across hers, once, twice, again. He deepened the kiss as he brought her hands higher to circle his neck. He felt the length of her pressed against him. The allure that was only Tara. No woman ever tempted him the way she did.

I find I like the feel of her next to me more than any other woman I've known. She is soft in all the perfect places. I want to touch her more intimately. Patience, I tell myself I need to have more. I've never had to control my mouth along with my hands when I've been with a lady. I've always taken what I want. Tara is different.

Groaning with his pleasure, Tara tasted of sweet red wine. In his arms, she left him with a heady sensation. Her nails skidded across his neck. Tara stood on the tips of her toes to get closer to him. She pressed herself close, closer still as if she wanted him as much as he wanted her. Case ran his tongue across her mouth, probing for entrance hoping she would part her lips.

Little devil.

She kept her mouth closed to him. He was certain she wanted to bedevil him. *Petite* witch. Her ploy was working. His fingers tightened around her waist before drifting lower to cup then squeeze her sweet fanny. Her gasp gave him entrance to her mouth. As if she hadn't meant to keep him from his goal, she rubbed her tongue over his. The sensation aroused. It was...

Exhilarating.

Exciting.

Blood pumped hard. Thundered in his ears.

Needing a deep breath, Case pulled away. He touched her forehead with his. "Bloody eyes, you're irresistible. You're not a little princess. You're a siren."

"That must be because I'm no longer a virgin." Tara didn't sound pleased with that statement. Bitterness coated her words.

What she said was true. Because of him, she was no longer innocent. With no thoughts except his pleasure, Case took that from her. He cursed, trying to ignore the venom he heard in her statement. Nothing changed. Tara was far from forgiving him. He understood this would take time. Even though she kissed him as if she missed him, with passion coupled with hunger, the resentment Tara felt was still fresh and ran deep.

A change was needed. "Let's go for a walk. The weather is wonderful. We can talk about the archery contest. The one you now remember." As they walked out the door and down the steps, he held her hand. Her fingers were long and slender. She wore one silver ring with a matching silver bracelet. Tara tucked her fingers through his. When she skimmed her fingers along the insides of his, the sensation startled.

My body flames with this tiny caress. I want to toss her skirts right here. The thought isn't one I'm proud of. I don't even care who would see. As in the cabaret when everyone watched the kiss. All eyes were on us. It would be the same now. I don't know where those thoughts come from. I'm not one to share in any way. Especially not this woman who is special to me in every way imaginable.

"Why didn't you say archery contest?" Her words were saucy. Adorable. If he could understand her better, he would love the way her moods swung. "You said competition. That's not the same."

"True. It's a matter of how you see the word...or the games you wish to play with me as your victim. We should set the competition or contest up tomorrow." He wanted to make certain they both understood how the winner would be determined.

"Ash, you know the man who is my cousin, he decided the park just outside the city would work quite well for what we need. There are not many people who visit there. We wouldn't risk an audience. Don't wish for people to watch. I would be nervous."

"Have you been practicing?" Struck by the fact she and Ash had things predetermined, Case didn't know if he was upset about her using the time he was away to hone her skills. Ash might have helped her with technique, given her pointers. Case was certain she was not up to his level. This should be over without having to set up a second round even if she practiced the time he'd been gone.

"Does it matter?" She tried to skip away from him. "I was very good before I met you. That hasn't changed. You will find that you won't win this easily, as you are thinking right now. I will give you sound competition. If you aren't perfect in the first round or the second you will lose."

He still held her hand while he weighed her words. Wasn't about to allow her distance. Case pulled her back to his side. Settled his arm around her shoulder, his hand rested where it had no business. "No...just curious. That's all. Will you shoot a perfect score?" He bent close so the next words would whisper across her ear. "I will."

I want to touch her breast, feel the hardened tip. Tara doesn't know how revealing her gown is, how dangerously low the corsage rests. I see the valley between her breasts. With the smallest tug, I would see much more than the rounded tops of her delightful jewels that are begging to be tasted. What would she do if I gave into my whim?

"You don't strike me as a man who is ever curious. My score will be better than perfect. The arrows I shoot will all end up in the center of the center," Tara told him, her voice prim. "You are set in your ways. You know what it is you want. Curiosity is for those with imagination. You are logical, always realistic, pragmatic as well as analytical. Your beliefs founded in what you know to be true. Sometimes your truths are not reality."

She would be thinking about the night he took her innocence away. In this assessment, she was right. "We should get a few things ironed out about the contest." He did imagine she exaggerated her skills. Nonetheless, he meant to approach this with the knowledge she might best him. If she did, he would be proud of her abilities. If she did, he would be having an off day. At the distance they first discussed he never missed.

"Such as? Not too sure I like where this is going," Tara said as they strode down the street. "What do we need to figure out other than how you will feel when I trounce you into the ground. I do have my forfeit for you picked out."

"Fairness. That's what this is all about. Nothing more. Either you have a low opinion of my skills or an inflated estimation of yours. I will guarantee you now, you will not trounce me."

"Rules...?" Tara questioned choosing to ignore his statement. Tomorrow, she would discover the truth.

I find this rather exhilarating. One might also say titillating. I would like the contest now. Waiting for the forfeit can be frustrating. Where Tara is concerned, I'm not a patient man. Though I understand that if I continue to woo her with caution, I will reap the rewards. I love to see her expression when I mention rules. Tara doesn't abide rules.

"Yes, the ones you pointed out. They are set in your favor until you fail to best me with the first two rounds. After that, it is my intention to end the contest on a resounding note." In the end, Case didn't intend to wait. He would put the targets at a distance her arrows would never reach. The last set was his choice. He wasn't about to prolong the win.

"I don't recall," she said looking at him as if she wanted to hit him. Her scowl created furrows between her eyes he'd like to stroke, smooth them out until her forehead appeared as it should.

"I'm certain you do. If I must, I'll explain what you yourself decreed. Correct me if I'm wrong. To elaborate, the first round, you pick the distance. If we are tied as you seem to believe we will be, you will pick the distance for the second round."

She tried to slip from his embrace. He held her snug next to his chest. "I remember. If we are still tied, you will march the targets so far from us I'll not hit the target let alone the bull's eye." Tara was muttering something about brute strength winning over finesse.

Case found he enjoyed that part of her too. Brute strength did have its advantages as did finesse. He had both. At her disposal there was only finesse. He still didn't believe she would hit the center of the target with all her arrows. That would take incredible skill. He could believe she might get lucky with one or two of her shots, not all ten. "So true, if we get that far."

"We will," Tara said with complete confidence that Case didn't understand who he was up against.

If she is as good as she claims, this contest will prove to be interesting. I will have to pay close attention. To miss a shot and lose would be too high a penalty to pay for my arrogance.

"You are positive. We will see on the morrow. I for one have high expectations for the morning." He stopped in front of the small café where they ate their first day in Paris. The wine had been delicious. He hungered for a different conversation. Something that would put him on a better track. He craved Tara. He cursed his callous behavior. "Wine as well as an aperitif to confirm the rules of the game as well as a toast to the best archer. Tomorrow?" Case nodded feeling his smile reach all the way to his soul. He felt positive he would win the forfeit. Tomorrow he would learn all about Grant. With that knowledge, they would be able to start over.

"Tomorrow will be fine. Ash has the contest planned. We'll do this in the morning before there are too many people in the park. You should send a message to Ash. He will undoubtedly be with Lou Lou now," Tara said. "He seems to adore that woman."

"Ash has this all figured out?" Case wasn't pleased by that bit of information. What could he do about it? Nothing. "I would rather the two of us...you and I...plan everything. Why does your cousin have a hand in this?" Case thought this to be private between the two of them.

"Why, yes." Tara smiled. "I suppose you would appreciate controlling everything. You do attempt to take complete charge of me. I won't let you do that, control me, direct my life the way you wish it to be. That I don't wish to be under your hand doesn't sit well with you."

Knowing what was in her head would be nice. She was taunting him with Ash. He wasn't going to let her words get to him. Ash was her cousin. It wasn't Jeremy involved. If it made her feel better, she could mock him with any person she liked. Case would let her words fly over his head. He was the only one who knew her intimately.

"No, Tara, what I do is attempt to keep you alive, not control you or direct you. The demands I make are to keep your heart beating. The need for absolute control has nothing to do with the guidelines I've made for you. Instructions you failed to follow, risking your life in the process. You've made a mockery of..." Frustrated beyond endurance, Case stuffed his hands through his hair, looking to the sky for heavenly guidance.

Tara tipped her head one way then the other as if she were sizing him up. "Case...I intend to win."

"You can try. I'm certain you will do your level best. I won't allow you to win." Case liked that about her. She did everything to the best of her female abilities. Those were not good enough to win against him in a man's domain...perhaps a lesser man.

She snorted as if she didn't believe a word he said. "What are we to do the rest of the day?"

He had many ideas. None of which he meant to explain to her while she still had her pique on. "Tomorrow, you will tell me all about Grant along with whatever happened to you two years ago. You will fill in the blanks you have left unsaid as to that day. I believe they are interrelated. It's the favor I'll request upon winning." He wanted to see her reaction.

Tara's face was a blank slate. She gave nothing of her emotions away. "When I win our contest, I will ask to know why you dislike all women. Why...what one woman did to you would make you jaded to all. Do you dislike all men because one was a cutthroat and liar? I know you don't judge all men because of the actions of one. Why do you do that with women?"

"I love women." He did. Though he understood what she was

saying. The truth was that it was more than one woman he based his opinions on. So far, his attitude was founded on all the females of his acquaintance as of now. He'd met no woman who could dissuade him. They were all cut from the same cloth...

Tara is different.

"On a superficial level, maybe. You don't love any woman other than physically. That doesn't mean you love or even like who they are. Women are a means to an end for you. Sex at your beck and call. Nothing more. I won't join that list of women."

She made a valid point. He would need to think about what she told him for more than a few ticks of the clock. The last part though...she would become his. They ordered. The wine arrived. The sweet confections followed. Case concentrated on the glass of wine then Tara. He needed to point things out to her, prepare her for her loss. "You won't win. Accept your fate. We don't even need to have the contest. You could accept defeat then we could move on bypassing the contest."

"So you think." Tara swirled the liquid in her glass, watching the play of colors. "Don't be too confident. Arrogance has been known to bring a man low."

"I know that for a fact." He drank long and deep before setting the glass on the table and sampling an aperitif. "You asked about the rest of the day. I have correspondence I need to dictate to you. Lord Montgomerie needs to be informed as to what is happening in Paris as well as my recent trip to the south of France. The fugitive was sent overland. He will arrive at Le Havre. The duke will need to have agents there to intercept. The French government will be apprised of the situation. Though I've sent a man with a letter. What I wrote will never explain everything in a satisfactory manner."

"Should we wager something more?" Tara asked ignoring Case. "I believe more should be..." She stopped speaking as she suddenly realized what she implied. Her face paled. "Never mind."

As she asked the question, Case saw the strained look on her features. If he guessed right, she wished she hadn't said anything. What was it she wanted to wager?

Case couldn't help the grin. He almost shook with his laughter.

Discovering her thoughts would prove delightful. Given patience he wasn't feeling at this moment, she would tell him more than she wanted. "We could wager more. I've several thoughts on that score. What do you have in mind?" Case loved the look on her face when he teased.

"Nothing," Tara muttered before she downed what was left in her glass. He poured more thinking if she was a bit muzzled, she would be even more intriguing. Tipsy brought forth pleasant ideas. A few feminine giggles would be delightful. A few more words she was loathe to tell him would be even better.

"Tara..." He leaned forward, wishing to touch more than look. "Thought you didn't lie. Tell me what you were thinking about." His body clenched with anticipation. "I'd be happy to oblige you. No matter your thought." Case leaned forward, capturing her hands. "Were your thoughts a *wee bit* indecent? Titillating? Even wicked? Are you a naughty girl for thinking things you shouldn't? Tell me. Did you wish for another kiss. Would you like me to explore you as we did the other night?"

She tugged her hands away. "I can't say anything more. Won't." Her face was flushed, her eyes crossed for a moment. She sipped her wine. Ate. Tara kept her eyes turned down. Seemed to study the floor where her foot moved in circles.

"Try." He lifted her chin needing to see her eyes. Case didn't want her to hide from him. He wanted her open as well as honest as she was before he made one of the biggest mistakes of his life. Before he rejected the most enthralling gift that was ever given to him. "You don't know what I'm assuming you meant to say. What you thought might not be quite so intimate as what I have in mind. Tell me."

She muttered something under her breath that he couldn't understand. His grin grew. Picking up her hands again, Case rubbed the inside of her wrists. Shivers. "I didn't understand what you said. If you dare, say it again."

"Rat," Tara accused.

"Scaredy cat," Case shot back.

That wasn't nice," she whispered as she turned away from him as well as the intimacy he offered.

"Tell me if you dare. Say what you want if you're not too afraid. I'd like to hear about this additional wager. What are you asking of me? If you ask more of me...well then, I can ask more from you. 'Tis only fair. Isn't that the way this started? You wanted to make all fair between us."

"I changed my mind."

"Doubt it but I'll go along with that thought. If you insist that is..." Case had never had a better time with a woman. Tara was softening toward him. He didn't know how long it would take, a few days, longer perhaps then she would be his again. When it happened, he wouldn't make a fool of himself.

"I insist."

"Are you finished with your wine?" Case realized he still had to speak about the days to come. He didn't want to ruin the afternoon. Now that he was home, she would have to abide by his rules. Tara should be told once more. Though he knew he would have visitors at the apartment soon. He understood his time was spoken for. This matter would need to wait for this evening or even tomorrow morning after the contest.

~ * ~

The next morning, Tara dressed in the attire she always wore when she hunted or practiced shooting. Case would not like what she wore. Case be damned. A handicap was never given. If she had to wear a gown, she would be two steps behind him. She needed comfort as well as free use of arms as well as legs. Tara didn't want to find herself hindered because of an excess of fabric swirling around her legs.

Ash stood by the door, her bow along with her arrows in hand. He grinned at her while they waited for Case to finish with the ledgers he needed to go over before they could leave. She was nervous. While she knew she was a good shot, she'd never been in a competition. Nervous energy could be a hindrance. Deep within she understood Case was exceptional. Damn, he was outstanding at everything he did. He would best her. Last night he had a point. She could concede then they wouldn't be embroiled in this travesty.

"Are you ready to show off your skills?" Ash asked her seeming to enjoy her situation. "Don't be nervous you are as good an archer as any man. You will show well. Case will be surprised at your expertise."

"Showing well is not good enough. I have to beat him." Tara wiped her sweaty hands on the britches she wore. "I have to win. There is too much at stake. I'm just too nervous. If it goes to the third distance, I don't stand a chance."

I know I'm making more of this contest than I should. Over the days he was gone, I couldn't stop myself from thinking. If I showed him a woman can excel at a man's sport, he might come to respect me. Found I want his respect. Want his love too. One out of two would not be bad. I realize Case cannot love. He has told me by his actions as well as his words more than once that he was not capable of love. While I don't want to change the man or expect something that isn't possible, I can still try for his respect.

Ash was staring at her. "I've seen him with other weapons. The man is more than good. Don't get your hopes up too high," Ash warned. He paused as if in thought. "What's at stake here? Do I need to be concerned for you? You're not gambling your virtue, are you?"

She'd already given away her innocence to an uncaring man. Her laugh was a thin sound. "Nothing I can't deal with." Tara didn't know if she could handle revealing Grant to him even though Case deserved to understand her better. He needed to know why she had been a virgin when everything about her screamed that she was not.

"Are you certain? We can call this off if you say the word. The man has no right to your body unless that's what you want him to have."

Tara laughed a soft sound in the stilted air. "Easier said than done. What I promised Case was to tell him about Grant. Nothing nefarious. He has no claims to my body, if that is what you were worried about." He claimed my body days ago then rejected me. He didn't just reject my body he rejected all of me. That was the part that was so difficult for her to accept after she fell in love with him. Now he sent her mixed signals.

When he looks at me with the deep bluish shimmer in his eyes, I know he feels different than he did that night. Sometimes I think I'm seeing something I want to see. Wishful thinking. That he still feels the same as before. I find myself asking why he would change his mind. I've done nothing different that would make a difference.

When I touch my lips, I remember every time he's kissed me. Recall the heat that rushes through me. The quivering and clenching of parts of me that long for his caress. That night when he loved me as no man has ever loved me, it was wonderful until it wasn't. I knew there would be pain. I just didn't understand the depth of hurt he could cause until he rejected all that I gave him. I thought my innocence would be more important to the man. It wasn't.

"Tara? Where are you?" Ash asked as he waved his hand in front of her face. "I feel as if I've lost you. Where did you go?"

"Thinking." She was thinking too hard. Focusing on the competition would be a better way to spend the time before she started shooting.

"Are we ready?" Case strode from his office prepared for the morning's contest.

The man was just as handsome as ever. He was dressed in buckskins that molded his powerful thighs as if they were a second skin. His white lawn shirt was open at the neck. Dark hair was revealed from the opening. Slung across his broad back was a quiver of arrows along with his bow. The bow was larger than hers. While the weapon would be harder to pull, the arrow would go much farther.

Tara felt inadequate. Afraid. She would have to muddle through then accept the consequences of defeat.

Who was she kidding? She would lose. All she could hope for was a good showing in the first two rounds. Was she prepared for the forfeit? She had to be. She gulped for air when he slanted his devilish grin in her direction. He also read the expression on her face. Knew the outcome, saw her fear coupled with the bank of nerves seeming to stretch her thin.

Stiffening her shoulders, she nodded. Tara didn't have one word for him. She needed to concentrate. When they reached the stable their horses were saddled.

"The first target is in place as are the first two marks," Ash volunteered with a quick glance to Tara then Case. "Jeremy is there to make sure no one changes them. As requested, the distance is thirty paces. I've counted off forty paces if this goes to a second round. If we go to the third one the distance is your call." Ash turned his attention to Case.

"Yes," Case said as he waited for her to leave. He followed making no comment.

Except for one time, he was always the gentleman. To Tara the two-mile ride to the field they chose took longer than expected. Her nerves didn't seem to settle. She didn't think they would until this was over. She found that her fists were clenched so tight around the reins nail marks were left in the palms of her hands.

During the ride she didn't speak to either man. Ash and Case chatted about politics between France and England. Tara thought of different ways she would speak of Grant. She wondered how Case would absorb the information. Before Case, Grant was her beloved. Her fiancé. She loved the man with all her heart.

When they stopped, she was surprised. She'd been so immersed in her brooding thoughts; she'd not known how close they were. Soon this would be in the past. The contest would be behind her. Tara pulled in a cleansing breath of sweet country air. When she looked to Case, he tipped his hat her way before he dismounted.

Before she could react, he was beside her, his hands on her waist, lifting her, startling her with his proximity, with the feel of his hands heating her. She slid down his length. Felt all his hard muscles. Though his body was hard, he seemed relaxed. Case was confident he would win. He was flexing his muscles. She wasn't going to allow him to intimidate her or make her more anxious than she was.

"Let me go," she told him, her voice quivering as she stared into his dark blue eyes. A lock of dark hair fell across his forehead. Tempted to push it into place, Tara refrained. "Please..."

As if he owned the world, he was smiling, "A kiss for good luck," he tilted her head. His thumb moved across her bottom lip.

"Your good luck or mine?" she questioned wondering who she was kidding. "I don't think kissing you would be appropriate. There are people watching." She was thinking of Jeremy and Ash seeing them together. She wasn't ready.

He touched her lip with his tongue. "My good luck. Why would I wish you luck when I don't want you to win? Hmm...? And...if you recall, there were people watching us at the cabaret. You didn't mind my kisses then. If I remember correctly, you told me you enjoyed being watched. You didn't mind the audience."

With that light touch he unraveled her, sent her nerves spinning. She couldn't deal with the repercussions. Tara found that she was shaking. "No...no kisses. I...no one knew who we were at the tavern. Jeremy and Ash..." She was mush. Thinking straight was not something she could do. "They know who I am."

Case's mouth framed hers. Moved. Dampened. He didn't seem to care about her answer. Unable to help herself and despite the feeble no, Tara's hands wound into his hair. She met his advances, reciprocated each caress. He was warm and strong. In his arms, she felt protected, even cherished though she understood for Case that was impossible. He ran his hands up her back then down. She remembered his caress, touching each bone down the long column of her back. She was naked then.

After he pulled away, Tara felt the loss. She didn't want to feel this way, not when she was trying so hard to keep her mind focused on the competition. Case set his forehead on hers. She closed her eyes.

His husky whisper sent tremors coursing. "May the best man or woman win. The kiss will bring us both good luck. *Bon chance*. Shall we start. If you cried off now, you wouldn't find yourself embarrassed by the loss."

This was what she waited for all the days Case was gone. The time was upon her. She would show her skills. They had separate targets.

"You may begin when you are ready," Ash said to both of them. "Take as much time between shots as needed. We are not in a hurry. In truth, I've all day though I don't know about the two of you."

Tara sipped in a long drink of air. She brought her bow and arrow cocked to level at her target. As she pulled back, the whizz of Case's arrow coupled with the zing of his bow string startled her. She pointed to the ground.

"Shoot all ten then I'll do mine," Tara told him, her voice along with her body shaking from the nervous energy that was sweeping through her. She understood if he did well, she would have to do the same.

I know my skill. At this distance, Case cannot best me unless I let my nerves beat me. We might tie. If that happens, we will move on to greater distance then again. I will lose. She was determined to prove her skill, even if this went to the third round.

"If that is what you want," Case said before he fired his remaining nine arrow, hitting dead center with each arrow. With each new shot, he stripped wood off one of the previous arrows. On his last shot the arrow splintered one of the first ones in the target. He sent it straight down the middle.

He bowed to her, a mocking smile on her face. "Your turn." Case stood back, his arms crossed as if to say the contest will be over with this round. His round was perfect. Better than perfect.

With tensions strained to their limit, Tara nodded several times. Each arrow landed in the center of the target, stripping wood from a previous one. Just as Case shot to perfection so did she. They would move on to the second round. At this distance she was good. Nonetheless, she could falter. So could he. If a breeze stirred at the wrong moment, the outcome could change. All factors needed to be considered.

When she finished, she smiled. Relieved she showed well, also pleased he did not best her on the first round. Ash and Jeremy set new targets at forty paces. This time she went first with much the same results. The only miss happened when one of her arrows hit one embedded then bounced off. She had nine in the center. That wasn't good enough to win if Case shot all ten of his to perfection.

Case tipped his hat. "You've done better than I thought. You are managing to make this a contest of skill. I'm surprised as well as pleased. A competent woman is always intriguing." He stepped up then unloosed all ten. All ten found the center.

It was over then. He won. She lost.

He cleared his throat while he pointed to the targets. "Believe we are still tied. If you were stronger that one arrow would have found it's mark dead center. I'm willing to give you those points. The game is as much about finesse as it is strength. You've shown admirable skill. Shall we go on to sixty paces?"

Sixty paces...

...Not fifty

"Yes," she said though she knew she wasn't any good farther than forty paces. The contest was over. However, she was not willing to back down so soon. She had to try. Maybe Case wasn't any good at that distance. There were other variables involved besides brute strength, including keen eyesight.

To Case, sixty paces was no different than the thirty paces of the first round. He recorded a perfect score. Tara took longer with each shot. She knew as soon as she missed once, the challenge would be over. Even if one missed the center, she wanted to send off all ten of her arrows.

"I'd like to shoot all my arrows even if I've ones that don't make the center. Wish to see how well I do shoot at the farther distance."

"Whatever you would like," Case told her, his arms crossed over his chest, confident now that he was certain of the win. "Now that this tournament is almost done, I would not begrudge you anything. Though I don't believe you should count yourself out before you've fired off the arrows."

"Thank you for that." She inhaled deeply, hoping to make the best showing possible. Held her breath. Aimed. The first arrow was far from center but at least she hit the target. She was afraid her shots would fall short. She adjusted her aim taking in the air currents then waited for a gust of wind that might help propel her arrow forward. The second one landed closer to the center than the first.

All her shots went the same way. Her last arrow hit the outer edge of the center ring. She was proud of herself. Her arm ached. If she had the strength, she would have done better. Now was not the time to bemoan her lack of muscle. Case was expert at many things. Ash told her he was proficient with many weapons. He was, after all, reputed to be one of her uncle's best agents.

When she finished shooting, Ash and Jeremy were gone. She was alone with Case, the winner. Beneath her ribs her heart thundered, knowing her time was up. She gave him a limp half-smile.

With a lift of her shoulders, Tara decided she would have to acknowledge his accomplishment. "You did better. Congratulations. Ash told me he and Jeremy would return to collect the arrows as well as the targets. We'll take our bows with us."

"Come, we've better things to discuss." He offered her his arm. "We can walk."

"Where are we going?" Her heart was lodged in her throat. Her breaths short little pants of air. She knew what he would expect now.

I can do this. I can tell him. He does deserve to know. I wished I could tell him for some time now.

"Your cousin along with your friend arranged a small celebratory feast for whoever won. In this case, the best man won. Not the best woman. What do you think? Are you hungry? Would you like to celebrate with me. No? We both need to eat."

Her stomach rolled. Tara understood she was too nervous to eat. Knowledge of the event two years ago rolled in her stomach. Needed to tell him everything then see how she felt. "Would rather speak of what you wanted to know first. After that I might be able to enjoy the feast. Don't feel much like celebrating or eating." She understood Case was the best at what he did. That was why her uncle employed him. She didn't understand why she ever thought she might defeat the man.

"Wine will help. Ash said he brought the two bottles he left with us back from one of the wineries near Bordeaux. Your cousin told me it was one of the best. The winery has been making wine for more than a century."

"I suppose." What she wanted was to hide. They passed through a thicket of trees as they walked on a path made of crushed rocks. A small grassy area was ahead of them. Trees shaded the spot. There was a fountain, sprays of water sparkling in the sunlight. Someone set a blanket on the ground. There were pillows arranged for comfort as well as a basket which must contain the food. She found she was curious.

"What do you think is in the basket, besides food?" Case asked as he brought her to picnic area. "Make a guess."

"I've no ideas. I would have thought you knew. You didn't

arrange this? Who did?" Beside the basket, she sat on her knees. Curiosity drew her to look inside. The bottle of wine and two glasses were on a shelf near the blanket.

Case poured the wine. "A toast?" he asked. "To both of us. To a contest well done." He sipped then set the glass down as he joined her. "Your skill is very good. As you might have guessed, I was surprised."

He sat next to her. His long legs stretched out in front of him while he leaned on a ledge behind him with one of the pillows at his back. His hands were folded on his stomach. His eyes darkened to a deep blue. A smile stretched across his face. He had every reason to be pleased with himself. He was relaxed while she had become a bundle of nerves.

"There is grilled chicken. Some type of chocolate desert. Strawberries. A loaf of bread as well as some *fromage*."

"Toast us. Take a drink of your wine. Relax for a while. I'm not going to insist this minute that you tell me everything in that pretty head of yours," he told her then set a pillow beside him for her to lean on. "I'm not in a hurry."

"I am," Tara murmured as she took a long drink. "I want to get this over with. The reasons before that I didn't tell you were not because the anniversary was some deep dark secret. It isn't. For me, the memories are too painful to think or talk about. The time changed my life in ways I could have never imagined. You already know some of what happened."

"An accident. That bad?" he asked as he seemed to be patient. "Despite the hurt it causes you to recall, I do need to know. We will get along much better when I've learned your truth. After I learn more about you, I might stop making assumptions."

She nodded agreeing with him. "No, it's not bad, just difficult to remember, harder to talk about. The memories haunt me." Tara felt moisture brim her eyes. She tried to push the tears back. Tried to find that place of calm she liked to drift to when memories intruded. Didn't want to think about the events that tore her heart into pieces.

"Anytime." Case topped off their glasses. He didn't say anything. Sunlight made the wine sparkle and shimmer. Sunlight shining through the leaves above cast dancing shadows around them. "Drink more wine if you like, if doing so will help ease the way."

Tara sat beside him, her legs tucked beneath her. Needing something to do with her hands, she smoothed them along her britches. All was silent except for the wind rustling the leaves on the trees and the splashing of the water in the fountain behind them. The scent of roses floated on the breeze coupled with freshly cut grass. The sounds along with the scents all soothed her tattered self. She drew in a large lump of air that sat inside her. She turned to face him. Set her hand on his arm. Despite her efforts moisture still pushed at her eyes.

"Two years ago...two long years have passed since I lost all my dreams for my future. One second, I was happy the next everything I ever dreamed of was gone. I lost the man I was in love with, engaged to be married to." Tears slipped from her eyes. Ran down her cheeks. Tara's throat was clogged. She tried to swallow, to push all the sadness away.

"Cry now if you wish." He touched a drop that slipped from her eye. Touched the liquid to his lips. "Salty. Let it go. You have me to lean on. I'm not going anywhere. Trust I will be here for you."

In time Case would leave. One more time, she'd be left with nothing except dreams of a future that could never be. He wouldn't always be here for her. She needed to enjoy as well as memorize every moment she had with him. Who understood better than she that in a blink the joy can be whisked away. After that all one had left were the memories.

"When it happened, I was five days from being married to Grant. That's who Grant was, my fiancé." Tara caught her bottom lip between her teeth. Pain would make her forget the loss. Pain would take her to a place where she didn't feel. She couldn't leave these thoughts to drift to that place now.

"You loved him so much?" Case watched and listened. His questions left her thinking about the past more than she wanted. That day when her world turned black. Jeremy understood the raw pain. No one else did. Jeremy and Grant were the best of friends. Jeremy lost Grant too.

"So much so I didn't want to live when he wasn't there to hold me or talk to me." As if anticipating the next question. "Grant died that day. I wanted to die too."

"This was an accident." Case picked up her hands. "An accident that has marred your life for two years. You have to learn to live again to trust another man. Trust in me."

Her hands were ice cold. His warmth seeped into her one small particle at a time. How could she put her faith in a man who would leave her? "An accident that shouldn't have happened. The horses pulling the wagon were spooked when a dog rushed onto the path barking as well as nipping at their heels. Grant did all he could to bring them to a stop. In the race over the rocky path, one of the wheels broke apart. I was thrown from the cart. Grant should have jumped. He didn't want to lose the horses. Must have thought he could save them. He believed he was invincible." She turned to look at him shaking her head. "Just as you believe the same about yourself. You are not immortal."

Case tucked her into his arms. Held her while tears slid down her cheeks wetting his shirt. Tara choked back the tears needing to finish the story. He rubbed her back as he made hushing noises. Sitting up, she wiped the tears away with the backs of her hands.

"Hush...you don't need to say anything more. It's done. Don't need to see you in pain any longer."

"No, now that I started, I have to finish." She cleared her throat thinking the worst was over. "He went with the wagon and the horses over the side of a cliff. The drop was steep, rocky. Jeremy told me was killed instantly. I don't know how he knew. I had multiple bones broken from my fall."

"Jeremy was there?" Case's voice sounded strained.

"He drove the wagon behind us. He was Grant's best friend. Grant was on an errand, picking up pots and pans for us to use in our new home, some furniture as well. Jeremy had a load of bedding and other things in the wagon he drove. Jeremy splinted my leg and my arm. He wrapped my broken ribs. There were two broken, others were bruised. After that was done, he drove me home. My parents were only there because of the wedding." Tara set her head against his chest her hand there also, allowing her emotions to spill from her. Except for a few times with Jeremy as her confident, she never spoke of that day. "My wedding was five days away. It never happened."

"That does explain the innocence I encountered," his voice was dry as he spoke the words. "If you were my fiancée, I would have never waited to make love to you for the wedding night."

"Grant wanted to make love to me. I wanted him to wait until after the ceremony. He conceded to my wish. I wish now...I wish we made love." Tara heard the intense longing in her voice. Felt Case cringe when she spoke the words.

"I'm glad you did not. Even though it must not seem that way to you, I treasure what you gifted me with. I do appreciate the gift even though I reacted badly." Case tilted her head to meet his gaze. With a light brush of his lips, he kissed her across her mouth. Touched. Savored as well as nipped. He ended the brief kiss as if the momentary caress meant nothing to him.

Tara wanted so much more from this man. She was giving him her heart. "When I was well enough to meet each day as if it might be a new one, mother and father left to chase another sunrise. Aunt Ella insisted I stay with them. Jeremy took me to London."

"Jeremy loves you. Why didn't you..."

She broke into his words with a simple explanation shaking her head. "I don't love Jeremy." She was quick to say knowing he could read a myriad of things into the few words. Tara understood then she loved this man. If she didn't, she would have never given him her innocence. "We are friends. Will never be more than that. What you don't understand is that a woman can be friends with a man. There doesn't always have to be sex between them or some concealed motive." Tara heard the anger in her voice when he was only being kind to her.

"If it means anything to you, I do believe you. Jeremy would take whatever favors you are willing to grace him with. He would have taken your innocence if you allowed him to do so. I did." Case seemed to think about that statement along with everything else she told him.

Yes, I trusted you with my virtue because I love you. You cannot love. I'm glad I did. Though I wish there had not been so much anger on your part. I would give you whatever you ask of me until you don't want it any longer.

"Can you eat now?"

I find he needs to change the subject to something he won't have to interpret. I will try to eat for his sake. I should be hungry. My mouth waters. Though the emotions of these last moments cause my stomach to churn.

"More wine? Yes. A piece of the grilled chicken. I'll try." Tara wanted to know what he was thinking. After all this emotion, she was exhausted. She wanted to close her eyes then sleep. The memories along with the tension of the contest drained her of energy. She felt weak.

Case propped up the pillows behind her. He refilled the glass with wine. After that task was finished, he found chicken for her to nibble on. She did eat. As did he. For a long time, nothing more was said.

The water in the fountain splashing against the rocks soothed. The wind rustling the leaves helped the ache in her heart as she tried to focus on the present. She blinked a few times trying to stay awake.

Case didn't talk.

"What are you thinking about?" Tara asked the question that was foremost in her head. She wished he would open up to her. Wished he would give her some sign his feelings toward her changed.

"Are you trying to tell me it's my turn to answer all the questions you've posed?" he asked as leaned back, closing his eyes. "I did not lose the forfeit. I need not answer anything."

~ * ~

Ash, Jeremy close on his heels strode into a fashionable restaurant on the Champs Elysée. After they were seated and their orders were taken, Ash spoke.

"Our little Tara will be fine. Case Ferguson is an honorable man. He won't ask for anything Tara doesn't wish to give. On the other hand, Tara is stubborn, knows her mind. She won't give him anything her heart won't accept."

"What is this forfeit," Jeremy asked. "I don't like Case. He wants more from Tara than she should be willing to give to him. He's not going to put a ring on her finger. I don't care how stubborn Tara is. She can be seduced. If the forfeit is meant for Tara to bed him..." Jeremy's fists clenched tight.

Ash understood all too well what Jeremy wanted from his cousin. Ash also didn't wish for Case to take Tara to his bed. She deserved better than a few nights with a lover who meant to leave her. Deserved a husband and children. Those weren't things Case would give her. By watching them, the seduction seemed to be in progress. "You aren't ever going to have Tara. I know she's made her feelings clear to you."

The huge sigh surprised Ash as much as Jeremy's statement. "I know. I just don't want to see Tara hurt. She still isn't all that strong. If she lets Case take her to his bed, it means she feels stronger about him than she should. If she falls in love with the man, he will break her heart. If that happens, she might decide her life isn't worth living. She's done that once. It was your mother who convinced her she should live."

"She's sturdier than you think. She is not going to let him take advantage of her. I'm sure she understands what he wants along with what he is capable of returning. She has a mind that is agile as well as quick." Ash didn't want to tell Jeremy he thought Case already hurt her. Tara had been so moody after Case left. He knew Tara went to see Madam Pipelet. He also understood what services the older woman provided for anyone willing to pay the price. Ash understood Madam Pipelet was a longtime friend to Tara. There were many reasons Tara might visit. She told him it was the jam.

He wasn't about to ask for more details even though he didn't believe her.

"The forfeit..." Ash tapped his fork on the table. "She was supposed to tell him about the two-year anniversary. She lost. I don't doubt that by now Case has been apprised of everything that happened on the day in question."

"That man treats her as if she is a tart. I don't like it," Jeremy said as he rearranged his silverware several times. "I should find a moment to talk with her in private. I could convince her of..."

"Case treats all women that way." Ash said with a bland tone. Case has secrets that he tells no one. Father knows. As Case's boss, he has to be apprised of everything that might put the man in jeopardy or cost a mission."

The drinks were served. Frothing ale spilled over the rim of the glasses as they were set in front of the men. A plate of bread along with butter followed.

"You should find another woman. Tara won't ever be yours," Ash went on to say as he spread fresh butter on a piece of steaming bread.

"True enough. Does Lou Lou have any friends?" Jeremy asked, a rakish smile gracing the firm set of his mouth. "Would rather have a mistress at the moment than a fiancée. Suppose I'll have to start looking for someone else to give my heart to."

"She does. Has a younger sister. Lou Lou was older than I thought. The family is destitute. Lou Lou is the oldest. She has six siblings she is supporting. I've taken to giving her things she can pawn or to bring so much food we cannot possibly eat it all. I know she takes the leftovers to her family's home. Her first thoughts are to provide for the younger children. She was a virgin when I took her. Clair, her sister, is one too. At least I would assume so. They are doing what they must in order to survive. I'm the beneficiary. Hope that before I leave for home, I can secure a job for her that she won't have to sell herself. Don't want to see her impoverished or at the hands of a ruthless man. Also, don't want to see her back in a cabaret."

"Their parents?" Jeremy asked.

"Both dead along with two of the children," Ash said wondering how life could be so cruel to some while it gave others everything they could wish for. "Would you like to meet Clair? I can arrange for a meeting tomorrow. If you would like to set her up, there is a townhouse close by that is for sale. She would be close to her sister. Believe the two would be grateful."

"Yes. Does she speak English."

"Passable. Lou Lou says she speaks better than she does. We will see. How is your French?"

"Passable," Jeremy said with no emotion. "What does it matter? I'm certain between the two of us, we will find a way to communicate."

Chapter Nine

Since Tara's reveal about the accident, their relationship was not as strained. Tara still held herself aloof at times. Case understood. As to date, she didn't comprehend what he wanted from her. He needed to have her relax around him. To be herself. She remained stiff as well as remote. In his arms that day, she sobbed, letting the past go.

I need to tell her my story. Tara deserves to understand why it is not possible for me to love. I want to hold her. Soothe her fears. She still has them. They are about me. I don't blame her. Wish that I could keep her safe the rest of her life. She deserves to have a man who can return her love. I knew the moment she told me why she didn't give her innocence to Jeremy that she loves me. How to deal with that knowledge? I've no idea. If I allow her the closeness I'm beginning to think she craves when I leave, I will hurt her more.

They were in the apartment they rented in Epernay. Tonight, if all went as planned, he would tell her his truth. Epernay was home to the best Champagne in France. There were underground cellars to explore. Many different houses of champagne to taste. Different flavors to enjoy including apple, pear, strawberry and cream. There was also an avenue of champagne where they could walk from one major, well-established house to another tasting as they strolled. He wanted her to enjoy this outing. After the fiasco at Versailles, he had a great deal to make up for. He intended to begin today.

"We've only one bedroom?" Tara asked while she wandered the room picking up different objects to look at them before putting them back in a different place. "I claim the bed." She smiled at him giving him a glimpse of the Tara he first met. The one who always spoke her mind. The woman who did not walk around him as if she tiptoed on eggshells.

Case would not be surprised if she began to plump pillows next.

Tara was nervous about tonight. He wasn't going to do anything with her unless he had her full consent. Didn't mean he wouldn't try to seduce or charm his way to experience her favors, the sweet charms he had caught a glimpse of. Nevertheless, he wasn't going to sleep on the sofa. "One bedroom. One bed. What to do about that deplorable fact? Do we share or flip a coin to see who gets the bed."

Tara stood in the doorway looking into the room with the one bed. "Flip a coin. If you were a gentleman, there wouldn't be a question."

"If I planned to sleep alone, I would have booked two rooms or made certain there would be two beds. I didn't. We have one room, one bed for a reason," Case told her his voice deep, husky with the raw desire he felt for this woman. Tonight, there would be no lies between them. Over the weeks their passion built to an explosive level. He didn't want to have to walk on those blasted eggshells any longer. They would come to terms with what they both wanted from each other. A change of subject needed to be approached. "Would you enjoy some champagne tasting before we find a place to eat? Before we haggle over the bed or sleep together. Do you suppose there is a sunset to watch?"

"Yes to both. I want to stroll through the city with you, drink champagne. Watch a sunset if the clouds don't get in the way." Tara began plumping pillows.

To hoot with laughter would not give her the confidence she needed. Case walked to her, took the red pillow lined with gold braid from her hands before tossing it to the sofa. "Looks best there."

"I don't know." Her laughter was soft, melodic. Seemed she understood what she'd been doing. Knew she'd been caught. "The pillow would look better in the bedroom. Don't you think?"

Tara didn't laugh enough. Case liked the sound of it. Remembered when she laughed more. It was before he was an idiot. "Do you wish to change your clothes before we find that champagne to taste?"

"No, I want to relax. I look at you and I..." As if embarrassed by what she might have said, Tara turned away.

He stopped her withdrawal from him, setting his finger on her mouth. "I do know what you want, little siren. It might not be what you need. Ash believes I've hurt you already. Jeremy thinks I will. Tara, both men are right. You must have information so you can make the decision for yourself. Be assured, I want you in that bed with me. I understand that is a lot to think over. We aren't wed. With any other man you would have expected a ring. If you choose to sleep with me, it will be your decision. I will accept whatever you decide. Rest assured, I do hope you decide to join me in the bed."

She would need to figure out how well she wanted to know him. Case knew she wasn't like the previous women in his life. She didn't lie. She didn't want him for what he could give her. Tara wanted to give to him. When that happened, he would take everything she was willing to grace him with. Even though he didn't know when he would leave, he knew he would.

He held out a hand. "Shall we?"

"The fresh air will be cleansing."

They stopped at the first major house they came to. It was the house of Ruinart. Inside they were greeted then given a table. Various cheeses were set on the table including Camembert, Conte and Brie. The first champagne had the taste of pears. Another tasted of strawberry. They both decided they liked the cream champagne the best.

"This is delightful," he said, sitting back, his hands on the table. His thoughts tumbling around in his head, he felt relaxed, anticipatory. She wore a yellow gown that brought out the amber color of her eyes. Her hair was pulled back into a loose chignon with wispy strands left lose to frame her face. Her eyes sparkled with the pleasure of the moment. He understood she was enjoying their time together.

"Are you going to tell me about yourself? Somehow, I got that impression. Why do you dislike the female gender." She bit into a strawberry. A drop of juice was on her lip. Case thought he'd rather lick the juice than talk about himself. He owed her some explanation.

The air he let rasp from his lungs resulted in a deep sigh. "I don't dislike you." If he could love, he would love this woman. She was everything he once dreamed about. Sweet and nice. Passionate. She was open to him. This woman didn't lie. "My mother never wanted me except for the multitude of chores I could do for her. Neither did my father who wasn't my father at all. She cuckhold him. Just as mother believed me to be useful so did father. When father died his sister came to live with us. She was about ten years older than I was. I thought she was beautiful. When she took an interest in me, I was smitten with the first bite of love."

"You fell in love with this woman? She must have planned your falling. That is why you hate us." She waved her hand in the air to stop his protest. "I'm sorry. This is your story to tell. You had the curtesy to listen to mine. I won't interrupt you. It's just that...it's not right that she helped you to believe something that wasn't true."

"You're right. She seduced me. That first time by a stream that was rushing to the ocean, filled with melting snow. She found me fishing." He closed his eyes as if remembering that time. "I cast my line in a still part of the stream. When I turned around, she was naked. The only women I'd ever seen without clothing were a few whores I paid for. This surprised me. I didn't think. All I could do was stare then drool. All my blood rushed to my groin with lightning speed."

The woman taught me how to give a woman her pleasure. Every night I slept with her. She also expected me to continue to work the fields. I did, thinking my work was for both of us. We brought in several crops that gained us a great deal of money. I loved danger though. Wasn't content to be a farmer. I found a man who was willing to pay me outrageous sums if I would find and bring in criminals. That was how I became a bounty hunter. Sometimes the man I hunted paid me more to leave him be. I always accepted the higher payment until I came into the service of Drake Montgomerie. With this man, I couldn't negotiate the price."

"You did? Is that how you became employed by my uncle? He wouldn't like a man who betrayed him. If you didn't do the job he expected of you, he would never send you on another mission."

"No, that was at a later date. I earned more money than I ever dreamed. Together my father's sister and I had a bank account. I thought the deed to the home in the highlands was in my name as was the bank account."

"It wasn't?" Tara asked as she continued to sip on the cream flavored champagne. She handed the empty glass to him for a refill. "We should buy a couple of bottles of this. It's very good." With a piece of

Brie between her lips she stared at him when he began to speak again.

"When I got back from a case that took me to Spain, I found that all the funds were taken from the account I thought I was part of, the home I grew up in sold, and the woman I thought I loved and who loved me was gone. She got her hands on what was rightfully mine with an advocate's help. Not certain how they pulled it off. There had to be some fraud involved. I'll never know. The advocate was the man she ran away with. The man she loved...maybe...maybe not. I was left with nothing. Knew myself to be a fool. Vowed I would never let another woman rule my life. After that I sought more danger. When your uncle discovered me, he told me I was the exact type of person he searched for."

"So, this older woman is the reason you cannot love." Tara's words were a statement not a question. "A man should never judge all women by one who hurt him."

"Not just this woman. Every woman I've encountered after that. They all wanted something from me. Some sought marriage. Some wanted me to set them up in a home as my mistress. They were looking for material wealth, not a man to care for them or love them. None of the women I encountered were interested in children. Some liked the thought of going to bed with a man they claimed was dangerous. Others just craved the orgasm I would give them. There was nothing else there except sex, raw and ugly. At one time I wanted more. Learned that for me there would never be more."

"You are dangerous. Not in the way you're saying. You're dangerous to my heart," Tara said with a voice filled with yearning. She pulled in a deep breath of air.

Case ran a finger along her jawline. Touched her with gentleness. If he could, he would never hurt her again. That wasn't something he would ever do...to any woman. Let alone this woman he cared for. "I understood how you felt about me when you told me why you never allowed Jeremy into your bed. Why you never allowed another man to claim your innocence. I was honored. Know that if I could give you my love in return, I would. I cannot give you what you want. I'm too jaded, my heart as well as my soul has been shattered by betrayal, too many times torn as well as ripped apart. If I pretended something different, we would come to hate each other. You have to understand how much I want you as well as the fact I would never take something you are not willing to give."

He noted the blood thundering at the base of her neck. She turned her face into the palm of his hand, her eyes closing for a moment. Felt moisture in his palm. His body ached for her, longed to ease her mind. He could not. Guilt swept into him. Guilt was an emotion he'd never felt before. Case wanted to push the sensation from his head. Replace the thoughts with Tara.

Tara placed her hand on his. Her fingers were small, her hand soft where she touched him. "It's alright. I understand what you say. For now, until you have to leave for some distant place, for some adventure you've never experienced, I want you also. I'll be honored to be with you in every way a man and a woman come together."

Case closed his eyes dwelling on her words. He opened them focused on her while he spoke. "I'm the one who is honored beyond anything I've felt before," Case said. "For the rest of the time I'm with you, I'd like you to be my lover." Case recognized the fact he tread on unstable ground. A woman such as Tara didn't become a man's lover. She should expect marriage. She deserved marriage. "You should tell me no."

"Just as you cannot love me or anyone else, I cannot say no to you. Whether you like hearing the words or not, I will tell you true. "*Je t'adore*. I want to know you intimately again. Want to know the pleasure you can give to me and I to you. I hope my being with you gives you pleasure too. Suppose I'm taking from you just what a jaded man would expect."

"No, if you tell me yes, I'll be taking from you. I'll be stealing your honor, your reputation forever tarnished. As long as this doesn't continue in London, no one will know what we do in France together at night. There is no mistaking the fact I want you in my arms as well as my bed. Every night for as long as I can stay with you. Will you honor me that way? Will you consent to becoming my lover?" He had no business asking this of her. He asked her to honor him with her body when he took her respect away. How the hell could he live with that? He didn't have an answer. That fact changed nothing.

"With all my heart I want to say yes," her murmured words were soft, sensuous. Tara was hesitating, thinking. "There is still that part of me that would..." Her thoughtful pause left him confused as well as frustrated.

"You're going to make me sweat, aren't you?" he asked lifting one eyebrow. Speculation would not give him the answer he wished for.

Case leaned toward her, his hand cupping her chin. He kissed her, brushed his mouth on hers. Soft lips met his. To Case the sensation was bittersweet filled with longing he couldn't hold forever. He understood he would never grow tired of her. In his future when he was alone, he would think of Tara, want her in his arms, his bed. With a light touch, her hand rested on his shoulder. Case loved the way she was both tender and sweet. Her innate honesty touched his heart. He should leave her alone. Should walk away from her life. Even Jeremy would be better for her because he would love her as she was meant to be loved.

I want Tara more than I ever thought possible. She will tell me yes. I will make love to her. Even now the thought that after he possessed her beautiful body, learned all the intricate curves, memorized them, left him cold and lifeless.

"Yes." Tara laughed that sweet melodic sound he was coming to adore. "If you had to sweat waiting for my answer, I believe I would like that. Sometimes a man has to come down a peg or two so he doesn't remain so arrogant. Sometimes a man needs to wait to hear an answer. He can't just assume all he wishes for will be his."

"You are a wicked *lass*, a *wee* siren to bedevil me." His body relaxed when he heard her answer even while his heartbeat picked up its pace. Case kissed her again, a brief chaste kiss meant to seal the bargain that was created here.

He stood, watching the slow rise and fall of her breasts. Knew soon they would be in his hands. He would hold their softness, caress the tips with his mouth, taste all of her. He would learn all her dark secrets. "Take my hand. We are going back to our room so we can finish this in private." His gut tightened with anticipation. Heat swept to his groin. He picked up the bottles of champagne he purchased earlier. On the way back they stopped at an *épicerie* for an array of cheeses along with a baguette. After that a *boulangerie* where they picked up croissants for the morning meal. "We are going to eat and drink tonight. Don't want you to go hungry. I'm going to keep you up until dawn. Naked, we will watch the sunrise from our balcony."

"You know I've an early bedtime." Tara skipped along beside him trying to keep up with his longer strides. "Did I say yes? I don't recall? Are we lovers then?" she questioned.

"Little tease. Not tonight you won't retire early. Though perhaps we will have to take a nap or two between our explorations." Case wanted her to investigate his body. Needed to feel her hands everywhere, her mouth also.

"I cannot drink champagne all night. You don't want me muzzled, do you? A headache in the morning would be terrible," Tara told him when he stopped at an intersection to let traffic pass by. "We will both wake up with a bad head. We won't see any sunrise."

"Neither can I. We will do other things during the night. One bottle will not be too much. Once one is opened, we cannot lose the bubbles. It has to be consumed. That's a rule." Case pulled her into his arms. His mouth found hers. Sucked. Nibbled. Tested her emotions as his body contracted with his desire. The flames Tara so easily aroused sent raw passion racing through him, straight to his swelling sex. Case wanted to show the entire world this woman was his.

This time after she opened for him, he tasted all the sweet flavors that were Tara coupled with the champagne they drank. His hands cupped her adorable bottom, pulling her body so she would feel his arousal caressing her belly. His member was blatantly hard. Her hands roamed the length of his back. She played with his tongue, danced then toured the depth of his mouth.

The conversations since the contest had him in a constant state of desire. The small touches enflamed him.

I'm a patient man. I waited. Tara came to me, wants me despite what I cannot give her. I'm pleased to have her for one night, a week maybe a month. After that we will go our separate ways. I'm hoping there will be no regrets. I will have to make sure I don't sire a baby. I would not want her life complicated in that manner. We will take precautions.

"Other things." Tara drew out the words as if questioning him. Her eyes were wide. Her lips damp, swollen from the few kisses they shared.

"Yes, many other things, different ways to give and receive pleasure so you don't get bored." The devil, he wanted to cup her breast, show all of Epernay that she was his. He wanted for Jeremy to understand that Tara would never want him. Jeremy would never possess Tara.

In the waning light of the day, he skimmed her back. Ran his hands along her sides until they were beneath her breasts. He cupped both soft globes, showing anyone who walked by Tara meant something to him. With his thumbs rubbing against her nipples, he kissed her deep and hard. Explored in the sultry dark recesses until the soft moan of pleasure rippled from her mouth into his. Again and again, his thumbs skimmed the tips of her breast. The tips were hard. Through the fabric, he squeezed then tugged. Case delighted in the way she pressed her soft body to get closer. There was no doubt in his mind. She wanted him.

A mewl.

A soft moan.

Tara sighed into his mouth.

Without help from his hands she pressed her hips against him. To toss her skirts then plunge inside her would be heaven to this man. This time he wouldn't hurt her. He would make everything right between them. She would climax. He would see to her pleasure, give her the orgasm she missed the first time they were together. Her fingernails raked across his neck then into his hair. She stabbed her tongue inside his open mouth. He took pleasure in the gentle nip, the bite she took. He sucked air wishing he dared bare her breasts so he could take them into the heat of his mouth.

Case deepened the kiss, holding her head tight. He pressed his knee between her legs, spreading them. He lifted his knee so his thigh rested at the juncture between her legs. He moved his leg with delicate precision across sensitive folds of feminine flesh. Tara responded. Her sweetness unraveled his senses. He pushed against her. If he didn't end this kiss soon, he would take her here at this busy intersection for all to watch. As it was now, heads turned. This was danger of a different kind.

With regret, he pulled away. "I want you now. Do you want me, little siren? Should we find a dark corner where I can have you to myself. Can I wait until I get you to the rental? Can you?" He had to have the answer. He wasn't going to push this any farther if she would have regrets.

"More than you want me. I'm burning up as if you lit a fire inside me. Deep in my most secret places I ache for you. My body hums with the desire you create with your kisses. I feel—"

He interrupted. "This time I won't hurt you. I promise. I won't disappoint or run out on you." Unable to wait for her smaller strides to reach the rented room, he swept her into his arms. His steps lengthened. She played with the buttons on his shirt, one then two came undone. He knew what she did. He fought to maintain his sanity. Before they reached the porch all the buttons were undone. She ran her hands across the expanse of his naked chest sliding lower then lower still. His stomach contracted with her touch. Tara wrestled with his belt buckle until it too was unfastened. Her hands slipped lower, touching him through the fabric of his pants. He grew harder. Minutes later he kicked the front door open. He captured her mouth with his while she teased him.

Tara's hand was flush on his chest. As if fascinated by his nipple, she played with the hard bud. Squeezed, twisted the tip. When he released her lips to stare down at her she spoke almost in awe, "They are so tiny," she said meaning the word. "You are so different. I love the differences."

"Not tiny like your dog who is anything but tiny which is his namesake." Case set the champagne on the floor before tossing her on the bed then fell down on top of her. Desperate to have her, he spoke. "If I can't control my desire, this is going to be hard and fast. Messy and loud. I'll try not to devour you. Though you aren't helping." Her hands finished unfastening his pants. She stroked him. He groaned his response to the pleasure. "After that we'll take our time. I'll love every part of you until you beg for more. I want you needing me with all that you are. Begging for me to find my way inside you." He bit then laved the spot at the base of her neck that told him how much she wanted him.

"Hard and fast? Messy and loud?" Tara questioned as his nimble fingers did away with the gown she wore.

"You will yell." He tossed the removed pieces onto the floor. She heard the swish of fabric along with the thud of her shoes. Cool air wafted over her naked flesh caressing her body, exciting her. She heated. Flamed to life. Her fingers gripped his shoulders.

She bit him. "So will you."

He laughed with his pleasure. She was soft everywhere. Between her legs she was wet with desire, raw passion. Tara flamed to swift heated arousal with little provocation. She was ready for him, gliding over him with raw heat.

"I should do this slow and easy," he murmured while he sucked on the tip of her breast, suckled and laved. Nipped with tenderness. His hand slid along her thigh until he could tug the rest of her underclothing from her body. He flipped her over to undo the corset she wore. Case liked her on her stomach. Her back was smooth and sleek, narrowing at the waist before flaring to wide hips. He loved to caress her rounded bottom. His hands slipped beneath her pantalets. Lower to caress then slide his fingers down her cleft. Into the softest part of her. The secret folds were swollen and wet. She wept for him. For the attention he would give her.

All she wore now were her stockings. He stood. In seconds his clothing was scattered across the floor. When she tried to turn over, he stopped her. Case loved her back. Loved kissing her down the length of her spine until he could nip her adorable butt then watch the muscles quiver. When he did, she cried out. He wanted to spread her legs so he could taste her intimately. Wanted her open to him in every way possible. Sometime tonight he would do so.

By dawn he would have tasted all of her, made love to her in many different ways. This would be a night he would never forget. Case prayed Tara would always remember this evening with fondness.

"Thought you said fast...messy as well as loud...I'm waiting," she said as once more she tried to turn. "And hard. I want you, Case Ferguson. Don't want to wait. Do your worst. Make this happen. Now!"

With his hands beneath her rear, he lifted her. Tara's legs were spread wide across his. He was between them. Case touched his lips on the cleft between her thighs. Brought her higher so he could see all of her. So pink and beautiful. He needed more. She needed more. One then two fingers slipped inside her. She was soft velvet. She moaned. Whimpered. Her hips rose to meet the small thrusts of his fingers. If he would have pleasured her this way the first time, he would have touched her barrier. Before he thrust inside her he would have known of her virtue. Would he have still taken her? There were no doubts in his mind that he would have done so. That night she would have been his. He would have had time to think. He would have treated her right. Not as he did.

Where loving Tara was concerned, he had only the one regret. He would make up for rushing out on her. For hurting her. Case understood Tara felt deep rejection by his actions. She was a woman who should never feel rejection.

"I did." Case turned her again. She faced him. He could see into her eyes. Read their expressions. Convention this second time would be more prudent than taking her in a manner that would surprise her. He settled her legs across his thighs. She was open to him, vulnerable in every sense. With trust in her eyes, she watched him. She caught her bottom lip beneath her teeth.

Tara's fingers touched his shoulders. She swept her pink tongue across her mouth leaving moisture behind. Dampness he wished to taste. He thought of spilling champagne on the tips of her breasts. As she breathed, the twin peaks moved. The sight delighted him in every way imaginable. The nipples were a soft pink surrounded by a softer shade of rose. With the liquid drops on the tips, he would suck her hard and deep into his mouth. Hard. Messy.

"Have you changed your mind?" she asked as she seemed to pant to drag in air. She was moving with restless need. Her body squirming.

"Maybe," he told her as he found the pearl in the soft folds that would soon welcome him. As he touched and massaged the hard jewel, her hips rose off the bed seeking more from him. "When you do that, arch your body, you are reaching for me. This will bring you to your orgasm. What this tells me is that you want for me to enter you. Is that what you want, little siren? Do you want me inside your body. Do you want to join with me?"

Her head was moving as her hips took on the rhythm he set with his fingers. His thumb circled the hard nub he pointed out to her. "Yes...I want you. Case, I need you. Please. Don't stop. Don't leave me! Don't be angry with me!"

Angry with her? "Never!" Leave her? Never again.

Bending over her he jerked a nipple into his mouth, drinking hard until she cried out. After that he switched his attention to the other breast. "Tell me what you want, sweet Tara. Do you like my mouth on your titties?"

"I can't...please." Tara's nails bit into his shoulders. She raked them down his chest leaving ten red marks. She held onto his hips. She spread her legs wider offering more of herself to him.

Case moved lower gazed at her intimately. He rose above her to take her mouth into his. Braced himself on his elbows. The kiss was hard demanding. Inflamed. She met his tongue with hers. Rubbed, played with it as he jabbed into her then out just as he would do later with his rod.

His fingers deep inside Tara, stroking her, he felt the clenching of her muscles, knew her climax would erupt. Her sultry thick moisture showered down on his fingers. She was aroused beyond what he thought possible. Tara was a welcome dream.

The first time he gave her a small amount of pleasure then pain. Everything would be different tonight. This joining of their bodies would yield pleasure, more pleasure after that more gratification than either could imagine. He wasn't going to stop until she understood she was his for the time allotted to them.

Tara was his. Until she wasn't. He understood. Case prayed she would also understand how it was supposed to be for them.

"I'm going to come inside you now," he spoke with a gentle ease as he prepared her. "I won't hurt you."

"No!" She sat up trembling. Her body shook with the need he gave her along with something else. "No, not yet!" Tara gulped air. Her entire body shook. "Wait."

"Why?" Case was shocked as well as unprepared for her denial. "What is it? Did I hurt you? Tell me."

"Hmm...well...I need a moment of privacy. Can you give me that? I've got to do something first. Before we..."

Case still didn't understand. "Tell me why. I need to know what you are thinking. After that, you can have anything you want. Do you not want to make love with me?"

She sat, leaning against her elbows, her legs still spread across his thighs. "It's not that," she looked to the door then to him. "I—I need," she swept her tongue across her mouth. "I just need to be alone for a second or two."

"What do you need?" Case realized what she was speaking of. He thought of it once before when she went to Madam Pipelet's home. "Never mind. I'll wait in the other room until you are ready."

"You will?"

"What you intend is best. I don't want a child out of wedlock. Don't wish for you or a baby I helped conceive to have the bastard stigma attached. I do understand." Naked he walked from the bedroom. Case understood he should have thought of protection. He wanted her too much to think with a rational mind. He wished she would have told him sooner. His grin widened. What this told him was that she had every intention of becoming his lover. She planned for this moment.

~ * ~

Beneath her breath Tara cursed. He aroused her to such a point she couldn't think. So enamored as to what was happening, she almost forgot. She was lucky the first time. Not only did Madam Pipelet give her the sponges as well as the vinegar to soak them in she also gave her a quick lesson on the best time to conceive. For her, today would be one of the best. If she made love without using protection, she would become a mother. Crossing her fingers, she set about soaking the sponges. She put four in the vinegar she poured into the small vial Madam Pipelet gave her.

I was afraid Case would object when I told him what I wanted.

When he understood, relief swept through me. Though I want a child to remember him by that isn't a good enough reason to have a child who would be labeled a bastard his or her entire life.

She understood some people got over the stigma and were able to move on with their lives. Her half-brother did. He was loved by two parents. He inherited a title. This babe would not. This child would have nothing except her love.

Before he spoke, Tara sensed his presence. His warm body was behind her. She felt strange standing next to him when they were both undressed. A current of energy swept up her spine. Her legs trembled while she thought her knees would give out. This was something she might have to get used to. He set his hands on her shoulders before turning her. The tips of her breasts brushed across his arm. His arousal jutted out from his body. She found she couldn't speak. Her throat was parched. If she could utter an intelligent word, she didn't know what to say. He ran his thumb across her bottom lip. The gesture seemed protective as well as evocative. His eyes sparkled with amusement.

"I will put the sponge inside you. It was my job to think about protecting you. I forgot. I'm glad you have what we both need." He held her with a light touch. If she wished, she could step away.

Tara blinked trying to come to terms with what he said. She couldn't fathom anything. Moments passed. "You...? Put it inside me? How...?" Tara never thought of that possibility. His fingers were inside her earlier. He would just... Bloody eyes, he would...he could...

"Yes." He ran his finger along the slender column of her neck then across her collarbone. He found the valley between her breast then moved on to her naval. He stilled his hand just shy of the juncture between her legs. He was making a valid point. One she could not dismiss. The caress was feather-light as he continued to traverse her body. Shivers wracked her. With two fingers he squeezed the tip of one breast then bent to suckle. "I hope you are still as aroused as you were before you stopped our love making. Lay on the bed. Spread your legs for me. You will be ready to receive me as soon as you do." Assuming she was in agreement, he took the sponge from her fingers.

Tara nodded, understanding it would not take much effort on his part to have her begging for her release since she now possessed an understanding of how that climax might feel. He brought her hands around his neck. She found herself flush against him. He was hard. His penis protruded against her belly. Her breasts pushed on his chest.

"Wrap your legs around me." He nipped her ear, kissed the sensitive spot behind while he strode to the bed.

When she did as he asked, his arousal nestled between her legs. Separated her most intimately. As he walked, she felt the friction in the most intimate part of her. With easy finesse he set her on the bed, came down beside her. With ease, he pushed her legs apart. Seeing her. Embarrassment heated her. Case set her feet so her knees were high. He had access to her. With care not meant to entice, he pressed the sponge inside her, Tara was certain he touched her womb. He pushed then withdrew those two fingers. With his thumb, tantalized the hard nub that sent her world spinning. A sound she didn't recognize whispered from her.

Case stroked and nipped tender sensitive flesh. He touched upon all her most delicate places until she was arching and moaning, begging with little mewls that should tell him how much she needed him. Her body crammed with overstimulated nerves brought to near bursting. Without speaking, he eased inside. Tara felt herself stretching. Her body accommodating his, easing his way.

Her legs were still around his flanks when he started stroking, moving in then out. Slow delicate precision turned to harder faster strokes. She held on tight as her body reeled higher then higher still. Her muscles clenched tight around him. He caressed, touching her womb, thrust.

Pleasure.

Pain. Sweet torture.

Deep throbbing desire consumed her as her body bucked against his seeking the ultimate release.

With a vibrant cry, her body climaxed. Blinding pleasure-pain pulsing, throbbing as she writhed beneath Case. With a rough growl he emptied himself inside her. Small pulses continued to command her body. Her arms around him pulling him closer, she didn't want to let him go. Tara buried her face against the hollow of his shoulder as her body calmed. This was something she never thought possible. Never experienced.

He ran his hands through the tangle of her hair. "You were perfect," his husky whisper sent a thrill of desire into her. She loved this man so much. Even more now that she gave herself so thoroughly to him.

Tara liked the way he felt inside her. He filled her. Loved being one with him. She felt a part of him. Heated her. A long deep breath of air enhanced her lungs. She nipped his shoulder. He rolled aside, staring at her. Braced himself on one arm as he stroked her with gentle care. Toyed with over-sensitive skin.

"You are still here," she said as she recalled the first time along with the near debilitating rejection she felt when he raced from the bedroom. "You didn't run from what we just did. I'm glad of that."

"Not planning to go anywhere." Case stood. Looked down upon her. "I'm going to get some refreshments. We will eat and drink. After that if you are amenable, we'll pursue a different way to make love."

She admired his body as he walked to the basin. His legs were long, his backside hard, buttocks small. The man was made of muscle. He washed himself then brought the cloth for her. "If you wish." He handed it to her. He brought two glasses of the champagne along with a small platter of cheese as well as the baguette. After he sat on the bed, he held a piece of Brie to her lips. She accepted.

"Believed you enjoyed the Brie more than the others." Case put what was left of the cheese into his mouth.

"I did like the Brie. Don't know if it was more than the others." Leaning against the headboard, they both drank and ate. She pulled the sheet up to cover her. He broke off two chunks from the bread. Tara didn't know how long this seeming calm would last or their discovery of each other. She meant to enjoy every moment she would have with this man. This seemed like heaven to her. For the first time in two years, she felt alive.

He held his glass to her lips, encouraging her to drink. Droplets trickled down her chin. Tara laughed, enjoying him more with each minute. The drops slithered down her chin then her neck. He poured more across her lips. She licked. Some of the drops settled between her breasts.

"Lay back, little siren. I'm going to taste you again." She did as she felt him adjust his position. "I'm going to clean you up. What do you think? Would you like me to sip the champagne drops? Should I consume you along with the wasted champagne? Devour all. Don't want to leave you in a mess."

"Case? You don't...?" she questioned when she felt the slow dribble of liquid across her breasts then lower to her belly. His lips sucked on each drop until her body quickened with the desire he aroused in her so easily. He nursed her breasts, drawing on each tip until they were elongated and wet. She'd never seen her nipples so large.

His fingers slipped between her legs. Moved with lethargy as she opened herself to him, wanting him. "You are soft and wet for me. Thick honey prepares you for my entrance. So ready. Will you always be primed for me?" With his long fingers he brought out the first sponge then inserted another one. Case meant to make love to her again. By the end of the night, she would be wilted, devoid of muscle along with energy needed to move or think.

With a quick deft motion, he flipped her over, pulling her hips up. Her forearms were on the mattress, her fanny high in the air. His hands bracketed her hips. "Case...is this...going to work?" Tara questioned him as he entered her from behind. She gasped with delight. He stroked. Pushed hard. Moved with slow caresses. Faster. Changed the tempo. Her mewl of pleasure rippled through the moonlit night. Held himself still as she pressed against him begging. She felt wet and hot. Tara needed him. Knew what she wanted. What he could give to her.

"Seems to be working just fine." Case laughed as he withdrew then entered her, thrusting to meet each begging pulse of her body. She cried out her pleasure. He growled. After they both climaxed, she rested in his arms again. He played with the long strands of her hair that fell loose from the bun she wove in her hair earlier today. "So soft. I feel as if I'm touching cool silk when I pull your hair between my fingers."

"I didn't know," she told him while she stroked his chest, curled black hair around the tip of her finger. "Are there other ways? Will you teach me?"

"Lots...we won't try them all tonight. Have to keep some surprises for another time." Case blew on one of her damp nipples. Her nails bit into his chest.

"I understand." Tara needed to ascertain everything about this man. Needed to know what he wanted. How he liked to be touched. To please him would be her enjoyment until he left her.

"Do you? I'm not so certain." He brought another long strand of golden hair to his lips. "Hmm...love the scent of your hair. Everything about you is lilies coupled with summer rain. You know the scent of the air when the drops falling from the sky are light and airy?" Case waited for her to answer.

The question was absorbed into Tara's head. "Yes, everything thing smells so fresh and new."

"That's your scent. I'll always think of you when it rains in the summer."

Tara needed to know yet she didn't want to find out. "How long will you be in Paris now that you got your man?" she asked curious about how much time she would have with him. Tara didn't want to count the days. When she thought harder about it, she didn't want to know when he was leaving. It would be best if she woke up one morning and he was gone. She wouldn't mourn him before he was gone from her life.

"Getting my man, as you put it, is not my mission in Paris. The act was secondary. I'm here on a diplomatic assignment that if you recall includes you. We've only been to one ball. We've barely mingled with the aristocrats we are supposed to court as friends. We will have to attend more to understand the gist of the politics at this time. We'll be here until Lord Montgomerie is satisfied with the knowledge I've uncovered or until there is some other fugitive for me to go after. At that time, I'll leave. Why?"

Case must know why she asked. She didn't want to answer. Didn't want to think about that time. For now, Case was hers. After he left, she would never see him again. He would vanish from her life.

Tara continued to play with the crisp dark hair on his chest wound her fingers into then out. It was her way of thinking without giving anything away by the expression on her face. "We will be able to sleep together when we're in the city?" She didn't want to think about sneaking around to be with him. "Ash will spend most of his time with his mistress. Doubt if he will care what we do."

"Yes, I'm sure he will. Ash won't be at our shared apartment. Nor will he pass judgement if he catches us sleeping in the same bed," Case told her. "Are you having second thoughts?"

"No, no second or third thoughts. Not for me. How about you?" She paused for a few seconds still toying with the hair on his chest. "Case," she stopped again. Braced herself above him. When she was looking at him, she said. "Don't tell me when you are leaving. I don't want to know. Don't want to have to think about the day or dread each day I have with you before that time. Need to enjoy the time we have together." The tears she wanted to avoid threatened at the thought of never seeing this man again. This man she loved with all her heart. How could this happen twice in a lifetime? Moisture clogged her throat. Tara fisted her hand on his chest. She tightened her body, willing the moisture to evaporate.

"You want me to walk out on you?" Case asked in disbelief. "I cannot imagine that would be preferable to knowing when I will go."

"Yes...no...leave me a letter or a note telling me you've gone. You can tell me where you are off to or not. I'll deal with everything else the best way I can. I don't want to cry before I know you will leave. Don't wish to worry over those last minutes I will have with you. Don't wish to live with dread."

"I don't like it. However, if that is what you want..." Case pushed hair from her eyes, lifting her chin higher. "Don't cry for me, little siren. I'm not worth your tears. You will be better off not loving me. I'm not a loveable man. Never have been. Never will be. Don't know how to love. I'm not a good enough man for you."

Tara tried to blink away the tears before he saw the pain in her eyes. Now that she tasted paradise, she didn't know how she would live without him. She would have to find some way to get through each day. It would feel much the same as when Grant passed away. She didn't want to see a new day without him. Was forced to do so because Grant was no longer with her. Now she would mourn the loss of Case as well. Once he left, he would never return. She would keep all her memories within the confines of her heart.

"Don't cry. I'm not worth tears," Case repeated as if his words would stop the rain of tears. "Don't shed any tears for me. I don't deserve them. You knew all along I cannot love. I will always cherish this time with you. Won't ever forget what we are sharing. Listen to me." His hand was set over hers. "Listen to me. When I've left, you need to find a man worthy of you. A man you can love and who can love you in return. Don't ever settle on a man just because..."

"No one can replace you in my heart. I've had two loves in my lifetime. I will have to make do with that. I'm luckier than most women. Some never find one man to love. As to settling for a man I can't love...no, I won't do that."

"Not as lucky as I was to find you." He kissed her, swept his tongue inside her mouth, sucked and nipped. He touched the surface of her teeth, tugged on her lips to get her to open more for him. He nipped kisses down her body, touching on all the sensitive places that heated her. She responded.

Once again, he settled between her legs. Instead of his fingers touching upon her to entice as well as create magical enchantment, his mouth kissed her. His teeth touched upon the nub. He bit then soothed. He laved then spread her legs wider. His tongue touched and thrust inside her. Tara cried out as her body felt the nerves tighten as the orgasm blinded her senses to everything except what Case orchestrated.

Seconds later, he produced another sponge. He was inside her, pushing her body to respond again and again. His roar of pleasure coincided with her cry as she climaxed. Found her body answering so easily to his demands. As she calmed, she rested in his arms. A fine film of moisture covered her. She was sated. Weak from the sensations. Didn't think she could move again. Her eyes were closed. His hand cupped her breast as if he owned the tender globe. He did. For now, as well as forever. There would be no one else for her.

They made love two more times that night. Each time seemed bittersweet to Tara. Thoughts of him leaving took over her sensitized brain. She tried to soak up each joining to remember everything, every caress, all the feelings as well as the longings. She would have to remember these fragile moments for a lifetime. Tara needed to remember for the cold nights she would have to spend alone.

The new lovers spent two more days in Epernay. Played in bed most of the night. Walked the streets visiting other champagne houses during the day. By the time they were ready to return to Paris, they had a case of various champagnes and flavors, many from the different houses they discovered on their outings.

In the carriage, she rested her head on Case's chest. She was tired yet felt completed. His arm was wrapped around her. He kissed her forehead then the tip of her nose. His hand played with the fabric of her skirt until she felt his fingers beneath. He slid his hand up her leg until he found the waistband of her underwear. He pressed his fingers across her belly. She understood what they would do for the next minutes.

"Lift your hips, little siren. I would prefer you naked beneath your skirts and petticoats."

"You are insatiable, Case Ferguson. Do you have a sponge ready also?" A couple of times they forgot the protection. Tara didn't know what that meant...if she was still safe since every other time they used the sponges. She would have to speak with Madam Pipelet as soon as she got the chance.

"I soaked a few before we left while you were enjoying your bath." He kissed her neck, ran his thumb along the length then across her collarbone. "I did anticipate the ride would be less boring if we found a means to occupy our time."

"You mean to do this? Make love in the carriage?" She was shocked by the thought then she wasn't. Case would dare anything. Inhibition wasn't part of him. She appreciated the danger inherent in being caught. Of course, she would be far more embarrassed than he. "What if we have to stop?"

"No problem. You will grin at the driver. We'll both be covered by your skirts. You can pretend you had to get close to me to feed me the bonbons in the bag next to you."

"You would think of everything."

He managed to wrestle her pantalets from her legs. She helped by raising her dress then wiggling as his fingers slid the length of her leg. Case took every opportunity to touch her in delightful and provocative places. By now, he knew everything about her, where he could touch her to bring the sensual heat to the greatest height possible. Even then it was no easy feat to get the blasted drawers off her feet. If the fabric didn't catch on one thing it caught on something else. When he finally removed them, Case stuffed the offending article in the corner then set her astride him. He undid his britches. She felt his heavy arousal. He was hot, pulsing, pushing against her softness. Case was eager to be inside her.

"You want to feel all those wonderful things. You can do this at your speed. Not mine. Take over the direction we should proceed? It is the orgasm you want. Isn't it? I've created a woman who wants her pleasure more than anything. Admit it, Tara. You don't care about my needs; you want to climax. The sooner the better."

Tucking her lips together she nodded, a smile on her mouth. "Yes...it's nice what you do to me. I like it when...oh...oh..." Tara shrieked when he started the seduction. He didn't sweettalk or charm. Case went straight to the part of her that would send her over the top.

Case touched her, danced his fingers on that most sensitive place between her legs, toyed with his deft actions. He pushed the sponge inside. "No chance taking today." He kissed her hard, touched her with demand.

Neither spoke of those few times they forgot the sponge. Before he left, they would have to speak of it. That was then. Not now.

"Do you wish to sit on me? As I spoke earlier, you will have all the control. This will be a wonderful way to spend the boring time for the ride home. It's your call," he said as he tugged on the sleeves of her gown. It was a simple matter to lower the fabric until her breasts were freed. "These are beautiful. So very kissable. Tasty. A man's dream come true," he murmured just before he curled his tongue around each one. He bit with temperate meticulousness then looked at her as if asking her if she liked what he did. Tara arched against him, giving him her answer. He already made her body hum with raw passion coupled with heated desire. The man could ignite her with the hunger, the gleam in his eyes he showered her with.

"Sit on you?" she was curious, thinking. Tara was delighted with the idea. She wanted him deep inside her. "Another way to make love? If you insist." She would do anything with this man. They would not be bored. Her gown lowered, Tara watched as her breasts bobbed and danced in front of him.

His fingers closed around both globes holding them still for the moment. He fondled them. Caressed the hardened tips. Traced the aureole around them. Once more, he bit. He licked. Soothed tender places. Case settled his head between the valley of her breast. He inhaled with a deep breath of air. She felt his tongue, felt the pressure when the palm of his hands glanced over the tips. "You taste just as nice as I remember. Though it hasn't been that long since I suckled here...and here." He paused. "Are you sore?"

This was a fine time to ask now that he had her aroused to a point she could no longer tell him no. To the point where her body vibrated with sensual need. Giving Case the only possible answer, Tara shook her head as she wondered if he would stop if she told him the truth. Well, she wasn't that sore. They would have to slow down sometime. She was exhausted. Lack of sleep had a way of doing that to a person. Reaching that point where her body exploded with unrestrained delight would tire any person.

His hands on her waist, Case lifted her. She felt the tip of him press against her. "Please," she whispered.

"Whenever you wish. I'll lower you onto me. Say the word then I'll be all yours. You do want me. Don't you?"

Her head was thrown back, her body crying out for release. "Now! Now, Case. Come inside me. Pleasure me until I can't breathe for the ecstasy."

Case guided her down until they were joined. Without moving she sat on him, enchanted with the feeling of him deep inside her. It was a heady feeling this control he gave her. She understood he could take over any time he wished. If he desired to do so, she would have no say. For now, he allowed her to set the pace.

Tara put her hands on his shoulders. With slowness that belied her escalating need, she rose on his member then traveled down. The sensation was exquisite. Hot. Sizzling. His hands tightened. She squeezed herself around him. Taunted. Teased. Drove herself wild. She wanted to make this good for him too.

"Have I told you before? I like the way you feel deep inside me. You are inflexible and scorching. I like to tighten my muscles around you. Do you like it when I do? Can you feel it? Case, I want to taste you. Can I do that? Take you inside my mouth?"

His body contracted at her words. He groaned as if he imagined the sensation. "Tonight. Tonight, you can do that. You can take me inside your mouth if that is what you would like. I would like you to taste me just as I've savored you."

Tara rose on him again, once then twice. When she looked at him there were fine lines around his eyes. His lips were pulled back across his teeth. Case looked as if he was in pain. "Am I hurting you?" She'd never seen him look quite like this.

"No..." The one word was another groan...a rumble. "You're so bloody slow. I wanted to give you control. Now...now..." He pushed up hard. She felt him drive inside her.

Her smile caught his attention. "Control. Too bloody slow...hmm..." She held still. Tara understood the problem was not so much about control. The difficulty he was having was about his orchestrating her climax before he lost the battle. He didn't touch her. Kept his hands around her waist. If he touched her, her body would soar. As it was, she was aroused but not so thoroughly she would climax when he decided. She needed this to be her moment.

Her body rested for a second. She felt as well as saw his frustration. The lines on his face deepened with his need. "Can I...?" he questioned but she wasn't certain what he asked.

"What?"

"Touch you?" his voice shook with emotion.

Despite the fact he gave her the management of this she had not expected him to ask permission. "Only when I show you what I want you to touch." Tara was enjoying this moment of domination. It was obvious to her that Case was not as pleased as she was. In the end they would both find satisfaction.

She moved again. Wiggled. Squeezed. Moved the tiniest bit up then down. She knew she was driving him crazy. Soon it would be over. Tara found she was reaching that point sooner than she expected. Took pleasure in his groan of desire. She moved closer. Captured his mouth with hers. Her breasts sashayed across his chest. The crips dark hair they encountered stimulated every nerve ending she possessed. Heat swept into her, igniting. Her body clenched around his. Flamed to life. Her face was hot as were her breasts and belly as well as lower in the most intimate places. She swept her tongue across his lips to find them open, waiting for her. Around her waist his hands clenched. If she wasn't mistaken, he tried to push farther into her.

"Naughty boy," she chided playfully. With her hands wrapped around his neck, she pulled herself up his large body. The tips of her breast settled on his mouth. She moved them across his open lips. He nipped. Licked. Wrapped his tongue around the peak. She stifled the whimper in the back of her throat. Could not hold back the next tiny moan as he thrust upward again. She no longer wanted to make the decisions. She wanted her climax. She wanted those blinding sensation when she lost control when all her nerves exploded to give her so much ecstasy.

"For a naughty girl," he said his voice soft as if he understood she was about to relinquish the choices to him. "You want your orgasm. You can hold out only so long. Tell me true. You want me to take over, to guide you to that point where you will cry out for me. Without my expertise, you will not reach that ultimate pinnacle."

"Yes..." She breathed deeply as one of his hands pulled up her skirt for better access. The other hand stroked her breasts alternating between one then the other. Twirling the tip between his fingers.

Case touched her, stroked intimately, worried the nub that would give her the orgasm she sought. She cried out when he thrust again. Harder and faster. Faster still until she thought she would never survive. She moaned when the pulsing nerves sent her into dazzling pleasures.

Case! Oh...oh! Hmmm..." It was over. Tara slumped forward, gorged by the exquisite vibrations. Her head rested on his chest. Each breath filled her lungs. He ran one hand along her leg. Her inner thigh his destination then the wet folds between them. Two fingers entered her. She jerked up. Her body went wild.

"Should we do this again?" Case asked, his voice gruff yet soft.

"Don't believe I would survive if you did this again." Despite her words she was going wild for more. The pulsing inside her grew hotter and stronger.

His laugh gave way to another kiss then his exploring hands left her aroused and needing him again. She didn't think she would be able to walk by the time they got back to Paris.

"You have to...oh...!"

~ * ~

Jeremy sat in the townhouse he purchased for Clair. He was pleased with this new acquisition as well as the young lady who was now his mistress. She was slender, her breasts larger than he would have expected from her slight frame. They were out of proportion. He didn't mind at all. Large breasts had always delighted him. Hers were exquisite. He was having a devil of a time waiting to see them uncovered. His hands squeezed as if in anticipation of fondling her delicious bubbies.

"What would you like? At your pleasure, I'm here to serve you." Clair stood in front of him, her hands folded in front of her. Long strands of her brilliant red hair swirled around her piquant face. Her nose was perky, slightly pointed at the end with a dusting of freckles across the bridge. The rosy cheeks, he assumed were that color because of embarrassment, reminded him of the cheeks on the ceramic dolls his mother kept on a shelf. Baby doll cheeks. Clair's mouth was as generous as her breasts. They looked swollen and pouty. He hadn't even kissed her yet.

She was an absolute delight to all his male senses. He couldn't have chosen a woman better suited to him. His mind went to Ash. He thanked him for the introduction. Jeremy knew the moment he set his eyes on her that Clair was perfect for him.

"For you to relax. You'll be exhausted if you continue to stand.

You're tight as a drawn bow string. Come sit down. Take it easy or I won't be able to give you the pleasure you deserve." While he wanted to pull her down on his lap and start exploring her soft charms, it was too soon.

Ash told him she was a virgin. With a doctor at attendance, he confirmed it before he introduced her. Jeremy meant to take every possible care in presenting her to the sweetness of lovemaking. He too would help her provide for her family. His generosity would be unlimited if she ended up being as giving as she seemed.

"Don't know if I can do that. Relax. You're right. I'm strung up tight something fierce." She turned her head in several different directions as if searching the room. "A brandy?" Clair questioned as if eager to find something to do with her hands.

The grin forming couldn't be helped. "That would be nice. One for you also." Jeremy wanted her to understand that while she was here to see to his pleasure as he would see to hers, she was not a servant in this house. Tomorrow she would meet her lady's maid as well as the housekeeper. She would also have a cook who would make certain there were meals prepared for her as well as him when he visited. He supposed he would have to list a few guidelines for her so she understood she was not to clean house or cook.

Seeming to feel a bit more at ease, Clair found the brandy then poured them each a glass. With some hesitation to her steps, she sat in a chair opposite. She smiled. Sipped. Coughed.

"It burns!"

Jeremy tried to keep the hoot of laughter behind his teeth. He failed. This woman was just what he needed to get over Tara. When he leaned toward her, he took the glass from her hands then set it on the table nearby.

"You've never had brandy before? You will grow accustomed to the heat. Soon, you might find that you enjoy the heady drink. As much as I want you to enjoy our time together." The answer was obvious but he meant to allow her to tell him. Jeremy thought that with some conversation she would grow more at ease.

"Never done any of this. Never been with a man...alone. This is the first time. Lou Lou has told me a few things to expect." Her hands were shaking when she picked up the brandy glass again. This time when she sipped, she swallowed waiting for the heat that didn't arrive.

"I understand why you said yes. What I want you to understand is that if I do anything you find uncomfortable you will tell me. I won't hurt you, Clair. Won't force you to do things that will demean you. Now, why don't you tell me about yourself." Jeremy sat back, his hands behind his head interested in the beautiful play of emotions across her face.

He realized she possessed a stubborn chin. The gown she wore was old, the fabric frayed around the hem as well as the ends of the sleeves and along the corsage. There was a hole in the side of one of her shoes. Tomorrow, he would take her to the dressmaker Ash recommended. She would have new clothing. He would make sure she was in fashion from the top of her head to the tips of her toes.

"There isn't much to tell." She looked to the ormolu clock sitting on the mantle of the fireplace as if she wanted the next hours to be over with now. "I've never lived anywhere except the small home where I was born. As you know, I've siblings that need protection. That's why I'm here. To make a better life for them." She waved her hands. "This is so nice. I'm afraid I'll do something wrong."

"Not possible," Jeremy was adamant on that fact. "I won't hurt you. You can't do anything wrong. All you need do is be yourself."

She looked up, her cornflower blue eyes wide, questioning. "Lou Lou told me the first time hurt her. She said that is true for every woman."

Running his finger around his collar, Jeremy coughed. He wished she didn't know about the first time. "True. All true. The first time will hurt a *wee* bit. After I see to your pleasure, you won't remember that first time. You will enjoy all that comes after."

With his words hurtling around in her head, she paled. "I don't like pain."

"Have another sip of that brandy. I brought food from the small cafe down the block. We have a light white wine along with fish. There are small potatoes and bread. I have strawberries for dessert. What do you think? Are you hungry."

"*Oui*, eating will keep my mind from later tonight. Though it would be nice if we got this first time done with. I don't like the waiting...the worrying. Once it is done, there will be naught to worry over."

"As soon as we eat." Jeremy chuckled, his voice turning raspy as he watched the delightful way her breasts were popping out from her old gown. He realized she must have had this one for a long time. She'd outgrown the dress. Several times she attempted to pull it up to cover herself more thoroughly. Every time she breathed, the gown slipped back to its comfortable position.

In the dining room, he sat next to her. Dished up a plate with a sampling of everything. When he sat next to her, she bent her head. The prayer she said surprised him in more than one way. She prayed for him as well as for her siblings. Before she quite finished, she thanked him for allowing her to become his mistress.

Jeremy saw moisture in her blue eyes when she looked at him. "I won't let you down. I promise. I need this position. The..." She stopped. Paled as if she believed she said something wrong.

Surprised again when she ate everything he put on her plate then looked with longing at the tray. Jeremy couldn't help the laughter. "You want more? Help yourself. You can have as much as you like."

By the time they finished she ate more than he did. Jeremy was certain she would have eaten the last strawberry if he didn't beat her to it. Despite the obvious nerves, her appetite was very good.

"There is no more?" she asked seeming to be surprised. "I do love..." Her look was sheepish. "...food."

Seemed his new little mistress wanted to eat to avoid the bedding to come. "*Non*, I'll tell the cook you have a healthy appetite. I thought you might have kept eating to avoid retiring to the bedroom. Hmm...you didn't though. Did you?"

"Oh *non*! I would not do such a thing. Though it did occur to me. I do wish to please you. Where I come from, one has to eat when there is food. The next day there may be nothing."

Those words startled him. He never thought about people who had less than enough to survive. He rose then extended a hand to her.

"I'm certain you will make me a very happy man. We will retire to the drawing room. I want you to feel more relaxed." Another bottle of wine might do the trick. She was more than willing to sample everything he gave her. At their meal, she drank all the wine that was poured into her glass. It was a generous portion.

"Alright," she murmured accepting his hand with a deep breath that revealed the color of her nipples.

After he sat, he pulled her onto his lap. "Drink," he told her handing her the second glass of wine he poured for her. She nodded and sipped. "It is very good, *oui*?" His French turned out to be better than her English. The weeks here improved his grasp of the language.

"You are very good." With a light, barely perceptible caress he ran his fingers along her arm then across the top of her partially exposed breasts. He felt the reluctant shiver. Saw the hesitation as well as alarm in her eyes when the sensation startled her. "I would like to kiss you everywhere I've touched you. Take another sip of your wine. What do you think? Should I do that? Relax. The wine will help."

"Kiss...kiss me everywhere?" Alarm bells were going off in her head as her eyes widened and she thought about what he told her.

"Kisses don't hurt if that is what you're afraid of. Is that it, Clair. Are you afraid? Let me try then you can tell me *oui ou non*. If you like it say *oui*. If not *non*."

To his delight she drank most of the wine left in her glass. The tension in her small body seemed to dissipate. "I guess that would be fine."

"Let me see," Jeremy paused while he played with her hand, running his fingers between hers with slow even movements. "Believe I've touched you here more than once. A kiss now to delight all your senses." He placed a kiss on her palm, touched her there with his tongue. She jerked but didn't say a word. "...and here." He placed kisses along her arm then back to her hand which he picked up. Each of her fingers went into his mouth. Jeremy felt tiny shivers vibrate from her into him. Pleased with his efforts, he smiled. "Did you like that? Should we try...?"

Clair interrupted him with a few whispered words. "You...you've touched me other places too." The undertone of her voice told him she was not immune to his sweettalking. Clair sounded as if she was asking him for more. She wanted him to kiss her more intimately.

"That I have. I will let you decide. Where would you like me to kiss you that I haven't already done so?"

Now, Clair looked alarmed. "Tell you...? Say the word. I cannot. "I'm a good girl... I used to be."

"*Non*, you would rather I guessed. Very well. I think I know what you would like." He brushed strands of her titillating red hair from her neck. With a gentle brush, he touched the pulse point at the base with his lips. He treated the experience with his tongue. Repositioning his lips, he sucked at the same spot, laved to soothe before sucking again. She squirmed. Her breath hitched. When he finished and saw the mark he left, he was delighted with his efforts. By the time he finished she might wish to wear a scarf for the next few days. Though he meant to keep that possessive mark on her for as long as she was with him. For however long he wanted her, he would own her.

"Did you like that?" Jeremy asked still absorbing her sweet scent into his nostrils. "Should I kiss you there again or move on to a different place?"

Clair moved on his legs as if trying to get closer to him. Her breasts were compelling him to kiss, begging as they pouted almost out of her gown. It would not take much to push the old fraying fabric low enough so he could taste the sweet hard tips, take them into his mouth. He wished to savor. This woman-child was delightful.

"I feel hot, very hot." Clair waved a hand in front of her face. "Is that right? I want to make certain I do everything how you would like it. Am I supposed to feel as if I burned?"

Jeremy almost yowled with laughter. Clair couldn't do anything better. "*'Tis verra bonny, my sweet lassie. Hot is good,*" he said with a lilting Scottish cadence. "Do ye want me to kiss you in more places?" He ran his finger across both her bottom as well as her top lip. "Now," he paused "This spot I'm touching you, would be a very fine place to kiss you. You could kiss me in return. You could put your sweet tongue into my mouth."

"I'd like that," she breathed into his mouth as he captured hers with his lips.

Since she'd parted her mouth, Jeremy took advantage by touching the inside with his tongue. He drew her lip wider with his teeth. Her small hands clung to his shoulders as he pushed her a *wee* bit backward. When his tongue entered into her, she rubbed hers over the top. He drew in a sharp breath. She gasped as he bit with gentle finesse. She wriggled, her body pressing nearer.

When he put a bit of distance between them, her lips were larger, moist and rosier than before. "Let me see. Where have I touched you with my fingers? Can you remind me? You can say the words to me."

Clair looked down as if thinking about the moments he let his fingers drift across the top of her gown. This time he meant to explore lower. With a shaking hand, she ran her finger across the top of her dress. "Here."

He lifted a speculative eyebrow. "I see what you want. *Lass*, I wish for that also. We are of like minds. This is good." Once more his hands roamed across the tops of her breasts, sneaking below, delving down the valley between those gorgeous globes. His body ached. His arousal needed its release.

Her head bobbed up and down. "*Oui.*" Her voice squeaked.

"Let me get a better look at your sweet charms. The places where I've yet to caress or kiss." Jeremy touched the fabric. With restrained gentle precision, he lowered the fabric that shielded her breasts from his gaze. She wore nothing beneath the gown. When he finished with the corsage, her breasts were naked to his gaze. "Beautiful. May I kiss them? Touch my mouth to the hard tips. Suckle until you would swoon with the pleasure."

For a moment he thought she would deny him. With the deep breath of air Clair tugged into her lungs, her large breasts swayed with an enticement he didn't wish to ignore.

"*Oui.*" Her breathless whimper gave him good reasons to smile.

Two to be exact. He might think of more later. Before he set his mouth on the two inviting peaks, he skimmed them with the palms of his hands. She gasped startled by the evocative contact on her over sensitized flesh. His hand on her thigh, he noticed her legs moving, separating. Instinct, played a part in this. Clair understood deep in the most secret part of her what she wanted. Again, she gave him multiple reasons to be pleased with this choice of his.

"This one first if that will please you." He squeezed the tip of her right breast rolled it between his fingers. The sound she made was somewhere between a moan and a sigh. "...or...this one." He repeated the attention to the left breast. Her head fell back as if inviting him to savor more of her.

"Oh...oh...*oui...s'il te plait.*"

Jeremy spent several minutes playing and toying with her breasts before his fingers whispered along her ankle then higher to touch behind her knee, higher still to glide to the waistband of her pantalets.

"Shall we take these off, precious one?" He played with the ribbon holding them snug around her waist until the bow came undone. Jeremy splayed his hand across the softness of her belly. Her stomach contracted at his touch. Her soft mewl told Jeremy she liked what he did. Clair was slightly rounded, not perfectly flat. She was flawless. The soft curve would be heavenly to kiss. "Lift up your hips and I'll get rid of these."

Without protest she did as he instructed. The sturdy white fabric fell to the floor. The material was coarse. Not meant for her delicate flesh. Jeremy wanted her wearing lace and satin, the softest cloth for her that could be found. Tomorrow, the new wardrobe would be readied as soon as possible. He didn't want the rough fabric against her soft skin.

He slid his hand along her inner thigh, moving upward until he touched her intimately. She gasped when he swept his finger between her folds. She was wet, thick, honeyed moisture drizzling down on his hands.

"You will kiss me there? *Non!*"

"In time." His thumb found her tight hard bud. Used it until her whispered sounds of pleasure filled his mouth. He withdrew his hand.

She placed her hand on his wrist. "D...don't...stop."

"It's time to go to bed." Jeremy carried her up the steps to the bedroom.

Chapter Ten

Case knew the time was coming when he would need to leave. With each passing day, he saw more and more tension in Tara's body. Blue smudges surrounded her eyes. She wasn't sleeping. When they made love, when they talked out on the balcony sipping wine, Tara knew he would be leaving soon. Tension was there...always there. The seasons were changing. August came and went. Leaves were turning different colors. Days were shorter. Nights longer. Almost twice a week there had been an engagement they were asked to attend. They mingled with all who held power. She translated correspondence every evening.

During the night Tara clung to him as if she didn't expect him to be around come the morning. Their lovemaking turned bittersweet. When evidence was undeniable that she didn't carry his child, he was both ecstatic as well as disappointed. A part of him wanted to have a baby with Tara.

He couldn't do that to her. Leave her with a bastard child to raise by herself. This was for the best. A man who could not love could also not have a child.

This morning Tara was eating chocolate croissants. She sat on the balcony sipping coffee while she broke off small chunks of the flaky pastry. All she wore was a lavender negligée he bought her after their trip to Epernay. After that gift, she insisted he buy her nothing more. Her request didn't stop him. He wanted her to have a few things to remember him by after he left. He bought her a silver bracelet surrounded by amber stones that were an exact color of her eyes. He was saving the matching necklace for when he left. He would leave the gift on the nightstand.

After pouring himself a cup of coffee, he joined her on the terrace. "We never went to Bordeaux. Would like to go tomorrow or the next day. We could stay for a few nights, a week if you'd like," Case asked while he studied the scene in front of him. He wondered if she would ever return to Paris. For him, the memories would be too raw too painful. It seemed they'd been everywhere. Watched sunsets along with sunrises from the most prominent parts of Paris to the least. He understood this wasn't a place where he could return for enjoyment. The memories would be too harsh.

Tara had roots here. She might return. Her family visited while she was younger. Madam Pipelet was a friend. What he didn't know was how Tara would be affected when he left the letter on her nightstand. Before that happened, he had a few more weeks to be with her. He accepted an assignment in Portugal. He would have to leave before he could see her home. Though, seeing her back to the MacLaren castle or London was never part of his plan. Drake would make certain her return would be safe.

Lord Montgomerie told him he could be assigned to London if he would prefer, even Scotland. Tara's uncle gave him every opportunity to remain close to her. He couldn't put her through that or himself for that matter. She meant too much to him. He couldn't live near her knowing he couldn't have her forever. Sometime he needed to relinquish his hold. Give her a chance to move on…away from him. No matter the precautions they took, in time she would conceive. Sponges soaked in vinegar held no guarantees. So far, they'd been lucky.

When she didn't answer right away, he spoke again, clearing his throat to garner her attention, "Well, would you like to visit Bordeaux? We could leave tomorrow morning, at the crack of dawn."

"I don't know." She held back seemingly reluctant to commit. Tiny set his head on her lap asking to be stroked. "I suppose it would be fun for a change of scenery. The wine would be excellent. We would be together, enjoying something new. Another memory."

There was a wealth of things she wasn't saying. Tara appeared lethargic. "Instead of champagne we could visit some wineries. See if we like anything. Catch a few places outside the city."

Her sigh left him wondering if she didn't understand this was his way of saying his goodbyes. As the weeks passed, they spent every day with each other. They made love every night. Case understood he would miss having her in his arms, holding her body close, feeling her precious curves pressed next to him. He could change his mind about the mission. He could change a lot of things. Case still couldn't love.

"This will be our last outing together." Tara held up her hands to stop his immediate response. "I understand. Have seen the missives from the duke even though you've tried to keep them from me." Her head was shaking, telling him to stay quiet so she could finish. "I wasn't trying to invade your business or to learn what I told you not to tell me. I feel the same as I did before. I don't want to know until it happens. Don't want more tears."

"You don't want knowledge that I'm spending my last night with you. I understand. Will that make it easier?" Case was certain the answer would be no.

"Yes," she murmured, her voice soft, light. She smiled for him. It was half-hearted. "Yes, it would be better for me to wake up and not see you. Know that I will never see you again, than to dread that day before it happens. Don't know how to explain myself or make my feelings clear."

He could hear the pain in the admission. Perhaps he should leave today. He didn't have to be in Portugal for three more weeks. He told Lord Montgomerie he would remove himself from Paris at the end of this week. He didn't know if he could do that. Tara would be left on her own to travel home. Crossing the channel, she would be sick. He couldn't hold her hair from her face when she lost the food she consumed. Case never thought he would have fond memories of that time.

As if she understood the direction of his thoughts, she placed her hand on his thigh. "I've Jeremy's promise he will see me home." Again, she stopped him from replying. "My friend," she sipped her coffee. "My friend, Jeremy, is quite enamored of his mistress. She pleases him more than I ever thought it would be possible. He's forgotten about me. That should make you happy." She paused to suck in air. "Clair is her name. Jeremy explained that he would take her with him when he left Paris. He's in love with her. Jeremy has found the woman he deserves. I met her the other day when you were mired in correspondence of the English language variety. Clair as well as Lou Lou are nice young ladies. Ash won't be taking Lou Lou though. Between the two of them when they return home, their family will never want for anything again. The female children will not have to prostitute themselves. The males won't become pickpockets. All that happened here is good."

Case didn't like the idea of Jeremy accompanying Tara back to London or anywhere else. The man had been in love with her. Could he change so fast? This very reason was why he didn't believe he could ever love. Love was fickle. A man could think himself in love with one woman and the next day be in love with a different one.

"Bordeaux? Do wish to go with me?" he questioned hoping he would have a week possibly more alone with her with no complications. His job here was finished. Case hoped to hold some remembrances close to his heart. If there ever was a woman he might fall in love with, Tara was that woman. She was unique in every way that counted. She fascinated him. Intrigued. Nothing in life was easy. Leaving her would be the hardest challenge he'd ever faced.

"I would like that. It will be our last adventure together. I hear Bordeaux is beautiful in the fall. The river running through the city is also lovely." Tara looked away but not before Case saw the moisture in her amber eyes.

There was nothing more he could say. He didn't want to hurt her. He wanted to take her into his arms. Needed to explain to her she would be happier without him. He couldn't do that to her. In any case, she would never believe him. "Can you be packed and ready by tomorrow morning? I'd like to get an early start. The travel will take more than one day. I've asked around. There are inns along the way where we can stay in comfort. We can sleep long into the morning if we wish. Make love if we desire. The driver is of course your uncle's man. He will be with us for the journey. His French is impeccable. He is the man who drove us to Epernay."

She looked at him, a soft smile on her beautiful face. "He knew we were making love inside the carriage. Do you suppose my aunt and uncle do the same?" She caught her lip between her teeth, the light in her eyes danced. "I can be ready. What would you like to do for the remainder of this day?"

What he wanted was to take her to the big bed they shared. If he could, he would keep her there until they needed food or drink then they would make love again and again until they were both sated. Case had time for that this next week. Take two if they wanted. They would take their time. Nothing need be rushed. After all, he had three weeks before he needed to report. If he wished, he could use every second of those weeks. They could remain in Bordeaux for more than the one week they spoke of.

Tara wouldn't protest. After he was out of her life, Case didn't want her to think all she meant to him was as a bed partner. Someone to slake his lust with. Yet... The devil, he didn't want to think of anytime in the future. The present was the most important. Together, they had the present. Soon, for them, the present would no longer exist. There would be no future for the two of them.

"We should visit Madam Pipelet. After that you should take me to see Clair. I would like to meet her if she is going to go with you and Jeremy to London. I need to understand what she means to this man who loved you so much he followed you here."

"We will travel to Scotland. I wish to go home, to MacLaren land. I believe Jeremy also wished to go to Scotland. He plans to marry Clair. I think that is sweet. She has curly red hair and the whitest skin."

"Why go to Scotland? There is nothing there for you except lost memories. You shouldn't have to contend with your past. Grant isn't there. In London you might be able to find a man to love." *To take my place. The thought of some man taking his place left him cold.* "There will be events for you to attend. You won't be lonely. Your aunt and uncle will help with that. You should find a man who can return your love." Case didn't like saying that or encouraging Tara to meet any man. When he thought of her sharing her love as well as her bed with someone else, his gut cramped, a green bug of jealousy crept into his head. The fact he was jealous astounded him. Where Tara was concerned, he wasn't supposed to have feelings. He did. Those feeling just weren't enough to call love. He cared about her. Hoped for her happiness. He chased then caught. Now the time at hand was to leave. He spent more time with her than any other woman.

She sighed, air rushing fretfully from her lungs. "You still don't understand. Case, in my life, I've found two men I love. We talked about this before. I'm not looking for a third man. Don't ever again want to deal with the pain that comes with love. Would never marry a man I didn't love." Tara sounded so matter of fact, Case cringed. "I've had one man in my bed. Don't want another. Can't bear the idea of doing what we have done with someone else."

"You need to—"

"No, I won't." Tara cut him off with a sharp scowl. Her words failing to penetrate his brain. "If something happens and there is a man I can love, I won't send him away. However, I'm not searching for anyone to fill my nights or my bed. You are the only man my heart can handle. Until I can forget about you, there will be no one else."

With his thumb he brushed away the tear slipping from her eye. "I'm sorry." There were no more truer words he could tell her. He couldn't tell her that her life would have been better if he never met her. Case didn't believe that. What he did believe was that his life would never be the same. "I never wished to hurt you. Never wanted to see tears falling from your beautiful eyes because of me." Looking at this woman, Case thought his heart would break. Splinter into thousands of tiny pieces never to be put together again. Tara was like no other woman of his experience.

She was sweet.

Honest.

More beautiful than either the rising or the setting sun she so adored.

"Don't you think I know that? You are good and kind. Vulnerable." Tara stood; her body revealed by the thin silk of her gown.

Her nipples tight hard buds. He'd savored their flavor more times than he could count. The rounded globes swayed and provoked with each step. Called to him. He saw all of her. Every part of her. If he lived to be one hundred, he would never forget the way she looked tonight. He wanted to pull her into his arms. To possess her. To reassure her. To love her. He could not.

"Yes, I've told you before." His voice turned husky. Desire

coursed through him. Raw passion followed. The devil, how he wanted her this instant. He tamped down the rising lust. He tried. Failed.

"I'm going to change my clothes. We can walk to the park. I will see Madam Pipelet before I leave for Scotland. Don't wish to go to her now. She will read my thoughts. She will sense there is more wrong than I would wish to explain." When she stood, Tiny followed, his tongue lolling from his gigantic mouth, drool flowing downward. "Should we take Tiny?"

"Whatever you like. He will serve as a chaperone in the carriage as well as the inn. We both understand he thinks he is human. He would expect to share the bed. He would hang his head on my lap in the carriage." Case laughed at his words. A chaperone was something they might have needed months ago. As it stood now, he'd been sleeping with her for almost three months. It was far too late for chaperoning. She would never be his except for this last week.

"I will leave him with Ash. He seems to enjoy having the dog with him. Lou Lou loves Tiny. She's never had a dog, a pet of any kind, so she adores him. Tiny worships the attention. They are well meant for each other." Tara disappeared into the bedchamber.

Case didn't follow. If he watched her undress, they would not leave the bedroom today or tonight. They would not be packed in the morning and ready to depart. He wandered around the house, picking up one thing after the other, thinking about leaving for Portugal then his thoughts turned to Bordeaux. Their last outing. If he could, he would take her to her home. He needed to be certain she found her way back without incident. Jeremy would see to her needs. She said she liked Clair. Nothing would happen to her. Fear for her shivered through him. His sixth sense rifled his instincts. New feelings for him.

He strengthened his will, telling himself one more time that Tara deserved better than the little companionship he could give her. She needed more than a man in her bed. She needed a man who would love her the way she deserved to be loved. With his hands behind his back, rocking on his heels, he gazed down the tree lined street. Once more, his mind wandered to all the sunsets they watched together then to all the sunsets they would never share. The way he always held her in front of him when the sun was appearing or disappearing. Tonight, if he had his way there would be one more for them to gaze at. One more for him to remember when he was alone or was with another jaded woman who wanted only what he could give her.

Tiny sent his head pushing against his clasped hands, nudging him. Case turned. "So, you're asking for more attention. If I didn't know better, I would think you understood we would leave you here for our little trip to Bordeaux." He rubbed Tiny's ears, slid his hand down the dog's sleek back. "You will be treated like royalty by Lou Lou and Ash. I've a very good resource that tells me how much she loves you. Almost as much as your mistress. Not that you aren't spoiled now. Lou Lou will continue the process."

He dodged a thin line of drool that was headed for his boots. Laughed. "You tried to get me, didn't you?" he asked as he continued to laugh. "You understand you are being left behind."

"What's so funny?" Tara stepped from the room, dressed in a light-yellow gown. The color was his favorite on her. A layer of lace trimmed the corsage as well as the ends of the short sleeves. The rounded tops of her breasts showed, inviting him to discover all she had to offer. The gown had nothing to fasten or unfasten. To touch her breasts all he needed to do was to pull the fabric down while sliding the tiny sleeves along her arms.

"Your dog is trying to drown me in his drool. Aren't you pal?" Case was having trouble removing his gaze from her. He flashed her a smile that would tell her how much he appreciated the feminine view she gave him. He continued, "Tiny very nearly succeeded. You look beautiful. The color becomes you."

Tara ignored his compliment fastening on his comment about her dog. "He has that way about him. Do I need a shawl? Do you think?" Tara didn't wait for an answer. She picked up a white lace covering that was hung near the door then a hat that would shield her face from the rays of the sun. Case placed the fabric around her shoulders before tying the ribbon securing her hat, further admiring the delicate view she presented.

I should leave. This is prolonging the inevitable, hurting her more than I ever thought possible. The harm is hard to admit. I've never felt anything for a woman other than lust. For the longest time I tried to convince myself it was lust driving me where Tara was concerned. When I learned her story, I understood more about her than I ever knew about another female. For a few days, I doubted myself. I understand now she means more to me than a way to quench my lust.

Before they left, he grabbed a dark blue tailcoat to go over his waistcoat when the temperature dropped. Carrying it over his arm, he lent her his other one. "We shall walk along the Champs Elysée. The Seine is beautiful with sunlight glittering off the surface. I love the way the water turns silver with the reflection of the sun. If you grow hungry, we'll stop to eat. Anything you wish."

The day was more than he could have asked for. They laughed at each other's jokes. Stared at the setting sun when the blinding orb slipped behind the buildings in Paris. He held her in front of him, just as he always did while they watched the vibrant display of colors. The setting was nostalgic. He would remember this until the day he died.

In a small café they sipped wine and ate pastries they bought at the *boulangerie*. He kept her close, his hand around her waist. Sometimes he held her hand in his, loving the feel of her fingers entwined with his. Case would miss the closeness he shared with her. Had never shared this with another woman. She knew more about him than any other living person.

Case kissed her after the sun disappeared. His mouth traveled across hers inviting her to deepen the kiss to open for him. He wanted to wait longer before they headed home for the rest of the evening. His body was hard pressed to keep himself in line. Once back at the apartment, Tiny came to life rubbing his big body against her legs then his.

"We should have taken the big fella to Ash tonight. He's got too much energy. He's been couped up inside all day. Tomorrow...I'd rather just be on our way."

"You don't want to stop. You are always so impatient." Her giggle surprised him. Her laughter had been missing the last few days.

That night they made love. In the morning, they got Tiny to his dog sitters then traveled to the inn where they would stay the first night.

During the ride, they made love in the carriage, sipped the last bottle of champagne they bought in Epernay. Ate more of the bonbons they bought in the candy store the day before. He would feed her one, letting his fingers slide along her lips then into her mouth. She would do the same for him.

"I know you have a mission. An assignment Uncle Drake gave you. I vowed I wouldn't ask where you would be." Her sigh surprised him just as her question did. "I don't want to know. So, never mind. I would worry too much about you. Whatever happens don't tell me."

Case tapped her on the nose, thinking of kissing her again. To his knowledge never before had a woman worried about him. "You've changed your mind twice. I believe in the last few seconds. I will do whatever you think will make you happy. Tell or not tell."

She leaned into him. Rested her head on his chest as if that would give her whatever it was she was craving at this time. "If I know where you are, I can imagine you watching the sunrise or sunset from that place. If it is somewhere I've never been, I'll still have the image of the sun in my mind as it sinks below the hills or the ocean. I'll remember how you hold me when we watch. How you kiss me. How you move the hair from the back of my neck then brush your lips there."

Case didn't wait for her to change her mind again. He discovered he wanted her to know. Just as he would know where she was. "I'm going to be sent to Portugal. Don't know the name of the city yet. I'll be in that country anywhere from a week to a month. It's possible I could be there longer but doubtful."

She sighed, snuggling closer into his arms as if seeking his warmth. "Are you hunting bounty? I would that you would tell Drake that you no longer wish to be put in danger. There are other jobs you would qualify for."

"You understand you shouldn't ask. Yes. I would never tell Lord Montgomerie something like that. The man would cease to employ me. As you know, I love the danger. Have always thrived on intrigue along with the thrills in capturing a fugitive. Enjoy the money also. Though I've no need of more." He ran his hands along her back, recalling the first time he saw her naked. The stab wound healed nicely. The devil, she saved his hide that night. She put herself in line of the knife for him. No one, man or woman, ever acted so selflessly in his safety. Even then, she thought herself in love with him. He hurt her that night. A regret he wished he could change.

He misused her. She gave herself to him because she thought she was in love. He took advantage. He continued to take advantage of her giving nature. She forgave him his transgressions. He took her innocence. That would be reason enough for Lord Montgomerie to fire him. To shoot him. Hang him from the yardarm of a ship as he threatened the McInnis.

Case could have left a week ago. Would that have been easier for Tara? It didn't matter. He couldn't make himself walk away from her until he had no other choice. He would stay with this woman until the last minute.

"I will worry," Tara told him. "I don't like that. I will wonder if you are alive or if you're hurt and need help."

"You shouldn't. If I could, I would send word to you every day that I'm fine. Though, if I even missed one day, you would think the worst possible scenario. In this job, there would be no guarantee I would be in the position to send you a letter. Besides," his sigh of regret was heavy, "Mail can be delayed."

"If you did, that would negate everything. I would wonder where you were off to next. What danger you would find in some other city. If you put yourself at risk for the thrills. No, once we break ties, we will break all ties. I couldn't bear it if I knew anything happened to you. I will need to pretend I don't want to know where you are. I will hope I can imagine that you remain hail and healthy."

Case understood she could ask her uncle, understood too that she wouldn't. Tara wished for exactly what she told him. For all ties to be broken. The thought of that happening stabbed him in the gut.

The trip to Bordeaux took longer than usual. It seemed they could not tear themselves from the bed even though they made love in the carriage during the day. He couldn't get enough of her and it seemed she felt the same about him.

They were insatiable.

In Bordeaux they visited all the sites. Walked the narrow streets. Shopped in some of the stores to buy souvenirs. Watched sunset after sunset over the river Garonne until the last day they planned to stay. He now had less than two weeks to get to Portugal which meant he had about a week left to be with her in Paris.

Through the people-lined streets, they held hands, never speaking of a future they wouldn't have. There were no tears that he saw, though at times when she was bathing, through the door, he would hear the soft sobs she tried to conceal. When he would enter to soothe her fears as well as her tears, she would turn from him telling him she didn't want him to see her this way.

When they were together, she didn't show her sorrow. Tara didn't cry when they were together. At times he thought she didn't care any longer. That hurt him. While he didn't want her to care so much for him, he cared for her more than he wanted to admit. Confusion as to his feelings twisted his emotional state. He understood he could refuse the assignment. Go with her when she left for Scotland. He'd never felt bewilderment before when it came to a woman. Always understood what it was he wanted from the female. By her actions, Tara defied his logical mind.

I would just be putting off the unavoidable. It is best I end our relationship as soon as possible before I manage to hurt her even more. There is nothing in the future for the two of us. We have no possible life together. Tara would never be happy married to a bounty hunter, a man who would be more committed to the English government than to her. Yet, I cannot bring myself to leave her. She is one with me. In some ways she has become part of me.

The thought of marriage never entered his mind. Case always got hung up on the notion of love. Taking the notion as far as marriage never entered his head until this moment. He suddenly felt confined. He was suffocating. Walls closed around him. He felt an urgent need to run far and fast from this woman.

By the time they reached Paris again, sorrow filled the days along with the nights. While there were no tears shed in his presence, Case knew they were just a breath away. She held them inside.

That night, when he made love to her, he memorized her body. With tender reverence, he kissed all of her. Tonight was the last he would have with her. Their last one together. He would never hold this loving woman in his arms again. He would be gone before she woke. It was the way she wanted his departure.

~ * ~

Tara didn't need to be told. By the way he made love to her, she knew he would not be in the apartment when dawn came. Trying to stay awake after he stopped loving her was impossible. The trip exhausted her more than she thought possible. She'd not been feeling well for the last month. She tried to keep her illness from Case. Doing so was easy because the sickness was sporadic and between their trip to Bordeaux and his job in Paris, he was busier than usual. She assumed he was tying up loose ends before he left.

Tara decided she was heartsick, nothing more. Stress always affected her stomach. He was leaving. They'd been back only one day. That night he made love to her as if it was the last time. It was all she could do to hold the tears at bay. When she woke that morning, his side of the bed was cold. She ran her hand over the spot where he always slept. She clutched his pillow to her breasts, drinking in the last remanence of his scent.

Case was gone from her life.

Sobs tore from her, long rasping cries ripping from her throat. She cried until all the energy that was left to her was to close her eyes. When she woke next, the sunshine spilled through the curtains into the room she shared with Case throughout the summer. Summer changed to fall. Leaves colored. Soon snow would cover the land.

Seasons changed.

Life continued.

Her life would travel a new path. It would be one of her choosing. She learned that more than two years ago when Grant was ripped from her life by an accident that also stole their future. This was different. Case chose to leave her. He didn't want her enough to stay with her even as her lover. Didn't wish to plan a future with her. While she would have preferred marriage, she would have remained true to him. She would have been happy as his lover. That was what she'd done. She became his lover until he chose to no longer want her. He no longer wanted her. Everything between them vanished.

To turn her feelings off was impossible for Tara. Her eyes sore and red from crying, she called for a bath. While the tub was filled, she stared out the window making note of the things she needed to do before she went back to Scotland. There were not that many. If luck was on her side, she could do everything today. She wanted to be on her way to Calais tomorrow morning.

First, she would need to see Jeremy. No, she would send a message to Clair's home telling him when she wished to leave. Ash would sell the townhouse for him. They could go as soon as everyone was packed. Drake wouldn't like it that she wasn't going to wait for him to make the arrangements. She and Jeremy could do that. She would be safe.

Second, she would say goodbye to Madam Pipelet. Tara didn't think she would ever be able to return to Paris. This would be the last time she would seek out the older woman. The thought of never seeing the lady again brought more tears to her eyes. Impatient with herself, Tara wiped the moisture with the backs of her hands. She hated goodbyes.

I'm not going to cry one more tear for that man. Neither am I going to spend time feeling sorry for myself or wallowing in self-pity. Life goes on. I knew. That was too easy to think.

No matter how many times she told herself those words, Tara understood these would not be the last tears. She couldn't help the sadness inundating her. Couldn't help the memories tearing at her. While she stared out that window, she imagined watching Case walking up to the house. He would have that natural arrogant swager she loved. No one walked to the house. Tiny nuzzled her hand. She bent down. Wrapped her arms around the big animal. Unable to stop herself, tears ran down her cheeks.

"No, no, no," she told herself. The dog turned to lick her cheek.

"You love me and I do nothing but feed you, walk you, and pet you. Grant loved me. He's gone. Now, I'm feeling sorry for myself because Case doesn't love me. He is also gone from my life. I knew he wouldn't stay. Despite that knowledge, I fell in love with him." She stood, walking back to the bed to once more hold his pillow in her arms, to breathe in his scent. She saw the letter on the nightstand. This was a letter she didn't want to read. Tara knew she had to see what was written.

The stiffening of her body surprised her. The missive would tell her what she knew. That he was gone. There would be no words that would tell her he might come back, might see her again. Tara didn't expect those words. So, why would she be disappointed. When she opened the envelope, a silver chain slipped out. The necklace had one large amber stone surrounded by silver. The gift matched the bracelet he gave her. Tara didn't want gifts. She needed the man.

For a few minutes, she held the necklace in her hand. It felt cold in her palm. The gift held no joy. The piece of jewelry slid through her fingers to pool onto the nightstand. Tara took the letter from the envelope.

Tara,

Off to Portugal. You know that. Take care of yourself.

Case.

She crumpled the paper. Threw the paper along with its curt message into the fireplace. Leftover embers curled and scorched the letter.

What did she expect? Words of love? A snort of pain-filled laughter followed the thoughts. Tara knew better than to think that way. She needed to file everything away to its proper place. The necklace she would never wear disappeared into her jewelry box to lay nestled against the bracelet she would never wear. To be reminded of him, was something she couldn't stand. As it was everything she saw or encountered or ate, reminded her of him. The three bottles of Bordeaux they didn't drink reminded her of Case. She would give the bottles to Ash and Lou Lou. They would appreciate the wine.

Third, she would write to her uncle to let him know she was coming home. He might still have time to arrange for a boat to meet them at Calais. That would be nice. The carriage along with his driver would have to wait for passage if Drake didn't have the needed time to take care of his niece. By the time all the necessary arrangements could be made on this end along with the overland travel to the port, she and Jeremy might not have to search for passage.

Did she have a fourth item to see too? Forgetting Case would have to be the fourth on her list. She stuffed in a breath of air wondering where he was. No doubt somewhere between here and Portugal. Tara didn't even know if he meant to travel overland or if he booked passage on a ship bound to that country.

"Your bath is ready," her maid informed her with a curtsy and a smile. "Let me know if there is anything else you'll be wanting."

There wasn't anything she wanted that she could have. Neither the void nor the emptiness in her life could be filled. "Nothing. You can leave a pot of coffee on the table along with a croissant. That's all I wish to eat."

The water steamed. The scent of lilies filled the air. *Summer rain and lilies.* Her maid added oil scented with the flower. Roses would be a fine scent to use in her future. Tara didn't think after today she would ever wear the aroma of lily again. No, this would be the last time. If something reminded her of Case, she meant to vanquish it from her life. Her hand settled on her rolling stomach. She must have caught something or eaten something that didn't agree with her.

When she finished with her bath and dressing, she left the bedroom she shared with Case for three glorious months. To her immediate surprise, Ash sat on the balcony eating croissants and drinking coffee. Tara didn't expect him to just show up though she knew he would come sometime today.

"Sit." He patted the chair beside him before dishing up a plate for her and filling her cup with hot coffee. "He's gone. Your maid said all you wanted this morning was a croissant. You need to eat more. You've lost weight."

She lifted her shoulders trying to hold back the relentless tears. The devil, was this going to be a constant struggle for her? "You noticed." Her sarcastic comment bit at her. Ash didn't need that from her. He'd done nothing wrong. She shouldn't take her anger as well as the frustration eating her out on her cousin.

"Case stopped by this morning on his way out of town. He wanted me to look in on you. See how you are doing. He was worried. By looking at you, can't say that I blame him. How are you?" Her cousin sat back, appearing to wait for an answer he wasn't going to get. He seemed to search her eyes for responses.

She ignored the question. Instead of replying, she set her gaze on the tree branches in front of her. They were gorgeous colors of yellow and orange. When she turned back, she was all business. "Will you write your father for me? Tell him I'm returning to Scotland. I want to leave as soon as Jeremy and Clair can be packed. I know it's short notice but I can't live here while Uncle Drake takes care of everything. I won't. I would go mad."

"Father has a boat leaving from Dover today to pick you up. It will be in Calais whenever you arrive. Seems your Case wrote to him before the two of you left for Bordeaux. If you don't wish to wait for Jeremy there is no need. As you know, Father will give me permission to hire two guards. That's all you will need."

"I'll be ready tomorrow morning. Will you inform the driver? I'm not certain where he stays. Case always took care of the arrangements for our excursions. As to the guards, if you can't hire any by the morning, don't bother. I won't wait around now that I know arrangements have been taken care of that will see me safely home."

"Be happy to do so. The guards are hired. They will be there for you. Both Mother and Father would have my hide if I let something so important slip. Is there anything else you would like? I have orders from the duke himself."

"I'm relieved. There is nothing else I want or need. If I think of something, I *ken* where to find you." She looked to the bedroom, understanding she would only have one more night here. One more night to sleep in that bed she shared with Case.

Ash touched her cheek with his knuckles. "You've been crying. The bounder isn't worth your love. While I like Case, you should have never let yourself drift under his spell. I should have been a better chaperone. That was my job here. I failed you. Now you're hurt again. What I did is unforgivable. I saw to my pleasures rather than your safety."

"Case told me that many more times than you can imagine. I love him anyway. No matter what you did or you think, you could not have kept us apart. I love Case even more than I love Grant. Didn't ever believe that could be possible." She would never blame him or fall out of love with him even if she could stop thinking about the man she loved with all her heart.

Ash issued a soft breath of air then a curse, his gaze concentrated on her. "It will be good for you to put distance from this place. Too many reminders of the man. Soon, you will see, you will no longer think about Case Ferguson. At least there are no repercussion from sleeping with him." Ash paused staring at her distraught face. "Are there?"

"No, we were careful. I had instruction on how not to conceive." Tara almost laughed at the strange expression on her cousin's face. She needed to explain. Though she didn't understand why. "What? You don't believe me? Madam Pipelet gave me sponges. Told me to soak them in vinegar. While they weren't one hundred percent, they would serve me better than nothing at all."

"My little cousin," Ash mumbled, his face turning a rosy shade. "You never fail to amaze me. Contraceptives and you thought of them."

Her cousin was embarrassed by her frankness. That surprised her. "I'm the same age as you," Tara retorted with a tad bit of indignation. "I didn't want to have a bastard. Thought Case would object..." She realized she said more than she should. This was not Ash's business. She held up her hand to stop him from the retort she was certain would be blasted her way. "Never mind. I've said too much. I have to go see Madam Pipelet today. I want to thank her as well as say goodbye."

"Alright then, I'll leave you to your visit along with the business of packing. I'll have the carriage here at eight o'clock sharp tomorrow morning. Nothing more will be said as to your unconventional relationship with Case Ferguson. No one need know except the two of you that you were lovers. Won't say anything to anyone. Neither will Jeremy."

Thank her lucky stars. "Thank you."

As soon as Ash left, she grabbed her wrap then set out down the street to see Madam Pipelet. Before she could get her hand up to knock, the door swung open.

"*Bienvenue*, Tara. I'm glad you are here to talk to me." She turned from the door. "I'm sometimes a lonely old woman. You are getting ready to return to Scotland? *Non*? Glad you came to see me."

"Gracious, does everyone know?" It seemed to Tara, her business was not her own. Ash knew, Madam Pipelet heard the news. She was certain Jeremy would know.

Madam Pipelet was bobbing her head as she turned to walk into the drawing room. "No rumors. Saw your man leave this morning. Heard he was headed to Portugal. Come in and sit down. Tell me what you need. I will give advice or anything else you wish. If it's just a cup of tea and perhaps a cookie well...you can have that too."

Tara understood because of her business, Madam Pipelet knew a lot of people. Her hand was in politics as well as the most fashionably wealthy. She catered to anyone who could pay her price. Of course, she would know more than the average neighbor. It seemed she knew all that went on in this area.

Tara couldn't help but smile at the woman. "Don't need or want anything. Came just to say goodbye. I'm not coming back to Paris."

"Ever?" One of her white eyebrows shot into the air. "You loved him that much? You are devastated by his leaving. From what you told me before, you understood this would happen. You foolishly gave your heart away despite the knowledge. *Amour*." The woman was shaking her head and tsking.

"No! Yes...I love him too much to return here to be reminded of him." Tara knew that for the absolute truth. Even this visit gave Tara memories of the first time she came to see her. "You recall when you gave me the sponges? He forbade me to come here by myself. He was forever giving me orders. Told me I'd be punished. He never got around to that bit of ridiculousness."

"You were forever defying him." She laughed, her chuckles seeming to echo around the room. "Made the man fit to be tied. He didn't understand how to handle your defiance. Yet...yet, your sprit was much admired by your man."

"I am, after all, twenty years old. I'm not married to the man. Didn't believe he had the right to give orders, to dictate my life. I've done as I've pleased since my parents left two years ago to see new sunrises."

"Thought maybe you needed help of a different kind. I take it the sponges worked. You do not have a little one growing inside you. This is good."

"Yes, I'm not pregnant. We were very careful except for that first week. We forgot twice. Two mistakes. I don't know. Maybe more. I didn't conceive." She was positive of that fact. There might have been other times in the middle of the night. Madam told her there were no guarantees even if they never made a mistake.

"You are certain. I can still give you something that would abort the child if that is what you would like to do. If I give you the vial, you will have it as a just in case. You don't have to use it."

"I'm certain." The heat rising to her cheeks told of her embarrassment. She never spoke of those times. Case never asked though he was well aware of the nights they did not make love as well as why.

"Absolute...certain?" Madam Pipelet asked.

"I've had..."

"Ah, but a woman's monthly can occur and she still might be pregnant. Sometimes that happens though it is rare. Have you had symptoms? Would you like something to take with you in case you are wrong?" she asked again. "You told me you didn't wish to bring a bastard into the world." She paused in thought. "Did your young monsieur change his mind? Is he coming back to marry you?"

"Oh, my...I didn't know. You mean...no I'm not. I can't be. I've no symptoms. *Non*, Case will not return to me. Our relationship was over when he left early this morning. I won't ever see the man again." She had been tired more so than usual. She lost her breakfast on occasion. All that could be stress or a *wee* bug picked up somewhere. She'd been under a great deal of strain with Case leaving. Most days she felt fine.

"Just you wait here. I'm going to get what you need. Keep the liquid in the vial I give you. When you know, you can take it. You must decide soon or it will only serve to make you very sick. It won't hurt you if you failed to conceive. Many of the women who come to me use it when they are uncertain. Sometimes they take it the night after. More protection, that is all."

Tara's head was bobbing. She didn't want to lose the child if she did conceive Case's baby. She wanted to keep the *bairn*. No matter, her family would love her child just as they loved Liam. She stood before Madam Pipelet could leave to fetch this potion. "No! I would never take it. I couldn't do that. Though I pray for the child's sake, I didn't conceive. I would not mind a little person to remind me of its father."

"Very well, it's your choice."

"I have to go."

"There are people where you live who can do the same for you. If you've a change of heart, seek them out."

Tara gave her a quick hug. "*Merci, au revoir*. I would finish the goodbye with until we meet again. That's not going to happen. I will think of you always." Tara felt the tears rise once more in her throat. She hated goodbyes. Loathed tears. Neither served any purpose except to make a person sad.

The trip home to the MacLaren castle was long and uncomfortable. Tara spent most of the time inside her cabin on the boat. The inclement weather did nothing to ease the horrible sickness she always had when she was on water. She spent the time indoors losing whatever she ate. The time she spent on top wasn't much better. Between the wind and the rain, she was always forced inside before the fresh air could make her feel better.

Tara had been home for two weeks. Her days were spent, riding and walking along trails she'd known since she was a child. She consumed time watching the little stream that meandered to the North Sea. There were moments in the middle of the night she heard a woman sobbing. If she walked to the battlements, she would see the outline of a woman. The apparition always cried. The ghost she saw must be the same one who helped her mother find Liam.

It was nearing the end of September. While the days were usually warm the nights turned cold. She missed her family. The devil, she missed Case more each day. The castle seemed so big, so lonely. Seemed she was always cold. Could never warm herself.

At Aunty Ella's request, Liam, her half-brother visited her for a week. During that time some of her melancholy vanished. While he walked the trails with her, he tried to talk her into returning to London with him. Tara flat out refused. As with Grant's death, she felt as if she now mourned the loss of Case. She didn't want company. Did not want to be encouraged to attend events she detested. What she needed was to be alone with her thoughts.

Every evening she climbed the steps to the battlements and watched the sun go down in the west. Each night her ghost appeared. Stayed with her until she left for her room. She became accustomed to the phantom. Peace would always settle over her. Through the trees the sunsets were not that much to look at. She understood why she liked the sunrises better. After the third week she took to climbing out of bed before the sun would rise in the east to visit the top of the castle. From one special place, the view of the ocean gave her reason to breathe. When the weather was clear or slightly cloudy the site was spectacular.

Tara recalled how Case's arms would go around her resting beneath her breasts. How he would brush her neck along with her shoulders with his lips. The last day of Liam's visit he was atop with her. The apparition vanished with her brother's presence.

"I'm worried about you, Tara. You're not eating anything." His long sigh of frustration caught at her heart.

She lifted her shoulders in a slight shrug. While she didn't want anyone to worry about her there was nothing Liam could do to change how she felt. "Haven't been hungry. A person doesn't have a need to eat if they are not hungry."

"While I've been here, you've only attended one meal with me. Believe that was dinner on the first night. If you are to stay healthy as well as alive, you must eat, Tara." Liam leaned against the brick, staring out at the ocean.

This morning the colors were vibrant.

"I've been tired. Usually after I watch the sun show itself over the ocean I go back to bed. That's why I miss breakfast. Once I rise again, I grab something from the kitchen to take with me." Tara didn't like lying to her brother. He was always so concerned and caring. He would make some lucky woman a wonderful husband. If he knew how much she did eat, he would tell their aunt and uncle. They would send for her.

What she did after the sunrise was to walk the trails. She would take her bow and arrows. Sometimes she would shoot at targets. She walked until her legs ached, until she had to rest. Until she could not take one more step.

"You don't look well. I'm going to have to mention this to Drake."

"No..."

When she started to protest, he shook his head. "Yes, Tara, you are not well. There are dark circles under your eyes. You are lying to me when you say you eat. I *ken* you are not speaking the truth about your desperate situation. I've watched you walk through the halls. The depression wrapping around you needs to end."

If only it was so easy.

"I will eat," she promised knowing she would try. Food didn't want to stay in her stomach. Tara didn't like the nausea or losing the contents. This was a constant problem. "I don't want you involving Ella and Drake. They will feel as if they need to come here. Or...they will send someone to drag me back to London. I would die if I have to go to that city. Let me stay here where I'm happy."

"I can't do that," Liam gritted out.

"Why?" Tara understood her protest was voiced to deaf ears. "I don't understand. I'm fine. Really, I am."

"I've already explained. I'm afraid for you. Tara, you've become little but skin and bones. Your eyes sport dark purplish shadows beneath them. You skin is nearly translucent you are so pale. With business to attend to, I cannot stay here any longer. If you won't let me take you back to London, I will speak to Aunt Ella. She can decide what is to be done. The matter will be out of my hands as well as yours. You need someone to look after you."

"Tell them whatever you want. I'm not going back!" Her back was stiff with hands fisted. Her resolution should be plain for Liam to see. No one could drag her back to London.

"Very well," Liam sighed. "Have it your way. I have to go. Be it known, I don't like this situation."

From the heights of the Castle MacLaren, Tara watched Liam leave. He was right about her. She ate little. Her clothes hung on her. She didn't eat because she wasn't hungry. When she did, food didn't remain with her. The woods beckoned to her just as the vibrant morning and evening colors of the sky. All she wanted was to be alone with her memories. There was nothing anyone could do for her. This was far worse than when she lost Grant. Just as in the situation with Grant, Tara no longer wished to live without Case.

Nothing changed for Tara as the days drifted by. With each passing week she grew weaker. Her body shook with fatigue. The hours spent in the woods were fewer. It seemed she didn't have the strength to walk to her favorite places. She began taking a blanket to the battlements. So, she wouldn't miss a sunrise or a sunset, she would sleep there with the spirit who's soft sobs kept her company.

Now, when she walked along the stream that ran nearby, she would go a short distance then sit on a rock. The water would run true and clear all the way to the sea. The ripples fascinated as well as mesmerized. She dipped her hand in the cold water, watched the drops flow from between her fingers. Tiny barked then set his head on her lap.

Where was Case? Still in Portugal? Had he been sent to some other country.

Was he alive and well.

This afternoon, the sun shone bright. The heat on her back felt good. Tara inhaled the scent of fall. Shifting breezes sent more leaves tumbling to the forest floor. When she closed her eyes, she didn't feel anything at all. Blackness consumed her.

~ * ~

Liam paced the small enclosed courtyard in the back of the

Montgomerie estate. He might have been overreacting. His sister, he knew well. Understood her better than Kenzie or their parents. If something didn't happen, and fast, this time she was going to die. This time she didn't have Jeremy with her to pull her back from the depth of her despair. This was the second time she fell in love then lost. For whatever reason, the second time she fell in love the man left her. When Liam saw her, he understood she was wasting away. Just like the time Grant died, Tara didn't have the will to live. She needed a reason to live.

No one died. Case was alive and well. The bastard wasn't suffering. Case chose to leave her. Liam understood he had to get assistance from people who could help her. Who could bring her back from the living dead.

"I tell you, Tara is not doing well!" Liam told both of them trying to keep hold of his temper. "She refused to return with me to London. Wants nothing to do with the family. Wants to stay at the castle and wallow in her despair. She is starving herself. She is all bones. Nothing else."

Ella tilted her head a bit to the side as if pondering Liam's words. "I knew she was enamored of the young man. Didn't think she would fall so deeply in love that she would stop eating. Would stop caring about her life. This is my fault."

"Jeremy pulled her out of the depression last time. Now he's in love with his mistress. Says he's going to marry the little redhead," Drake said with a slight chuckle in his words. "I would be surprised to see that happen. They've moved into a townhouse here. From what I can tell, Clair's status is still one of mistress. Perhaps we should send Jeremy to Tara."

"I don't think Jeremy can help this time. So...getting back to Tara. Can you make her come here? I understand you can't go to her," Liam was walking back and forth, pacing the small area. Nervous energy assailed him. He needed to take charge since his parents were off to God knows where. He didn't.

"I've a new charge coming to stay with us. Maybe I can go get Tara. How, pray tell, do you believe we can make her come here?"

"I don't bloody know!" Liam was beside himself with angst.

"Maybe I'll go back. She is more important to me than business that can always wait. My solicitor can handle most things. Suppose I could hogtie her and give her no choice in the matter." Liam turned to Drake. "Don't know what the man does for you. Don't want to know either. This Case Ferguson fellow has to be the root of all Tara's problems. Can't you order him back? Tell him what is going on with Tara."

Ella spoke up, shaking her finger at her husband as if Drake would agree to such nonsense. "Doing so might make matters worse. You know that. If he left her once, he could leave her again. Thought they would be good together. It seems to be obvious to anyone with eyes, they are not. Did get a short letter from our neighbor in Paris, Madam Pipelet. She was also worried about our Tara. Said Tara's heart was broken when Monsieur Ferguson left her for his assignment in Portugal."

"Why does one lovely young woman have to suffer so much heartache?" Elizabeth asked as she strode onto the patio. "She is not deserving of this second tragedy nor the first. Yet she is continually forced to deal with life that is beyond her control."

"Elizabeth, you are looking lovely today," Liam said, his arms outstretched for a serious hug. Elizabeth, his aunt and uncle's daughter was too young to understand all that Tara was going through. Though she did seem to have a handle on the situation. Liam thought often that it was too bad they were relatives, fairly distant but too close for him to consider for a wife. He thought she was a lovely young lady, intelligent, spirted too. She was too young for her coming out. In another year she would be seventeen. Though she always seemed older than her actual age. Living in this household had to make a child older as well as wiser than their age.

"I don't know. You are right about one thing. Tara has had enough heartbreak to last several lifetimes," Liam added still hoping he could find someone who would go after Tara. Force her to come to London where there would be family to care for her. He had to admit the only person who would be able to tug her from the debilitating depression would be Case. Case wasn't coming home. Something had to be done.

"Well, we have to do something," Ella spoke up, her scowl one that couldn't be ignored. "Anyone have a suggestion?"

"You could send me," Elizabeth offered flashing a smile that could send a man to his knees. "Can make up some excuse that I need to get away from the hectic scene. Tara would understand. Maybe she would feel protective. We did always understand each other. If that happened, she might snap out of whatever is plaguing her. Tara has always taken other's problems to heart. As long as I've known her, she has never put herself first." Elizabeth tossed the thought out.

"With enough guards on the carriage, it could work," Drake mused. "I could send you well protected. This just isn't the right time for me to leave London or I would consider accompanying you. It's been a while since I've been in Scotland. Wouldn't mind a visit to the MacLaren castle."

"Not that long," Ella said, with a snort, her scowl deepening. "You do remember the wedding of Nicki and Ian McInnis. Don't you?"

Drake laughed acknowledging her words as if he'd had a grand time then.

"When can I go?" Elizabeth asked, impatient to move on.

"In a week. I'll make the arrangements," her father told her.

Chapter Eleven

With the back of his arm, Case wiped sweat from his brow. Even for the end of September it was blasted hot in the south of Portugal. The man he'd been sent after was ensconced deep in the bowels of the boat, confined where he could do no further damage. He did his job. Now he was headed home. With fair winds he might arrive in London in a couple of weeks. He was eager to set his life straight. When he abandoned Tara, he'd been a fool. An idiot. He called himself a dozen names over the course of time. Nothing made what he did right. He prayed she would forgive him.

One week after he left on this new assignment, Case realized his feelings for Tara were stronger than he could admit to himself. Two weeks after, all he could think about was returning to her. He wrote to Lord Montgomerie telling him this would be his last assignment. Told him he would check in for his debriefing then find Tara. Didn't go as far as telling the man his intentions. Tara would need to agree with his plans.

Now he was on his way home. He would deliver the fugitive to the proper authorities in London. He would see Lord Montgomerie to officially end his career as a bounty hunter. After that, he would ride hell bent to the MacLaren castle. Case hoped he would be able to convince Tara how much he needed and wanted her. Prayed that he could set right what he wronged. Would tell her over then over again how much he loved her. Would speak the words until he convinced her. He would never again do something so foolish as leave behind the woman he loved more than life. On board ship, he watched the weather, watched the winds as they changed their tune each day. Every moment he spent waiting was one too many.

Once they docked in London and he had the fugitive in the proper hands, he made his way to the Montgomerie townhouse. No one was in residence. He was sent to the country estate. Case hoped he would find Tara there. Prayed she wasn't living alone at the castle.

Tara wasn't with her aunt and uncle.

The few minutes he spent with Lord Montgomerie, he learned how concerned they were for Tara's health. Seconds passed while his heart forgot to beat. It was explained to him what Liam found when he visited several weeks ago. His inbound breath caught half way to his lungs, froze there. He was told Elizabeth visited Tara and was promptly sent home. Tara didn't want anyone with her. She wished to be alone with her thoughts...with her life. Ella explained she mourned his loss just as she mourned the loss of Grant. With this knowledge, ice filled his veins.

While Case waited for Black to be saddled, he paced the stable, swore beneath his breath at having to wait over long for his horse. He didn't know what he would encounter when he reached her. Praying the depression both Liam and Elizabeth spoke about was not as serious as they led him to believe.

Case understood they blamed him for her state of melancholy. Bloody hell, he blamed himself. Guilt ate at him. Fear for her was a constant pounding in his head. He arrived a day and a half after leaving London. After he dismounted, he tossed the reins to a stableboy who appeared from the door. Every extra minute it took him to find Tara was a minute wasted.

"Take care of him, rub him down, feed and water him. I rode him hard." Case strode to the castle, storming through the entrance. "Tara!" he bellowed out. "Tara!" Where the devil was she? He slammed through a door then another calling out her name. He raced up the steps stopping only to toss open one closed door after another then hollered her name.

His heart raced. Liam told him Tara spent time on the battlement. At the top of the castle there was no sign of her. He picked up a quilt that was still damp with the morning dew. Holding it to his face he caught the scent of roses. That wasn't Tara. Her scent was all about lilies and summer rain. It was October the summer rain changed to falling musty autumn leaves and stormy weather.

He stood at the top of the castle staring out at the ocean, his gaze sweeping the area around the castle. Soft sobs caught at him. While he knew the crying wasn't Tara's, he searched for the source. A ghostly apparition hovered in the air above him. The woman floated, lingered over him, sweeping around him. She seemed to beckon to him. His imagination was getting to him. He fought off the shivers created by this image. Tried to direct his thoughts back to Tara.

Liam also told him she liked to walk the forest trails with Tiny. Too bad the dog was so friendly. Often, she walked along the stream. She'd done that since she was a child. Tiny hadn't been in the home either. Tara wasn't in the castle. She had to be taking one of her long walks.

The woman soared down to the earth. His heart lodged in his throat when he saw Tiny bounding down the trail that followed the stream he'd been told about. This spirit floated beside the dog. The two were on the path where Tara liked to walk.

If Tiny was there, his mistress would have to be close. Tearing down the steps he raced through the rooms to the ground floor, through the outskirts of the small village where different shops catered to visitors. Tiny met him, standing on his hind legs to greet him, slurping at his face as if he was meant to be the big dog's next meal. The sobbing ghost lingered, waited. Moved in the direction of the stream.

"Down Tiny. Where is she? Take me to Tara!" His voice sounded too urgent, too terrified. He stole a breath of air while he watched. Waited for the dog to respond to his command.

As if the big animal understood, Tiny dropped to all fours then turned onto the trail skirting the stream. The apparition followed. Within minutes, Case saw her. Tara was sprawled on the ground. Her body lay in an awkward position. Her hair was fanned out around her, amber-blond strands against the green of the moss. She didn't move. He couldn't see her breathing.

"Tara!" Panic swamped him. Gripped his senses. Blood pumping through his veins pulsed, frantic. He stooped over her, pushing the dog to the side as he tried to find a pulse. Relief swept through him. With no thoughts of anything except Tara, he scooped her into his arms. Cradled her as close to him as he could get her. Against his chest, he felt each labored breath. When he reached the castle gate, the stableboy was there as if waiting for his return. Get the doctor in the village. Bring him here. Tell him this is an emergency. Go!" Case waved him off. "Hurry!"

The boy nodded before running into the stable. Case heard the pounding of the horse's hooves as the boy left for the village. Men from the various shops lining the way to the main house opened their doors to see what was happening. The kitchen maid stepped through the door when she must have heard him.

"Miss MacLaren?" she asked, her eyes wide. "Is she not feeling well? What can I do?"

"Wait for the doctor. Don't move from this spot. Take him to her room when he gets here." For a few tension-filled moments, Case looked confused. Blood pounded in his head. He'd never been here. Bloody, bloody eyes, he needed directions. "Where is her room?"

The woman blushed as if she understood the impropriety of him taking Tara to her bedroom. It was not the time for recriminations. With Tara passed out in his arms, nothing untoward was going to be happening.

"On the second floor at the end of the hall. It's on the right. Kenzie's is on the left," she said her face turning rosy. "Oh, my...the doctor you say. The little Miss is going to be alright. Isn't she? What's wrong with her?"

Case took the time to nod. When he reached the room, he set her down on the bed. Tiny sat at the foot, his big brown eyes watching. The devil, she was pale. Her body so thin. In his arms, she felt as if she was a skeleton of her normal self. Liam told him Tara lost weight. He had no idea the loss was this much. Nothing anyone told him prepared him for this first sight of Tara. With gentle strokes he brushed her ill-kept hair from her face. Again, just as Liam descried, purple smudges surrounded her eyes. Her skin translucent. Her hair dry, brittle. She was dying. He thought about her past. How once before she almost passed on from grief. How with the loss of Grant, she told him she didn't want to live.

What the devil did you do to yourself? I did this to you. I take all blame for your condition. He was an arrogant bastard. Both words were so *verra* true. *Never did I believe you would starve yourself over me.*

He could curse his actions a blue streak. The curses would do him no good. They would never change this. Again, to reassure himself, he touched his finger to the pulse point at the base of her neck. His breath caught in the back of his throat, still relieved he could feel the beat of her heart. He didn't know what to do next.

His breath heaved as he paced the room thinking of what should be done. When he stopped at the window, the sun was beginning to go down. On his boot heel, he whirled. Went to the armoire to retrieve a sleeping gown. Case was certain the little kitchen maid if she knew what he was planning to do would frown. He undressed Tara then slipped the gown over her head. My God, he could see her ribs, all her bones were poking out. Sitting by her side on the bed, he held her hand. Stroked the fingers. He remembered other times when she returned the caresses. Case needed to keep her close to him in any way he could. Her fingers felt like icicles in his hands. He brought them to his lips, kissed the back of her hand. Found the pulse again just to reassure himself.

The soft moan drew his attention. Case prayed she would open her eyes. Instead, she moved. The movement was small. Tiny set his head on his thighs. His big brown eyes were huge. Worried. The dog whimpered. Tiny understood his mistress was in distress. The sobbing ghost was no longer here. Perhaps she had been his imagination.

"You're troubled too. Aren't you pal? If I have anything to say about this, Tara will be fine. She is going to be good as new. We'll all walk those trails she loves. We'll go to London to see the duke and duchess. We'll get married." Case didn't have that much confidence. It helped him to hear the words. He stroked Tiny's head as they waited either for the doctor or for Tara to wake up.

Hours seemed to lag while they sat in the room, watching Tara breathe while in truth when he looked at the clock only twenty minutes passed.

"They are in this room." It was the maid leading the doctor. The woman stopped at the door. "Is there anything I can do?" she asked while her hands were winding in then out of her gown. "She is special *ye ken*. All who live here love the *wee lassie*. *Dinna* wish anything to happen to her."

Case knew how special as well as unique Tara was. He also understood the wrongs he did to her. He should have never seduced this woman. Wanting her more than he needed to breathe was no excuse. She was fragile, special, unique in every way. He was a cad. Didn't deserve this beautiful woman. Tara loved him when he didn't merit her love. He prayed she would not pay a horrible price for giving her love to a heartless bastard to find the coveted emotion tossed back in her face as if the sentiment meant nothing to him.

"You can wait here," the doctor said as he motioned for Case to move. "I will have instructions for you."

Bloody eyes he didn't want to move from her side. He needed to hold onto her. Case nodded as he stood, his reluctance obvious. He stepped away giving the physician room to work. While Case watched he held his breath as long as he could. With each of the man's movements, he grew more worried.

The doctor listened to her heart and lungs. Case assumed that was what he was doing. He ran his hands along her arms then legs as if searching for broken bones. Touched upon her torso then lower to feel her belly. "Did you change her into the gown. The stableboy told me you carried her from the woods."

"Yes." Case felt the words deep within. Saw the recrimination in his eyes. "Yes, I did." Tiny sat beside him. He wasn't going to deny the truth.

"Did Miss MacLaren have any wounds on her body? Was there any bleeding? You might have cleaned it before you put the night dress on her." The doctor looked at him, as if assessing his character.

"No. Nothing, no wounds, no blood. Nothing that would indicate she was physically hurt." Case felt as if he wallowed in a haze of the unknown. He understood Tara's pain was emotional. She mourned for a man who was not worthy of her.

"Good. Did she seem to have bruising to her ribs or anything broken," was the doctor's next question.

Again, he formed the same answer. Tara appeared unhurt when he found her. "No, nothing that would indicate internal trauma. To me, she seemed fine. Sleeping just as she is now, her breaths slow as well as labored." He hesitated with his next question. "What is wrong with her?" Case asked, frantic with concern coupled with all the fears that raced through his head since he found her.

She is pining away, her body wasting with time. Tara will die soon. You have to be there for her. She will die if you don't care. Those were Liam's words to him. *She can't live through another lost love.*

"Rest easy, young man. There is nothing wrong with her that rest and food won't cure. Take care of her. I *ken* you care about what happens to this young woman. When she wakes, make sure she eats soup. Nothing too heavy. From the looks of her, it's been a long time since she has enjoyed a meal." He nodded to the maid. "Have your cook keep soup warm. Not too hot. A broth. If she wants more give her a small amount at a time. A pieced of bread, a bite or two of cheese. Make sure she can handle a *wee* bit of solid food before you give her more. Can you do that, *lass*? Go tell the cook. Go now." The physician turned his attention to Case. "Who are you? What is your relationship with the MacLaren *lass*?" His voice was stern as if the man was about to embark on a lecture in propriety.

Case ran his finger around his collar unsure. He wasn't going to lie. "I love Tara MacLaren. If she'll have me, I'm going to marry her." There was no hesitation after he realized his exact feelings for this woman. Her emotions for him that he abused. Even the word marriage didn't send a bolt of terror through him nor did he stumble over the word as he would have a mere few weeks ago.

"Good. Stay with her. She'll need to hear those words when she wakes up. While there are no wounds on the outside to make her sick..." The doctor paused. His hard-edged gaze penetrated him, giving rise to the guilt he piled on top of himself. "It is not my business. If you love her take care of her. I'll come back tomorrow afternoon to check on her. If she takes a turn for the worse, send for me. This family has been good to all of us living around the castle. Here, we take care of our own. Don't disappoint."

He found himself nodding in agreement. While Case didn't wish to leave Tara, he walked the doctor out thanking him for everything. At the bottom of the stairs, the man stopped. "There is something else you should know."

Fear reverberated between his ears. His mind raced to all the worst-case scenarios. "What?"

The doctor patted him on his hand. "Tara is pregnant. Is it your child she carries?" There was no condemnation in the older man's voice. Just fact.

"Yes. How far along is she?"

"That I'm not certain. I would need to ask some pertinent questions of her. If one knows the signs, it is clear that she carries a child. She may be pencil thin but the swelling in her abdomen tells me much. I've known this *wee lass* since she was born. I delivered her into her mother's and father's waiting arms. They were thrilled to find a girl in their arms."

I'm going to be a father. I should have known. Should have seen the evidence that week when we were in Bordeaux. She told me she was tired. I knew there were times when we forgot the sponges. Too many times. A couple days she lost the little breakfast she ate. We always thought we were being careful. Not careful enough.

As the man rode from the castle, Case seized a long deep breath of the crisp, cool fall air. His fists tightened. He was a man determined. Tara would get better. If he had to, he would force feed her. He would lay atop her if that would make her sleep. He would baby her, treat her with all the pent-up loving feelings he possessed. Case knew he had much to atone for.

Tara's room was directly above where he stood in the courtyard. As if she called to him, he looked to the window. In his best dream, she would have been looking down at him, smiling. Perhaps waving for him to take the stairs two at a time to reach her. The window was empty except for the fluttering curtains coupled with a *wee* bit of candlelight. He must write the duke to tell him what was happening here.

With a long, drawn-out sigh, he walked to the kitchen. Case checked on the soup. It seemed all the employees were eager to give aide to the *wee lassie*. Chicken broth simmered on the stove. Fresh baked bread was sliced and steaming on the counter. Feeling both enthusiastic as well as reluctant to see her, he hesitated on the first step.

All kinds of scenarios swept through his head at blinding speed. Tara, when she woke, should toss him out on his ear. She should yell at him. Rant then rave if it would make her feel better. He would allow that. The devil, he prayed to any God who would listen, that she would not continue down this path she took. First, he needed her to wake. Second, he hoped she would listen to him when he told her how he felt. He would get down on his knees then apologize a thousand times if that would make her feel better. He would tell her all he knew about himself changed after he left her behind in Paris.

Sluggish steps took him to her room. The doctor was right to ask him about his intentions. He'd always taken so much for granted when it came to women. Always assumed they were made from the same ilk. Tara was pregnant with his child. Case was having trouble believing the news. Once, not too long ago, he didn't think he would have children. Didn't believe himself to be competent as a father. His only role model had to be the worst father in this world. What would he know about raising a child? Nothing.

This woman, sleeping in her bed, who was wasting away, taught him how wrong he was about everything he'd taken for granted since the woman he once thought to marry ran off with another man. Taught him that no one should be judged by something another person did. Tara taught him about unconditional love. Her perspective on life was always bright, filled with laughter along with love...until he stole her happiness.

Tara had to wake up. She had to get well. He needed to hear her laughter. See her smile. Take in the scent of summer rain coupled with lilies. Hold her in his arms. Kiss her until she kissed him back.

After he reached her room, he stood inside the door staring at her small form. Case couldn't remove his gaze. He wished she would sit up, sweep the hair away from her face and tell him how much she missed him. Tara was stretched out on her side, her hands clasped below her cheek. This time when he watched her, he could see the easy rise and fall of her breasts as she breathed.

"Tara...sleep, rest. In the morning when you wake, I'll give you something to eat." Case hoped his voice was soothing, not expectant. The doctor told him he needed patience. She might sleep the night as well as most of the day tomorrow. It was her body's way of healing. Over the past weeks since he left her, she'd been under tremendous trauma.

Her soft sigh pleased him. She adjusted her position on the bed. Some of his tension eased. Case wanted to believe that she heard his voice. That she felt better because he was here. He lay down beside her. Pulling her into his arms, he buried his head in her hair, soaking up the foreign scent of roses. As if by instinct, she turned then nestled against him. He held her as close as he could, listening to her breaths in then out of her lungs, hearing the steady slow beat of her heart.

The sun dropped.

The moon rose.

Tara slept. Peace filled Case.

I will not rush her to wake. She must have the time to heal. Case closed his eyes.

When he woke, Tara was still cradled in his arms. Her head was no longer nestled in the hollow of his shoulder. Sunrise flitted through the lace curtains that hung on her window. Shadows danced on the floor. Case felt her move so she could see him better. Felt the warmth of her breath as it flitted across his face.

She touched his cheek. "Case?" Tara explored his lips, his nose, ran her fingertip across his eyebrows. "Am I dreaming? You are really here?" Her soft voice whispered across him.

The delicate caress of her fingers surprised him. "You're awake. No, this is no dream, Tara. I'm never leaving you again. If you will have me, you're stuck with me. Forever."

Tara stiffened. She pushed on his shoulders needing to get away from him. "Go away. I won't let you..."

He placed a fingertip on her lips. "I've no intention of doing anything that will harm you. You're distressed, surprised. You've been through too much. Rest assured, I'm not going away. Ever."

Case put distance between them stepping from the bed. Giving her the room she needed. Later, there would be time for explanations. He pulled the bell cord near the bed. He smiled at her. "It's time for you to eat. We'll see what your empty stomach can handle. After you've eaten your fill, we will either talk or you will nap. What we do next will be up to you. If you would like a bath, that is also an option."

"You can't tell me what to do!" Her anger was obvious though misplaced. Her little hands were fisted.

"Foolish woman. If you continue to abuse yourself, I will. I can force feed you. Tell you how to spend your time. You need to get healthy again." He smiled at the way she scowled at him. Case wondered when he should break the news about the *wee bairn* she carried. He hoped she would be as pleased as he was. Tara might know the truth. The thought displeased him. She might have meant to keep the information to herself.

"You called?" The maid dropped a small curtsey. "What can I do for you?"

"Your mistress would like soup to begin with. I'd like something a bit heartier. Seems I missed the evening meal." *Missed several before that in my rush from London.* "Make it enough for two people. If she keeps the soup down and would like more, there will be plenty. You won't have to make a second trip. Heat water for both a bath for Tara as well as myself. I'll take mine in Liam's or Kenzie's room. You can attend Miss Tara in here."

With a bob of her head, the maid left. When Case turned, Tara was sitting up in bed, her expression unreadable.

"You were curt with her."

"The woman...?"

"Very young woman," Tara corrected. "She is about fifteen. If you're going to accuse her of something, you shouldn't."

"She allowed you to starve yourself," Case ground out, furious this got so far. Didn't wish to argue with her. "She should have sent for someone. You could have died last night. No one would have gone looking for you."

"Who? Who would she send for?" Tara questioned. "Liam visited. He tried. I wasn't hungry. My brother wanted me to return to London. I refused. Elizabeth came. I refused. Whatever blame there is, is on my shoulders."

"Because of me. You starved yourself because of me!" Case didn't want to hear the answer to the question or confirmation. He didn't want to be angry with her or to yell at her. Tara had this way sometimes of getting under his skin.

"Because..." She lifted the frail shoulders; he'd kissed not so long ago. "Because I was wallowing in self-pity. Now that you have roused me from that deplorable state, tell me when you're leaving so I can prepare myself." Her anger might be good. Case had no doubts now that she would rally.

"I'm not going anywhere. I'm here to stay. Forever." She was going to have his child. Even if he hadn't discovered he loved her, he would not leave. Even if he didn't *ken* the child that was in her womb, he meant to stay.

"There is no need for you to feel sorry for me. I'll not starve. Don't want you to stay out of pity." Tara's brows drew together. "Where did you find me? How did I get here?" Her questions began to unravel from her. She was curious. That was good.

"Tiny found you for me." He wasn't about to tell her about the sobbing ghost that followed them to her. "He took me to you. You'd fallen asleep, fainted from lack of food. You were lying by the little stream. When you would have woken up was anyone's guess. You would have been all night in the woods. Cold. Vulnerable." He cringed at that thought. "I carried you here. Summoned a doctor."

By the way you're carrying my child.

That was too much for him to tell her. Case wanted her to understand he came to her because he couldn't live without her. He didn't want her to believe for one moment he was in Scotland because he sired a child. When he started his journey back to her, he didn't have a single notion she was pregnant. He would have to convince her how much he loved her.

Though he would have been here if he'd known. In Kenzie's room he penned a letter to the duke as well as The Duchess. With their blessing, he told them he intended to marry Tara. If she would allow it, he wanted to bring her to London for the wedding. Hoped she would be able to plan something with her aunt. The ceremony could be anything she wished, fancy or subdued. She could invite the entire city or only family. All was up to her as soon as he got her to agree with him.

~ * ~

Tara was a mass of confusion. She woke in the man's arms. A man who she never thought to see again. Case was here, all flesh and blood. Strong where she was vulnerable. He left her feeling warm as well as loved until she reminded herself he was incapable of love. Months ago, Tara decided whether he could love or not made no difference. She had enough love inside her for both of them. Now, waking up beside him, she felt as if he'd never been gone. It floored her to think she was so weak she fell asleep in the woods. Her father taught her to use caution when she wandered alone. She remembered sitting down to rest. That was all.

The feelings surrounding that moment were vague. One second, she was watching the water in its rush to the sea while wondering how she could live without the man she loved. Tara realized this was the second time in just over two years a man brought her to thoughts of death. She should never let a man control her to this extent. She didn't want to die. What she wanted, she couldn't have. She wished for Case. Needed the man. Would have to find the means to live without him. As far as she understood, nothing between them changed.

He left her for his bath. Tara had a bath waiting for her. Hot water steamed in a tub nearby. The soup settled in her stomach quite well. One piece of bread with honey and butter didn't like it where it was. She should have stopped with the soup. Bile rose. Tara raced to the basin on the shelf by the window. Lost the little food she consumed. Her body felt so weak. She didn't know if her legs would hold up while she walked to the tub.

She sank to the floor with a soft sob. Depression. Fear. This sickness was one of the reasons she didn't eat. The last week nothing stayed in her stomach. She'd gone from trying the tiniest bits of food to nothing at all. No food worked the best for her. She didn't want Case to know. Tara rang the cord. One of the house maids arrived within seconds.

With no words offered, she held out the basin. The maid bobbed then took it from her hands. This wasn't the first time the maid had to empty the washbowl. She tried to keep it minimal. During the last month, Tara discovered it was much easier to lose the contents of her stomach in the forest. None of the animals asked questions. She didn't have to explain anything to the servants. Nothing needed to be cleaned.

Rinsing her mouth out with the tea that was left earlier, she took off the nightdress she wore then eased herself into the steaming water. Tara set her head on the lip of the tub. Her eyes were closed.

What was she going to tell Case? If he stuck with her the way he did in Paris, she couldn't hide the sickness from him for very long. She didn't know if the tea she drank would stay put. Tea most often did remain where it was supposed to be. The broth would have stayed if she hadn't eaten the bread.

The water was scented with the rose oil she started using. Tara still preferred the scent of lilies. The aroma was softer, not so vibrant. Case was back. Before she went back to the scent of lilies, she would have to see how long he intended to stay.

When she swept the wash cloth over her breasts, she winced. They'd become so tender. She didn't understand why. This wasn't her time. Even though she'd not been eating, her belly was rounded.

The swift intake of air left her to gasp then cough. Tara thought of the times they forgot the sponges. Sometimes she still had one deep inside her when they made love for the second or third time. There were other times when they'd been out seeing sunsets that when they opened then closed the door of their apartment behind them, they could never wait to reach the bedroom. Too many times to count they made love on the floor with their clothing strewn about the room. After that Case would retrieve a sponge. She always decided those times didn't count because the vinegar was there almost as soon as he left her.

She supposed they did count.

Tara couldn't deny the fact she conceived. Madam Pipelet knew more than anyone. She told her it might have happened. Even if they never forgot, Madam Pipelet told her nothing was one hundred percent infallible.

How will I tell Case? He didn't want a wife. Didn't want a child.

Couldn't love her. Tara didn't want to have to call her child a bastard. If Case didn't want to stay with her, they could pretend they married in Paris. If he would allow her to do so, she would use his last name. After that he could do as he pleased, go wherever it was he wanted to go. Take any job the duke offered. He got off on danger. He loved hunting bounty. His work was important to him, more so than she.

Her unhappiness lingering, she lifted herself from the bath. The towel was warmed near the fire. Before she wrapped the material around her, she looked at herself in the mirror. There was a definite bump. She ran her hands down the swelling. Moisture clogged her throat. Tara found she had too many mixed emotions to deal with.

"Miss..." The knock on the door startled her out of her musings. With a quick motion, Tara wrapped the towel around her. "Mr. Ferguson would like you to meet him downstairs when you are dressed. What should I say to him?"

Tara let out the deep breath of air she held in her lungs. The time was fast approaching where there would be one less secret between them. "Tell him yes. I'll be down as soon as I'm dressed. Spent too much time soaking up the hot water."

She bobbed a curtsy then left.

Tara sat down at her mirror. Studied herself. There were sunken hollows where her cheeks should be plump. Dark circles rimmed her eyes. Where her skin used to be rosy, it was now pale, translucent. She looked as if she was on death's doorstep, the grim reaper waiting for her. Perhaps that was where she'd been headed. If she died, so would the *wee bairn* before the child had a chance at life.

Guilt.

Blame.

Regret.

Those emotions no longer held a place in her heart. She needed to live if not for herself but for the child she carried.

I never thought I'd see Case again. Here he is, waiting for me to show up downstairs. I didn't think I conceived either. Now that I know I have, the thought pleases me...as it should. No one in the family would think ill of me when they discover how the bairn came about. No matter what anyone would say to her, this baby was conceived in love. Liam was born a bastard. Ryder, my father, adopted him. Gave him the MacLaren name. Liam inherited the title that was passed down to him from his grandfather. He is the earl of Rothen. Liam will not care about the parentage of this baby I carry. Neither will my parents. All will love the child. Nothing will be amiss.

A few minutes later, her hair was tied behind her head with a ribbon. A few curling strands framed her face. The dress she wore hung on her. Even her breasts, which were larger when she stared at them in the mirror, didn't fill out the bosom because she lost too much weight in other places.

When her stomach rumbled, she cringed. The need to eat suffocated her less than the knowledge she would lose whatever she put in her stomach. Pulling in a deep breath of air, she walked down the steps then into the study. She didn't know why she looked for him there. Seemed a fitting place for Case. When they were in Paris, he spent almost as much time in the office as in her bed. At the thought, she smiled. This might be a new beginning for them if what he told her was true. If he meant to stay. When he told her, she didn't believe him.

Case sat on a chair behind the desk. He wasn't working. His hands were behind his head, his long legs stretched out in front of him. He didn't stand when she entered. His face was a mask she couldn't read.

After he sat forward, he spoke. His voice was harsh, gruff and to the point. "We have to talk. You and I."

Yes, that was true. Tara just didn't know how to begin the conversation or how much she wanted to tell him. Some of it depended on what he would have to say to her. She felt hesitant. Wary. Afraid this was all a fanciful dream. "Suppose now is as good a time as any."

Tara eyed the tray that held a pot of tea along with a few scones. They must have been brought in for her. Case never ate except at meals...or in bed with her when they had champagne or wine.

"How do you feel?" Case asked as it seemed to Tara he meant to get straight to the point.

That was a good start. He put the first question on her shoulders. Tara would turn it about. "Why are you here?" Case didn't need to know that she felt as if she'd been throwing up for weeks, not days. He didn't need to know she regretted starving herself. She didn't do it on purpose. How do you tell someone the reasons you chose not to eat when they were confusing?

Case chuckled. "You haven't changed. When you don't want to answer one of my questions, you ask me something. Very well, I'll be honest. I'm here because I discovered I didn't want to live without you. I decided the only way I could do that was to marry you. When I was in London, Liam apprised me of your condition. I raced here. Good thing I only stopped for a couple of meals. If I did otherwise, you would have spent the night in the forest. I would not have found you until this morning. Anything could have happened in the woods." As he spoke his voice grew harsh. He sounded angry as he finished. "You need to take care of yourself. If you won't do it, I will do the job for you."

"I'm sorry you decided to deprive yourself of a meal or two on my account." That was lame. At his confession, she should be jumping for joy. He wished to wed with her. It was what she wanted for so many months. "I cannot marry you." He didn't ask. All Case did was assume she would bend to his will. Before she joined with a man for the rest of her life, she wanted to hear the word love mentioned in the scenario.

I want to marry the man. Why am I sabotaging this? If I had any sense at all, I would tell him marriage was what I also wanted. What does it matter if he loves me or no. If he doesn't ever leave again, that would be heaven? I couldn't live with myself if he chose to stay with me because he thought I needed his protection. He cannot love. I cannot change him. Cannot marry him no matter how much I want to.

Case stood, his size intimidating. That was something he'd never done to her before. Intimidate. "You will marry me. I've made arrangements with the duke and duchess for the ceremony to take place in London at Ella's discretion. We will be wed with your family around you. If you wish, friends will be invited. If you only wish for the duke and duchess to witness the wedding, that would be fine also. As soon as you are able to travel, we will leave."

"I didn't say yes." She lifted her chin, the stubborn streak in her that her father told her would one day get the best of her. This could be the day. She was denying herself what she wanted most out of stubborn pride.

His soft curses echoed around the small room. "You will because that's what you want. Tomorrow, we will leave for London." In a blink, he did an about face. Changed his words to suit the moment.

What happened to when I was healthy? He never demanded anything of her before. Baffled at him, she bristled at his attempt to control her life. If this had been a proper proposal, she would have agreed. A man was supposed to get down on one knee. The devil, he was supposed to ask not tell. There should be a ring to put on her finger. Tara thought of Grant's romantic proposal. Comparisons were ugly. Grant was her past. Case might well be her future if she didn't get in the way of herself.

Marriage to Case was what she wanted. Tara needed to backtrack. "Alright. I'll marry you."

"You have to eat."

"I'll try." Eating was something she could make no guarantees about. No, eating was something she could do. It was keeping the food in the proper place that proved difficult. Why wasn't he pleased she agreed to marry him? Why was that scowl still on his face. His dark thick brows were still drawn together.

"You can begin with one of the scones. They have blueberries in them. Heard the *wee* berries are very good, healthy," Case seemed out of place speaking of healthy foods.

Hesitant to eat so soon after losing her breakfast, she nibbled. She sipped her tea then nibbled again. "It is good." Tara didn't lie. She just didn't think she could eat more. She was afraid if she did there would be a mad dash to the nearest basin. The devil, she didn't know where one was. She might throw up all over the beautiful blue carpet.

"I want you to finish that." Case pointed at the poor scone.

"Give me a minute. A little bit goes along way." Tara nibbled again. Somehow in the five minutes it took her to eat the pastry, she found the food didn't object. With a long sigh of relief, she thought the scone would remain.

"That wasn't so hard, was it?" Case asked while he watched her.

What he didn't know, she wasn't going to tell him. "No." Tara set her hands in her lap, waiting. Silence clung to the air. Her stomach rolled. She supposed he would have to find out sometime. Without another word, she ran from the room. Thankfully, her maid anticipated her needs. She handed her the basin. Tara kneeled, bent over.

Case was beside her, stroking her back. "What is it?" He ran the back of his hand along her back. After she sat up, he wiped her mouth with his handkerchief then gave her a cup of tea. "Sip this."

Nodding, she complied with his wishes. "I'm sorry." Tara didn't know what else to say except to toss out the words that might send him running in the opposite direction. She supposed she was pleased he proposed before he knew about the child. If she could, she would keep the news from him until they were wed. No, that would be wrong. Case should be allowed to decide for himself if he wanted to find himself shackled to not only her but a child as well.

"There is nothing to be sorry about. How long has this been going on? Your maid told me you lost that piece of bread along with the soup you ate this morning."

He scooped her into his arms just as she shrugged. "I don't know, a few weeks maybe longer. I was so tired. I've lost track of the time. It's hard to eat when you know the food is going to come right back up."

"Are you pregnant?" Case asked as if he had suspicions. "Is that why you're not keeping the food down? We need to find the right time of day for you to eat. Fill you up then. Spend the mornings sleeping. I would like to leave for London tomorrow. Can you do that? We can leave after lunch. We don't have to travel very far at one time. We'll take it slow. Give you lots of time to rest. You can sleep in the carriage."

Since she didn't know when the morning sickness would end, she couldn't answer. "I just realized it this morning. I saw my rounded belly in the mirror after my bath. I guess. I don't know for certain. Does it matter?"

"No." Case was shaking his head.

"Now that you know about my condition, do you still wish to marry me?" The shakiness in her words startled her. "You never wanted a child. You told me that."

Tara was in his arms as he strode into the study where they'd been talking. He sat down, cradling her in his lap. "More than anything. I was part of this. You know that." With more gentleness than she'd ever known from Case, he set his hand on her abdomen. "More than anything...I want this child of yours...of ours."

"Why now?" Tara needed answers. Honest answers.

He sighed while he appeared to be thinking. "The moment I left Paris, I missed you. Spent the trip to Portugal thinking about you every second of every day, recalling the sound of your laughter along with your special scent. The nights without you in my bed beside me were the worst. The moment I touched foot on land, I wanted to turn around and take the same ship back to Paris. You wouldn't have been there."

"You had a mission that needed completion."

"That too. It was an assignment that was fraught with misinformation. Took me longer than normal to locate the man and bring him back. Of all things, the time I cared when I finished, it was the time when everything would go wrong."

Her hand rested on his face. "You missed me? I missed you too. I spent so much time standing on the battlements watching the sunrises along with the sunsets, remembering when you used to stand behind me, your arms around me. I didn't mean to starve myself. Though I did miss you so much. I did forget about eating...then I couldn't keep the food in my stomach."

His husky voice reached deep into her soul. "That is good to know."

"When I started losing the contents of my stomach, I thought I was sick. I found there were times of the day I felt better. I would try to eat then."

He didn't stop the soft chuckle she felt that vibrated through his body. "Think that's why it's called morning sickness."

"Yes, but mine got worse. About two weeks ago I was sick all day long. Was afraid to eat at any time of the day even though I *kenned* I should."

"Is it better now?" He lifted her chin. "You've more color than I saw yesterday. The circles around your eyes are not so dark as they were less than twenty-four hours ago."

"I'm tired. Never felt so tired in my life." Tara leaned against Case, rested her head on his chest. She didn't mean to fall asleep. Lying with him, hearing his heart beat against her cheek, she felt as if she'd come home.

When she woke, shadows from the setting sun ran across her room. Case sat on her bed. He kissed her cheek then picked her up.

His voice husky with emotion, he said, "We're going up to the battlements. We'll watch the sun as it goes to sleep. After that we will see what you can keep down. I've ordered tea with honey, chicken soup with goodies in it instead of just the broth, bread as well."

She stifled a shudder that was sweeping through her despite the fact she tried to stifle the sensation. "I..."

"You have to try. This might be the time of day that you can eat. What do you say?" Case didn't give her a chance to answer. He made his way to the top of the castle then set her down. Just as they always watched the sun, he held her. Her back was pressed against his chest, his arms below her breasts. He swept hair from the back of her neck before he brushed soft kisses there.

Tara felt the sweet sensations she'd known in France. Her stomach rumbled. They both laughed. As soon as the sun disappeared, Case lifted her in his arms to carry her back to the bedroom. He set her at the small table that was now covered with several varieties of food.

"This feast smells divine," she told him hoping the food would stay where it was supposed to be. As a just in case, the washbowl was set nearby.

"Are you hungry?" Case asked as he dished up soup for both of them then placed a piece of bread along with a slice of cheese on her plate. "There are some sliced apples if you have room when you're finished with this."

Sucking in a deep breath of air, she looked at the wealth of food sitting in front of her. "I'm famished." Tara was still afraid to take the first bite. Case was watching. With hesitation, she dipped the spoon. Tasted the broth avoiding the carrots and chicken along with the potatoes.

She waited.

He watched with a smile on his face.

"You should eat too. It's kind of hard to eat when someone is watching you." She gave him a slight smile then took another spoon full of broth.

It seemed Case took her words at face value. He tucked into his soup then the rest of the meal. Case sipped the tea even though Tara knew he didn't like tea. He much preferred the coffee they had in Paris. The scene might have been funny at another time. An hour passed. She consumed most of what he dished up for her. For the first time in too many days or weeks to count, she felt satisfied.

"How is that little belly of yours doing?" Case asked looking at her as if he wished to touch.

To Tara's surprise, his hand rested on her stomach, his fingers spreading out. "So far I'm feeling fine."

"Good, some apple slices?"

"One, I don't think I can hold any more food."

She chewed trying to savor all the juice of the apple. Tara felt fine. "Time for bed. Whenever you wake in the morning..."

"I know. We will take our time."

"Was I too highhanded?" Case asked. "Telling you we were going to London for the wedding. Thought you would like to have some of your family there. Was I wrong?"

"As usual, you were right."

~ * ~

As the days passed Tara's morning sickness diminished. Ella flitted about, thrilled to help plan the first wedding of her sojourn as The Duchess. Drake left for the country estate muttering that he couldn't take all the people coming and going from the townhouse. He was going to go mad. Told Ella he would visit in a week. She told him he had to be back in London in two days for his fitting. He grumbled but left with a smile on his face.

In the dressmaker's salon, Ella watched her niece as she showed off the wedding gown she'd chosen. The lace around the corsage was exquisite. Her dress was made from white satin. She refused to have it covered in pearls. Tara's bouquet was made up primarily of lilies.

Ella kept Case away from Tara and kept her so busy she would fall into bed at night exhausted. He wasn't allowed to sleep with her. She understood if Case chose not to fall into their plans, he would be in her bed.

She sighed while she sipped tea in the parlor with Ella. "Didn't think we would ever get to the wedding day. This all seems to get more complicated. Where is Case?"

"Appears he's gone with Drake to White's. They don't cotton that much to sitting around. Drake needs to put distance between him and all the preparations."

"Tomorrows the big day," Ella said. "Will the two of you go back to the castle?"

"No. Case wants to buy land in the highlands. He has a place in mind. Saw the land and house up for sale in the London Times. I think it was his old home. He won't tell me. I refuse to ask."

"Then...you know about his childhood?" Ella asked.

"Some of what he was willing to tell me. Don't *ken* if I know everything."

"You should understand. Drake was behind this. He bought the land. When Case told him he was finished with the secret service, he put the ad in the times. Made sure Case saw the advertisement. Believe Case suspects. He isn't going to mention this. If you wish to tell, him I'm certain it is fine."

"I see." Tara wasn't at all certain she saw anything. Though she was heartily glad for the manipulations. If having his home back in his hands would please him, she would also be happy.

Ella clasped her hands. "I always thought the two of you could heal each other. Believe this worked out the way I planned."

Epilogue

The wedding was everything she imagined it would be. All her dreams were coming true. After Grant died Tara never expected to fall in love. She never needed fancy or elaborate. Saying I do to the man she adored as well as in front of the people she loved went beyond all she wished for. In this instance, she allowed Ella to have a major say in the venue along with the decorations. The ceremony was held in the ballroom on the third floor of the country estate. As to her wedding gown, she kept the dress simple.

Case told her he thought she looked beautiful. To Case, she was beautiful inside as well as out. Her ivory gown belted just below her breast hung in smooth lines. He was pleased to see the gentle swell of her belly. If he didn't know she carried his child, he would never guess.

Beaming with what appeared to be brotherly affection, Liam gave her away. She'd always been close to her half-brother. Dressed in his wedding finery, Liam looked every bit the lord of the realm that he was. Her maid of honor was Nickie McInnis. The two cousins had always been close. Growing up they didn't live too far from each other. Many times, they'd spoken of this day, their wedding day. Of all things, Ash was Case's best man. Those two were the only attendants they had except for Ella and Drake's youngest children, Charlotte and Cole who were the flower girl and the ring bearer.

Case told her was going to build her a mansion in the highlands. It would be high on a craig where they could watch both the sunrises along with the setting of the sun. She told him all she wanted was a home large enough to have as many children as they wished for. Since those words he wondered how many she wanted. He could well afford as many as she liked. She told him true that she had everything she'd ever wished for. All she ever wanted was a family and a man who loved her. He'd not told her those words...expressed his love for her. He meant to do so today while they watched the sunset from their bedroom balcony.

When they reached the highlands two weeks after their wedding, he wanted her to remain in Inverness while he built a small cabin where they would live until the home was finished. The cabin would become a guest house. Hoped all her cousins would come to visit. She told him she'd divorce him if he made her stay somewhere without him. She never wanted to be alone again. So, in the end, she traveled with him to the highlands. For the first days they slept in a tent. The sleeping arrangements were a *wee* bit rustic as well a tad romantic. They made love every night then she would sleep incased in his arms. He would listen to her breathe, to the sound of the beat of her heart. He would remember how he might have lost her because he was too stubborn to realize what he held in his hands.

As a wedding gift, Drake sent carpenters along with supplies to build the two-room cabin where they would stay while their home was built. The cabin went up in less than a week. Before they moved in, wagons of bedding along with dishes and furniture arrived...a wedding gift from Ella. Beth told him she never felt so blessed as she did now. Other gifts arrived from her parents along with her cousins. He was always amazed at her family.

Tara told him she had everything she needed to be happy. The first thing Case intended was to rip down the hovel where he grew up. The home harbored too many bad memories to allow the frame to remain standing. That task was fine with her. The two of them didn't need reminders of a past best forgotten.

With all the help from the duke along with The Duchess, the new home was built in five months. She was, she thought, about eight months along. She would give birth in her new home. Her parents heard about the marriage while they were in Singapore. They would be home as soon as possible. Hopefully, her mother would be there for her for the birth. Tara couldn't count on that.

Case wrote to her parents. Neglected to tell them about the problems they went through on their rocky road to finding happiness. Every day he did as much as possible to make amends for his lapse in judgement. Every day, she forgave him because she loved him. Case knew she loved him. He still could not conjure up the words to express his love to her.

Now, they stood on the balcony of their new home. They would watch their children grow here. Would grow old here. It was a fine day for watching the sun descend behind the misty craigs. The sky was a beautiful cerulean blue. A few clouds dotted the sky. There was no rain threatening the view.

"This is our first sunset from our new home," Case told her as he led her onto the balcony. "Do you think this one will be as striking as the ones you watched from the battlements of the castle McClaren?"

Tara turned to look at him, the roundness of her belly pushing against him. He felt the *wee bairn* kick. Since those first terrifying days after he found her in the forest beside the stream, she thrived. It did take some time for her to regain the weight she lost. Now, she blossomed. He couldn't be more delighted.

She laughed. The sound trilled from her as if she didn't have a care in the world. "If you would recall the sunsets could barely be seen since the woods got in the way. The sunrises were spectacular. We will have to see what the morning brings. Not at all certain I can get up early enough to watch a sunrise." Her hands pressed against her belly.

Moving so her back was forced against him, she seemed to wait for him to enfold her in his arms as he used to do. Before he placed his hands on her expanding belly, he brushed her hair aside. His lips drifted across her nape. He felt her shivery response. The doctor told him he could still make love to his wife. Doing so would not hurt the babe.

"Tomorrow morning then...who will wake whom?" he queried while he continued to kiss her. "My son kicks. Seems he's in a hurry to leave."

"Well, he must wait for another four weeks. Don't want this *lad* to be early." She pushed back against him.

He didn't wish for his child to rush the due date either. They weren't certain as to what that was as they had been careless. He was glad of that fact. Wanted this child more than he would have ever thought.

"If you conceived that first time," he could be coming today. Curious, he asked, "Have you felt any contractions?"

"Not one. I don't believe he was conceived that first time. Don't want to think it could have happened that night. Perhaps that time in Epernay when you couldn't keep your hands to yourself."

"Perhaps," he didn't care when although he understood why she didn't wish for the babe to have been conceived when he'd been horrible to her.

"Tara..."

"Hmm..." she pointed to the radiant colors above the tops of the craigs.

"I never told you..." he paused as if he didn't want to tell her. "I saw the castle MacLaren ghost sobbing on the battlements."

"You what?" she turned in his arms as if she needed to see into his eyes.

"Yes, I saw her. She was sobbing. Along with Tiny she helped me find you. Vanished though, after I got you back to your room."

"You believe?"

"I wouldn't go that far. Certain she was part of my imagination."

"Hmm..."

He wouldn't know what she meant by the last hmm... The sun would set. The colors were vibrant. Maybe this night foretold only good things ahead for them.

"I love you, Tara. You are different from any woman I've ever cared for. The woman who tells no lies."

Once more Tara turned in his arms. "You know I love you. I would say the words every day for the rest of our lives."

"Tara with no lies. I love you forever."

Coming Soon
by the Author
At Rogue Phoenix Press

Kerrie's Love Forever
Naughty Book Six

Scotland 1838

The wind caressed her face, sent her hair flying behind her. The exhilaration keen. Hooves pounding, thundering. Kerrie Johnston pushed the horse harder, faster. She was one with her horse, Dex. Thrills chased down her spine with the exciting race through the forest. They would fly out on the meadow soon, headed for home. The huge stallion sired by her mother's favorite horse, Fiacre, trampled the grass. Battered the ground beneath his hooves. She lay flat against the big stallion's neck. He leapt the log lying across the narrow woodland trail. She felt as one with the magnificent animal. Soon, she would need to slow him, walk him. Allow him to cool down. They would both breathe again. She sipped deep the forest air she loved. The fragrant smells were a profound part of her.

"Good boy," Kerrie whispered to the stallion stroking the animal, his hide sweaty. After they returned to the stable, he would need tender attention. As she understood the necessity, she slowed the pace to a walk, praising the animal as they continued. A deep breath of air filled her with the scent of pine. Four days were left to her. If she could enjoy every second with her horse, she would do so. She treasured the time alone with her thoughts. Sometimes she was a solitary soul. Loved the moments she had to herself.

The London season she didn't want awaited her. She was no debutant. Nor did she wish to call herself on the shelf though she was. Her stomach churned at the horrific knowledge of what was going to happen to her. Dancing with fops at the ball who had the sole purpose of shopping for a wife was not on a favorite to do list. Riding the wind. Feeling Dex beneath her. Those were what her dreams were made from. Her parents didn't know she took this slight diversion into the hills behind the country estate where she was supposed to become a lady. She would never simper. Would never bow down to man's whims.

If her father discovered she had left her entourage in the village below, he'd be furious. Even more so if he discovered she was alone. Kerrie didn't need or want babysitters. Didn't need to be protected or sheltered from the big bad world. She wasn't a helpless female. That's all her entourage was. Protectors of her virtue. Hah! The guards he sent as traveling companions weren't needed. She understood they were a precautionary tactic. Her father suspected she would do something to deviate from his plans. Before riding up the path to the Montgomerie hunting lodge, she sent Aunt Ella a note as to her plans, telling her the anticipated arrival would be delayed a week. If she dared delay it further, she would do so. If she could put her debut off forever, that would be better. She anticipated with glee the time alone. Time to collect her thoughts then figure out a way to avoid a marriage, any marriage. She didn't have room for a man in her life.

Fathers always worried about daughters. Haden had two to worry over. Though Kelsey, her younger sibling, always did what she was told. Kelsey was a father's perfect daughter. For the most part, so did she, do what was expected. This was not one of those times. Before she was whisked into the carriage, she told her father this was not what she wished for in her life. Her parents thought she needed a husband. The devil, she turned twenty this year. She didn't care about the label of on the shelf. If and when she ever wed, it would be for love, not to gain a title or wealth. A love like her parents experienced was what she was holding out for. Kerrie understood she would never find that type of love at a debutante's ball. Wouldn't find love anywhere in London either. She needed a real man. What did she want with a dandy?

Nothing.

It wasn't as if she didn't have a few suitors. She did. Their kisses did nothing for her that would send her heart soaring. The caresses never sparked anything within. While the kisses were nice, that was all she felt. Nothing else. No flicker of desire. No flames she couldn't resist. Kerrie wanted something that would cock her toes up.

Kerrie leaned over to caress Dex, stroking the animal's neck. She'd been surprised when her mother allowed her to take the stallion with her. She also realized the allowance was to ease her into the acceptance of her destination. She had no choice except to go. Telling her mother she didn't care about a husband, would never hold water. The words would be a lie. The fact was she wasn't about to settle for a relationship without love. Most of all she didn't want a man with a title. That was the last thing she wished to have. A title would inhibit everything she longed for in life. There were too many rules that went with a title. She didn't like rules. Didn't need the obligations. She saw what Aunt Ella went through. Her aunt was a duchess. That title was just down the line from the king and queen. No, no man with a title would be hers. A man like that wasn't about to give her a second look. She was, after all, a *wee* bit, no, a lot rough around the edges. Her manners weren't lacking. She had her own way of doing things.

London... She was going to live with Auntie Ella now known as The Duchess. The one and only Duchess. Her aunt was in charge of all the female relatives who were sent to the city for their coming out. So far, she had sponsored three of her cousins. She was the fourth. As far as Kerrie was concerned, she didn't want a season. Didn't want to be sponsored by anyone, even The Duchess. Back in the little village at the bottom of the hill were three trunks filled with all the new clothing her mother had made special for her introduction. Kerrie thought the expense was a waste of good money. Though her father had more money than he needed. Money that could have been spent on the stables or purchasing new horseflesh to breed.

At the end of the trail, she found a boulder to sit on. This was one of her favorite places. It overlooked a canyon that fell away to a stream far below. Yesterday, she walked down to the stream with a fly rod in her hand. She caught two fish for her dinner that night. Since she didn't bring the cook with her, she cleaned then fried the rainbow trout herself.

What she did would allow her travel guards to help her bring enough staples to last the week she planned to stay here.

The food was plentiful. She could also fish in the lake next to the Montgomerie hunting lodge. She possessed a clean aim, hitting a rabbit or bird with her rifle. However, cleaning and skinning an animal was not enjoyable. While her family had permission to visit the lodge whenever, they always wrote of their plans ahead of time to make certain they would be the only ones staying. Didn't find sharing amenable. This time for Kerrie the visit was unplanned. Knowing what was expected, she did write. Nonetheless, she was afraid someone would be at the lodge. When she reached the village below, she knew she would be fine. All the servants who worked at the lodge were at the village. No one was expected. She would be alone. Exactly what she needed to prepare herself for the dreaded season.

Thinking of the boring period ahead of her, she tossed a small rock over the edge of the cliff listening for it to land even though she understood she wouldn't hear a sound. The drop was too far. In this spot the stream tumbled across large boulders. The water rushed down to the sea. She breathed in deep. The scents as well as the scenery touched her. Moved her. This serenity was all she needed. Balls, dinners, recitals, held no happiness for her. The crush of the season was horrendous. She cringed thinking about all those perfumed bodies in one area.

The noon hour had come and gone. She was hungry. For a few more minutes she leaned back, the autumn sun beating down on her face. From the summer, her skin was tan more so than what a lady wanted. She was no lady. Never claimed to be. Her best friend in the whole world scolded her for forgetting her bonnets. A bonnet got in the way of riding in the manner she liked. Dex moved restlessly beside her. She wished she could ride forever. Riding was her one and only joy.

With a heavy sigh, Kerrie looked to the horse she adored. Smoothed her hand along his neck. "Time to get back, Dex. Are you as hungry as me? There will be something special waiting for you. After you eat, I'll bring you apple slices as well as the carrots you so enjoy. First thing though is a good rubdown. I did work you hard."

After she stood, she smoothed her hand down his long nose. Except for the white mark running down the center of his nose, he was pure black, his coat glossy from the tender care she gave him. His dark brown eyes stared at her, waiting for the treat he knew he would get. The juicy morsel would come later. The stallion knew that fact. He thought if he stared at her with his big brown eyes, he would get it sooner. Today, if she had apple slices or carrots in her pocket, he would receive his reward.

"You're such a fine fellow. Every girl's dream. Too bad there isn't a man out there as special as you are." Kerrie reached into her jacket pocket coming up with pieces of a carrot. She smiled at him. Until now she forgot about the treat. "For your good behavior." Dex had been right. She always gave into those bottomless dark eyes. Would give the big stallion everything since he always gave his all.

Dex gobbled up the treat. Using a log, Kerrie mounted, swung her leg over his back. The movement hiked up her skirts to her knees. She didn't care. They were alone in this small piece of paradise. Not that she would give it a second thought in other circumstances. Riding near her parents' property she rarely met anyone. They lived away from the small town near where she grew up. She bent close to his ear. "Shall we race one more time? As soon as we leave the woods for the meadow, we will test your strength. Your stamina. A brisk race across the field is in order. You are in need of a *wee* bit more exercise." The smart trot she set him to brought a bob of his head telling her he was just as ready as she was. Dex understood every word she spoke. He was an incredible animal. He would be the means for her to build her stable.

He shook his head, nickering his approval. She kept the pace slow through the woods. Dodged fallen logs. Jumped over ones that lay across the trail. Once they reached the meadow in front of the lodge, she gave him the go ahead to race. The hunting lodge was a small dot in the distance. She inhaled as they set off. Her heart raced, the thrill of the run inherent in every part of her.

Exhilarated.

The grin of enjoyment swept her from the inside out. Wind tore at her hair as his speed increased. Leaning over, Kerrie urged the big stallion faster. Faster still. They flew over the grassy field. Together, they raced the wind for the second time today. Next year Dex would race with the three-year-olds. Dex would win just as his father won every race her mother entered. Would become a legend. This horse was unstoppable. He belonged to her. This was all she wanted from her life; the horse, a stable that would be hers. A husband to demand things of her was not something she had room for. Did not want to be the oldest debutante for the season.

Hoofbeats that weren't Dex's thundered behind her, too close for comfort. Her heart lurched. Deep inside she panicked. She was supposed to be alone. No one should be here. Who the devil could be shadowing her? Kerrie turned to look over her shoulder. She grimaced at the sight. He was chasing her. His mount gaining on her. She needed to urge Dex faster then faster still. This wasn't right.

A man...

No, it couldn't be. His face was stern. His lips pressed together. What she saw of his expression before she turned her attention to the race of her life was anger. This unknown person had no reason or right to be furious with her. No reason to race after her. What the hell did he want? Fear thrashed inside. Wind stung. Her hair whipped around her face.

This man was the interloper. He didn't belong.

"Faster, Dex, please. Faster. Go! Our lives might depend upon your speed. You're the fastest horse in the British Isles. I'm willing to bet on that fact." Kerrie's heart leapt. She cringed against the horse trying to make herself small. Dex was tired from his earlier run. He might not win this race. Her confidence no longer soared. He was up against a formidable enemy. One she didn't wish to confront.

Seconds ticked by, one after the other. Hoofbeats still pounded behind her. When she peeked again, the man was closing on her. She bent closer to the horse's neck, knowing the stallion didn't have more to give. He was exhausted. Earlier she put him through his paces. His big body heaved. Would want his oats as well as that good rub down she promised him. He would give her everything he had. His valiant heart wasn't enough. She needed to face whatever was in store for her. She would never run her horse to the ground. About to pull up on the reins, she felt the man beside her.

The shriek cried out from deep inside her when, without warning, she was lifted through the air to land hard on the stranger's thighs. "No!" Kerrie pushed at the arm that circled her waist, holding her against a hard chest. Squirming she twisted, pushed, kicked as well as hit at the man. She punched him hard in the jaw. His head snapped back. She didn't care if she fell. This was far worse than finding herself trampled.

"Stop it!" He shook her as the stallion slowed. His words furious. "Stop it! I don't mean you harm. What the bloody hell do you think you are doing? That horse was out of control. He's too big for you. Too strong."

Kerrie swung. Her fist hit his jaw. His head jerked back for a second time. He dumped her on the ground. She landed on her backside so hard air rushed from her lungs. Moisture rose to her eyes. "Hellion! I saved you! What do I get for my efforts? A broken jaw!" He rubbed where she hit him. Stared down at her as if she was insane.

Kerrie couldn't help from gaping at the audacity of his words. Her feet firmly planted on solid ground, her hands on her hips she felt a bit of bravado. This man was an arrogant bastard. "Saved me from what? Just what exactly do you think your highhandedness saved me from. You could have killed me! Could have been thrown beneath the hooves of your horse. You are too wild. Too reckless. Arrogant."

He swung his leg over then dropped to the earth beside her. Good God, he was tall. Broad shoulders. Narrow of hip. Thighs muscled. Lips thinned into a flat line. Blue-grey eyes simmered with heat. Flashed sparks of fire in her direction. She was taken aback by his words. Despite her determination to stand her ground, she stepped back from him. His stance was too overpowering. She couldn't meet him eye to eye. Would need to find some other way to state her case against his bravado. He had no rights here.

"Your horse was running wild. You are a *wee* bit of a thing. Scrawny arms. No muscle. There was no way in hell you could keep that huge stallion in line," he spoke with infuriating calm. His voice held her enthralled for a moment. Talked as if he knew what was what. "Before you broke your pretty neck, you needed help. I came to your aide. No thanks from you. I rescued you." He threw up his hands. "What the hell were you thinking?"

"You're crazy. I'm no damsel in distress who needs help from the likes of you. I had everything well in hand! Didn't need a man to save me from the horse I've ridden for two years. Dex obeys my commands.

He understands." She didn't intend to back down from his tirade. The man was wrong.

"Could have fooled me." His fury was no longer flashing sparks.

The eyes that stared at her turned smokey. His gaze ran over her as if he assessed her abilities. *Scrawny arms. No muscle. I'll show him muscle.* He seemed more annoyed than anything.

"Come along, I'll take you wherever it is you need to go. Are you one of the servants here? If so, you shouldn't be playing super horsewoman while there is work to be done in the house."

Come along? Not on his life or mine. How dare he speak to her in that manner?

Kerrie didn't have words to combat him, his highhandedness. His smug grin. His arrogance. Her anger had not died. "I did. I fooled you. Now I'm the one who has to walk back because of your highhandedness. I hate walking." She began the trek to the lodge. Which wasn't that far. She could have ridden into the stable. Because of his actions, she walked. Brushed Dex down. Given him his evening meal. This man kept her from attending to her stallion as he should be tended to.

"You're telling me you had everything in hand? That you weren't in trouble? I don't believe a word. That animal has to be sixteen or seventeen hands. A little slip of a female can't handle an animal that large. Besides, if you were taking everything in hand, you were running the animal into the ground. A good horseman would never do that."

A wave of nausea swept through her. In all her life she'd never overtaxed an animal. In this case, his statement might be too close to the truth for comfort. Only because she was running from him. Unable to say anything else, she made an unladylike snort. "How would you know? You were chasing me. I feared for my life. Thought you were a madman. Still do." Kerrie felt more than ready to blast the man out of the water. Instead of giving him what for, she held her tongue after that last statement. She'd said too much. Arguing with this beast of a man would get her nowhere. She still didn't know his intentions. What the devil was he doing here?

"I know. Now, come along. Let me give you that lift to wherever you're going. You don't have to walk unless you're so stubborn you'd defy my generosity. Didn't you just tell me you abhorred walking?"

Come along. Infuriating beast.

Self-absorbed male.

"Would rather walk than be anywhere with you." Kerrie was beginning to dislike this man, this handsome man, she amended, wishing he weren't so arrogant as well as annoying. Wishing he didn't believe his every word was gospel. Wishing he didn't intrigue all her senses. He was too handsome...too masculine. Too…

"No?" he questioned her. One more time in less than five minutes his hands were on her waist. He tossed her onto his horse. With no effort on his part, he leapt up behind her. The reins were in one hand. His arm was around her waist pulling her close. He guided the animal toward the lodge. In a different life, she might admire his skill with his horse. Might enjoy the heat pervading her body when he touched her.

No!

At his obvious destination, she groaned. He couldn't be going to the lodge. While she had permission, at the same time she didn't have authorization. Ella wouldn't have known until today she was here. The duke might have given this man permission to vacation at the hunting lodge. Her note would have reached Ella only a day or two ago. He would have arrived this afternoon while she was out exploring the territory. The servants from the village would begin to assemble. Her long-awaited relaxing vacation before London would be over.

"Seems your horse..." the man began but he cut himself off. His huge arm squeezed against her stomach.

"Dex."

"Seams your horse is headed for the stable. Did you steal the animal? Gives me more reason for concern. Are you a thief?" His audacious question infuriated her more than his highhanded assumption she needed help.

The bristling couldn't be helped. He made too many suppositions to satisfy her. She meant to set him straight. "He's mine. My horse. No, I didn't steal the animal. If you want proof, I don't have any. Never thought I would need a document. Raised Dex from the moment he was born. My mother gave him to me."

"How would you..." He looked over her clothing, ran his hand along the fabric of her skirt. "How would you afford that fine of an animal? You're dressed in clothing suitable for a servant. Not the owner of as fine an animal as that stallion. Believe you lie. Care to speak the truth? Could summon the law. Hold no respect for females who lie."

The groan she hid behind her teeth. He wouldn't send for the law. The sheriff in the village knew her. Knew her family. Would give her away. His question was legitimate. Dressed as she was, his rush to judgement didn't surprise her. "I don't always wear old clothes. Dex needed to be put through his paces. I dressed for work not a day of leisure. Not for a ride in the park or down a country lane. Don't wear my, 'ride in Hyde Park', ensemble when working out the animals. No reason to dress up when I'm working."

The air from his bark of laughter ruffled her hair. This was too much. She sucked in a breath of air when his arm tightened around her again. "Snippy little thing, aren't you? You need to learn to curb your tongue before it gets you into trouble you can't find a way out of." He spread his fingers across her belly. Heat flared in her. He took liberties he had no business taking.

"Stop calling me little! I'm not. I'm grown. A woman. Not a child. I'm not small." Kerrie didn't understand the burgeoning anger. The fury his words elicited. Understood the way he acted coupled with the words coming from his mouth had a way of irritating her. Rubbed her wrong. He talked to her as if she had no brain in her head. She was a woman grown.

This time he chuckled. His arm pulled her closer to him, pressed below her unfettered breasts. She pushed away to no avail. "When the description fits, I'll use it. When a person acts like a child they'll be treated as one. You, my dear, were acting as if you had no wits about you. A child would behave in that manner. Not a grown young woman. "He moved his arm up. Her breasts pushed against his forearm. He should be able to tell she was no child.

He made her feel like a hoyden. Just what did he expect her to do when she turned around to see a stranger chasing her? She needed to approach this from a different angle. It was time to learn a few things about this man who was invading her space, her life, her future. "What are you doing here? If you don't mind my asking," she questioned hoping to get some information from him that would dispel her fears. He was still an unknown entity in her life. The man could force her. Have his way with her. She had no protection this far from the village and her entourage. The devil, she couldn't point that out to him. If she said as much, her words might put ideas into his head.

"You took my question right out of my mouth. I'm assuming you work here or in the village below. You've taken privileges that were never meant for you. Presuming you are getting ready for my arrival. Am I wrong?" He steered the animal they were riding on toward the stable. Kerrie straightened trying to keep her back from touching him. Everywhere he touched, heat flared.

"You're wrong on all counts. You know nothing about me. Your assumptions are all wrong." She cringed when she thought about tonight. He would persist until he discovered what she was about. Who she was. While this wasn't meant to be a secret, neither did she wish to broadcast the fact she didn't travel to London where she was supposed to be. Kerrie understood this man deserved the truth. Giving him her truth would not be forthcoming until he proved himself to be trustworthy. He could be the worst of the worst.

"Enlighten me then. What am I wrong about? I'm a reasonable man. I'll listen. Decide what to believe as well as what not to believe." He persevered with the line of questions that she wished to ignore.

The man let her slip to the ground. She stalked to Dex's stall where she began to rub him down. Kerrie didn't want to look at this infuriating person let alone acknowledge his presence. She needed to ignore him. Pretend he wasn't there. Knew he wouldn't be here without the duke's permission. A man took the reins of his horse. She supposed all the servants she'd told had the week off would be up here working. So much for her wish for peace and quiet. She might have well as gone straight to London.

Talking to him was not an option at the moment. Any words that would fly at him from her mouth would offend him. Her standing in his eyes would diminish. With his watching over her, staring at her as if he wished to devour her, she couldn't think. If she offended the man too much she would be sent back down the trail to the village. If she desired to remain here, she would need to find a way to coexist with him for her remaining days. She could charm as well as any woman. Flirting was second nature to her. Used the ploy only when necessary. Though she loathed doing so. This was for her good...not his. She didn't want anything from the man except to be left alone. If she were to find a *wee* bit of luck, she might be able to send him packing.

Minutes later when she finished seeing to her horse, she strode to him intending to bridge the widening gap between them. Kerrie held out her hand. With a deep breath, she began, "I'm Kerrie Johnston. Who are you?" This introduction seemed prudent. A name for him a necessity. She hoped he didn't have a title behind his name. Men with titles were loathsome. Give her a peasant any day over a lord or the realm and she would be happy.

"Nice to finally have a name for you. Sterling Talmadge at your service. My friends call me Tam." He brought her hand into his. Instead of shaking it, he brought it to his lips to kiss the back. He then turned it over to stroke the palm with his thumb.

Shocked, outraged by the strange feelings that centered inside her, Kerrie tugged. A man should not take wicked advantage of a situation...of...of a lady. He let go with a wide grin that pronounced the cleft in his chin. "Mr. Talmadge," she acknowledged with a slight quiver to her voice. Glad that he bore no title in front of his name. "Believe we have quite a few things to discuss. I..."

"You don't belong here, Lady. If you are not a servant then who are you? Some usurper who found a cozy place to call home? A woman who needs to hide from someone? Perhaps a lover? That still doesn't explain that magnificent horse you tell me is yours." He stood with his feet braced apart. His beautiful eyes shot daggers at her. This man wasn't going to credit anything she said.

Obvious, he didn't appreciate her any more than she liked him. "A friend of the family, the Montgomerie family. Ella is my aunt, my mother's side. Drake is my uncle by marriage to Ella. You understand. Right? My mother and father have a standing invitation to visit this hunting box. I took the invitation to heart which is why I'm here. Didn't wish to be in London." She was about to tell him too much. "What about you? Why are you here?" She tried for bold as well as brash.

"You're here without your parents?" The voice of disapproval flashed at her. "A lady doesn't go someplace like this without a chaperone. Rules…the unwritten code of society…is important. You are quite the risk taker. Maybe you're not as innocent as you are supposed to be."

Kerrie bristled. "That obvious? Nope. No parents for me. They trust me to say no to a cavalier man. Unless you don't take no for an answer to anything. Quite capable of taking care of myself." She couldn't help the sarcasm ebbing from her. "I've never needed a chaperone. Don't need or want one now. If you are applying for the job, there isn't a job. If you think I might want you, you are sorely mistaken. Don't need some unknown person in my presence to tell a man no."

"A little slip of a girl with no protection. Don't believe the duke and duchess would approve of you being at this hunting lodge by yourself. I'll wager they don't know you are here. Nor do your parents. Do you have a husband?"

She coughed, shocked by his assumption. "Good God no!" She bit out before she could bring the words back behind her teeth. Whether she was married or not wasn't his business. The fact he asked was rude beyond anything a gentleman would enquire.

Bloody everlasting hell he sounded sour, even bitter. Right before her eyes his disposition changed. Even with the ardent disapproval in the tone of his voice coupled with his words, his lips seemed to be twitching as if he held back a smile. What could he find in this conversation that was amusing?

Unless the blasted man laughed at me. I am old enough to be on the shelf. I should be able to go anywhere by myself that I please. I'm not going to give him more reasons to chastise me.

"I'm twenty," Kerrie blurted out again then wished, for a second time, she'd kept her mouth closed. Before she told him her life story, she was going to have to curb her impulsiveness with this man. She didn't understand what was happening to her. Never acted this way. She was quite capable of keeping her story behind her teeth.

"That old." His chuckle rumbled up from his gut, the grin he sported broad. "So young. Still," He rubbed his chin with long sculpted fingers as if thinking. His nails neatly cut as well as clean. "A woman of your wild nature should have a chaperone despite your advanced age."

"Yes. That old. My age is not your business. Neither is a

chaperone. I'm independent." She didn't like the tone of voice or the deep base laugh she heard after her words. Kerrie went back to rubbing down Dex before she gave more of herself away. She needed to keep her mouth shut.

"Means you're well versed in a great deal of things. Am I right? You are of such a great age. You must know men well. What they want. All about their needs." His gaze lingered a little too long on her mouth then her breasts. He assessed her. She bristled.

She whirled when he first began to speak now facing him. She didn't wish to see into his eyes. Didn't understand the second meaning to his words. Knew there was something wicked underlying those innocent phrases. What the devil did he mean by what he said? Her face heated. She set her hand on her blazing cheeks hoping she could cool them.

"Yes, I'm proficient at many tasks. For starters, I ride quite well. I train horses to race at Newmarket as well as other places. I'm an experienced..." Her shoulders squared. She tossed the brush into a barrel. Her hands fisted on her hips, she shouted at him. "What do you mean by that?"

His grin grew wide. His white teeth flashed in the dim light. "Good to know you're experienced. Maybe you can teach me some of those tasks you merit applauding at. You could always give me pointers on riding. Something a man likes to understand all the intricate details along with the subtle nuances. Might make my stay here more relaxing as well as interesting if you offered a few lessons...in riding. Could use some new knowledge of the carnal type. A woman who doesn't have a chaperone...my, my, my. This must be my lucky day."

Not wishing for this man to see the heat of embarrassment staining her cheeks, Kerrie turned away from him and concentrated on the grooming of Dex. Picked up each hoof to check for pebbles. This wasn't at all what she anticipated for tonight. Relaxing. Bah! That was also the circumstance she looked for by traveling here before moving on to the city. After she felt a bit more in control, she resumed the conversation. Stupid of her.

"I've no idea what you are saying or implying. Don't understand why you find humor at my expense. I'm going into the lodge now. After

I've changed my clothes, I'll start dinner. I can make enough for two if you wish to eat with me. If not, you're on your own. I don't care what you decide. I'm trying to be polite."

"You're not staying in this lodge tonight unless it's in my bed." His voice was bland as well as irritating. "I haven't believed a word that has come from your sweetly kissable lips. A mouth I would like to taste among other places on your lush sculpted body."

Her back stiffened. She stepped away. Bumped into the back of the stall. Stumbled. Righted herself. "I am staying. Won't be lying in your bed." The nerve of the conceited man. She made a note to start down the trail tomorrow. She understood when she...no...she wasn't going to give into his dictates. Wasn't going to run. She would stay. Fight. What authority did he have to kick her out? Demand her presence in his bed? None over her. If she didn't allow him authority, he couldn't force her to leave."

By the time she was out the stable door, she heard his curses. Kerrie smiled. The man was just as she imagined, all bluster and orders with no backbone. When faced with an unwilling victim, he didn't know what to do. Willing or otherwise she wasn't going to become his prey or fall at his feet. Nor was she about to join him in his bed.

Mr. Talmadge caught up to her by the time she stepped inside the lodge. He grasped her by the shoulder to turn her around. She stumbled. Managed to keep her balance by bracing her hand on his chest. Confronted him with her intentions. One more time, "I'm changing my clothes. After that, as I said I'll fix dinner." By the looks of him, she doubted if he could cook.

"No, you won't. The chef Drake employs is in the kitchen as we speak. Fixing my dinner. If you wish to eat tonight, you should tell him he needs to make enough for two people. The man doesn't allow interlopers in his domain, the kitchen. You will have nothing to eat if you don't do what I've suggested. Whether you eat or not makes no difference to me. You will still be in my bed."

She was flummoxed. Perhaps he did have a bit of backbone. All Kerrie could do at this time was nod her head. This was a nightmare. She did as he told her then walked the stairs to the master chamber where she left all her belongings. She would have to move to a different room. That was fine. Sharing a room or a bed was unacceptable.

Shock hit her in the gut when she saw what he did while she was out riding. A few unladylike curses left her mouth. From behind her, she heard unconcealed laughter. He followed her.

All her clothing was lying on the floor outside the door. She whirled, her hands fisted at her sides. He stood at the top of the steps leaning against the balustrade, relaxed, arrogant. His little half smirk told her he enjoyed her discomfort. Seemed he trailed behind her to see her reaction. Kerrie found herself shaking her finger at him with disbelief. "You didn't. Of all the conceited..."

"I did. If you want this room you have to share. Share with me. As I told you earlier, I'm willing to make concessions. You can even put your clothing back. There is plenty of room for two people."

"You've..."

His brow arched. He had every right to kick her out of the master chamber. No right to tell her she had to share his bed. While she fumed, she caved. Picking up her clothing, she marched to the guest bedroom at the other end of the hall.

"You've dropped your drawers," he laughed.

Kerrie marched back, grabbed her pantalettes from him then retraced her steps. Her back stiff. Her face flamed. Mortified.

"Wouldn't mind sharing. If you change your mind, you do know where to find my bed," he called after her retreating back.

A wise woman would leave in the morning. Without trying, the haughty man got her hackles up. She made plans to stay the week. Stay she would. She wasn't about to back down. Before she changed her clothes, she needed a bath. A dip in the lake would make her feel clean again. Kerrie hoped he wouldn't see her sneak down the back steps. She gathered soap and a towel along with clean clothes. Her heart hit a rapid stride as she picked up her pace.

Opening her door a crack, she peaked out. There was no one in the hall. On silent bare feet, she whisked her way to the backsteps then down. She stopped for a moment to slip on a pair of slippers then quick-stepped her way to the end of the lake, the part that couldn't be seen from the front windows.

Kerrie understood she might have only a few minutes to take care of the bath. In the cold water, she wouldn't wish for more than that. With speed born of desperation, she stripped to her chemise and pantalettes. Didn't dare submerge herself naked. With her favorite soap in hand, she walked into the water. Dipping under so her hair would be wet, she lathered the soap through the long hair. It seemed to take an eternity to wash all of her. Afraid he would see her, she kept her back to the house. Didn't know what she would do if he discovered her bathing in the lake. Another confrontation so soon would be heart stopping painful. This bath in haste was far from relaxing. She needed a soak in a hot tub. If she asked, he might have ordered one for her. She wasn't about to go into the kitchen to heat her water or take a bath in the scullery as she did the night before as well as the one before that. Hauling buckets of water upstairs was a difficult task. One she needed to avoid.

After she realized she'd been daydreaming as well as wasting time, her heart lodged in her throat. She raced out of the water to the towel she left on the bank. Thank goodness it was still there. While she knew he'd not left the house through the front door, there was always the possibility of the back. Once she pulled her gown over her head, she heaved in a deep relieved breath of air. Naked, well, dressed only in her underclothing, she was too vulnerable. No man ever saw her without clothes. He thought she gave her favors away. How stupid of him. She didn't tolerate ignorance. The man was also judgmental.

The sun now was dipping behind the trees surrounding the property. As she walked back to the house, she saw him standing in the upstairs window of the master chamber. Heat spread across her face. How much did he see? He might have been watching her bathe. Another inferno blazed. Her gut clenched tight.

He was still watching. Biting her lip, she straightened her shoulders. She wasn't going to give him the satisfaction of witnessing her humiliation. Thinking again of him watching her bathe sent another wave of heat, flames licking all over her body.

By the time she reached the servant entrance, he was there, holding the door open for her. The smile on his face was wicked. He would think the worst of her. Would make more comments she didn't understand.

"Enjoy your bath, Miss Johnston? Must have been chilly. It's the wrong time of year to bathe in the lake." His voice was solemn which surprised her. "If you asked, I would have ordered a hot bath for you. Much more relaxing. If you were sweet, I might have joined you. My bath was hot."

His formality surprised her. Behind her breath Kerrie muttered a few choice words she hoped he wouldn't understand. "Didn't wish to put you out. After what you said earlier, I had no idea how you would respond."

"I had a bath," he told her again his voice whiskey smooth. "We could have shared. Wouldn't have put me out at all. I would enjoy sharing most anything with you." He didn't wait for her to answer. His hand sat with firm possession at the small of her back. "Come along now, dinner will get cold if we don't attend to it soon. I've been waiting for you. I'm famished. Been a long day."

Come along. I am also famished. I've not eaten since breakfast.

Her hair was wet. Needed drying before she wanted to eat. It didn't seem he was giving her a choice. He pulled the towel from her hair then made an attempt to towel-dry the length. Her hair was too thick. She would need to sit in front of the fire and comb it for the strands to dry. Doing so would take most of an hour.

"After we finish our meal, I'll brush your hair for you." He ushered her into the dining room. "Would enjoy that."

Brush her hair? That was the last thing she wanted him to do. The man was too handsome. Too intimidating. Too exciting. Worst of all he set strange notions stirring inside her body she didn't understand. If she were with Aunt Ella, she would ask about those feeling. She wasn't. She could never ask this man who would either smirk or laugh at her questions. Who might take advantage of her lack of knowledge. She didn't trust him. Not one *wee* bit. If given a chance, he would run right over her.

"No...no." Holding up her hands as if the tiny gesture would sway him from the course he was set on. "Y- you c-can't brush my h-hair. It...it w...wouldn't be proper." She stammered out the words, berating herself about letting his presence get the best of her.

Again, the brow was lifted as if he speculated about another idea she wouldn't understand. His expression told her if he thought it best for him to brush her hair, he would do as he pleased. "Whatever pleases you. It is a tangled mess. I'm very good at brushing hair. Used to brush my mother's when it was so tangled a comb couldn't be drawn through the length. She never had the patience to do it herself. With my lovers when we finish, there hair is always smothered in tangles. Love the feel of the silken strands while they glide between my fingers. Ever had a man brush your hair? I would be your first."

Her body quivered at his words. The thought provoked. "You brushed your mother's hair?" *His lovers? When they finished? What did they finish?* She choked. His statement took her by surprise. Her eyes widened. He didn't seem like a man who would care so much about a single person that he would brush anyone's hair.

"Yes. The fact surprises you. I can see it in your eyes. Mother was older. Her arthritis was terrible. When she was tired, she had trouble holding a comb or brush. With my lovers...they enjoyed the additional attention. My fingers gliding along their scalp, well that always led to more fun. We'll start with a comb. It's easier to untangle hair with a comb than fingers."

The man had her steaming again. It seemed to be a constant state when he was nearby. "You're not brushing or combing my hair!" She found herself yelling at him. Mortified that he would believe he could say the words and expect her to allow whatever it was he commanded.

"We will see." He held out the chair for her. "This dress is much more in fashion than the last one. The fabric is acceptable as is the modest decolletage. You look stunning by the way."

"Thank you, I was pining for your approval." She managed to bite her tongue wishing she could hold the sarcasm back. If she meant to stay her allotted four more days, she would need to do something about the way she replied to Mr. Talmadge. Nicer, even more polite would work. Sugar coated words were too obvious a deviation.

His snort of laughter told her he didn't care about sarcasm. It seemed he enjoyed her antagonism. A challenge she didn't want to give him. She didn't know why he brought out the worst in her.

He splashed wine into her glass then into his own. Holding the glass high, he said, "I propose a toast." He waited for her to reciprocate before he continued. "To a few more congenial days together. May they proceed in much the same way as this afternoon." He added almost as an afterthought, "I came here to relax. Would like to believe it's possible."

"Mr. Talmadge," she paused while she thought of the right words, "if we stay out of each other's way, I'm certain this arrangement will work for both of us." She grinned at his scowl of displeasure. It seemed he didn't want to stay away from her.

"Call me Tam."

She nodded, "Mr. Talmadge." Delighted in the scowl of an expression he shot her way.

She saw that he gritted his teeth.

~ * ~

Even though she was the most disagreeable woman he ever met, Tam had no intention of staying out of her way. For some reason she intrigued him. Fascinated all his masculine senses. More than anything irritated him with her unladylike behavior. For all he knew, she could be the spawn of the devil. Nonetheless, he saw something refreshing, unique in the way she tackled life. She made him smile when he least expected it. After that she scared him near to death with her antics. When he first saw her tearing across the flat meadow, afraid for her, his heart leapt to his throat. He did believe she needed help to keep the huge stallion in line. The lady was so tiny. Too small to be riding that stallion or any stallion. If it was possible to feel scared to death, that would describe his reaction. If he had a say about the animal she rode, he would never allow her on top of a huge horse such as Dex. He didn't have a say.

Once he set her across his thighs, he was mesmerized by her bare legs. An immediate need to run his hands along them flooded his senses. His masculine nerves twitched. Her legs were long, slim and white. He imagined them wrapped around his flanks. His callous speech to her surprised him. It wasn't his habit to degrade a woman's reputation as he did hers. Much to his chagrin, this woman brought out all his worst instincts. Even at that baiting as well as teasing she was enjoyable. She never seemed to take him with the seriousness his words deserved. He adored the way her cheeks turned rosy with embarrassment. If he didn't miss a guess, she was clueless to the challenges along with the not so subtle innuendos he tossed her way.

She didn't like him. That part puzzled him. In his recollection, he'd never met a woman who acted this way toward him. If she knew he was a titled aristocrat, a marquess until his father passed, she would change her mind so fast it would make his head spin. Women were like that. Tam didn't doubt that salient fact for a moment as he admitted to himself he was jaded where women were concerned. The mere mention of his title had women dancing attendance, fawning over him, hoping to catch his attention. As of yet, he never met a woman who didn't worship a title along with his money. Whenever he could, he kept his aristocratic inheritance to himself. Doing so wasn't easy. Most places he traveled he was recognized. It was obvious this woman didn't know who he was. Tam meant to keep their relationship that way. He wanted her to know him. To understand who this man was, with or without a title.

For his part, he wished to learn as much about her as he could. What he did understand was The Duchess was her aunt, the duke her uncle. That would make her what...? When she introduced herself, she didn't put the title lady in front of her name. No, she was Kerrie Johnston, plain and simple. Wondered if she was related to the Johnston shipping magnate living on the eastern coast of England. That might attribute to the fact she owned that magnificent animal. Once at Newmarket he heard a reference to the Johnston stables. Heard also it was run by a woman. Could that woman be her mother? It certainly could not be her. She wasn't old enough. No matter, obvious to him, the girl was given everything she wanted. Was spoiled from the top of her pretty little head to her tiny toes he'd not seen yet. He could imagine tasting her toes.

Interesting.

What could he do to change her dislike to him...perhaps lust for him? Lust was a heady thought. He reminded himself he didn't like the way she acted or the risks she took even though in too many ways to count she was adorable. A few tumbles in the big bed upstairs with her would be enjoyable. He would have to use all his available charm to sweettalk her into his arms, after that beneath the sheets. Doing so would be hard unless he could change her aversion for him to something a bit more positive. He would need to temper his speech. Hold back on the commands. Tam had to admit he got off to a bad start when he snatched her from her horse. As things now stood between them, she wasn't going to fall into his waiting arms anytime soon. Where it concerned him, her hackles were up, all her defenses in place. She bristled when she saw him. Turned her chin up. The woman persisted in a battle she didn't need to fight. One she couldn't win.

While Tam stood at his window watching her as she disrobed then bathed, it took all his strength of will not to join her in the swim or bath as it turned out to be. Nothing could stop him from observing. A gentleman would never stare. Where this lady was concerned being a gentleman would never do. The sight of her slim body was just as delectable to his senses as he imagined while he held her this afternoon. Staring at her backside...her well-shaped butt as she waded into the lake sent all his senses reeling. On the other hand, when she left the water, her camisole as well as the pantalettes she wore plastered against her feminine curves, inflamed every masculine part he possessed. She was rounded in all the places he appreciated the most. There was enough light to point all that out to him.

While she dressed, he decided he would meet her at the back door. Her knowledge that he watched her bathe then dress seemed necessary for his plans to move forward. Let her wonder how much he witnessed. She would never be certain. The meal was quite good. The chef Drake employed was a master. The man created palatable dishes from everything imaginable. Though he couldn't help but wonder at Kerrie's cooking skills. He decided he would send the chef back to the village for more vacation days. Spending a bit of time in the kitchen with this woman might be fun. Working side by side. Tam imagined many different scenarios that would keep them busy.

He would keep the maid. Needed to have someone to tidy the lodge. Send the cook home, yes. The stableboy needed to stay. Without one...he paused in thought. Kerrie was a tiny woman. The top of her head didn't reach his chin. For that matter didn't reach his armpits. Her stallion was huge. She must saddle that big horse of hers by herself. The beast stood at least sixteen or perhaps seventeen hands. Until he arrived with the stableman, there was no one to do the duty of saddling for her. Her ability left him in awe. Unless she had some trick, she would be hard-pressed to heave a saddle onto the stallion's back. Her arms were not that big around. Muscle was lacking.

A trick.

She would have some gimmick.

Across the table from her, he watched. Her light brown hair was streaked with touches of the sun, red in places as well as ash blond to white. Her pert little nose tipped up at the end. The lips he wished to taste were full almost too full for a woman her size. He would like to see them swollen from his attention. Her eyes were the same color as the whiskey in the crystal glass he poured himself while he watched her. When she strode from the lake, he noticed the firm round globes tipped with hardened buds. They were the size of fresh peaches ready to be plucked. He was the man to do that.

After she finished the first glass, he refilled both his as well as hers. She slanted him a cross-eyed stare which produced a short chuckle he would never hide. This woman was his delight. So different from the women of his acquaintance. Pushing his plate away, he leaned back in the chair. Rested his hands on his belly.

"If you are finished with the meal, would you wish to retire to the sitting room? I'm ready to comb out your hair. It is beginning to dry. All the strands will be tangled together. Quiet a mess. I can fix that for you." To his surprise, her hair was curly. The few tendrils that dried while they ate curled with beguiling tenacity around her forehead. He needed to feel the texture, run the stands between his fingers.

She choked on a sip of her wine, sending a few drops from her mouth. With the napkin at her plate, she wiped the tiny red drops away. "Didn't I tell you I don't want you to comb my hair? Do you have trouble recalling facts? Perhaps your hearing is lacking."

"You don't need to be rude. I'm just trying to be nice. Come along, now. Sit by the fire." Tam stood. Held out his hand. The maid he hired turned up with both her brush as well as her comb. He held them as he motioned toward the door. "If I don't do the honors, no one does. Not even you. Your locks will remain a tangled mess. Is that what you want?"

"You've confiscated all my combs? How rude?" She muttered the last words while stomping off to the sitting room.

A gentleman, Tam never claimed to be, though he could be

gallant from time to time. What she told him implied she might have more than one of each. His maid assured him she did not when he excused himself from the table for a brief chat with the woman. He grinned, charmed by the flash of her amber eyes that deepened to a whiskey hue when she didn't like something. There was no further protest. Kerrie understood she lost this bout with him. If he had his way, he would allow her the win every now and then just to keep life from becoming a bore. He didn't want her to believe she would never get her way. He could afford to be generous.

She did plop down on the hearth. He wanted her between his legs. Cuddled right up to his groin. He wished for her to feel his arousal, the proof of his willingness to bed her. If she noticed, he would enjoy the flood of color to her face. At this juncture in the building of their brief but pleasant relationship, she would never succumb. The fight was on because he did want her...and...he wasn't about to lose the battle.

"Not on the hearth." Tam sat down. While he was leaning against a chair facing the fire, he patted the place in front of him. Shaking her head as if he was giving her a choice amused him. He would seduce her his way, not hers. This would take time since to him it was obvious she still held doubts concerning his charming self. He still believed she was disagreeable as well as annoying. However, she captivated every male part of him.

"Why? You don't like me. Why would you wish to do any of this?" she asked, the puzzle in her expression there for him to read.

"I've never said that I didn't like you." He wasn't going to point out to her that she didn't care for him very much either. "You're a beautiful woman. I admire stunning women." That was a fact that could never be argued. Like was such a tepid word to use between two passionate individuals. Some of the women he bedded before, he didn't like. However, he never slept with a woman he didn't lust for. This woman made his heart pulse. Heated his body with his imagination of what was beneath her gowns. He imagined since she was a niece of the duke and duchess, he should be careful how he approached her. If he didn't take precautions, he could find...hell he was risking a marriage by pursuing this course.

Rethinking would be prudent.

Tam didn't think he could do anything less than pursue his immediate plans. Damn the possible consequences. If something happened, he could sidestep as well as any man.

Kerrie blinked a few times as if she tried to understand the gist of his comments. Tam patted that place in front of him where he wanted her. In lieu of speaking, she sat where he insisted. One small step at a time. As much as he wished to hold those ripe peaches of hers in his hands, he wasn't about to caress her with intimacy until she begged. His hands around her hips, he pulled her close. She touched his body against hers. Her little rump delighted him as she wiggled to get comfortable pushing against his inflamed groin.

She cleared her throat. "How long are you staying?" Kerrie asked with a soft sigh as he began to comb through the tangled strands. Inhaling, exhaling with each gentle stroke she supported herself against him. Her hands were on his thighs.

"Depends." He held a strand in his hand, working his way from the bottom until he untangled the length. She sipped her wine. The pattern repeated until he was satisfied with the job. He put the comb on the hearth before picking up the brush.

"On what?" To Tam, with no apparent reason she sounded angry. For the time he was combing her hair, he believed she relaxed. Felt the softening of her body. She was stiff again. "Don't be so vague. You owe me a decent answer. I came here to be alone. Your presence put a decided damper on my plans," she snorted as if she didn't like the gist of his comment.

That was something else that intrigued him. Her tiny unladylike snorts of disapproval. This wasn't the first one she gifted him with. Now he understood what she wanted from him. She wished for him to leave. Not until he'd seen this relationship to the proper conclusion. With a smile, she couldn't see, he said, his voice soft close to her ear, his lips touching. Whispers floating along her flesh. "I'm leaving when you leave. Won't have any female going down that trail alone. A woman needs protection. Even if she doesn't think she needs a guard at her back." He wasn't going to elaborate about thieves as well as the possibility of an abduction. Kerrie should be brilliant enough to figure out something of that nature. Also, some of the other consequences of going it alone she might encounter.

"No, you're not!" She recoiled, turning to glare at him, breaking the subtle mood he created. "I won't have it. You are not going with me!" Each word was punctuated with a jab of her finger against his chest.

"Look at the fire, little one. We will see. My company is not so bad." Her return to her uncle, a good friend of his, would be done his way. Not hers, no, never her way. She might not return with her innocence intact. Nonetheless, she would return alive, unscathed in any other way. Drake wouldn't appreciate losing a niece to cutthroats of any kind. Hell, even the animals could be dangerous to her wellbeing.

He kept the chuckle to himself when she obeyed his command. Perhaps this little lady was more biddable than he thought. When he started brushing her hair, she settled into him again. A lady who enjoyed her creature comforts. From what his mother told him, the strokes were soothing, calming her when the day was at an end. He pushed her long hair over her shoulders so he could continue brushing while she leaned on him.

"This feels so good," Kerrie murmured seeming to forget her aversion to him.

That was fine by him. She came both ways, hot and cold. One moment she bristled as well as glowered at him, the next she sighed in contentment. Kerrie wasn't as immune to him as she let on. "There are a lot of things we can do together that will feel this good. With your go ahead we could explore the possibilities. Tonight, if you like."

"What things?" She'd pushed away from him again, her golden eyes taking on a bedroom, dreamy kind of look. He imagined that's how they would look when she woke in the morning or after good sex. "What are you implying? I'm not..."

It seemed she wasn't at all certain of herself or what he wished for. "We could start with the discussion about the bed in the master chamber. Take the wine upstairs along with a few of those delicious cakes," he spoke close to her ear. Felt the shiver of delight pass through her. The female part of her body hummed to life. Once she agreed, Tam held no doubts about her passion. She would be a delight as a lover.

"I'm not sharing your bed if that's what you are getting at. I'm not..." She stiffened again retreating to the chilly voice he wished to have no part of. Kerrie resumed her position against him. "Remember, I don't like you. Don't lovers have to like each other first? I don't have any intention of giving into carnal pleasures."

"No, just lust for each other. Like plays no part between lovers. That is all that is needed. Lust. It's a wonderful condition. Hot. Wet. Sex." Inside he was chuckling at her naiveties.

"Mr. Talmadge?"

"When you leave here, where are you going? Did you tell me before? If you did, seems I've forgotten." He asked trying to remember if she mentioned a destination. He would escort her wherever it was she was headed. He wasn't about to leave her to her own devices that would get her into more trouble than she could handle.

"Don't recall if I mentioned it to you. None of your business. Since you asked and you were nice, to London. Supposed to find a husband. Don't want one. Especially one with a title. Want to marry a man who can do a good day of work. One who doesn't believe he is entitled just because there is a title in front of his name. Who doesn't mince around at balls or hold his handkerchief with the tips of his fingers. Don't wish to have a dandy as my husband. If I did want to marry someday, I want a real man."

Tam kept his yowl of laughter behind his teeth. No, he needn't tell her he was about to become the next Duke of Sherburn. She would run the opposite direction. Good God, what she described was not that far from the truth. He would have to show her not all titled aristocrats were dandies. He found he was pleased she didn't want a husband. Though, from what he'd seen of her so far, the little piece of baggage needed someone to look after her. Recalling how she rode Dex, seemed she didn't have an iota of common sense. To keep her safe. A husband would do the trick. Didn't all women wish to marry? Have children? Why didn't Kerrie? He wasn't thinking straight.

"Why don't you want a husband?" Tam asked, curious if she would give him a good reason. "All women wished for the security a husband could bring, a meal ticket." He laughed while he felt her back stiffen. Wished he could watch her eyes flare as well as her brows knit together. What other emotions danced through her brain? They were suited. He didn't want a wife, at least not yet. He had a few more good years of bachelorhood in front of him.

She didn't turn around. The sight of her expression would be nice. He imagined her flashing eyes. Full lush lips thinned in displeasure. From this vantage point he recognized the tilt of her chin.

"I've a million and one reasons." She wiggled against him, adjusting herself, inflaming him further. "I don't need to explain my reasoning to you. You mean nothing to me. I don't even know anything about you."

"Why don't you enlighten me as to one or two reasons. Assuage my curiosity. I'll be certain to let you know if I believe them to be valid." Tam ran his fingers through the silken length of her hair, brought a few strands to his nose to catch the scent she favored. It was something he would tuck away in his memory. The fragrance was vanilla. Unusual. Most women seemed to like something stronger.

"Well..." she paused, moved again, caressing his hard length with her backside. He was tormenting himself. Wouldn't do anything different. Though he couldn't guarantee where his hands would roam. He felt a male urge to cup her breasts, test the tips.

It seemed she was experimenting. Trying to figure out things. A sudden flash of possible insight caught him. "Do you have siblings? A brother or two? Younger? Older." An answer to this question could give him a few clues as to what she was doing with her bottom.

"How many questions are you going to ask me? I haven't answered the first one yet." Her indignant huff brought more amusement to the forefront. Kerrie turned the question back on him. "Do you have siblings?"

"If that's how you want to play this, let's start with siblings. We can get to the husband question later. It's not a topic I'll ignore." His hands settled on her shoulders. A light massage would relax this little bedeviler of men a bit more. Her head fell forward as he orchestrated his magic. Dictated her reactions. He heard the soft sigh as he worked the knots from her muscles.

"Don't understand why that would matter. If you must know, I have one sister. Her name is Kelsey. Oh...that feels so good." Kerrie sighed again. She was falling into his plans with seeming ease. He never thought her seduction would be this easy. Perhaps he deluded himself.

"No brothers, then you wouldn't have seen..." Tam decided not to go that route. They would be here for several days. He didn't want to shock her until she liked him.

"None..." Her little mewl of pleasure made him grin.

Tam wondered what she would sound like in other circumstances begetting pleasure. He set her away from him, intent on putting distance between them before he took something that wasn't offered. If he wasn't going to find relief tonight, he didn't need more sexual stimulation. She should retire for the evening. For Tam, a swim in the cold lake would help.

Placing her on a large chair facing the dying fire, he filled both their glasses with the sweet wine that was stocked in the kitchen. "Here, you can give me all the reasons you don't want a husband."

She pushed hair from her face. "I don't appreciate being told what to do. Imagine you've noticed. A husband would have rights I'm not willing to give to another person let alone a man. To do so, I would have to trust the man. Except for my father as well as my uncles, I've never met a man who could be trusted."

"That's only...relatives don't count." If she were his, she wouldn't ride Dex unless he was on the horse's back with her. She would never like that dictate. His word would stand. As to Dex, his command would be law. He couldn't think of anything else.

"Well..." She drummed her fingertips on the arm of the chair. Her face turned the rosy hue he enjoyed.

She was about to embarrass herself. How she would do it would please him. "Well?" he parroted anticipating an enjoyable answer.

"I heard these two women..." She downed half her glass of wine then a bit more. "I wasn't eavesdropping you know. I don't make a habit of listening to conversations that don't involve me. They were talking about." She looked up stopping then blinked a few times. "I'm not telling you this." She finished her glass of wine made to stand up, wavered then sat back down."

"Embarrassing?" He grinned anticipating what was yet to follow.

"Mortifying," she stated with a firm voice. "I don't understand what they were speaking of but what they said was strange. A man poking...never mind." Kerrie waved her hand in the air. Her face turned the color of a beet. "They were loud, laughing. I wasn't listening in on a private conversation, mind you."

"If you can't speak of sex maybe there is a third reason you don't want a husband." He sipped his wine watching the play of emotions on her face. Her eyes widened. "Is that what they were talking about? Sex?"

"Imagine so." Tam didn't intend to say anything more to this delightful innocent. He was going to have to rethink his approach along with his intentions. With each tick of the clock, he liked this lady more than she annoyed him. "A third reason?"

"Don't want to share a bed with anyone. A man would take up too much room. I'd end up on the floor if I wasn't careful. Men snore. I'm certain it's difficult to sleep with all that noise next to your head."

She would end up beneath her husband more often than on the floor. If she became his, he would never push her from his bed. He would pull her close. Hold her tight. Explore all her feminine delights. "Is that all? Beds can be made to fit two people with lots of room left over."

"Why don't you want a wife?" she asked, holding her glass out inviting him to pour more wine into it. "Don't you think it's your turn to answer a question or two? I've held up my share of this question answer interrogation."

"You're going to get foxed if you keep that up." He evaded the question. Poured more wine for her enjoyment. He would never complain if she became a little tipsy.

She lifted the fragile shoulders he'd been massaging a few minutes ago. The gesture was delightful as well as intriguing. Some of the best parts of her moved with the upraising of her shoulders. Tam found himself fascinated. They'd gotten off to a rough start today. Tonight was turning out better. The conversation interesting. The possibilities intrigued. He began to make plans.

"I don't care," Kerrie told him. She was leaning back, her head settled on the back of the chair. With her eyes closed she seemed to enjoy the small conversation between them. "Why don't you wish for a wife?" She persisted.

"I do want a wife. It's my duty. Need an..." Tam didn't want to get into the part about needing heirs. He was twenty-nine. His father would pass soon. The duke questioned him many times about a possible woman in his life. To this date he never met a woman he could live with or wanted to live with the rest of his life. When he did wed, he meant to be faithful. He understood enough about himself that while he might not love his wife, he would care about her. Tam wasn't certain if love existed or how love felt. As the new duke when the title became his, he had a duty to continue the line. Before he left for the hunting box, his father reaffirmed that fact. His father hoped to see a wedding then a grandchild. Just as Kerrie was going to find a husband she said she didn't want, he was going to London in search of a wife.

"Duty..." she sat up staring at him with a puzzled expression. "Don't tell me you're one of those fops? An aristo playing at being a man?" Kerrie paused for a beat. Looked at him. "You don't..." she cut her words short. He wondered why.

He took umbrage at her assumption. "I would never presume to tell you that. A fop? Do I look like a mincing dandy? Have you ever seen me hold a handkerchief between my fingers then bring it to my nose?" Tam didn't understand why he was offended by her questions. He was. "I've never played at being a man." He was all man. Male to the tips of his toes. He never needed to pretend in any way.

Kerrie relaxed back in the chair. Her breath left her is a soft release. "That's a relief?" she sighed again. "No, doubt if you would have to make a game of being a man there would be repercussions. If I discovered you were titled, I'd leave first thing in the morning. Would make certain to leave without you knowing."

"Why? Do you have thoughts of marriage with me?" Tam grinned wondering how she would respond.

She took her time, slipped her tongue across her bottom lip soaking up a few errant drops of wine in the process. She was foxed. He didn't have one doubt in his mind. She sat up seeming outraged. "Good...God...no! You don't like me? If I did agree to marriage with a man, it would never be to one who didn't like me."

They were back to that. Tam reminded her just to point out a noticeable fact, "You don't like me either."

"True...though I do enjoy the way you brushed my unruly hair. Could get used to the attention. I did like the massage too. Every night would be nice... My legs...they would love that kind of attention. The muscles do get a workout controlling Dex. Sometimes they cramp." She flushed when she mentioned a massage on her legs seeming to realize after she spoke the placement of his hands that might entail.

At the thought of any part of this delicate woman getting a workout on that horse left his stomach sour. Tam understood for the time being, he needed to hold his tongue on this matter until he was ready to make a decision regarding his possible relationship with her. Enraging her would set his plans back. If he kept her from her horse, she would be furious. Her safety was more important than her anger. He cared about her. How much he didn't yet know.

His mind wandered to thoughts of massaging those legs every night. He knew what would happen when he did. She didn't. By the rosy blush tinging her cheeks Kerrie might have some idea. He doubted that fact.

"It's best you go to bed before you imbibe too much." He took the wine glass from her hand. "Can you walk?"

She pushed against the arms of the chair before falling back. "Of course I can walk."

Grinning, he waited to see the result of her efforts. He meant to allow Kerrie to come to her own conclusions.

When she tried again then failed, he swept her into his arms. Hers went around his neck. By the time he reached the second floor her head was nestled against this chest as were her breasts. He pushed the door to her room open with his foot then set her on the bed. Stepping back, Tam watched her wondering what she would do next. He was leaving everything up to her.

When she didn't speak or make a move, he said, "Unless you want me to help you with your nightgown, you will have to sleep in your clothes." His hands were on his hips as he waited for her answer. In this possible endeavor, he was a willing man.

She twisted then leaned forward presenting her back to him. "Just undo the back of my gown. I can take it from there. I accept your help."

Tam stepped back, shaking his head as if to say no. Instead, he swore beneath his breath. Did her bidding then stomped from the room slamming the door closed on his way. The simmering anger was not something he understood. He alone orchestrated this scenario. If he'd left well enough alone, he wouldn't be hard as steel. Needing to be deep inside her. She escalated him.

Downstairs, wishing she was in his bed, he gazed into the fire. Not many of the burning embers were left. Instead of finishing off the bottle of wine, he poured himself a generous amount of brandy. Unless he got foxed, sleep wasn't going to come to him tonight. Maybe by dawn he would sleep. His body whirred with life. If he could find a suitable woman besides the one upstairs, he would take her to his bed. He adjusted his pants then stared at the ceiling while he inhaled long deep breaths. This lady was working her way into his heart. He didn't want another woman.

The only relief in sight was the lake. Tam hoped the water was cold enough to slake the lust burning in him. Frigid would be perfect to relieve his needs. Shirking out of his clothes as he walked, they landed wherever they came off. By the time he reached the dock, he was ready for the plunge.

A long shallow dive brought him into the water. He swam beneath the surface until he could hold his breath no longer. After he surfaced, he gasped for air. The lake was damn cold but not frigid enough to ease his need for the enchanting woman upstairs. When she bathed a few hours earlier, she gave no indication how cold the water was. His little Kerrie was tougher than she appeared at first glance. He still wasn't about to reconsider her horse. If she was his... She would be his, she wasn't going to ride that beast. The decision was made. Like it or not, he would make sure she didn't ride Dex.

Since he was immersed in the coldest water he'd been in for years, he made the most of the event. He swam across the lake before returning. When he climbed out, he stretched out on the dock. He watched a few clouds ghost the moon. Stared at the twinkling stars. Tam loved it up here. Wished this lodge was his. He meant to buy a place like this for himself. Decided he would.

His laughter echoed across the lake. What would he do if she came down for a swim? He was naked. Brought no towel with him. His clothes were scattered from here to the house. Imagined he could dream about making love in the lake with only the water separating her body from his. That was one place he never tried. Wondered how it would feel to only have water between them. A fantasy, one or two, might be nice. Might keep him going through the night. If he fantasized enough, he wouldn't go to her room to find out if she was as soft and warm everywhere as she looked.

~ * ~

"What are you up to this time, Ella?" Drake, duke to The Duchess of London, asked with a wicked grin. "All I have to do is look into those beautiful eyes of yours and I know you're having wicked thoughts. You're plotting something. Can't keep secrets. Need to tell me or...might not make love to you tonight."

She would know he could never keep that promise. So, she continued in the vein that she thought would reap the greatest rewards. Ella plucked at her skirts, keeping her face down, her lashes lowered. When she looked up, she said with innocence in her voice. "Why ever do you ask? You believe I'm up to something? What could that be? I wonder?" She was smiling through her teeth as if secrets abounded in her head. They usually did. His woman possessed a lively imagination. It seemed once she decided to accept her nieces as charges for their seasons, she became an extraordinary matchmaker. Ella handpicked the man she hoped would work for each of her charges. Funny that she always made the best decisions. For Ella nothing was left to chance. She researched. Dug into the man's background. Of course, she knew her nieces from birth. Understood all their likes along with their dislikes. Ella understood their needs too. Something far more important.

Drake understood the look. His wife was plotting the next wedding. They just managed to get Tara wedded to Case. Now it seemed Kerrie Johnston would arrive soon to begin her journey to find a husband. Kerrie never made a secret of the fact she didn't want or need a husband. Just like her mother, she was happiest tending to her horses. She despised men with titles. No one understood why.

Indeed, her carriage should arrive in a few days according to Kerrie. That was odd because he remembered the missive from her father, Hadden, who told him the arrival date. The two didn't match. He received two different messages. The one from Kerrie arrived a day or so ago telling him she didn't leave as soon as expected. She would arrive a week later.

An idea plummeted to his head. He wasn't positive but things were no longer adding up. Ella must also understand that. He tapped a finger on his chin. "Did you know, or did you read the correspondence I had from Sterling Talmadge that was sitting on my desk?" The little sneak. There wasn't a doubt in his mind that she read every word. He scrubbed his hand across his jaw still thinking, still wondering if some shenanigans weren't going on here. Chance might also have a hand in his imaginings. He would never put it past his wife to put these two in the line of fire. They might well be perfect for each other. He had to admit to that. Tam wanted a woman who wasn't after him because of his wealth coupled with his title. Kerrie didn't wish to be burdened with a title. If they fell in love, both could be assured what they felt for each other was true love. The if was a big one. The lie even bigger if it was continued.

Ella's smile was all sugar. "Should I have? Did you want me to read it? Would be pleased to do so. Only if that is what you want." Ella had that devious innocent look he learned about years ago. With her head tilted just a bit to the side, he understood the significance. She was plotting a union. It must be Sterling and her niece Kerrie. They might not appreciate her efforts. If they fell in love, they would thank her later. Drake knew Sterling was far too serious for a woman with such boundless energy as Kerrie possessed. He did need a woman with backbone, a woman who would laugh with ease. That was Kerrie. So far, Ella pegged every match right. Her record was unblemished. Not that there hadn't been problems that needed fixing before the happy couple could say 'I do.'

"You know better than to tamper with the papers on my desk." He would laugh except this was an issue he needed to make certain she understood. They'd been married too long for her not to comprehend all the delicate matters that crossed his desk. Reading the wrong paper could possibly put her life in danger. He wouldn't' stand for that. He would need to take better care of the paperwork.

The look of outrage on her face brought out a bark of laughter he would never hide. She snorted, very unlike a duchess let alone The

Duchess. She did have her reputation to uphold. "Would never touch one piece of paper on your desk. I'm shocked speechless to hear you ask that question." Her apparent indignation caused him to chuckle anew. He knew she didn't tell the entire truth. She wouldn't touch but she would manipulate.

Now he was getting the gist of what happened. One of his letters must have drifted to the floor or his chair. Provoked by a wave of her hand or unprovoked. He would never know the truth. She might have had the maid sweep her feather duster over the top until something fell off. If that happened, his wife would have no qualms about reading whatever flew away from his desk. She would be innocent of all but curiosity. She didn't lie.

"What is it you did, Ella? I know there is something I will have the answer to sooner than later. Something I will have to explain away." Drake imagined that Ella would have all bases covered. Not only was she a passionate woman she was also very intelligent. She did love seeing her nieces wed to respectable men. Men who would complement the woman, love her as well. Taking over her Aunt Charlotte's job was the joy of her life. She had so many nieces that would come to London for a season. That didn't count all the nephews if they failed to find suitable wives on their own. Ella was more than willing to urge the progress along.

Her bright smile could send him to his knees. At this juncture in time what he wanted was to toss her skirts then have her here on his desk. He would do the sweeping of the papers despite the fact he would have to sort through all the ledgers.

She lifted small feminine shoulders, "Just set the wheels in motion. That's all. Promise you, they will find love together. The letter fell on the floor. I couldn't help myself. I did the read the missive. Nothing from all your secret dealings. Nothing important. If I knew it to be correspondence of the secretive sort, I would never look."

"You gave Kerrie the go ahead to stay at the hunting box even though you knew someone else would be there." His words were not a question. He understood for a fact that was what she did.

"No, Kerrie never asked. Her driver sent word that she intended to take a week at the lodge. I never wrote back that it would be occupied by Sterling, letting chance take its course. Whatever could be wrong with that?" Ella looked so proud of herself. He wasn't going to burst her bubble.

"You understand our niece despises titled lords. It's one of the reasons she was loathe to have a season. Sterling Talmadge is a marquis soon to be a duke. He will not be to her liking."

"Sterling isn't the usual aristocrat. Something happened to Kerrie she won't speak of. Storm was certain it had something to do with the viscount, whatshisname, that visited the village last year. She is quite lovely. Exceptional. Unique. The man made a pass at her. She snubbed him. The next time he saw her he tried to force her. From what I've heard one of the village lads stopped the rape. Now she believes all titled lords are all cut from the same cloth. Except you, of course."

"That's the way of it. Don't think she was violated? Not that it would matter to a man who fell in love with her. She would tell him. Wouldn't she?" Drake paced the room, looking to his wife then his desk. He would have to be more careful about his correspondence from now on. If it was that easy for his wife to peruse his desk, what would happen if someone meant the government harm. Sensitive papers still crossed his desk. Two years ago, their home was ransacked by a man seeking information. He had his enemies. Wouldn't do to put Ella in harm's way or his children. He thought of the French count who despised him. The man threated him.

"What do you think is happening at the hunting lodge?" Ella asked with that dreamy expression on her face telling him she was thinking about love. Also remembering their stay at the same place. The ultimatum that brought them together.

"I hope the two of them are not scratching each other's eyes out. I fear for Sterling if Kerrie discovers he's about to become a duke."

"Kerrie will suffer if he gets all autocratic about her riding. It's not normal for a woman to ride a horse such as Dex. You would never have protested if I rode him," Ella poured them both tea. Set a lump of sugar in each cup. "She will rebel. We both understand Tam's archaic notions about females. I believe Kerrie is just the lady to set him straight about those outdated notions."

At everything his wife spouted, Drake groaned. "I need brandy not tea. Do you think we should pay a surprise visit? Help ease the tension we know will grow between those two?" Drake asked while he slid a generous amount of brandy in his cup.

"Heavens no! We might interrupt something important. Something that might embarrass all of us." Ella's demure smile didn't surprise him.

Little minx, Drake didn't think anything would embarrass his wife. She would always find a way to turn the situation around. "That is why we should interrupt. We don't want the babe before the right amount of time." As if he'd cared when it came to his relationship with Ella.

Ella's peered over the rim of her tea cup an impish grin on her face. "If the two are right for each other, there is nothing wrong with a dalliance before the wedding to cement the relationship. We cannot be judge or jury given our relationship in that same hunting box." When she looked up with brows drawn together Drake understood he was about to be reminded of his sordid past along with what he did with her in that same lodge.

He held up his hands in surrender. "I concede."

Christel and Ryder's Story
by the Author
At Rogue Phoenix Press

Christel's Sunrise
Twelve Dancing Princesses Book Four

He Made Her An Offer...

Life has thrown Christel McClellan some experiences that could have devastated a less determined woman. Beautiful, self-assured and fiercely independent, she is trying to forget the loss of her stillborn child. But is the child alive?

She Couldn't Deny...

Life is carefree for Ryder MacLaren who loves to see what is on the other side of the sunrise. Laird of Clan MacLaren, he is wealthy, handsome and happily unencumbered...until stunning Christel McClellan enters his life. When he hears her story, he believes the child she thought dead has been sold to a wealthy buyer.

Also by the Author
At Rogue Phoenix Press

Nick's Tender Rogue
Naughty Book One

Once a McClellan lass

Beautiful, naughty and audaciously daring, young Nickie Gray is a McClellan princess through and through—as wild and reckless as the most incorrigible of her male cousins. Now that she has reached a marriageable age, Nickie has set her amorous sights on a most unsuitable male—the notorious rake and womanizer known to all mamas on the debutante scene in London as dangerous. When her chaperone tells her all rakes are off limits, she finds the challenge one she sets her mind to.

Always a McInnis rake

Not expecting to find a ravishing woman throwing herself at him yet blatantly willing to accept whatever overtures she makes, handsome Collin McInnis is thrilled by the brazen escapades of this naïve creature and is willing to experience her high-spirited advances with no expectations of commitment. On the high seas, he is bested by a vivacious beauty whose love of freedom and adventure rivals his own...and by an inescapable tidal wave of passion that threatens to engulf them both.

Dream About Lyssa
Naughty Book Two

When Lyssa Andrews sees the earl sitting behind his desk scowling, she knows she will someday put a smile on his face. The handsome brooding earl isn't playing the same game. He resists her outrageous comments and questions until she is ready to give up. Lyssa didn't come to London with the intent to find a man. Now, though, she is willing to chance love with the stodgy earl of Blackmore.

Raised by the Sioux when his father sought adventure then fell in love with a Sioux maiden, Kane has been betrayed once by a white woman. He isn't about to give his heart to another, especially one who is as white as newly fallen snow. Despite his best efforts, he can't deny Lyssa's intoxicating effect on him. Now Kane will risk his very life to protect the innocent beauty who has seduced him with her tender love.

Deke's Magic Kiss
Naughty Book Three

She would risk everything to become a practicing doctor

Annie Lundin's dream of practicing medicine and a life of dignity and self-sufficiency vanishes in the small Kansas Territory town of Denver City. When the men of the town refuse to become her patients, all she has left to fight for is her practice. She is thwarted from every direction. She didn't mean to fall for the dark, handsome sheriff. Didn't mean to ask for his help. Annie needs Deke Sullivan to protect her from the dark secrets that follow her from Boston. In return she offers all she has—herself.

He would stop at nothing to win her love and trust

Raised by the Cheyenne, Deke Sullivan was churlish, overconfident, and dangerously handsome. His life changed when his Irish grandfather discovered him. He was sent to West Point, fought the

Seminole in Florida as well as some on the planes where his loyalty was divided. A woman is the last thing in the world he needs. Especially a woman who belongs in Boston, not the rugged Rocky Mountains. He has commitments that don't include a woman. The moment he sees Annie her intoxicating beauty changed him forever. Love has a way of changing the rules.

Chasing Still Water
Naughty Book Four

The single kiss behind the church changes Chauncey Lakeland's life forever. At that moment, Chauncey knows Still Water Runs Deep is the only man she can love. Someday she will prove to him she can be courageous as well as bold. She decides that when he leaves for Dakota territory she will follow. Chauncey has every intention of being with this man she just met. She isn't going to risk losing him. No matter what it takes, Still Water Runs Deep will be hers. Now, she is willing to take a chance on love with the Sioux warrior who kissed her then stole her heart.

Still Water Runs Deep, a Sioux warrior, is a man intent on living true and loving deep. His greatest challenge will come with the woman he is destined to love. In Chauncey's stubborn determination to follow him into Sioux territory despite the danger, he realizes the fire in her soul. Wrapped in her arms he discovers both his heaven and hell. Even as she risks her life to be with him, he must keep her with him.

VISIT OUR WEBSITE
FOR THE FULL INVENTORY
OF QUALITY BOOKS:
http://www.roguephoenixpress.com

Rogue Phoenix Press

Representing Excellence in Publishing

Quality trade paperbacks and downloads
in multiple formats,
in genres ranging from historical to contemporary romance,
mystery and science fiction.